GW01459092

TO
SAVE
HER
HUSBAND

BOOKS BY ELLIE MIDWOOD

The Violinist of Auschwitz

The Girl Who Escaped from Auschwitz

The Girl in the Striped Dress

The Girl Who Survived

The Girl on the Platform

The White Rose Network

The Wife Who Risked Everything

The Undercover Secretary

The Child Who Lived

I Have to Save Them

When the World Went Silent

The Photographer's Secret

ELLIE MIDWOOD

TO
SAVE
HER
HUSBAND

bookouture

Published by Bookouture in 2025

An imprint of Storyfire Ltd.
Carmelite House
50 Victoria Embankment
London EC4Y 0DZ

www.bookouture.com

The authorised representative in the EEA is Hachette Ireland
8 Castlecourt Centre
Dublin 15 D15 XTP3
Ireland
(email:info@hbgi.ie)

ISBN: 978-1-80550-144-2
eBook ISBN: 978-1-80550-143-5

To guardians of democracy—past and present. Truth, freedom, and kindness will always prevail.

PROLOGUE

Austrian-Hungarian border. March 1938

The train rattled through the twilight, the rhythmic clattering of wheels against tracks underscoring the tension that hung heavy in the air. Aurelia sat beside her husband, Max, their hands intertwined, a fragile lifeline in a world that felt increasingly precarious. The two other couples that shared the compartment with them held onto each other with the same mute desperation —Austrian citizens just hours ago; now, refugees without any rights, hoping to outrun the Nazis that had poured over their country's border earlier that day. The landscape outside the window blurred into a series of indistinct shapes, a haunting reflection of their own lives—once vibrant, now marred by fear and uncertainty.

Finally, the last stop before the Austrian-Hungarian border. Suddenly lightheaded with nerves, Aurelia looked around. The air itself seemed to vibrate with anticipation. Her foot tapping in time with her wildly racing heart, Aurelia sensed the same unease radiating from the other passengers. Whispers floated through the compartment, a blend of hope and anxiety. Aurelia felt her heart pound against her ribcage like a caged bird desperate for freedom.

"Do you think we'll make it?" she asked, glancing at Max, whose face was etched with concern.

He squeezed her hand, his eyes steady. "Our papers are in order. We should. Just stay calm."

But as they pulled into the station, Aurelia's heart sank at the familiar sight of plain-clothed men standing on the platform. The Gestapo. She'd seen enough of them in Berlin in the past few years to instantly identify them even without their uniforms. It was the manner in which they carried themselves, assured of their unchecked power, and also the eyes. It was the eyes that always betrayed them: cold, searching, utterly devoid of all emotion—those were the vultures' eyes, just waiting to pounce on their prey. Through the window of their car, Aurelia watched as they moved with purpose, their faces impassive, eyes scanning the train with predatory intent.

"The Germans only crossed into Austria this morning," Max murmured, his grip tightening around her hand. "How in the hell are they already here?"

Aurelia tossed her head, her throat dry with mounting fear. Because the elections before the Anschluss had only been for show. The Nazis had known the outcome for months now. They'd been preparing, implanting their agents everywhere. And as for the Austrian SS? They were just as old as the German ones. Frankly, she would have been surprised if they weren't here. And, in her own twisted way, she, Aurelia, had helped make it all happen.

As the train came to a halt, the doors slid open. The Gestapo officers boarded, their heels thudding against the metal floor—each step a nail in their communal coffin. Naturally, they began with the private compartments: people who could afford them had the most to hide and the most to lose.

"Papers!"

Aurelia jumped as she heard one of them bark in the next compartment. The atmosphere shifted, a palpable tension filling the air. Their fellow passengers scrambled to comply, fumbling with documents, their expressions a mixture of fear and resignation as they waited for their turn. Aurelia's blood drained from her face as she listened to the steps move down the aisle, nearing their compartment's door.

"Max," she whispered, "what if they—"

"Shh," he whispered back, his expression a mask of calm. "Don't forget who you are. We'll be fine."

As if she could ever forget. It was that cursed name of hers that had got them into this mess. How desperately she'd tried to shed it, but it kept coming back, like a snake's skin, enveloping her anew and strangling her all the same.

"I'm Aurelia Laub—" Aurelia tried to speak, but the door slid aside, cutting her off.

The officer in charge—a tall man with a sharply defined jaw and ice-cold blue eyes—fixed Max and Aurelia with his piercing gaze. He recognized them; Aurelia could see it at once.

"Papers," he inquired, politeness personified.

Still, his voice sliced through Aurelia's hopes like a knife.

She reached into her bag, retrieving their passports, together with Max's American certificate of naturalization. Should she have just produced the certificate alone? But he didn't have a visa to travel to Hungary as an American citizen; as an Austrian, he didn't need one. No; she did everything right.

Meanwhile, the officer scrutinized the papers, his eyes narrowing as he flicked through the pages. "Herr Laub," he said, looking up at Max. "Would you kindly step off the train, please?"

Aurelia's heart sank. "What? No! His papers are in perfect order!" Panic surged through her as she stood, gripping Max's arm tightly. "He's done nothing wrong! Why are you taking him off the train?"

The officer remained unfazed, gesturing for Max to follow him. "I'm merely following orders, Fräulein von Brandenburg," he said with the same mock-apologetic smile. "They give me a list with names, I check papers against the list. Apparently, Herr Laub is needed by one agency or the other for further questioning."

"Further questioning?" Aurelia echoed, her voice rising. "You can't just detain people without good reason! Besides, he's an American citizen."

"He's also an Austrian one," the Gestapo man pointed out, smiling wider. "So, Austrian law holds." He quickly caught himself, chucking. "I beg your pardon, *German* law. Austria is a part of the German Reich as of today. But I'm sure you've already heard that much."

He motioned for two other officers to approach. They moved with a practiced efficiency, gently but firmly guiding Max away from her. Aurelia felt her entire world tilt on its axis, her heart racing as she struggled to keep her grip on reality.

"You have no right!" she cried, trying to prize their hands off her husband's shoulders in the narrow passageway. "What are you charging him with? He's done nothing wrong! Just let us leave; you'll never see us again anywhere near Europe, I swear! We just want to leave, that's all!"

Half-turning to her, the Gestapo leader beamed at her as his underlings led Max through the car door. "Oh, you are welcome to proceed with your travels, Fräulein von Brandenburg. You aren't on the list."

In one last surge of desperation, Aurelia lunged at the Gestapo agents, set on pulling her husband away or to die trying right there, on the platform. Momentarily surprised, they subdued her, though, with the utmost care not to inflict any injuries, for which there would be hell to pay. She screamed at Max to use his chance and run—she'd just keep fighting them if needed—but he only stood there, the believer in human rights, the damned idealist she loved more than life.

"Ari, quit it, please," Max urged, smiling at the agents almost in embarrassment. Despite the angst in his eyes, his voice remained steady. "You'll only make it worse. Go to Hungary like we planned. I'm sure it's a simple misunderstanding. As soon as they let me go, I'll find you."

But as the leader escorted him to the unmarked car, Aurelia followed stubbornly.

The officers repeated their mantra, "You're free to go, madam," as if their words could erase the horror unfolding before her.

Aurelia's resolve hardened, fueled by a fierce determination. "Like hell I will!" she declared, her voice unwavering. "Wherever you take him, I'm coming with you."

The lead officer raised an eyebrow, clearly taken aback by her defiance. "That's not how this works. You can leave now or—"

"Or what?" Aurelia interrupted, her voice rising. "You'll arrest me too? I don't care! You think I'll abandon my husband to whatever fate you have in store for him? Take me with him!"

The officers exchanged glances, momentarily unsure of how to proceed. But Aurelia stood her ground, the fire in her eyes burning through the veil of fear. She couldn't lose him—not now, not when they were so close to freedom.

With a resigned sigh, the Gestapo leader put his mask of a smile back on. "As you wish, Fräulein von Brandenburg. As you wish."

ONE

In the airy drawing room of the Laub villa, tucked away in the greenery of the Grünewald, Aurelia picked her way through the remnants of the election party, stunned as though by a physical blow. As far as the eye could see, little flags and confetti littered every surface, along with the leftovers of rubbery food and empty bottles of champagne swimming upside down inside silver buckets. The ice had long turned to water. The guests had left while the world was still full of hope, while the ballots were still being counted. So sure were they of their victory, they had celebrated like those unsuspecting Pompeiians with the volcano already rumbling under their very feet, ready to annihilate them all.

In Aurelia's hand, a newspaper was rolled into a cylinder as if to conceal the results confirming the inevitable. Hitler's Nazi Party—the NSDAP—was now in charge of Germany. Lowly Brownshirts that belonged in the cheap beer halls where they spewed their hateful propaganda before getting into fistfights with the Reds would now occupy the majority of the Reichstag seats. Their hysterical leader, whose silly mustache Aurelia mocked so perfectly to the delight of her friends at the exclusive table at the Horcher—one of Berlin's finest restaurants, in which Hitler himself couldn't afford to step foot—would now be the Chancellor. That clown, a literal convict, in charge of the country—*her* beloved, cherished country, for which Aurelia had fought, along with the freedom fighters of the early twenties, against those wishing to turn the clock back to the Dark Ages. It was an abomination. A nightmare. A bad hallucination from a poorly prepared opium from a seedy Oriental haunt.

She needed to talk to someone. She needed to break this silence before it would break her.

"Love?" Stopping in the door of her husband's home office, she called to him, her voice soft but laced with urgency. "Have you seen the morning papers?"

He must have; her filmmaker husband was an early riser, particularly when busy actively shooting a movie. On filming days, he could exist on virtually no sleep at all, preferring to curl up right on the set's floor to catch quick cat naps, while Aurelia, his cinematographer, marked the next camera's positioning for the following scene. They were in between projects now, but Max—an Austrian who was more Prussian in his self-imposed rigid discipline than any actual Prussian Aurelia knew—still spent each morning at his desk, his brow furrowed in concentration as he scribbled notes for the script of their upcoming film, *Caesar*. The project consumed him, a world of creativity that he was eager to dive into, inspired by something Aurelia had mentioned to their friends at a game of cards.

"Not yet," he replied absentmindedly, glancing up only briefly. "I'm trying to finalize the script before we offer it to the studio next week."

Leaning against the doorframe, Aurelia gazed at her

husband, just as infatuated with him as on the first day they'd met.

Her childhood friend, Zara, now a wealthy art gallery owner, had invited Aurelia to the premiere of Max Laub's film, *The Last Letter Home*, in 1928. Having only heard of Laub in passing before, Aurelia had stared at the screen awestruck, wondering just how it was possible for someone to film precisely what she was feeling. The story of a Great War soldier who had set off to the front as a young and naive patriot but gradually grew disillusioned with the command, war, his very country and world order itself had hit hard, square in the chest. Aurelia, who had always prided herself on her stoicism, had broken into actual sobs at the scene when the young soldier, facing his French counterpart in close combat, had dropped his weapon, choosing death over senseless slaughter, resonating deep within her very soul. She had clutched Zara's arm after the credits rolled—she had to meet the man who had made it.

Zara had indulged her, but Herr Laub had his leading actress hanging off his arm and Aurelia was going through a divorce from her husband, Arthur 'Art' Nachtnebel, that she had hoped to keep private, but which her half-brother Wilhelm's political affiliations had blown into a rather public and scandalous affair. In short, they had barely exchanged a few words that night. Still, Aurelia had felt herself falling for the man—or, perhaps, his talent, she couldn't quite tell—and falling hard.

And who could blame her? Max Laub was a striking figure, a man whose presence commanded attention even in the most crowded of rooms. In his mid-thirties, he stood tall, his athletic frame exuding an air of confidence and charisma. His dark hair was slicked back with a practiced ease, framing classical features. Chiseled cheekbones and a strong jawline lent him an air of sophistication, while the subtle curve of his lips often hinted at the warmth of a gentle smile.

His most captivating feature, however, was the soulful, intelligent brown eyes that shone with creativity and passion. They seemed to hold a world of stories, a depth that drew people in and made them feel as if they shared a connection, however fleeting. Yet, there was a shadow that lay just beneath the surface of those expressive eyes—a scar that ran over his left brow, a remnant of his days in the war. It had left him nearly blind in that eye, a painful reminder of the past that he concealed with remarkable poise. He had learned to navigate life with a slight tilt of his head, his gaze often shifting to accommodate his blind side, but the scar only added to his allure, telling stories of resilience and survival.

Certainly, he bore the marks of the Great War but chose to sleepwalk through the turbulence of current German politics instead of taking an active interest in it—sometimes to Aurelia's great annoyance.

"The Nazi Party has won the majority in the Reichstag," she said, pushing herself off the doorframe. "I bet Big Brother is delighted."

Despite the two von Brandenburg siblings growing up together and sharing at least one parent—their father Otto—to Aurelia, Wilhelm was *Big Brother*, a title which she uttered with a sneer, her mouth full of distaste.

She hadn't spoken to him in over a decade after running away from her ancestral home, and particularly after discovering Wilhelm's name among the emerging Nazi Party leaders. They found themselves on the opposite sides of the political barricade—Wilhelm marching along with Hitler in their attempt at a nationalist coup, while Aurelia marched for democratic freedom. As both siblings gained more publicity, it was inevitable for their familial connection to be uncovered by the warring sides of the two factions' press.

Before long, a journalist from *Vorwärts* took great pleasure in asking Wilhelm von Brandenburg his thoughts on his sister posing for her husband Art Nachtnebel's canvas as naked as the day she was born. The painting was titled "Germany" and, in both the public's and critics' eyes, represented quite accurately the post-war, half-starved state of their country, mournful and on her knees, vultures circling overhead.

With a somber look, a certain Joseph Goebbels, the Nazi Party's new mouthpiece, had spun a story that had little in common with the truth: an anarchist Nachtnebel had confused an innocent aristocrat, Aurelia von Brandenburg, turned the poor child to drugs, corrupted her morals by exposing her to his so-called "artistic," Dadaist movement and generally used her as a prop to get at the conservative class he personally detested.

Through the same paper, Aurelia had asked her brother who confused him for Wilhelm to pivot so sharply from an exploiter of the working class to its most ardent supporter.

It was only natural for the Nazis to grind their teeth over Aurelia's personal choices. After all, she was their poster girl—a striking embodiment of classical Nordic beauty. Then in her early twenties, she had possessed long, flowing blonde hair that cascaded down her back like a golden waterfall. Her features were delicate yet defined, with high cheekbones and a strong jawline that gave her an air of elegance. Her blue eyes reflected a depth of emotion that was often hidden beneath the surface. However, her appearance belied a spirit that fiercely rejected any societal norms. Unlike the polished, conventional beauty celebrated by her half-brother and his Nazi Party, Aurelia had often used her skin as her artist husband's canvas, her intricate tattoos a declaration of her identity as a free spirit and a rebel. Contrary to Nazi-promoted female modesty, she was unafraid to embrace her body, happy to pose nude for her husband's art, which he sold to support the unemployed. Goebbels called it exploitation; Aurelia called it an expression of vulnerability and solidarity with those who suffered in the wake of economic despair.

TO SAVE HER HUSBAND 11

The siblings had exchanged barbs over the years—always impersonally, through the press—but Wilhelm had taken it to a whole other level when he had claimed that his sister had married half-Jewish Laub just to embarrass him in front of the Party. Max had found it amusing; Aurelia, now truly enraged, had officially changed her name to Laub. As for the Party—whose opinion Wilhelm was so concerned with—its leader Hitler had turned out to be Director Laub's admirer. In the four years since Max and Aurelia had been married, Wilhelm hadn't spoken to her once; she was dead to him.

Aurelia didn't mind the estrangement in the slightest. But now his Party had won the majority of the seats in the Reichstag. Wilhelm would be the one wielding power over her and the rest of German citizens.

Max paused, the pen hovering above the page. He turned to Aurelia, surprise flickering across his features. "They did?"

"Yes," Aurelia replied, dropping the newspaper atop his notes like a dead rat, the bold headline screaming for attention. "Look at this!"

He took the paper, scanning the article with a furrowed brow. "This is... unexpected," he finally said, his voice flat, devoid of the emotion Aurelia had anticipated. "Oh, well... I'm having trouble with the finale. It's just not turning out right. Do you want to brainstorm a bit together?"

"Brainstorm?" Aurelia echoed, incredulity rising in her voice. "Max, this is our country! The very foundation of our democracy is crumbling before our eyes and you're worried about a finale? People are frightened. This isn't just some passing phase! The rise of the Nazis means a rise in hatred, in division. This isn't just politics, it's life and death."

With a sigh, he set the newspaper down, removing his glasses with his other hand to rub his eyes. "And what do you want me to do about it? We can't change the outcome of an election. All we can do is keep telling stories that matter."

"Stories that matter?" Aurelia pulled back in disbelief. "What good are stories if the very fabric of society is unraveling? If we don't stand up against this, who will? Are we just going to sit back and watch as our country falls apart?"

"I'm sorry I'm not living up to your expectations and taking to the streets with the Molotov cocktails. Perhaps you should call your ex-husband; he might just be making some for today's protest."

He must have regretted the words the second he uttered them. Instantly on his feet, Max tried to gather Aurelia into his arms while she hissed at him to piss all the way off, already heading for the door.

"I'm sorry, I'm sorry, I'm sorry," he kept saying like a prayer into her temple as she struggled against his embrace. That's how he always was on the rare occasions they fought—instantly apologetic, sincere regret radiating from him in waves, refusing to let her go until she'd forgiven him. "That wasn't fair. It has nothing to do with you or Art. I spoke from a place of my own inadequacy. I have always admired you both greatly for the courage to physically fight like you did in the twenties. I'm not comfortable in crowds. I can direct actors, not people from the street. I'm too soft and middle-class for that. What I *can* do is make movies." His voice was soothing, asking for her to see his point. "Think of it this way: *Caesar* is a reflection of our times. Wasn't it you who first put the idea in my head after drawing parallels between Caesar, Mussolini, and Hitler? Each of them started off wishing to build a powerful empire but turned—"

"—Into dictators instead; yes, I know." Aurelia's voice rang with emotion. She was still taut like a spring but not struggling to release herself any longer. "Caesar's senate was reduced to a mere rubber stamp, ending all political discussion, precisely as is the case with the fascists in modern-day Italy. Both Caesar and Mussolini are the sole architects of any policy, and political success is no longer something won from the people but rather earned by brownnosing Caesar or Mussolini. And that's precisely whose blueprints Hitler and his Party are using."

Max smiled, his arms around his wife softening. "And there you have it. Making *Caesar* is our own way to educate people, to engage with the very issues we're concerned about. Films are such a powerful tool: they deliver a message better than any political agitator would. The Nazis may have won the majority of seats in the Reichstag, but Hindenburg is still the President and von Papen is still the Chancellor. Germany is still very much a democracy, with constitutional rights, free press, and freedom of assembly. All we have to do is make people understand how easily a democracy may fall, like it happened in Caesar's times, so that in the next elections they don't vote against their own interests. And that's precisely what I'm planning to do with this film."

Aurelia sighed, acknowledging his arguments. The main reason why she had divorced Art was because of his all-or-nothing nature. He was a good comrade to fight alongside but a lousy husband because of it. He was gone more than he was present; he gave away all of the money earned from his art, leaving nothing to even feed his own family. He loved humanity so much, Aurelia took second place to his noble goals. Aurelia still admired him, but her heart belonged, unreservedly, to Max Laub.

Turning to face him, she buried her nose in the collar of his shirt, inhaling the heady scent of his skin, pine aftershave, and cologne.

"And what if it's not enough?" she whispered, kissing the outline of his jawline, feeling him inhale sharply under her lips. "What if we're a little too late with our movie? Then what?"

"I can't think straight when you're actively trying to seduce me in my own office." He lifted her effortlessly by her hips and set her down on his desk. "If I weren't such a jealous, possessive husband, I'd just venture to suggest you go to the Reichstag and kiss every Nazi there to make them forget what they came for."

"Oh, is that right?" Aurelia parted her legs, pulling her husband closer by his leather belt, her nimble fingers already undoing it. *"Take one for the team,* as Zara's American husband called it?"

"The country is in danger, Frau Laub." Aurelia shivered against his breath on her bare skin. "You may just be going to have to make some sacrifices here."

"Shut your mouth, Herr Laub, or put it to better use."

As she lost herself in passion of their lovemaking, Aurelia had no idea just how prophetic those words uttered in jest would be.

TWO

The slogan "Men are willing to fight; women must be there to nurse them" stood on a platform in front of an election site, guarded by two Brownshirts. Undeterred by November sleet and gusts of wet wind, one was handing out leaflets to the voters passing by on their way to yet another Reichstag election and the other voicing the Party's words through the mouthpiece in his gloved hand.

"Abolish the humiliating and unjust Treaty of Versailles. Abolish Weimar-era feminization of German society. Abolish the liberal government selling Germany to Wall Street Jewry. Return man to his rightful place in the army and woman to her rightful place at home. Reject Jewish eugenics aimed at eradicating German people through their policies of abortion and birth-control devices. Vote National Socialist. Vote German. Vote tradition."

Aurelia's nostrils flared, her countenance resembling that of a hunting dog catching sight of particularly despicable rodents. Threading her arm through the crook of Zara's elbow, she pulled her childhood friend as far away from the offending view as possible. After all, Zara was so well-bred, she would go and take a leaflet and say "thank you" on top of that, just because her English governess had taught her that it was the right thing to do.

The two women had grown up in the same circles, their fathers' hunting lodges side by side, only Zara had always been the sensible one, in contrast to Aurelia's wildness. Zara, with her cold, rational mind, never took the idiotic risks Aurelia was infamous for. Unlike Aurelia, Zara had married well right away, to a nouveau riche American called James and chose to invest in art—both in the New World and on the continent—and had quickly expanded her chain of galleries, making a name for herself as one of the most regarded new art connoisseurs.

Back in the 1920s, while they had never really lost touch, they had rarely seen one another, dedicated to different causes. Max was a big reason why they had rekindled their friendship, meeting by accident at a house party. Aurelia was there with him—the director and screenwriter Zara had introduced her to during the premiere of his film just a few months ago.

"You're looking well," Zara had noted when Max had stepped away, finally letting go of Aurelia's arm, which he had kept touching all evening. "Though, I must admit, I didn't expect to meet you here."

"The crowd is much too bourgeois to my taste?" Aurelia arched a playful brow. "Don't call me a sell-out just yet. I simply traded artistic bohemian circle for a cinematic one. I'm working for the UFA studios. Learning cinematography," she had said over the noise of the room. "My marching days are over. Germany's doing well; no one needs soup kitchens anymore. I basically sleep on the set. Our director happens to be a despotic *Arschloch.*"

Aurelia had shot a glance in Max's direction, which must have told quite a different story, for once she had turned back, she had seen Zara hiding a grin behind the rim of her champagne glass. Indeed, just a year later, from being Laub's assistant, Aurelia had turned into a co-creator and cinematographer and, another year later, she had become his wife. Zara still held a special place in her heart for Max Laub for bringing her childhood friend back to her.

The Brownshirt's voice pulled Aurelia out of the past and back into the present as it reached both women marching toward the entrance.

"Women shouldn't vote; women should be at home with their husbands," he said with a foolish, well-meaning smile, almost kindly.

Zara had almost managed to pull Aurelia away, into the safety of the school building, but some grandfatherly figure just had to go and stroke his beard and nod.

"Indeed, that's precisely how things ought to be."

Aurelia twisted herself out of Zara's grip and swung to face the men, eyes wrathful and full of cold fury. "You look like you won't even make it to the new year, old man. Should you be voting for the next government, you'll see only from God's blue skies? As for you two, I can understand why you need to force women back into homes: the only way you'll ever get a wife with that attitude will be when your Führer mandates her to become one under threat of the death penalty."

Leaving all three groping for words, Aurelia shoved the heavy door open and pushed Zara in first—in case one of them decided to ask for seconds. Her own skin toughened in the metaphorical fires of the twenties' civil unrest, Aurelia had no trouble mouthing off. Zara, with her refined manners, was a different matter entirely. For that very reason, Aurelia made it a point of honor to protect her from any verbal assault.

"You could just ignore them, you know," Zara said, pulling her blue velvet gloves off to produce her passport for the election site worker, sat with a ledger in front of him.

"That's what they count on—women remaining quiet and obedient. It wasn't her sweet nature and compliance that got Clara Zetkin into the Reichstag and has kept her there for thirteen years and counting, it was her big mouth." Aurelia signed in the ledger next to her name and took a ballot from the election worker, winking at him. "Guess who I'm voting for?"

"Isn't Zetkin a communist?" Zara wrinkled her high alabaster forehead as the two headed to the voting booths.

"So?"

"Aren't you a social democrat?"

"Zetkin used to be a social democrat. We're fluid, me and old Clara."

The booths were separated by thick blue curtains. Pulling one closed after herself, Aurelia heard Zara's voice through the partition: "It feels like we're having elections every month. Where's Max, by the way? Why isn't he exercising his civic duty?"

"He doesn't know left from right in the government and doesn't particularly care," Aurelia snorted from her booth. "Sometimes I wish I didn't."

"James doesn't care either."

"He's American. If I were him, I wouldn't give two hoots about some other country either. Oh, look! Wilhelm von Brandenburg, NSDAP, for the Reichstag." Pulling the curtain away for a moment, Aurelia poked her head and bared her brilliant teeth at the nearest election worker. "If I draw something obscene next to his name, will it disqualify the ballot?"

"Yes."

"Rats!"

In the next booth, Zara burst into chuckles.

Moments later, they pulled the curtains open simultaneously and stepped aside, making way for other Berliners.

Much like Aurelia and her friend, other voters also seemed none too pleased to be returning to the voting site on their day off just because Reich Chancellor kept playing his political games.

"Coffee house?" Zara asked, subtly guiding Aurelia toward a different exit. Aurelia thought of following her gentle lead—she knew it wasn't that Zara was afraid of the Brownshirts; it was more that it went against her noble nature, open conflicts of any sort—but the SA men's comments just wouldn't let her rest.

"Yes, coffee and cake, and some Austrian one, the kind that Max's *Mutti* used to make, not this watery Berlin business." Noting Zara's growing alarm, Aurelia winked at her as she undid her coat and revealed a camera hanging off her neck. "But first, a photo—to celebrate our exercising our civic duty and all. Here, you hold it. It's your American Kodak, you should know how to operate it."

"I do." Zara exhaled, examining the new portable miracle as they stepped outside.

"Here, right in front of the slogan," Aurelia called, gesturing enthusiastically toward the Nazi banner rather to the Brownshirts' confusion. "Center it good; who knows, maybe one day it shall hang, enlarged and framed, in one of your galleries. And count to three so I know when *not* to blink."

Seeing the camera at Zara's eye, the Brownshirts naively straightened with their arms along the seams, good little soldiers. Suddenly, just before Zara called "three," Aurelia pulled up her sweater, exposing her spectacular breasts and making obscene gestures with both of her hands right under the words, "women must be there to nurse them"—just in time for Zara to capture the priceless shot.

Breath catching in their throats against the wind, they sprinted wildly through Berlin's backstreets, chased by the Brownshirts' curses and the policeman's shrill whistle until they collapsed against one another in a fit of stifled laughter in a confession booth of a small Catholic church.

"Like good old times," Aurelia wheezed, her teeth in the

wool of Zara's coat, sleeve. "Remember old Reinhardt, your father's overseer, chasing us with a horsewhip when we let all of the pigs out? The ones he readied for slaughter?"

"Oh, Papa was so mad at me when Reinhardt came to him to complain!" Zara, too, appeared to be swayed by the pull of the old memories. Aurelia, with her wild streak, had always been an instigator, but Zara was only too willing a participant in her friend's antics. "You couldn't let your pigs out, you had to let out mine!"

"We had no pigs. Father was big on hunting, not farming. He preferred his livestock already slaughtered."

Aurelia's smile was quickly twisting into a grimace of old distaste and resentment, as was always the case whenever her surviving family was mentioned.

To stop her from falling into the pit of old memories, Zara caught Aurelia's chin with two fingers and looked into her eyes, almost as dark as Zara's in the twilight of the confession booth. "He only caught half of them, old Reinhardt. The rest, they were long gone into the forest. Got to live a while longer, thanks to you. Good old times."

"Yes," Aurelia nodded, caught between the past and the present and belonging to neither.

In the very last democratic election in early 1933, Clara Zetkin was no longer on the ballot—or the Reichstag. Only a few months later, there was no one else left in the Reichstag except for the Nazi Party.

THREE

Berlin, Germany. February 1933

The evening in Berlin was bitingly cold, but inside Zara Whitby's art gallery, warmth enveloped the guests as they gathered for the opening night of Art Nachtnebel's latest exhibit. The gallery—a converted townhouse adorned with high ceilings and large windows—was filled with the soft glow of strategically placed lights illuminating the artwork that lined the walls. Yet, despite the elegance of the setting, a palpable tension hung in the air, an undercurrent of unease that even the brilliant hostess in her sequenced dress could not dispel.

The artist himself was absent, as was his habit. He had never made himself comfortable among the glamorous crowds, finding his only peace in either the solitude of his studio or among the masses in the streets. Ever since Zara had discovered him, a pioneer of the emerging Dadaist movement of the early twenties, he hadn't once collected any proceeds from the sales of his works. At first, it had been Aurelia who used them to organize soup kitchens for the starving people of Berlin and, after the couple's separation, Zara. As Art's fame grew, so too did the prices for his work. Now, he could not only feed the needy but fully sponsor two orphanages and a private office of veteran affairs that took care of his fellow soldier fraternity. Art chose to live in the attic of that very office and feed himself with whatever the veterans grew on the building's grounds.

Aurelia stood beside her husband, Max, as they surveyed the room, her heart heavy with the weight of recent events. It was February 1933, just weeks after Hitler's appointment as Chancellor, and the stormy clouds of uncertainty loomed larger than ever. As they exchanged polite smiles with other guests, Aurelia felt the dissonance between the joyful celebration of art and the grim reality of the world outside. But, her own depressed state aside, she still put on a smile for the others' sake. The more paintings Art would sell, the more funds he'd have for his charities and, let's be honest, half of the crowd was here to ogle her, Nachtnebel's former muse, with a famous director husband in tow. Years had passed since the Nachtnebels' quiet, nondramatic divorce, but they still piled into any event at which Aurelia's "new" husband appeared to support her old one. Contrary to their expectation and perhaps to their disappointment, there had never been any animosity between the two men, only a mutual respect of one artist for the other.

"Look at this," Max said, gesturing toward a striking piece that dominated one wall, as if to confirm Aurelia's last thought. It was a powerful rendering of a hyena standing on a mound of fallen soldiers' bodies, a swastika armband wrapped around its leg. From its thick neck, an Iron Cross was swinging as the beast cackled—a scavenger preying on the sentiments of a fallen nation to stuff its belly with that very nation's blood. "Nachtnebel has truly outdone himself this time."

Aurelia nodded, taking in the impressive mixture of oil brushstrokes, cloths sliced likely off his own old uniform to create eerily realistic, mangled bodies and wilted petals sprinkled liberally with red—Art's own blood, if she ventured to guess. He'd gone a tad mad after the war, but then again, who wouldn't? Max threw himself with the same abandon into his films, starving and depriving himself of sleep to create equally powerful messages for the public.

"Frightful, isn't it?" she asked, turning the champagne flute in her hand closer to her chest.

"Frightful, but hauntingly beautiful," Max replied, his voice thoughtful. "And just in time for all of... this." He gestured vaguely around, meaning the suddenly somber-faced Berlin and the entire country that was holding its breath.

Just mere weeks ago, Germans had refused to believe that drastic changes were coming. As antifascists rang alarm, Hitler supporters waved the "fearmongering" off with astounding nonchalance. Nothing would happen to their precious rights under the new Chancellor. He would simply rid the nation of bureaucracy and set the economy back on its feet, bringing production back into Germany and reducing unemployment. What were these social democrats moaning about anyway? Did they not want their country to be strong, something to be reckoned with after their disastrous policies of the past decade?

But as Hitler's cabinet went from having only three Nazi ministers in it to becoming the full-fledged NSDAP arm by the end of February, as police leaders were swiftly being replaced by Hitler's loyalists, as this new police force began raiding and closing the offices of any independent newspapers, no one could quite ignore the astonishingly rapid erosion of democratic rights. Still, most Germans continued, business as usual, slapping the "Hindenburg is still the President" band-aid on the republic's severed artery.

As the guests mingled, Aurelia's gaze drifted to her childhood friend, Zara, who moved gracefully among the crowd. Zara was particularly radiant that night, her sleek black pageboy cut complementing her striking features.

"What do you think?" Zara approached the Laubs with her

dazzling smile. "Quite a piece of *résistance, non?*" she inquired in perfect French with a nod to the painting.

James, Zara's husband, stood nearby, his broad shoulders and easy smile offering a comforting presence. As an American, he remained somewhat insulated from the immediate threat that loomed over Germany.

Deep inside, Aurelia envied his ability to engage with the evening as if everything were fine and dandy, but she knew that the reality for at least three of them was far from it.

"We, Germans, are cultured, educated people, aren't we?" Aurelia responded with her own question.

"I would like to think so sometimes." Zara rolled her eyes: clearly, the last election proved to be an exception to the rule.

"How did we end up electing a poor person's version of Mussolini instead of highly qualified politicians who actually know how to govern the country? Social democrats actually had a step-by-step program on how to reduce post-market-crash inflation and boost the middle class. They have been working tirelessly on regaining the trust and friendship of England, France, United States. Germany was finally becoming something—"

"Not according to Hitler, it wasn't."

"Hitler is an idiot who couldn't even make it into an art institute. What does he know about politics?"

"Nothing, but that's not the point." Zara shrugged her bare shoulders. "He represents the past, which is familiar and secure despite all of its shortcomings. Social democrats with their progressive views represent change, which is much too rapid, much too painful, and much too alien for the majority. They know how it was back in the day, when Keiser was in charge, when Bismarck's armies commanded the whole of Europe's respect, when Nietzsche glorified their Nordic, masculine exceptionalism. They don't want to be friends with France, they want to conquer

France. They don't want social-democrat-approved legalized prostitution, they want free sex from their wives who can't work, can't vote, can't leave the kitchen without their permission."

"They are appalled to see my naked tits painted by my ex, but they will line up at the nationalist gallery to see that same very teat being suckled by a blonde-haired babe—that sort of thing?"

Zara snickered, her hand stacked with bracelets at her mouth. "That's one way to put it, I suppose."

"You're laughing."

"What else am I to do?"

They grew silent. They ought to be enjoying the pleasant champagne buzz, but both were oddly sober, clear-headed, as though after a cold shower.

"I know Big Brother must be thrilled," Aurelia spoke at length, eyes riveted to the cackling hyena. "The Nazi bastard has just been appointed Prussia's Minister of Interior."

As the night wore on, the atmosphere grew increasingly somber. Guests whispered among themselves, their conversations punctuated by nervous laughter and sidelong glances toward the door. The truth was that fear lingered just beneath the surface; it seeped into their interactions and tainted their shared moments of joy.

"Have you heard about the raid on the Communist Party office?" a woman murmured to her companion, her voice barely above a whisper. "I hear they jailed them all."

"Apparently, they're saying that anyone who opposes the new regime will face consequences," her friend responded on an undertone. "Social democrats are next, rumor has it."

Aurelia felt a chill run down her spine at the mention of protests. She turned her attention back to Zara, who was now discussing the paintings with a small group, gesturing animatedly. The passion in her voice was infectious, yet Aurelia could sense the tension in Zara's shoulders, the way her smile faltered for just a moment when she caught Aurelia's eye.

"Are you all right?" Max asked Aurelia quietly, noticing the concern etched on her face.

"I'm fine," she replied, though the tremor in her voice betrayed her. "I just... I worry about all of this, Max. It feels like we're celebrating at the edge of a precipice."

As if on cue, the celebratory atmosphere within the gallery was abruptly shattered by a sudden commotion at the entrance. A group of guests crowded around the door, their voices rising in alarm, a wave of anxiety crashing over the gathering. Aurelia felt her pulse quicken as she exchanged worried glances with Max and Zara.

"What's happening?" she asked, her voice tense.

"I don't know," Zara replied, her brow furrowing as she stepped toward the crowd. "Let's find out."

As they moved closer, the murmurs turned into frantic whispers. Someone shouted, "The Reichstag is on fire! It's burning!"

A chill ran down Aurelia's spine, her breath hitching in her throat. "What? How could that happen?"

"It's chaos out there," a man with wild eyes exclaimed, his voice trembling with a mix of fear and disbelief. "They say it's an attack—an attempt to undermine the government!"

Without thinking, Aurelia grabbed Max's hand, her heart pounding with urgency. "We have to go see it."

Max hesitated for a moment, his expression torn between concern for their safety and the gravity of the situation. But knowing that his wife would just set off on her own, he went to grab their coats from the cloakroom.

Together with Zara and James, they hurried out of the gallery, the biting chill of the February night air hitting them like a wave. The streets of Berlin, once vibrant with life, now felt charged with an electric tension. As they made their way toward the Reichstag, the thickening crowds of people echoed their dread, a collective heartbeat pulsing in the darkness.

Aurelia's heart sank as they approached the iconic building, towering against the night sky. Flames licked at the structure, bright orange and yellow against the inky backdrop of the heavens. The fire roared, crackling with a ferocity that sent sparks spiraling into the air, illuminating the faces of onlookers who gathered in horror.

"Oh my God," Aurelia breathed, her hand flying to her mouth as she took in the scene. The Reichstag, the very symbol of their democracy, was engulfed in flames. She felt a wave of nausea wash over her, the reality of what was happening hitting her like a physical blow. "This can't be happening," she whispered, her voice trembling. "Not the Reichstag..."

Max stood beside her, his expression grim as he surveyed the chaos. "We were just filming this," he spoke quietly, his voice laced with concern, "when the Roman Senate went against Caesar's wishes, he decided to storm it."

"And after he emerged victorious, there were no more checks on his power," Aurelia echoed, feeling heat on her face even in the cold of the night. "He declared himself a sole ruler. Out of a republic, Rome became a dictatorship."

Max, too, appeared to be spellbound by the macabre spectacle. In the lenses of his glasses, democracy itself was turning to nothing but ash. "Whether it was incidental or not, the Nazis will use this as an excuse to tighten their grip on power."

As they stood there, the flames continued to rage, consuming the building with a ravenous hunger. The sound of shattering glass mingled with the distant screams of panic, the acrid smell of smoke filling the air as it curled around them, choking out any semblance of hope. Amid the mounting panic, firefighters were hastily unrolling their hoses to douse the flames.

"It's them red bastards," a man declared, appearing among

the crowd as though out of thin air. "Commie scum, to be sure, unhappy with the fair and democratic elections."

Aurelia's very blood chilled as another one quickly echoed this sentiment, though much louder this time.

"That's what they always do, damned anarchists! Burn anything they don't like."

"Shut it!" Aurelia yelled, her old revolutionary self summoned in an instant. "Quit spreading rumors, you brainless oaf! Are you the fire chief by any chance? No. The SA are already beating the communists right in the streets under the protection of the police so quit your jawing before more people get hurt!"

"As they should," another man responded with a shrug. "It was them, red scum, all right."

How had she not noticed them before, brawny and clean-shaven, strategically placed throughout the crowd as though by design?

"It *is* the Nazis," she hissed to Max and Zara after pulling her friend close. "These are plain-clothed SA; we fought them plenty in the streets, back in the day. I'd recognize them in a second."

"What's happening?" James inquired in English—his German was rudimentary at best—as he shifted his curious eyes from his wife to the burning building and to the Laubs.

"Ari's saying that the Nazis must have started the fire and will blame it on the communists," Zara explained to him in his native language, her dark brow drawn in thought. "Which wouldn't surprise me. They thrive on chaos and fear. This could be the catalyst they need to justify their actions."

The crowd began to swell with agitation, voices rising in anger and fear. "They're attacking our democracy!" someone cried. "It's a terrorist act, on German soil!"

"Fear not, good German citizens!" a familiar voice sliced through the night like a blade.

Aurelia had heard it on the radio more times than she cared to count, agitating for Hitler during every single preceding election. She recognized the orator as well: it was his face that glared off every edition of nationalistic *Der Angriff*—Dr. Joseph Goebbels. And here he was in the flesh. Swiftly climbing on the ledge of a fire truck, he addressed the crowd, making up for his short stature and unimpressive build with the beautiful, hypnotic voice that could easily sway the masses.

"The *Führer* is here and the situation is under control," he declared, arm raised in the air as though to pacify the vulnerable citizens of Berlin. "Our police leaders have already informed me that the perpetrators were swiftly apprehended and detained. Unfortunately, this was indeed a case of incendiarism. Communists have made the last attempt to cause disorder by means of fire and terror. But fear not! The NSDAP's vigilance has frustrated their malicious plans to overthrow the democratically elected government and seize power. Minister of Interior von Brandenburg is already working closely with the *Führer* to ensure that any last threat to public safety is eliminated. Tomorrow you shall awaken to a new dawn of a new, safe Germany! *Heil!*"

Pale as a ghost, her eyes like glass, Aurelia watched in abject terror and helpless rage as, one by one, hands around her flew up in Nazi salutes toward the red, infernal sky. The republic she'd known was falling apart like a house of cards in front of her very eyes.

Unsure of what he was cheering, James tried raising his arm as well, only for it to be slapped down by Zara.

"Never—and I mean *never*—do that again," Zara spoke through gritted teeth.

As the columns of smoke continued to rise, illuminating the night sky like a beacon of destruction, a profound sense of loss washed over Aurelia. It was as if the fire was consuming not just the building but the very ideals they had fought for—the hope of a democratic Germany, the promises of freedom, and the future they had envisioned.

"Stay close," Max urged, wrapping an arm around Aurelia's waist as they watched the scene unfold. She leaned into him, seeking comfort in his presence as the reality of the night pressed down upon them like a suffocating blanket.

As the flames continued to roar, they mourned in silence what was being lost: the Reichstag and with it, their carefree past, now reduced to ashes.

FOUR

The early spring of 1933 brought a reluctant warmth to Berlin, the chill of winter slowly giving way to the promise of blooming flowers and longer days. Aurelia and Max drove through the bustling streets, their city the same and yet alien at the same time as the political landscape continued to shift beneath their feet. The air felt electric, alive with the chatter of citizens, yet the undercurrents of tension ran deep as the Nazi regime began to solidify its grip on power.

They arrived at the elegant home of director Arnold Fanck —a celebrated figure in the world of mountain films—where an intimate gathering was set to take place. When they entered the lavishly decorated sitting room, Aurelia smiled as she took in the warm atmosphere, lively with laughter and animated conversation. Fanck stood near the fireplace, his commanding presence drawing the attention of the guests as he regaled them with stories of his adventures in the mountains.

It was Max who had introduced Aurelia and Arnold, the two directors' friendship dating back to the early twenties when both had embarked on the same professional path. Though, even if the path might have been the same, their films couldn't have been more different. Whereas Laub was celebrated all over the world for his epic historicals, there was no one who could rival Fanck when it came to filming his native mountains and ice. Well, almost no one. His former protégé Leni Riefenstahl's name could be heard in film circles more and more often, becoming synonymous with cinematic innovation. That night's gathering was his present to her—a belated celebration of her directorial debut, *The Blue Light*, which had premiered just before Christmas of 1932.

It was only natural for Leni to play co-host to Fanck. With her tall, athletic frame, she moved with a grace that seemed almost ethereal.

"Ari, Max!" the actress-turned-director cooed, opening her arms to the couple after Fanck had welcomed them into his home. Her hair, a rich chestnut hue, fell in soft waves around her shoulders, framing a face that was both classically beautiful and hauntingly intense. "I haven't seen you since forever!"

"Well, you were busy filming again after your great success." Charming as always, Max kissed her on both cheeks. "Congratulations, by the way!"

"It wouldn't have been possible without these two beautiful people," Leni said with a smile addressed to Aurelia and Fanck.

"Fabulous work, Leni." Genuinely proud of her fellow artist —it would have been a stretch to call them friends—Aurelia pulled Leni into a warm embrace. "I couldn't take my eyes off the screen. Your heroine Junta reminded me of myself in my younger years—just as feral and just as misunderstood. And the juxtaposition of the villagers' greed, close-mindedness, and corruption, and Junta's desire to simply live her life as a free spirit—magnificent!"

They had met back when Aurelia was still married to Art and Leni was still begging directors for parts that went to actresses who were blonder and didn't mind getting undressed, both in front of the camera and later, in a more intimate setting, in front of the director. Aurelia remembered very well the grudge Leni held against "that bitch Marlene," who had got the leading role in *The Blue Angel*, which could have been hers. It was Leni, after all, who was a professional dancer, not Marlene. She must have classed Aurelia with the same crowd when the two had stumbled into one another at some or other artistic dive —who could remember now which one? The places were all the same back then, obscured with the sweet smoke of hashish or something even stronger and peopled with the same characters, dressed as extravagantly as someone from Max Reinhardt's play and invariably drunk.

Leni later confessed to Aurelia that she had disliked her at first sight because she looked just like Marlene, all long, bare legs through the slit of silk dress and bedroom eyes that drove men mad. But then they had somehow got pushed much too close together in an improvised bar operated by an extremely handsome transvestite and Aurelia had fixed those catlike eyes of hers on Leni and Leni had suddenly felt as if someone stared straight into her soul.

Aurelia remembered the night very well; remembered shouting over the music to ask what had got Leni's panties in such a twist, and for some reason Leni had blurted it all out, about that whore Marlene and the producer who had promised her the world but, while Leni was still arranging her clothes back in order, had reduced the promise to twenty American dollars—for an abortion, if she would happen to need one, and for some stockings, or whatever. And she didn't even sleep with him for the part, she wasn't that kind of a girl, she genuinely liked him and thought he'd liked her too, saw the potential in her—

"They can all go hang themselves." The verdict came from Aurelia, seductively hoarse and strangely hypnotic. "Don't depend on anyone. You want a film? Go direct it yourself. Cast yourself as a lead."

Leni had stared at her in a mixture of astonishment and mistrust. "I thought to myself, that broad was drunk and speaking nonsense of things she knew nothing about," she later admitted to Aurelia. "Why should I listen to her mad ravings that she won't even remember tomorrow?"

But the tiny seed of an outrageous idea had already planted itself deep in her very core.

"Who's going to let me?" she had asked, just to quarrel, just because the broad looked like Marlene in the dim light of the dive.

But the broad had only grinned savagely and breathed her sweet breath right into Leni's mouth. "Who's going to stop you?"

And now, look at Leni—fresh from Davos with her second film under her belt while the first one was still gathering crowds in theaters.

"And leaving once again soon," Leni pretended to roll her eyes, but they shone with too much impish enthusiasm. "Hitler has commissioned me to create a documentary about Horst Wessel!" the director exclaimed, her voice dripping with pride. "Can you believe it? I did try to talk my way out of it," she claimed with another theatrical roll of her beautiful eyes. "I tried telling him that I can't work on commissioned films as I'm an artist first and foremost and I must have a deep personal connection with the subject to film it, but he insisted that he wanted only me for that particular task."

Aurelia, whose face was growing longer by the second, felt her entire body turn to stone. "Telling who?" she repeated very slowly, as though giving Leni a chance to take her comment back before it was too late.

"The *Führer*, naturally!" Leni laughed, her excitement bubbling over. "I've met with him in person quite a few times now," she added in mock confidence, which was anything but. "You should hear him talk—"

"Oh, I've heard him talk," Aurelia cut her off, her eyes darkening. "Heard every single speech calling for ethnic cleansing, destruction of the opposition, concentration camps, banning of free speech and all else to that extent."

Leni waved her hand dismissively, her laughter ringing out like a chime. "Oh, Aurelia, you always take everything too seriously. He doesn't mean it when he says it. It's just slogans to get him elected. Nothing will come of it, you'll see for yourself. Hitler is a darling and such a charming conversationalist. You wait till you get to know him in person—"

"I won't."

Leni heaved a sigh, as she moved to steer Aurelia away from the curious guests.

Max must have had enough of Leni's enthusiasm as well. "Where's the bar?" he demanded with put-on brightness as he took Fanck by the elbow.

"Hold your breath and let me tell you something before your next monologue. You remember Sokal, my former producer?" Leni asked Aurelia once the two women had seated themselves on a bench by the window.

Aurelia shrugged, opening her golden cigarette holder. Not even five minutes at the party and she already needed a smoke. This country was turning to a dung heap of a show indeed. "He's the one who sponsored your *Blue Light*," she said, lighting her cigarette without looking at Leni. "The film about a free spirit who goes against all conventions; an early feminist who chooses freedom over marriage, wealth, and society's acceptance." This she uttered with a very pointed look at the director as if to drive the point across—*just how does one go from creating an anti-establishment picture to the nationalistic propaganda in a matter of months?*

"He did bankroll it," Leni confirmed, ignoring the rest of Aurelia's remarks. "But now, while I was in Davos filming, he left the country, taking its negative with him! And not only that,

that Jew is showing it all over Europe without paying a single Pfennig to me!"

"Do you blame him for leaving?" Aurelia arched her brow at Leni. "With your boyfriend Hitler's anti-Semitic ethnic cleansing talk?"

Leni heaved another big sigh, drawing her eyes toward the ornate ceiling. "It's a bit too dramatic, leaving just because someone said something."

"Have you been in Berlin lately? No, you were in Davos. Well, allow me to fill you in: SA are actively boycotting Jewish businesses. The newly established Propaganda Ministry is nationalizing all of the press, closing whoever disagrees with them. All Jewish professionals are finding themselves out of work due to decrees your wonderful Party pumps out with envious regularity. So, I would say, no. Leaving under such conditions isn't *a bit too dramatic*, but you wouldn't know of it because it doesn't concern you personally. You could have asked Sokal why he left and maybe offered the proceeds from the *Blue Light* to him yourself, as he damn sure could use them now that he's virtually homeless, but you're too absorbed in your own life to give a crap about anyone else's."

Her cheeks aglow, Leni drew herself up, shifting away from Aurelia and the sting of her words—Aurelia could almost sense her discomfort.

"This is why I've always been apolitical," Leni finally chirped, putting the smile back on like an ill-fitting mask. Noticing a waiter, she motioned him over and took two glasses of champagne from his tray, offering one to Aurelia. "It always gets people into fights. Let's not talk of it tonight. Better, tell me: what did you like the best in the *Blue Light*? From the point of view of photography. Yours is always so stunning, I would truly appreciate your honest opinion."

Aurelia watched her through ringlets of cigarette smoke and considered arguing further—but what good would that do?

"How much money do you need?" she finally asked, her eyes softening.

"Oh no, I'm all right, really." Leni tossed her head, the quarrel seemingly forgotten. "Don't mind my complaining, I just wanted to get it off my chest. It's not even so much Sokal himself; because he left without paying me, now I can't pay another person, Béla Balázs, who worked with me on the script..."

"How much?" Aurelia repeated, keeping her voice purposely discreet. She knew how sensitive such matters could be to artistic people, who, for the most part, were always scrabbling for money and even if they weren't at present, they still remembered how difficult it was, not to have any. "Better I give it to you than you mix with those... people."

Leni pressed her hand in gratitude but shook her head with finality. "Thank you, Ari, really. But I have already said yes."

"She wouldn't have taken your money," Max spoke once they had entered their home later that night. "Even if she didn't agree to that Horst Wessel documentary."

With their dogs Loki and Astrid nosing at their masters in great excitement, Aurelia looked at her husband. "Why on earth not?"

Max grinned, kneeling in front of his wife to help her with the buckles on her shoes. In her narrow dress, with the dogs slamming their bodies against them both, she didn't stand a chance to remove them by herself. "She resents you, that's why," he said.

"Whatever have I done to her?" Aurelia demanded in frank disbelief.

"She said it herself, it was you who gave her the initial push to get into filmmaking. It had never crossed her mind until you came along with your larger-than-life ideas." He held up his hand while Aurelia muttered something against this. "Let me finish. Then, while she was away filming, she probably half-expected to hear that you got shot at one of the protests or the other. Instead, you went and began working with me, soon to have your name alongside mine on UFA studios billboards."

"So? It's not like I stole her spotlight as Germany's first female director. I'm a cinematographer, not a director."

Also, unlike Leni, Aurelia actively avoided the spotlight despite the tabloids' obsession with the juxtaposition of her pure Nordic beauty and her rather rebellious personality. No matter from which side Aurelia considered it, she failed to see the reason for Leni's resentment.

"And another thing," Max continued, straightening up with one last appreciative glance at his wife's now-bare ankles. "You and me, we work like a well-oiled machine. You know exactly what I mean when I explain what I want from the scene and I know exactly what you mean whenever you suggest something." He gestured Loki and Astrid after himself, heading to the kitchen. "Let's go, you beasts. Let's see what Frau Abel left for you in the fridge. Meanwhile, Fanck," Max picked up where he left off, "despite working with Leni on several pictures, was either purposely obtuse or simply couldn't see what Leni had in mind for her independent project when she asked him to help her edit it. He didn't even consult her, just edited the entire affair himself. Remember how upset she was, telling us that she would have to rummage in a refuse bin to fish out whatever he sliced off and reassemble it all back together if he hadn't singed through the film with cigarette butts?"

Padding after him in her stockinged feet, Aurelia muttered, "I did offer to come up with her to his studio and slice off a piece of something very dear to him to teach him a lesson."

Max barked out a laugh as he pulled open a fridge door and Aurelia leaned against the countertop, sinking back into the past, reliving the scene he had reminded her of to find clues to the present.

"Little harsh, Ari," Max had protested that day, theatrically shocked, from the driver's seat. They were heading from Babelsberg, where they had picked Leni up, to Fanck's house doubling as his studio, in which he had so brutally sliced Leni's first independent project, according to her complaints.

Aurelia had tried to see them both from Leni's perspective. They must have presented a wonderful contrast, Max Laub and his new wife. He, middle class and half-Jewish, speaking and dressing with a learned refinement European bourgeoisie so desperately lapped up during their tender years in order to pass for nobles; and she, blue-blooded as they came, with ancestors hailing back to when Goths rode on horseback through present-day Berlin, tough as nails and with mouths to match.

"Harsh?" Aurelia had swung round toward him, her long, manicured claws digging into his knee. "Wasn't it you who threatened the new head of the UFA to quit if he dared censor your latest creation?"

"I threatened him to quit, not cut his manhood off," Max had responded without taking his intelligent, bespectacled eyes off the road.

"That's because he only raised the possibility of censoring certain scenes the new Reichstag majority may find unfavorable to Germany's moral well-being." Aurelia had swiped at the errand strand of her blonde hair tossed about by the warm July wind. "Would you react just as calmly if you walked into your editing room and he was there, slicing pieces of your film into the waste basket?"

A shade had passed over Max's forehead, wrinkling it, as something dark gleamed momentarily in his eyes.

"No, you would have stabbed him in his hand with those splicing scissors, that's what you would have done," Aurelia had finished for him, looking very self-satisfied at predicting such an outcome correctly—Leni must have seen it plain as day written all over Max's countenance. "So don't call me harsh. Your blood runs hotter than mine."

"No, you're cold like a snake," Max had commented with an elegant arch of his dark brow. "All poise and feigned indifference until your fangs are in someone's jugular."

Aurelia's lips had curled at his words as she'd moved away from Leni riding with them in the front and pressed herself against him. Leni must have barely caught the wind-torn sentence as it slipped off Aurelia's lips against his neck, just above the stiff white collar of Max's shirt: "You know just what to say to a girl, *Herr Direktor*."

Suddenly, Aurelia had realized what was going through Leni's mind as she'd pretended to be very interested in the peony someone's maid was cutting as they passed by yet another villa. It wasn't discomfort at their open affection but a spasm of desire to have this very kind of love—physical, almost tangible to those in its presence, and envied by the rest for its fiery purity.

The gravel of Arnold Fanck's driveway had crunched under the wheels of Max's Mercedes. Aurelia recalled seeing Leni looking at the villa colored pink by the rays of the descending sun, with the woods looming up ahead. Just like Max with Aurelia, it was Fanck who had given a chance to a waif-like, dark-haired girl to assist him with directing all those years ago. It was Fanck who had taught Leni all she knew. But he had never loved her like Max loved Aurelia. He never saw the world through the same eyes.

Aurelia understood it then, the reason for that resentment: it wasn't that she had everything Leni secretly coveted, it was the fact that Aurelia was everything Leni wanted to be. Bold, uncompromising, brutally honest with herself and others, and infuriatingly, astonishingly unafraid. Of anything. People were drawn to her for that very reason, lovers and haters alike. To add insult to injury, she could pick and choose the company she kept, the films she made, the morals by which she lived, while Leni had to sell her talents to the Nazis to ascend the career ladder, standing on the broken backs of yesterday's benefactors.

It couldn't have been an easy path. Aurelia was just beginning to wonder how she would feel in a similar situation, but her husband's hand found her knee in the dark and she forgot what she was thinking.

FIVE

Her two dogs in the front seat, Aurelia pulled into her designated parking place in front of the UFA studios in Babelsberg—Berlin's answer to Hollywood, sans picturesque hills and brush fires. The beasts, whose chains she wrapped twice around her wrist to lead them inside, weren't technically dogs. They were very much the progeny of Grünewald's increasingly rare gray wolf population, orphaned as pups after someone with a rifle had shot their mother in the middle of winter. Aurelia had come by them by sheer chance—almost entirely snowed in, shivering against their dead mother's cold body, three of their siblings already frozen stiff. She'd scooped them up at once and snuggled them, cold as icicles, trembling something frightful, against her breast.

Aurelia and Max's idea was to nurse them back to life and release them as soon as they were old enough to fend for themselves, but the wolf siblings had different thoughts on the matter. After Aurelia's tender care, the bottle feeding, the warm baths, the heat of her body as they snuggled up against her in their sleep, the pups had decided that this was their mother now and acted accordingly, following her close on her heels no matter where she went and baring their fast-growing teeth at anyone who dared come a tad too close.

They liked Max well enough, but for Aurelia, they would kill and die. In spite her best intentions, Aurelia had to submit to the idea that they now had dogs, Loki and Astrid. Frau Abel, their housekeeper, was frightened stiff of the "beasts", as she called them, but Heinz, their elderly groundskeeper, often delighted himself and the pups by playing tug-of-war, which they sometimes graciously allowed him to win.

For the past few months, the Laubs had managed just fine, keeping the wolves confined to the fenced-in interior of their estate; however, with the recent regime change, there was too much of a traffic increase with all kinds of new officials and their underlings coming and going—someone from the forestry department, someone from the census taking department, some Party agitators asking to sign support for who knows what. The point was, if Aurelia didn't want to deal with someone's torn limbs, she had to keep her loyal beasts where she could keep an eye on them at all times.

"Hey," she growled in a low voice in response to their low growl and wrapped the chain around her wrist a third time just in case.

Berthold, Max's assistant-director, came to an abrupt halt at the sight of the beasts standing level with Aurelia's left hip, and she was not a short woman by any measure. With tousled dark hair that framed his face in loose waves, Bibi, as he was affectionately called by those on the set, had an intellectual appearance. His deep-set brown eyes held a warmth and intensity that revealed a fierce dedication to his craft. Despite the pressures surrounding him as a Jewish man in a rapidly changing Germany, he maintained a spark of optimism that set him apart from those who had succumbed to the prevailing pessimistic mood—perfectly justified, as far as Aurelia was concerned. Like most of Max's crew, Berthold had been with him for years, starting off as a score writer but eventually falling in love with the film industry so much he aspired to make his own films now. Max was only too happy to teach the fellow Austrian expat everything he knew.

"Are those..." the young man swallowed, taking an involuntary step back. "Loki and Astrid? The dogs Laub always refers to?"

"The very same. I would advise strongly against looking them in the eye—they take it as a challenge of authority."

Berthold swiftly looked away from two pairs of amber eyes with a murderous glimmer in them. "Are they... wolves?"

"Wolves? No." Aurelia looked convincingly mortified. "Keeping wild wolves is against the law. These are harmless Siberian huskies."

Siberian huskies were thrice smaller in size and had tails curled in the friendliest of manners, but Aurelia herself had only seen them once in Soviet Russia, at the dacha of one of the government officials the German artistic delegation had been invited to after a modern art gallery opening. Berthold wouldn't know what they looked like; neither would anyone in Babelsberg.

He didn't appear pacified in the slightest, but nodded conciliatorily, more pressing matters than dog breeds on his mind. "Your ex-husband is here."

"Art?" Aurelia arched her brow, following Berthold inside.

"You have some other one I don't know about?" Max's assistant walked like a crab, refusing to turn his back on the "harmless huskies." After opening the heavy door, he promptly hid behind it to hold it open for his boss's wife from the safety of the other side.

"No, but—" Aurelia wrinkled her nose, a sense of foreboding settling over her.

Art had long ago devoted his life to humanity. For as long as Aurelia had known him, he'd been distributing his art, his time, his money, and all his efforts to save people. There was no lofty pathos to his noble goals, neither did he imagine himself Christ's second coming in an old Great War tunic. He simply offered his all to the needy until they could take care of themselves. Same happened to Aurelia, really: he had picked her, a runaway, up off Berlin's street, given her a home, his name, and a reason to live, and parted ways with her as soon as she'd matured into the woman Max Laub eventually met, wishing her all the best.

Sometimes Aurelia wondered whether Art had loved her in the first place. Sometimes she was certain that he had simply felt sorry for her, just like he did the others. At any rate, he wasn't the person to pay casual visits just because he was in the neighborhood.

Trying to shake the feeling of unease off, Aurelia tossed her head, allowing her eyes to get used to the darkness.

She had been coming here for years, but the studio's assault on one's senses would never dull as one crossed the invisible line from the real world into an imaginary one. Inside the pavilion, surrounded by shadows and thick ropes of cables snaking around the concrete floor, was a snapshot of a life the way a director conceived it, transported straight from the creative brain and onto the soundstage, with every detail as he willed it to be, every figment of his imagination transforming into a living and breathing person, speaking the words the omnipotent god that ruled this underworld put into their mouths. He breathed life into these actors, moved them like figures on a chessboard and rolled the camera while they fell in love, flew into rage or ecstasy, killed or died until they moaned that they couldn't give anything more to him. But he squeezed them in his vise-like grip and drove them to near desperation until they finally produced something so masterful that he would raise both his hands, with his artist's long, sensitive fingers, in the air as though to frame this very moment, and whisper, "Now *this*, ladies and gentlemen, was *beautiful*."

"I would die for him just then," Willy, one of Max's leading actors, had confessed during an interview. "I would hate him for weeks for putting me through this torment, for forcing me to repeat scene after scene, but there would always be that one moment when I felt like I was empty, I had nothing else to give, and he would give me one last shove—and after we were done, I knew I'd produced my best scene yet. And he knew it. Everyone knew it. I would literally lay my life for him in the moment like that."

Aurelia understood exactly what Willy was talking about. That's how she had fallen in love with Max.

And he'd regarded her so coldly at first, when she had come to ask him for a position of an assistant mere weeks after seeing *Last Letter Home* together with Zara and falling in love with what he had created on film—the impossible, arrogant, condescending Max Laub. "I know you. I know *of* you. You're an anarchist and a staple of Dadaist dives. You're unreliable. You will miss deadlines and won't show up at early-morning screenings. I arrive at the studio at five—isn't that when you just go to sleep?"

"Try me." She'd thrust her chin forward as a challenge, eyes feverish and dry. "Just one single chance, that's all I'm asking for. If I blow it, I blow it. You'll never see me or hear from me again."

He'd tilted his head to one side, the faint scar above his left eye barely visible in the shadows of the studio. A Great War wound that had left him partially blind—but of that, she'd only learned when they were already married. He knew how to hide his weaknesses.

"Forgive me for being so blunt." He had tried to soften the blow. "You're a beautiful woman. You're a great model. I bought your husband's *Aurelia in Wonderland* painting and there was quite a fight for it at the gallery."

"The 'Eat Me' one, with the cupcake covering my modesty?" Aurelia had passed her hand over her forehead, suddenly tired and annoyed—of her own wild reputation, which she had helped to create. She had never regretted baring herself for Art's canvas and, if anything, prided herself on getting a reaction out of the conservative circles she so passionately detested, but now it suddenly seemed to hinder her professional prospects.

"It hangs in my office, just above the working table."

"I bet your housekeeper loves it."

He'd grinned at her, as charming as it was rumored, and reached out to brush the hair she wore long and straight against the fashion. Aurelia had swatted away his hand.

"I don't want to sleep with you." She had licked her lips. She did want to sleep with him, very much—ever since she'd laid eyes on him directing a scene while waiting for a chance to speak with him. But if she did sleep with him, that was where it would all end, forever. "I want to work with you. Give me a chance."

A shadow had passed over his face, wiping off the charming grin, turning the embers in his eyes to ice in an instant.

"Be here tomorrow, at four fifty-five sharp, with a thermos of hot coffee. Bring lunch with you; times are hard and we make do with what we have. Wear trousers and comfortable shoes—you'll be climbing and crawling a lot. And a sweater, too. The studio is unheated."

A lip between her teeth to suppress a grin at the memories, Aurelia tied Loki and Astrid to a concrete column supporting the structure and wondered what Art could possibly want.

"Where is he?" she asked Berthold.

"In the storage."

"The storage?"

Berthold shrugged. "He had all of these paintings with him he insisted on hiding."

Bracing herself, Aurelia headed to the back of the pavilion, where the sets and costumes for Max's current picture were kept.

Art jumped out of the depths of the clothes racks at her like a jack-in-the-box and grasped Aurelia's shoulders with hands that were trembling beyond his ability to control them. In his mid-thirties, he possessed a memorable appearance: his blond hair, often overly long and unkempt, framed a face that bore the marks of a man who had seen too much. His intense gray eyes remained perpetually haunted with the memories of war. He was dressed in a simple shirt and worn trousers; yet, despite his modest attire, he carried himself with a defiant air, his fighting spirit emanating from his very being.

"Lia, thank God!" he cried, uncharacteristically frantic. "You know I wouldn't have come to you if it wasn't so important. You have to help me. You have to come with me, right this instant, while we still can do something about it! I grabbed everything I could from the studio, but everything I have in the attic—ugh, it's literally every wall, everything is dripping with art! You remember how we had it, don't you? Art instead of wallpaper and panels—that's how you wanted it and that's how we did it and it looked so very beautiful—"

"Art!" Aurelia grasped him back, frightened with his agitated state and hoping to still him. This was not like him, at all. The Art Nachtnebel she knew faced off SA thugs without a trace of fear, undeterred neither by the knives nor guns they loved to brandish. "Deep breath. Coherent sentences. I can't help you if I can't make head nor tail of what you're saying."

His gray eyes wild, he tossed his head, pale as ash, beads of sweat breaking on his forehead. "You don't understand, they're destroying my paintings! The anti-fascist ones—they gutted them with bayonets in front of the gallery manager. Slashed them and took them all to burn! Zara called me after he called her."

All blood leaving her extremities, Aurelia felt her fingers dig into her former husband's flesh. The entire pavilion suddenly ceased to exist, their world narrowing to the catastrophe enveloping them with lightning speed. She had recently attended that exhibit with Max; she had felt her breath being stolen at the powerful sight of a Nazi hyena salivating over market-crash-shaken Germany.

"Who did?"

"Who do you think?" His voice was sheer poison, but directed at someone else entirely; Aurelia felt that much. "The Brownshirts! The money from the sales was supposed to go to support the immigration efforts of the Jewish community and to see them through at least a year of the application process. Most of them got laid off, what will they live off?"

Neither of them noticed Max appearing by their side, as if from thin air. Dark brows drawn, he pushed his glasses back onto the narrow bridge of his nose, all composure as always.

"What's going on?" he demanded in the same polite tone he always employed whenever his union and non-union employees would come to near blows over the matter of overtime, which one group invariably requested (they were paid double for it) and the other just as ardently protested (their overtime was billed as regular hours).

Art dropped Aurelia's arms from his and wavered unsteadily, as if she were the only force that kept the ground from going from under his feet. "The Nazis marched into the Whitby galleries and confiscated nearly all pieces displayed there. Took all of mine that Zara had. Slashed them and put them into a truck bed. From what I learned, there will be some big pyre later tonight, to burn the so-called "degenerate art." That clubfoot Goebbels from the Propaganda Ministry has gone all medieval, imagines himself a grand inquisitor, no less."

Not a single muscle betraying his emotion, Max checked his wristwatch. "It's not even noon yet. Do you know where exactly they took their loot?"

Art shoved his hand into his trench coat pocket and produced a crumpled leaflet with a swastika on it. "Opernplatz. Some pimple-faced Hitler Youth gave it to me by mistake." Art's jowls worked under his skin as he passed the leaflet to Aurelia.

Down with un-German, degenerate art, crimson words called from its frontispiece as Aurelia smoothed the paper out with ice-cold fingers. *Join our student brotherhood in the first step to purify the great Aryan culture from the cosmopolitan, pacifist, and Jewish filth! Head into the nearest libraries and bookshops and remove the books authored by those listed underneath. Should anyone interfere with your patriotic effort, call the attention of any SA or SS member—they shall be patrolling the streets en masse. Bring all the books you can carry and follow our torch-bearing troops to Opernplatz—*

Aurelia's trained eye skipped the rest of the propaganda and scanned the list of newly banned writers and artists. Heine, Mann, Remarque, Marx, Hemingway, Brecht, London, Keller—the Nazis didn't seem to discriminate between political and fiction writers, German or international, Jewish or gentile. Anyone with a dissenting view was suddenly an enemy. The same went for the artists: Chagall, Matisse, Picasso, van Gogh—world-renowned geniuses also found themselves among the "degenerate" ranks. And right after Matisse, in perfect alphabetical order, Arthur Nachtnebel, her ex-husband, the original Dadaist, the man with whom she had narrowly escaped her mother's sorrowful fate.

"Well, at least you're in great company," Aurelia commented with a sardonic twitch of her lips.

Art only raised his eyes at her, eyes full of unspeakable torment, and to Aurelia, he suddenly looked like a man mortally wounded, helpless, even if still grinding his teeth at the enemy.

"Don't despair, old fellow," Max said with an amiable clap on Art's shoulder. "Not all is yet lost. I have a set decorator who can repair anything, including slashed canvas. Let's head to the Opernplatz and try to reason with them. We'll stop at the bank first, so that if reasoning doesn't prevail, we can count on money to work its magic—"

"No," Art stopped him abruptly, somber and sober like Aurelia had never before seen him. "I have no car. I borrowed a bicycle from a friend but still could only bring a handful to hide here. Let's stop by my place first. The bulk of my work is still there. Take all the paintings from here and from my studio and hide them somewhere they won't think to look."

Aurelia saw Max's mouth open to ask the same question that burned the tip of her tongue—do you really think they'll go that far?—and close shut like a clam.

"We have a spacious wine cellar," Aurelia spoke at last. "We'll store them there."

SIX

At the Nachtnebels' former residence—if the tiny, stuffy attic could be called so—they worked fast and in silence: Art taking precious canvases out of simple wooden frames, Max rolling them into tight cylinders and tying them up into neat little stacks, Aurelia taking the stacks into the car, near which Loki and Astrid were pacing, chains trailing on the gravel.

In the east, the twilight was just beginning to gather when they climbed into the Mercedes, Max and Art sharing the front seat and Aurelia sharing the back one with the dogs, her knees pulled up to her chin. Concealed under layers of furs, the remainder of Art's canvas lined the floor. With a wistful feeling, Aurelia almost regretted he was so prolific, that mad dissident former husband of hers. They couldn't fit all of his paintings into a single trunk.

Once safely inside the gates of the Laubs' mansion, Loki and Astrid roaming the grounds, they moved inside, one funeral procession, carrying the body of slaughtered Dadaist art on their shoulders. Only dim wall sconces lighting their way, they filed out of the hallway, through the kitchen and down the stairs into the wine cellar. Down below, the air smelled of earth and stone and it fitted the somber occasion somehow. Unconcerned over his tailor-cut trousers, Max knelt in front of one of the wine racks, pulled out three bottles of Château Mouton Rothschild and, depositing them with utmost care on the stone floor, reached for Nachtnebel's canvases.

"We'll stack them all here for now," Max said, carefully depositing the first few rolls onto the rack. "I hope you don't mind these French fellows for company." He tried to lighten the mood with a jest, nodding at the collection of French wines.

"Unlike the old government, I never had any quarrel with them," the artist grumbled after a long moment of contemplation. "Enjoy it while you can. The new government is already saying it wants to get even."

The night was still young when they turned from Wilhelmstraße to Under den Linden, but the torchlight procession was already in full swing. With traffic ground to a halt, they abandoned their car and hesitantly allowed the crowd to pull them into its current. Animated, wild-featured faces all around them, they felt themselves strangers among the people they lived with side by side. Without exchanging a single remark, they found themselves grasping each other's sleeves so as not to be separated in this torch-bearing march spewing hateful slogans along with black smoke into the sky slowly bleeding out above the Brandenburg Gate.

Once they reached the Opernplatz, the people's river flowed into its basin, forming a circle around the towering pyre at its center, still unlit. Black-clad SS stood watch over it with torches at their shoulders, facing the crowd.

"If they're standing guard, not all is lost," Max turned to his companions, his face alight with purpose. "There must have been threats issued of counteraction. Let's try to make it to the speaker's podium; perhaps, we can talk sense to someone with authority."

Austrian to the marrow, Max was already politely apologizing his way toward the front, whereas any Berliner would simply elbow his way forward, cursing out anyone who'd give him a dirty look.

"They aren't standing guard to protect it," Art muttered near Aurelia's ear so only she would hear it. "They're just making sure the crowd doesn't push too close forward in its desire to do away with the dissidents and stumble into the flames."

"I know," Aurelia said.

"Why are we following him then?"

"Max he's..." Aurelia searched for the right word. "An idealist. He believes only the best in people. Unlike us, he had a happy childhood and when parents love you like that, you don't see the world like we do. And I won't be the one to tell him."

"He'll get clipped in the mug if you don't."

"He won't."

"He's Jewish, Lia, and looks it."

But Max had already removed his elegant hat and held it against his chest, greeting one of the SS thugs in his well-bred manner.

"Good evening, *Herr Offizier*. I am terribly sorry to bother you while you're carrying out your duties, but could you perhaps take a moment of your time and simply point me in the direction of a person in charge of the event organizing? My name is Max Laub, I'm a film director, and I desperately need to have a word with him."

The SS man narrowed his eyes at Max, regarding him for a very long time. Finally, having decided something for himself, he unclenched his jaw to utter: "Are you a scheduled speaker?"

Max hesitated just enough for Aurelia to push her way

forward before he could speak the truth and ruin it all with his damned honesty.

"Yes, we are. My name is Aurelia von Brandenburg. I believe my brother, Ministerpräsident von Brandenburg, is here. I demand to see him, *now*." No polite asking in her voice, no suppliant tilt of the head. She spoke to him like a woman who'd grown up in a household that considered everyone else beneath them if they didn't share the privilege of belonging to the same class. Aurelia loathed employing the same tone that was the only one her father could communicate with, but if this was the only one they understood, so be it.

The SS man clicked his heels at once and, having motioned to one of his comrades to mind the gap created in the line, set off toward the back of the podium, guarded much heavier than the pyre. Aurelia gazed after him, not wishing to acknowledge the mixture of amazement and hurt in Max's eyes fastened on her impassive face. This was the first time she had publicly uttered the hated family name she'd shed more than a decade ago and particularly after it began making the rounds in nationalistic circles with her half-brother's rising to power as Hitler's right hand.

Not that Wilhelm wanted to have anything to do with her, his half-sister from that mad woman his father had made a mistake to marry. Thankfully at least, Maria had offed herself, saving the family from the embarrassment of having to lock her up in an asylum. Would be nice if Aurelia followed her example —these were the last words the brother and sister exchanged the final time they'd seen each other what felt like eons ago.

Art snorted, not bothering to hide his amusement. "Do you seriously think he'll come over for a chat? With you?"

Still as an arrow in a taut bow, Aurelia nodded with calm self-assurance. "He will. Even if just to gloat."

"He won't give you anything." Art drew himself up

suddenly. "And I don't want you to even consider humiliating yourself by asking. Let the lot burn. To the devil with it all."

He was still clasping her sleeve, but Aurelia's eyes had already sought her brother out of the crowd. He towered even over his entourage of handpicked SS men, making his way toward the podium, near which he paused, a grin slowly spreading on his undeniably handsome face. He was the bridge that helped Hitler reach from filth-infested beer halls to high-ranking army and nobility. It was Wilhelm who had opened the bursting purses of aristocracy and funded Hitler's campaigns for the past ten years. It was Wilhelm who, with the aid of the Nazi Party, had bought himself the position of the de-facto president of Prussia—the place his ancestors used to own and rule. With social democrats in power, he would have been one of the shunned, the former oppressing class, a ghost of the past epoch, belonging in the dusty libraries and museums together with the Kaiser. But with the Nazis, he was a feudal prince once again, with the entire army at his disposal.

There was a ten-step distance between them. Wilhelm waited for Aurelia to come to him.

For a few moments, she considered. Aware of the Minister of Propaganda Goebbels making his ascent to the brightly lit podium, aware of the sea of arms rising to greet him in the Nazi salute, aware of the deafening shouts of "Heil" rolling over her like the waves of the North Sea, Aurelia stood perfectly still.

Smiling wider, now laughing, Wilhelm shook his head and made a step forward, feeling charitable in his new uniform with its golden sash and a diamond-encrusted sword. Aurelia stepped toward him as well, obstinate to distraction just like her mother was, playing the familiar game that used to drive him up the wall when they were mere children.

They finally met in the middle, face to face, taking each other in with the unhealthy obsession of mortal foes.

"You look so much older, sister. I'd say your mother looked

better in her coffin, but since she put a shotgun to her head, I'd rather rephrase it to, your mother looked better just before she pulled the trigger."

Aurelia smiled at him sweetly and poked him in the sash. "And you look so much fatter, brother. Too many state dinners and not enough horseback riding? Mind you don't end up like Daddy, with both legs missing from diabetes. How is he doing, by the way? Still polluting the air?" Her expression was a picture of mock-concern.

"Father passed three years ago. You would have known it, had you been reading anything besides *Red Front*."

"I don't read *Red Front*."

Wilhelm arched his brow, feigning surprise. "No longer a commie, eh?"

"Never was."

He tapped his temple. "Smart words, sister. Such associations are no longer in fashion. May even land you in jail, God forbid."

Aurelia yawned at the threat without covering her mouth. "Enough with the courtesies. Aren't you going to ask me what I'm doing here?"

Wilhelm put his finger to his lips, all theatrical contemplation. "Let's see. Seeing that you're here in the company of both of your husbands and seeing that one of them is on the list, I would venture to guess you'd like his paintings back."

"Close, but no cigar." Aurelia smiled brightly.

To anyone watching them from afar, the siblings would appear cordial and at perfect ease with one another—a long-lost family connection mending itself at the dawn of the new regime's reign. Who would go and slander the new Führer now, accusing him of stoking hatred? Just look how he had brought these two together.

"No?" The President of Prussia pulled back, blue eyes wide and innocent. "You've got me intrigued. What is it then?"

Aurelia stepped even closer to him, taking one of his gold buttons into her fingers. With everyone's attention riveted to Goebbels, she could speak to him heart to heart.

"You love money more than anything, Willy, brother. You're not a Nazi any more than you're the regular soldier you pass yourself for. Had the Reds had a program that didn't abolish private property, you would have traveled around with Trotsky—don't argue, we both know it for a fact. You were probably busy in the past few months, buying the election and securing yourself all sorts of government posts that would allow you a deeper dip into Germany's coffers, so you wouldn't have time for a little research. So I'll save you the time. Arthur Nachtnebel's *War Pigs* was sold at a Christmas auction in New York for a quarter of a million dollars. His *No Man's Land* was sold for over three hundred thousand. The *Portrait of Guts and Bone* went to a museum for half a million. Another one—I don't recall the name—sold for another quarter of a million. Feel free to contact Zara Whitby—she's Art's dealer—and she'll produce the exact receipts for you. What you're about to throw in that pyre, brother, costs over two million dollars. Are you really that stupid?"

Money was always a safe bet with Wilhelm. Blood, friendship, art for art's sake—nothing touched him. Had she tried appealing to his conscience, he would have laughed in her face and personally thrown the paintings in the fire. But now that she'd put a price on them, the cogs were quickly turning in that cold, calculating mind of his.

"I'm afraid you're too late, sister," he said eventually as if probing the ground. "Herr Minister's"—a disdainful toss of the head at Goebbels shouting into the microphone—"men took the task on a bit too ardently. The paintings are all slashed."

Aurelia shrugged as if this was of no consequence. "Nothing that can't be restored. I bet they'll fetch even more now, with their 'wounds' and the story that they nearly escaped the pyre."

Wilhelm licked his lips, glanced over his shoulder with barely perceived annoyance. "Even if so, how do you suggest I pull them out of there?"

"Aren't paintings on the top? They burn slower than books. It would make sense to leave them on top, where the flames will be the hottest, to consume them faster. Besides, oil paintings burn so beautifully."

"Oh, you don't have to remind me of that. I remember quite well how your mother set fire to a portrait in the living room."

Once again, Aurelia shrugged, unconcerned. "Must have been a really rotten portrait."

Wilhelm cursed quietly under his breath, his eyes fixed on the pyre. "Why would I agree to it? How would I even go about selling them?"

"How everyone else does. Anonymously and through a dealer."

"You have answers to everything, don't you? And what's in it for you?" He looked suddenly suspicious.

Just like he wouldn't understand any appeals, he wouldn't understand *"Art is my ex-husband and I feel bad for him."* So, Aurelia spoke to him in his language instead.

"I'm not stupid either, brother. You're a big man now, with lots of power in your hands. One hand washes the other and all that. I do this for you now and, who knows, maybe you'll do a favor for me in the future?"

"Such as not jail you once someone conscientious puts you on the list?"

"Something to that extent, yes. Art's paintings are signed with a big red X in the corner instead of his name—they're easily identifiable. Now wrap it up and fast; your comrade over there is just about done whipping the crowd into a frenzy. Even your SS won't be able to contain them soon."

Wilhelm von Brandenburg must have seen it too. He quickly motioned to someone from his entourage and gave him orders in his clipped manner.

"There are some paintings that were put in there by mistake. They're all labeled with an X to mark them out of selection, but someone who is about to be dismissed from service piled them up all the same. Fetch several men and pull them all out, and be snappy about it if you don't want to fish them out when the fire is already lit."

The adjutant snapped to attention and bolted toward the rest of the President's escort. Before long, they were crawling all over the pyre, pulling Art's antifascist collection out of the communal grave.

Not a soul questioned anything.

With the paintings safely locked in the trunk of his staff car, Wilhelm von Brandenburg ascended the podium and gave a signal to light the fire alongside the Minister of Public Enlightenment.

Their faces awash with infernal heat, Aurelia, Art, and Max watched the pages churn and fly into the black air—the last embers of freedom turning to ash before their very eyes.

"Where they burn books, they shall soon burn people."

Both Aurelia and Art turned to Max in surprise. He'd been silent this entire time, silent and very still, like a man who had returned from the war to find his house in ruins and his entire family dead. Only, instead of just one home, the whole country was burning to the ground before his very eyes.

"Don't look at me." He smiled with tragic solemnity. "I didn't say it, Heine did. There he is, the old man. Burning."

With that, he bowed his head at the pyre, turned on his heel, and only then put his hat back on.

He was done with this funeral. He was going home.

SEVEN

The Laubs' and the Whitbys' weekly Horcher dinner was a somber occasion this time. James, his pale-blue suit in stark contrast to the sea of black and brown uniforms, barely spoke at all, his mind already back in New York. Zara hardly touched her shrimp, nursing her third martini and replacing cigarettes in her golden holder, one after another. Aurelia was loudly crushing ice between her teeth as she stared down a uniform occupying the next table, who was clearly bothered by the sound. Only Max tried to inject some life into the conversation, reminiscing on last year's vacation to Long Island and prattling about James's antics on his sailboat, snapping his fingers whenever an English word eluded him.

He spoke French like a native, thanks to a French governess that had raised him back in Austria, but English still gave Max trouble. Nevertheless, he insisted on speaking it since James's German was even worse.

"You brought the boat so close to the Statue of Liberty, you almost stabbed her toe! And then you insisted we disembark and have a picnic on Liberty Island, in the middle of the night."

"We were all so drunk," Zara murmured, expressionless.

Her lined almond eyes stared, unseeing, somewhere past Max's shoulder. A Berlin-New York style icon, she hadn't bothered curling her short, dark hair today; simply parted it sharply on one side and brushed it back. Her burgundy lipstick matched her nails, but Aurelia couldn't help but notice a few chips on their always immaculate edges. She was back to biting them, like she used to when they were young girls.

"*Give me your tired, your poor, your huddled masses yearning to breathe free.*" James quoted from memory the lines etched onto the bottom of the Statue of Liberty. His unfocused gaze fixed suddenly on Max. He smiled brightly—that open, all-American smile that had stolen Zara's heart all those years ago. "Why don't you come stay with us again this summer? The house is too big for just the two of us. We'll sail again, go down as far as the Florida Keys—or, hell, Cuba even! And when we grow bored of the ocean, we'll rent two suites at the Plaza and go see a new Broadway play every night, take boats out in the park, drink forbidden booze at speakeasies—it'll be fun!"

Zara shifted in her seat. "Yes, come stay with us! Lia, you can help me set up new exhibits for the fall; there will be so much to do now, with all those paintings being shipped from Germany. Speaking of," she lowered her voice, leaning closer to Aurelia, "your special goods are on the way to New York, all arranged to be sold at a private auction my manager is setting up. The buyers are already lining up, after I let slip that I'll be selling newly banned Nachtnebel. Some don't even want the canvas fixed. They want to exhibit them as is, with bayonet slashes, in between two panes of glass."

"I'm glad I wasn't wrong about that," Aurelia said.

"You know us, Americans," James said, stabbing a shrimp with a good-natured chuckle, "anything banned makes us drool. Just look at how popular we made the Prohibition."

"Ari can go if she likes," Max said, touching his wife's wrist with affection. "But I'm afraid I'm a bit tied up."

"I thought you'd finished filming," Zara said, signaling the waiter for another martini. To Aurelia, several drinks in, she still looked perfectly sober. Events of the past few weeks must have strained her nerves to such an extent that alcohol had no effect on her whatsoever.

"We did, but now I have to edit the entire thing."

"*I* have to edit?" Aurelia repeated, arching her brow at her husband. "Am I fired then, *Herr Direktor?*"

Max grasped her hand and kissed it with passion, his eyes gleaming momentarily reddish-brown behind his spectacles. "Never, my love. I'm just saying, why lock yourself up in a stuffy editing room with me if you can sun your beautiful body by the ocean with your friends? Take the dogs with you; they love swimming. I'll finish everything up here and will—"

He was interrupted by one of the uniforms from the neighboring table—the same one who kept throwing dirty glances Aurelia's way. Shoving his chair aside and clearing his throat, he stood before the friends' table with his hand resting on his leather belt. "Are you all foreign nationals?" he inquired loftily. He was young, younger than anyone at the table, yet held himself superior. Uniform did that to people; Aurelia had learned it as early as she learned to walk.

"We're Germans," she responded coolly, "but my friend's husband is an American who doesn't speak German, so we speak English on his benefit."

The officer offered a thin-lipped smile in response to that. "He'd better learn it then. Germany's official language is German. Foreign nationals are required to speak it and particularly if they're married to German nationals. It's the law."

"Never heard of it," Aurelia countered.

"It's new."

"I bet."

Under the table, Max's shoe touched the tip of her foot— *don't make any waves, will you?*

But the SS man had already fished a small notebook out of his breast pocket. "And your name is...?" he inquired with a pointed look at Aurelia, his mechanical pencil poised over the page.

Aurelia couldn't help but notice how interested all the civilian patrons suddenly became in their respective dishes—heads lowered, shoulders hunched. A pathetic herd, she smirked. That's how they'd ended up with that moron controlling the entire Reichstag, looking away and keeping their heads down when they shouldn't have.

"Aurelia von Brandenburg."

Aurelia stared at Max, who was the one who had uttered her name—her family name—instead of their shared, married one.

"Yes, like President von Brandenburg," Max answered the SS man's unasked question. "She's *Herr Ministerpräsident*'s sister."

The SS man chewed on something but then snapped his notebook shut without putting anything down, clicked his heels, and returned to his table.

"The hell did you do that for?" Aurelia hissed at her husband as soon as the SS was out of the earshot.

Max shrugged and poked at his steak tartare without meeting her gaze. "Von Brandenburg is a better name to have now than Laub."

"I like Laub."

"I know."

"I only introduced myself as von Brandenburg to get Art's paintings out of that pyre for him."

"I know."

"After he gets his money, I want nothing to do with my brother, whatsoever."

"I understand."

It had always infuriated Aurelia, this studied compliance of his. No matter how spoiling she could be for a fight, he yessed her to death until there was nothing for it but to let the matter be.

"What happened?" James asked no one in particular, having grown tired from turning his head this way and that without anyone explaining to him what the trouble was.

"They want us all to speak German," Zara muttered, downing her fourth martini. "Apparently, it's the new law."

"*Ich kann sprecher Deutsch,*" James said, carefully stringing German words together.

Aurelia saw the glare Zara threw at him through the cigarette smoke rising from her holder before speaking under her breath, "Oh, shut up, James."

"*Ich spreche...*" James insisted.

Zara stared at the Laubs across the table, ignoring her husband as one would a child who knows not what he's talking about. "Why don't you both come with us?" Zara asked. "Stay for as long as you want. There's plenty of work to be had in New York, or in Hollywood if you like."

Aurelia looked at her husband, the fire of a wild child of the twenties igniting in her eyes. "Why the hell not? Nothing holds me here. Let's go."

Max claimed that it had always amazed and confused him in equal measure—this spontaneous nature of hers. She shed her former selves like a salamander its skin, moving onto a new adventure without a single glance back. Nothing bound her, neither the land, nor family; certainly not profession. She grew bored of people, places, and certain life choices just as she grew bored of things and discarded them, no matter how desirable she considered them not that long ago. He admitted that he feared this thrill-seeking of hers as well, feared that she'd grow tired of him someday. Perhaps that was the reason he loved her with such abandon, because deep down, he suspected that domestic bliss would never last with someone like Aurelia. One day, she'd be gone—what a fearsome, terrible thought!—and then what would he do with his empty, pitiful life that would lose all its color?

"But, Ari, my film," he pleaded with her softly, smiling, suspecting the worst.

But she only nodded and kissed his hand in turn. "So, I'll stay then until it's finished. We'll edit it together and then we'll go to New York."

"You don't want to go without me?"

"No, I don't want to go without you."

Inside Max's chest, his very heart blossomed into a carpet of flowers.

EIGHT

The summer sun hung low in the sky, casting a warm golden light over the cemetery as Aurelia Laub walked hand in hand with her husband. Ever since she was a child, she had always found comfort here, alone among the silent gravestones over-grown by moss. No one could find her here—a young girl surrounded only by the dead, slumbering deep and at peace under the ground she remained on. No wonder her mother, Maria, had chosen the serenity of the cemetery over life at Otto von Brandenburg's estate; the headstone under which Maria rested was warmer than the walls of Aurelia's childhood home.

"He did it out of spite, you know," Aurelia spoke softly as they made their way through the neatly arranged gravestones, the soft crunch of gravel beneath their feet echoing in the still-ness. "Buried her here, in her family's plot instead of the von Brandenburgs' familial vault."

"Your father?" Max asked as they approached Maria's grave, a modest stone marker nestled among the shadow of apple trees.

Aurelia nodded, caressing the headstone with her hand. "He said she didn't deserve to be among the von Brandenburg family after she took her own life. Even if it was him who drove

her to it." A sneer touched fleetingly upon her lips before
turning into a smile full of infinite sadness. "Instead, he did her
a favor. I know she's happy to be rid of him and can finally rest
peacefully like she deserves. Hello, Mama," Aurelia spoke to
the headstone softly, her voice barely above a whisper as she lay
flowers atop the grave before settling next to it with her legs
crossed. "What have you been up to lately? Haunting
Wilhelm, I hope? I know I will when I'm dead. Him and his
cronies too."

Max knelt beside her, his presence a comforting anchor. "A
bit too soon for such talks," he spoke to her gently.

"That's what she must have thought when she married
him." Aurelia took a deep breath, feeling the rush of memories
flood her mind. "She was much too young to marry in the first
place, but my grandfather died too soon, leaving my grandmother with five daughters and only a small government
pension to support them. They were all beautiful girls, but it
was their curse as much as a blessing. My mother had to marry a
man thirty-five years her senior to ensure the rest of her family
didn't go completely destitute... so that at least her sisters could
marry for love. She was only sixteen."

Aurelia heard Max's breath catch in the silence that
followed. They'd been married for quite some time, but she had
never divulged any details of her family's past, brushing it with
vague strokes only and sweeping under the rug what she didn't
care to remember. Not that she thought he wouldn't understand; Aurelia simply hesitated shedding the armor she wore to
keep anything—anyone—from getting under her skin. As Art
had once taught her, people who have nothing and no one to
lose are the most fearsome. Ungovernable. And she had liked
being ungovernable... until Max had come along. She still didn't
care what happened to her; it was him that she worried about—
more and more, with each passing day.

"I could never understand how some men can, in good

conscience, take children for brides," Max spoke with a disgusted shake of the head.

"Because young girls are much more pliable and easier to mold into whatever those men desire. That's precisely what he was doing with her—pruning even the slightest independent streak in her to shape her into a perfect little bonsai tree to exhibit in front of his friends," Aurelia hissed with disdain before tossing her head and resting her back against the headstone, warmed by the sun, reminding her of her mother's embrace.

For some time, there was silence between them, interrupted only by the chirping of the birds nesting in the trees overhead and the occasional cry of a frog also warming itself in the sun by the lily pond nearby. Her eyes closed, Aurelia heard Max stretch his legs next to her. His wedding band was warm against her skin when he found her hand and pressed it.

Prompted by the tenderness that made her heart swell, Aurelia felt words slipping easily off her tongue in this moment of shared intimacy: "Have I ever told you the story that about a gypsy cursing the von Brandenburgs' clan?"

"No?" Max sounded surprised.

Aurelia grinned, shadows playing upon her face tilted toward the sky. "During the Franco-Prussian war, my father and his father fought on the Kingdom's side under von Bismarck's command. And if you remember anything about the man, he was strongly in favor of iron and blood instead of diplomacy. On the battlefield, Bismarck was just as ruthless. One day—Big Brother told me this, believe it or not—the cavalry regiment under my grandfather's command encountered a gypsy camp in the field von Bismarck fancied for military purposes for the upcoming attack. Wilhelm doesn't know for a fact whether it was Bismarck's order or our grandfather's initiative, but the point is, my father rode into it with his men, sabers unsheathed, and began to slaughter men, women, and children alike. When

the carnage was over and my father was on the ground supervising the removal of the bodies, an old woman grasped him by
the boot and, with her dying breath, cursed his entire bloodline.
He laughed at her then but must have remembered the old
gypsy when all of his children began to die after his firstborn,
Wilhelm. There were seven of them altogether, the last one not
only not drawing his first breath but taking his mother with him
as well."

Next to her, Max shivered momentarily. "You know just the
stories to tell in the cemetery," he grumbled half in jest. "You
should have waited for night to fall for a better effect."

"Say what you will, but Wilhelm's wife also died without
giving him any children. I never got pregnant either—not that
either of us wants any children."

Max shrugged, kissing her knuckles. "We'd make lousy
parents. Much too busy and self-absorbed. We barely have
enough time for Astrid and Loki with our schedule. And particularly now, with everything going on. There's too much uncertainty in the world to bring children into it. I'd rather take
Nachtnebel's route and donate to the orphanages once I get us
out of the *Caesar*'s budget hole I got us in." He chuckled softly.
"I swore to provide for you when we married and now look at
me, up to my neck in debts, worse than your ex-husband."

"Money comes, money goes," Aurelia mused philosophi-
cally. "We wanted to produce *Caesar* ourselves so that no studio
would have any say over the message. Fortunately, the bank
agreed to use the house as collateral to issue us a loan."

"Thank you for agreeing to it."

"It wasn't my house to have any say in what you do to it.
You bought it long before I came along."

"It is yours. All of mine is yours."

"I'd say all of mine is yours as well, but I'm afraid, I can only
offer you a family curse."

"I'll take it," Max agreed surprisingly easily, wrapping his arm around Aurelia's shoulders. "I was thinking, when we release *Caesar*, we can use the proceeds to sponsor families as well. You know, the ones Art mentioned. Those who want to immigrate."

Aurelia blinked her eyes open and saw her own smile reflected in her husband's face. Once again, as happened so often between them, he was voicing precisely what she was contemplating. And around them, like an invisible embrace, her mother's presence like a blessing.

"She would have liked it," Aurelia whispered, fingers of her free hand feeling the ground with all its life sustained by it.

"Your mother?" Max smiled after seeing Aurelia nod. "Tell me more about her. What was she like?"

"Slightly mad, just like I am." Her quiet laughter poured like a melody into the molten golden air shimmering around them. "She loved her horses. Loved the water—we'd spend hours by the lake in summer. Loved animals, all kinds. I don't remember her ever as much as killing a spider. She'd catch them and release them outside instead. She loved me. She took me everywhere she went, even though we had a governess, but I can count on my hand the number of times she would look after me instead of my mother."

Her eyes veiled with memories Aurelia wished so desperately to have more of.

"I was only seven when she... when she left us." She sighed, growing melancholy. "Not that I blame her. My brother pretended she didn't exist; she could live with that. It was my father who took wicked pleasure in snuffing the tiniest sliver of joy she had. She had her favorite mare—he shot the mare. She took care of a cat that had just kittens in the barn—he found out and wrung their necks in front of her. In front of both of us."

At once, Max's hand wrapped around her shoulders, his grip reassuring. "Oh, Ari, how absolutely terrible! I'm so very sorry. It must have been incredibly difficult for her." He added softly after a pause, "To feel that escape was the only option."

"It must have been," Aurelia replied, her eyes dry but tormented beyond belief. "I sometimes wonder what she would have been, if she were free."

"I know precisely what she would have been." Max's lips caressed Aurelia's temple with such tenderness, it made her heart ache. "You're living that life right now, for both of you."

Aurelia looked at him, her gaze filled with love and gratitude. "You always know what to say."

"Unless it comes to scripts. It was you who finished *Caesar*."

"What would I do without you?"

He smiled, brushing a strand of hair behind her ear. "You'll never have to find out. We're in this together."

As they sat together, side by side, Aurelia felt a sense of peace wash over her. In the midst of grief, they had found a moment of connection—a reminder that love could endure even in the face of loss. Together, they would carry on the legacy of those who had come before them, honoring their memories while forging a path toward a brighter future.

With a final glance at her mother's grave, Aurelia whispered, "I love you, Mama. One day, I shall make you proud."

"You already did." Max regarded her in surprise, helping her to her feet.

"Not yet." Aurelia dusted herself off, her eyes on the horizon. "But one day, I will."

NINE

With the first day of film edits almost behind them, Max remained in his chair while Aurelia was arranging for the screening of the scenes they'd just cut. It was a great film. Maybe their best yet—a groundbreaking exploration of one of history's most iconic figures. Only, instead of glorifying Julius Caesar as a great leader and military genius as most of their predecessors had done, the Laubs had gone for a more nuanced and critical portrayal. Their Roman emperor was no hero, but a tyrant and dictator whose thirst for power had led to the erosion of the Republic he'd claimed to protect.

Was it a gamble, portraying ancient Rome as an allegory for the struggles facing Germany, particularly with the new Chancellor in charge? *Gamble* was putting it mildly, Max thought, playing with the slices of film that hadn't made it into the final cut. The international press were already salivating over it; the German press was conspicuously quiet.

"To hell with them," Max muttered, swiping the film slices into the waste bin. That much was expected. The Laubs hadn't made *Caesar* to appeal to the Nazis, neither had they made it to openly challenge them. No, *Caesar* was a film for the people—

German and the rest of the world—encouraging them to question the nature of power and the responsibilities of leadership. It was a warning tale, urging viewers to remember the lessons of history, and recognize the dangers of unchecked ambition. Max expected the firestorm to erupt upon its release.

Intoxicated by the process—films were his drug of choice—Max began to look through the scenes arranged for the following day's edits. His eyes stung with strain, particularly the bad one, but the smile on his face grew all the same as he savored Aurelia's cinematography like rare, rich wine. Even on narrow strips of film, her touch was powerful and atmospheric, with sweeping shots of Rome's majestic architecture juxtaposed with the stark realities of its political turmoil. She loved playing with shadows, which sometimes drove Max to distraction, but this time he had to admit, the high-contrast lighting she had used really did marvels to emphasize the moral ambiguities of Caesar's character. If he had any money left, he'd gladly offer her a raise.

Max hadn't told Aurelia anything yet, but he had requested for her name to be put alongside his in the opening credits, instead of acknowledging her as a cinematographer only. Berthold was supposed to deliver them to the studio today. Giddy in anticipation, Max picked up the phone and asked the operator to connect him with the Babelsberg tech lab where Bibi worked.

A film by Max and Aurelia Laub. He could almost see it before his eyes while he waited for the connection.

As the husband and wife had popped the champagne on the last day of filming as their personal tradition had it, they knew that they had not only crafted a compelling cinematic experience, they had also taken a stand for the values they believed in—a stand that resonated deeply in a world teetering on the brink of chaos. It was only fair to share the credit for it like they shared everything else.

"Herr Laub?" An unfamiliar voice answered instead of Bubi.

"Yes, erm..." Max regarded the phone in his hand, confused. "Who am I speaking with?"

"Martin Helm."

Max muttered a greeting, growing impatient. "I need to speak to my assistant, Berthold Wolowsky. He was supervising the work of my artist, Stern."

A pause. "I'm your artist, Herr Laub. Apologies, but no one told me about any supervisors."

"Since when?"

"Since this morning. I used to work just with Fräulein Riefenstahl, but now you two share my services for a while, I'm afraid."

With a rush of blood to his head, Max tossed it, annoyed. "No. There must be some sort of mistake. Stern has always been my artist. I only work with him. Is he ill? I spoke with him just yesterday and he was fine."

"I really can't say, Herr Laub." Helm's tone was sincerely apologetic. "They simply told me that I work for you now."

"Who told you that?"

"Herr Kranz's man."

Max's scowl grew deeper at the name of the UFA studios executive. They'd had their share of run-ins over the years, mostly concerning the budgets Max could never stick to and his refusal to submit to censorship, no matter how lax, but Kranz had never taken such liberties as appointing Laub's personnel. In fact, Kranz had all but stayed away from Max and his sound-stages ever since Laub began securing his own producers and became a household name that could guarantee a box office hit. Even when Hitler's new policy purging all Jews from countless positions had sent shockwaves through Babelsberg, Max's own pavilion remained a safe haven for them. If they weren't on the UFA payroll, there was nothing the Nazi thugs could do but grind their teeth in helpless ire. It was Max, personally, who paid his staff. Therefore, it was only him who could fire any of them.

Max thanked Helm mechanically and hung up. With a growing sense of unease in his stomach, he picked up the receiver again.

"Max Laub. Herr Kranz, please. It's urgent."

"Herr Kranz has already left."

"Call his home. It's urgent."

Background hum as the operator was trying for a connection.

"No one is answering, Herr Laub."

"Who's left at the office?"

"It's past eight, Herr Laub. Everyone's left for the day, except for the technical personnel." The girl sounded as though she wished she had gone home too.

Max slammed the phone down and headed to the viewing room, only to find his wife arguing with the projector operator—also some new fellow, not their regular one.

"Max, can you make sense of what he's telling me?" Aurelia turned to him, her eyes flashing in the dark room like those of a cat. "This gentleman I'm seeing for the first time in my life is saying there's no score to use with the opening credits—and no opening credits either—when I personally arranged for the score to be delivered here for tonight's viewing."

Married or not, when it came to work, Aurelia retained the attitude of a precautious employee who prided herself on irreproachable work ethics. The very thought of Max suspecting her of the slightest shortcoming still visibly mortified her, even though she should have been well aware by now that he would forgive her even if she set his entire pavilion on fire.

"I know it wasn't your fault, because I personally arranged for the opening credits and they aren't here either." Max fixed the new operator with his dark eyes. "Whatever happened to my projectionist?"

The new one, with cheeks and jowls drooping like molten wax, mopped the sweat off his brow and pulled the pale blue uniform gown together defensively. The garment, that had obviously come off someone else's shoulder, positively refused to close over his rotund form. "Just like I told Frau Laub here, I don't know diddly-squat about any such person or any scores or credits. They pulled me out of a motion pictures theater where I was working weekends only and now I'm stuck here in this godforsaken UFA—it took me an hour and a half by train and bus to get here this morning—minding this booth until I'm dismissed. Speaking of, when am I going home?"

"As far as I'm concerned, you may leave now. No skin off my nose," Aurelia said through her teeth.

Max, too, waved the man off. Both of them knew how to operate the projector. Without a score and opening credits, that was all there was to it.

Left alone in the darkened room with only a few chairs in it and a single ray of bright light emanating from the projection booth, the husband and wife exchanged looks.

"All right." Max heaved a sigh. "Let's see what we have."

Both watched it straight from the projection booth. The film opened with grand scenes of Caesar's military triumphs, showcasing the lavish parades and celebrations that accompanied his conquests. However, as the narrative unfolded, the tone shifted dramatically. The camera lingered on the faces of the common people, capturing their fears and disillusionment as Caesar's power grew unchecked.

"Here comes your alter-ego, Brutus," Max said, playfully nudging Aurelia with his elbow.

It was one of the film's most striking elements—Max's portrayal of the conspirators who planned Caesar's assassination. Instead of painting them as antagonists, Max and Aurelia had framed them as heroes fighting for the preservation of democracy. Unlike the cardboard cutout villains of the past, Max's assassins were portrayed with depth and complexity. There was no senseless stabbing planned out of sheer malice; on the contrary, their motivations were rooted in a genuine desire to protect the Republic from tyranny.

The climactic scene of the assassination wasn't edited yet, but Max knew it would be shocking and reverent, the tension palpable as the conspirators confronted Caesar in the Senate.

The only thing that was missing was the film's score. It was a brilliant affair composed of stirring orchestral arrangements, which accompanied the emotional highs and lows of the narrative, heightening the impact of each pivotal moment. In a striking contrast to the grandeur of Caesar's triumphs, the music softened during the assassination scene, lending it a haunting quality that lingered in the minds of viewers long after the credits rolled. Bibi had produced it, having created the baseline notes on his violin right after reading the script. Max still remembered the goosebumps raising the smallest hairs on his skin after he'd first heard it.

"Bibi's disappeared from the tech lab, along with Stern," Laub spoke softly after the first part of the film had ended and the screen went blank.

"Bibi and Stern?"

"Yes. The fellow I spoke with said Kranz's man told him that we'll be sharing him now with Riefenstahl. He used to be her artist."

"I don't want Leni's artist!" Aurelia protested at once. "Don't get me wrong, she's a great director, but she makes mountain pictures. Completely different from our historicals. He wouldn't know what we want."

Max began to pace the room, as much as the narrow space allowed, thick carpet muting the steps of his shoes. "Those are *my* employees, Ari. They're on *my* payroll. Who could have pulled them and why?"

She watched him, silent. Then, "Do you want me to call my brother? See if he knows something and can exert some influence if needed?"

"No." He swung round to her, sharp as a razor. "I'll sort it out myself. I'll go see Kranz tomorrow, in person."

When she nodded, Max could swear it was with relief.

TEN

Kranz's office as a UFA executive was a world unto itself. Max never felt comfortable inside this imposing space that used to reflect both the ambition and anxiety of the twenties, but now, in 1933, had turned into something altogether different. Dark wooden furniture dominated the room, with a large, polished desk positioned at its center. Its surface was cluttered with the remnants of the current week's work: stacks of scripts, contracts, and correspondence, all waiting for the executive's discerning eye. A typewriter—Max's constant personal companion that never left his desk—was notably absent: Kranz occupied too important a position to bother typing his own correspondence.

True to himself, Kranz made Max wait. Annoyed with this obvious pretense to be occupied with more important matters, Max made himself comfortable, pulled Kranz's personal ashtray close and lit his pipe. Kranz's good-looking secretary hurried in and out, piling up correspondence on the executive's desk. Left to his own devices, Max scanned the room.

From his last visit, he remembered the walls adorned with framed posters of successful films, vibrant glimpses into a bygone era of German Expressionism and the burgeoning sound era. Now, with Expressionism declared a degenerate art movement, the posters of Arnold Fanck and Leni Riefenstahl's mountain films were positioned front and center. Max supposed it made sense, with the Nazis' desire to return the nation "to its roots." Mountains and nature scenery was *en vogue* now, instead of the urban style of the twenties. Out with the scantily clad Marlene Dietrich and her gender-ambiguous *Blue Angel* dancers, in with the muscular Aryan mountain climbers.

Max suppressed a yawn and scratched his temple, more doubts about his *Caesar* creeping in. The Propaganda Ministry would love the entire Roman warrior business with the parades and uniforms—of that he had no doubt. But Caesar revealed as a dictator instead of the brilliant leader everyone had portrayed him as for centuries? Max shifted in his chair uncomfortably.

As he considered his film from this new perspective, Max couldn't ignore the symbols of loyalty that had crept into Kranz's office since his last visit—a small flag on his desk, a photograph of the *Führer* just behind his chair. Certainly, there remained hints of the man behind the title. A family photograph sat at the edge of his desk, capturing a fleeting moment of happiness. Occupying the entire wall, a small library of film texts and scripts revealing his enduring passion for storytelling. But when it came to the choice between creating and conforming, Max sensed he knew where Kranz's priorities would lie.

"Laub, my good fellow." A booming voice interrupted his musings.

Kranz had finally decided to make an appearance, holding his hand out for the director and imploring him to remain seated as if the two were bosom buddies. He was a man of average height and wore his baldness like a badge of honor instead of trying to conceal it, having his head shaved daily by a barber, who then treated it with a soothing lotion and a splash of expensive cologne. Made-to-measure suits crafted from the best

Italian wool and colorful silk neckties made up for his otherwise bland features were his typical attire; though, today, Max couldn't help but notice, he was dressed in more subdued tones. As they shook hands, Max also glimpsed a new shining Nazi Party pin in Kranz's lapel.

"Herr Kranz."

The UFA executive feigned offense. "Whatever did I do to you for you to address me as Herr? Come now, Laub, we've known each other for years and always called each other *du*. Why suddenly such ceremonies?"

"I thought it was me who had offended you somehow." Max was a good actor himself. He had no trouble adopting Kranz's jovial, friendly tone. "Seeing that half of my staff is suddenly missing."

"Laub, my friend, I have nothing to do with it whatsoever." Having seated himself in his leather armchair, Kranz lifted the glass under which several papers were tucked atop his desk and extracted one of them. A brilliant rectangle of emerald cloth remained where the paper used to be, now pushed across the desk toward Max. "Officers from the Ministry came, handed me this, made me sign it and told me to continue business as usual since they'd be taking care of everything."

"Propaganda Ministry has officers now?"

"Uniforms and all," Kranz confirmed and pressed his lips together.

His pipe set aside, Max carefully perused the executive order. With each word, his blood ran colder and colder until his very fingertips turned to ice. With the Ministry taking over the control of the UFA in the interests of the public enlightenment, all persons of Jewish race were to be dismissed from their positions effective immediately.

"I can't choose my own staff now? Even if I'm the one paying them?" Max had to take his glasses off and polish them, his own eyes blurring the words as if to refuse to acknowledge their meaning.

"Anything affiliated with the UFA is strictly regulated now. It's not just you, Laub. I must submit screenplays for the Ministry's censor office approval. I can no longer decide what to make and what not to make."

"But they are *my* specialists." Max still couldn't grasp it.

"But they used to work in the UFA labs, UFA screening rooms, UFA pavilions."

"But the studio was not the one paying them."

"Doesn't matter."

"I need those people! They've been with me for years. They know how to design my sets, how to develop my rushes, how to write music that would fit the picture like a glove. Who's going to do their job?"

"German specialists."

"Like the oaf they pulled from a part-time weekend job who is now supposed to be my projectionist?"

Kranz spread his hands helplessly. "I'm certain it's a temporary hiccup. We'll just have to train more German specialists and, in the meantime, try to make do with what we have."

"What we have is not good enough," Max said, separating each word. "Not for a Max Laub film, it's not. Consider me as a self-important bastard, but I won't be risking my name and my reputation just because someone decided to hire based on an Aryan blood principle all of a sudden."

"Lower your voice." Kranz, the omnipotent demigod of the UFA who used to decide which films the German and international public would see and which weren't worthy of his stamp of approval, stole a glance at the closed door. In that moment, Max saw him exactly for what he was: a guardian of the silver screen, yet a prisoner of this new Nazi era's demands. "The world outside is changing. The fabric of our art is changing together with it—"

"It's not changing," Max interrupted Kranz, pulling forward and speaking through his teeth, yet softly, to the point of self-loathing. "It's going to the devil is what it's doing. And we're going with it."

"Your *Caesar*, it's finished, isn't it?"

Max fell to the back of his armchair, feeling oddly defeated. "I have just begun editing it."

"Good. You only need minimal staff for it. Can Aurelia splice it for you instead of Wolowsky?"

Max sighed. "She can."

"Can Riefenstahl's artist make opening titles for you?"

"I suppose I can ask him to emulate Stern's previous work." Max wiped his hands down his face. He felt the beginning of a migraine pulsing dully behind his eyes. "But what about the score? I can't use my original score?"

Kranz took pity on him. After all, Laub was one of his biggest earners. Laub's pictures over the years had paid for Kranz's Grünewald villa, his Austrian winter lodge, his summer house at the North Sea and his car and his boat and both mistresses.

"You can still use the original score," he said confidentially. "Just credit someone German with it. Not Berthold."

ELEVEN

Berthold Wolowsky, also Austrian-born and Viennese-educated, seemed strangely understanding when Max stopped by his home later that day after leaving Aurelia in charge of editing. She'd asked him if he wanted her to come as well, but Max felt that this was a visit he had to pay alone—he owed Bibi that much.

Berthold had left the Vienna Philharmonic to join Max on his one-way trip to Berlin over a decade ago and had been writing scores exclusively for his films when he wasn't busy touring the world with his string quartet. Max had never personally liked the violin, but Bibi played it with such skill and heart, Laub invariably felt tiny hairs rising all over his arms as soon as Wolowsky's bow touched the strings. Bibi was in the middle of composing something heart-wrenching when Lisl, his wife, showed Laub into the living room.

"You decided to play at funerals, or what?" Max teased his old friend, pulling him and his violin into a hug.

"I would, but German corpses must be seen off only by persons with the correct racial profile, else they won't make it into the Valhalla," Berthold responded in the same tone.

Max wanted to laugh but only cringed instead.

Berthold put away his instrument, revealing callouses on his long, nimble fingers. "Coffee?" When Max failed to respond in time, Bibi winked at his wife, visibly pregnant with their third child. "Put some brandy in it. He looks like he needs it."

After the second cup, it all came pouring out of Max—the conversation with Kranz, the executive order from the Ministry, the names of people who had been fired and friends that had left.

"My head is spinning. I feel like the earth is coming from under my feet," Max admitted.

"All your trouble is because you were raised as a gentile," Berthold announced, lifting his index finger in the air. "Too many Brothers Grimm tales and not enough stories of our people's trials and tribulations. Had all the ways we've been hated and persecuted been hammered into your head at the yeshiva, you wouldn't have been surprised in the slightest at this turn of events. A Jew being kicked out of his workplace? What else is new?" He rolled his eyes, unimpressed. "And don't be daft, take the score. I've already got my money. Who cares if it bears my name or not?"

"I do."

"Feeble-minded idealist."

"Max, tell him to accept the Universal Studios offer." Lisl stuck her head through the doors to the living room, wiping her hands on her apron. In the kitchen, something delicious was roasting. Lisl was a Berliner but had quickly learned to make Berthold's favorite Austrian dishes the way he liked and always prided herself on showing off her skills whenever Max or any other of his fellow Austrians visited.

"You got invited to the Universal?" Max livened up.

"I'm not going," Bibi cut him off categorically.

"Why on earth not?"

"Because they only issue a visa for me for the first two years and only then, after I establish my life there, can I bring my family. Would you have left Ari for so long? You two don't even have children, so let's not consider them. But just Ari alone; would you?"

Max opened his mouth, about to make a joke that Ari could certainly take care of herself if left alone more than he could, but then he remembered that Ari was very much German, with a high-ranking Nazi for a brother in case of emergencies, and closed it shut.

"We would take care of Lisl and children," he managed instead.

"You're half a yid yourself." Berthold snorted. "Wait till that comes to their attention. Taking care of Lisl," he repeated mockingly. "Who will be taking care of you?"

Max blinked at him. "I'm not Jewish. My mother converted to Catholicism to marry my father and he is as Aryan as they get. I was baptized right after birth—"

"That makes you half a Jew, regardless. And that's only in the Nazis' eyes. According to the Jewish law, mother is Jewish, baby is Jewish. No one cares if she converts a thousand times, she's still a Jew. And that makes you one."

Max could only stare at him while Berthold tried to get his mirth under control. Max's reaction seemed to amuse him to no end, even if Max himself felt as if he had just been punched in the gut.

He wasn't feigning his stunned state. He had never made a secret of his ancestry, but before Hitler came to power, no one had seemed to be interested in it in the slightest. He must have recited the circumstances of his birth to countless outlets, both German and international, and it had not once occurred to him to count himself among the Jewish artists whose fame had exploded in the twenties. He was raised in a very Viennese, very Catholic household. His governess was French and a Protestant. He had attended a regular school, certainly not yeshiva. He had not once set foot inside a temple. He had only begun calling his wife by a Jewish pet name—Ari—bestowed upon her by his elderly grandmother shortly before her passing —only because Aurelia herself had insisted he call her that from that point on. It greatly annoyed Aurelia's brother and his cronies who used to hail her looks as some Norse goddess, so Max had complied until the name had stuck for good, but still...

"I'm not Jewish," he repeated, but puzzled and more unsure of himself than ever.

"Just take the damned score and welcome to the club."

Mark Stern, too, carefully removed his name from the opening credits and offered them, in a small film can, to Max, free of claim to any artistic rights. He knew this wasn't Max's doing. No hard feelings. Any other artist would just make a mess out of them and that Stern couldn't possibly stand. He also knew Max would call when the situation changed for the better and it would—soon, hopefully.

German democracy was being dismantled brick by brick in front of Max's very eyes. Together with the film can, he carried out of Stern's home some heavy doubts concerning that last statement of his.

Blaming some pitiful communists and immigrants for burning the Reichstag, the Nazis took it over under the pretense of protecting the public. Blaming the subversive message threatening the very soul of the German society, they burned the books of anyone who disagreed with them. Blaming the international Jewry for their "attempts to ethnically cleanse German society, infiltrate and overtake it with their lax abortion laws," the Nazis banned the procedure and encouraged German women to have as many German children as possible, so that their land would once again be populated with the people God intended for it.

By the time he reached Babelsberg, Max's migraine had turned so vicious, he left the credits in Aurelia's capable hands and went to lie down in one of the dark rooms, leaving the "work in progress; do not enter" sign at the door.

TWELVE

"Here's your deposit slip. All the proceeds from the sale, minus the gallery's fee, are now in the account you provided, in Swiss currency after being exchanged at the current rate, as per your instructions." Aurelia pushed the slip across Wilhelm's desk.

She remembered the old oak wood surface very well. It used to stand in their father's study, passed down from their grandfather, who had worked at it back when the soil on which their familial estate stood was still called the Kingdom of Prussia. Aurelia moved forward with the times; Wilhelm, it seemed, took great satisfaction in turning them back. The title might have changed, and the Kaiser was no longer in charge, but Wilhelm was still in his splendid uniform, signing orders as the President of Prussia, at the same desk his forefathers did.

"Did you really have to drag this old relic here?" Aurelia picked at the carved wood with her nail.

Her half-brother pocketed the slip, smiling like a cat with the proverbial cream, and caressed the desktop as one would a woman. "It felt appropriate for the office I hold. Thank you for the deposit. Frankly, I'm surprised. Didn't expect to see a Pfennig out of it. Thought you'd up and bolt across the border, together with both your husbands, and that would be the last I'd see of you."

Aurelia regarded him, looking bored. "Yes, you did. Else you wouldn't have those paintings out of your hands. And, across the border? Really? As if you haven't issued travel restrictions against all of our names to all border patrol agents."

Wilhelm widened his frank blue eyes at her. "My, Lia, I would never!"

Aurelia rolled her eyes.

"You know, I've missed you." Wilhelm was suddenly on his feet, chuckling. "Have a drink with me, for old times' sake. What's your poison these days?"

It wasn't in Aurelia's plans to stay any longer—just give the brat his money and forget the whole rotten affair like a bad dream—but for some reason, she remained seated.

"Got gin and tonic?"

Wilhelm reached under the desk, looking offended. He was the President of Prussia and Hitler's second in command. There was literally nothing in this country he didn't have.

Summoned by an invisible signal, a young adjutant appeared in the door and clicked his heels behind Aurelia's back.

"Gin and tonic for Fräulein von Brandenburg and a glass of champagne for me."

The adjutant snapped a sharp salute and disappeared once again.

"I'm still Frau Laub, Wilhelm."

He waved her off, unconcerned. "You were married so many times, I lost count of your last names," he said airily, all playfulness.

"They know who I am, *your people*. I'm a public figure."

"Here, you are my sister and they will address you as such, with all the respect due to the name we've carried proudly for centuries."

"Why are you so obsessed with the past?"

Wilhelm leaned against the desk, his shadow blocking the sun from the French windows. "Because there was nothing for us in the future, Lia," he spoke at length, grave like the Bismarck's bronze bust just next to his hip. "After the Empire was torn piece by piece by the Brits and the French, what was left for us? With the Kaiser gone, we couldn't pay the soldiers under our charge."

"Father could have paid them out of his pocket."

"His pocket?" Wilhelm laughed. "What pocket? All of our fortunes were tied directly to the Kaiser. He paid for our soldiers, we trained them and sent them to die in his name. Do you think it's cheap, training and maintaining a cavalry regiment? Do you realize how much money goes into it? The barracks, the equipment, the food, the pension—for them and their families; and don't even get me started on the horses. Do you remember the stables we used to have? Do you remember how many men we had to maintain to tend to the horses, in addition to the soldiers?"

"You had all this land left, plus the land given to you as a dowry for your wedding." Aurelia hadn't been invited to her brother's wedding but had read about the event in the early Nazi paper. And the very next year—an obituary for Frau von Brandenburg. Aurelia wondered if it was painful for Wilhelm to be reminded of his wife's untimely demise, but there was nothing whatsoever in his gaze testifying to it. Knowing her brother, she was beginning to suspect that he had married the girl for money. "Father could have turned it over to the farmers and collected profit from them."

"We are military men, Aurelia. Always have been and always will be. We aren't farmers."

"I didn't suggest you pick up a plow yourself. I said, rent it out until you have enough money to maintain whatever lifestyle you want. I imagine, it wouldn't have taken much, since you didn't have to maintain any regiments anyway after the war."

The sound of the door opening interrupted their heated discussion. The same adjutant, elegant to distraction, held out Aurelia's drink to her with a soft muslin napkin wrapped around its bottom, all the while balancing the ornate silver tray with Wilhelm's champagne on the tips of his left hand's fingers. After receiving his glass, Wilhelm barely motioned his chin to dismiss the young man.

"Thank you," Aurelia called after him, but only heard the same sharp snap of heels at the door.

"Now is that discipline or what?" Wilhelm was back to his grinning.

Aurelia hated seeing such a strong familial resemblance in his features, hated seeing her father's features in herself instead of her mother's. But that was her mother's trouble all along: she wasn't strong enough—not to endure her marriage, nor to pass on her genes to her daughter. She was like a canary, her poor mother: beautiful and fragile, beating herself against the bars of the gilded cage until she had killed herself, finding the freedom in death she couldn't have in life. And yet, that damned von Brandenburg blood called to her from the depths of her half-brother's beating heart. In spite of herself, she toasted her glass to his, smiling at the sudden onslaught of memories flooding her after the very first sip.

Wilhelm helping her onto a gorgeous Arabian stallion, black as obsidian and still sweating after a vigorous gallop. The smell of the horse's sweat and the heat of its body she could feel even through the saddle. She was only five and he had to put her onto the saddle sideways, her short legs barely reaching the other side of the horse's wide back.

"Don't be afraid, he's not going anywhere without my permission," her brother laughed, a teenager himself but already a skilled rider. "Take a hold of his mane. I'll be holding the reins for now."

"He's moving!"

"Well, he is a living horse, not a wooden one. Are you holding onto him? Good. Now, give him a kick on the side. Harder, he didn't feel anything. Harder!"

"I don't want to hurt him."

"You won't hurt him any more than a fly landing on you hurts you. Go ahead."

She kicked and the stallion made a step forward, almost sending Aurelia flying back, had it not been for a fistful of horse hair in her small hands. For the first few moments, she was still finding her balance, but then such sheer happiness bubbled up from inside her. Little Lia began to laugh in wonder, observing the world from her new vantage point, making a beast of an animal move with a single kick of her tiny heel.

Without their father's knowledge, Wilhelm trained Aurelia until they could ride into the forest together, taking felled trees with ease and shared laughter, racing one another and holding mock contests in dressage, to the soldiers' amusement and admiration. She was a born rider, everyone said so. By the time Otto von Brandenburg discovered his daughter in riding breeches in the middle of a stable, it was too late for him to do anything about it.

"What are you smiling about, little sister?"

Aurelia swirled the contents of her glass. "I was thinking of the dressing-down you got from Father for teaching me to ride."

"Not for teaching you to ride, but for teaching you to ride in a male saddle."

"Why did you do it?" she asked, lifting her gaze to him. "Because you didn't have a brother but still wanted a riding partner? Or were you going through your own rebellious stage with Father?"

"Have you considered that I did it simply because I loved

horses and the way riding made me feel and thought to share it with you? You were such a damn sad child, Lia. Between your mother carrying you around like a china doll that could break from a sudden wind gust and Father making you learn piano and ballet, for both of which you had neither talent nor discipline... I don't know. I felt sorry for you, I suppose."

The words hit like a fist to a gut. Aurelia didn't want this sentimentality. It was easier to hate him, cast him together with his despicable circle, but he had to go and say these things to her and unwittingly sew doubt in her heart.

"I have to go," she said, rising to her feet and finishing her drink in one go.

"Thank you for stopping by." Wilhelm smiled at her like he did on all of his official portraits. The moment had passed. The mask was back in place. "Don't be a stranger."

"I suspect you won't let me," Aurelia muttered.

THIRTEEN

August 1933

Not one to rise early, Aurelia placed an order with the Romanisches Café for Max's lunch while still in bed and got on the road at eleven. The day was splendid for a drive in the car and she took the top down before climbing in.

She was making her way through the Grünewald, her wolf dogs lolling their tongues on the passenger seat beside her, when she spotted Leni speaking with someone on the side of the road. Aurelia slowed down next to a stranger's car and honked as she called Leni's name.

"Shirking work, Riefenstahl?"

Leni's shoulders jumped with a start. With what looked like relief, she released the grip she had on her closed arms and waved back, revealing an armpit sweat stain on her pale blue dress. "Lia, hi!" Her voice came out in a screech of enthusiasm that was all but genuine. "Are you heading to the studio by any chance?"

"Sure am." Through the tint of her sunglasses, Aurelia noticed the hairs rising on the wolf dogs' tensed backs and wrapped their chains around her wrist, not liking one bit the unblinking stare they had on the stranger's back. Small in stature, shorter than Leni in her heels, he tipped his hat in Aurelia's general direction without turning to face her. If anything, she thought he pulled the hat even lower onto his face to obscure it further. Sensing what only women and animals sense around shifty characters such as this one, she reached out and pushed the door open, offering Leni a chance for an escape. "Need a ride?"

The man tried catching her wrist, provoking a low growl from Loki and Astrid, but Leni freed herself with a pearl of nervous laughter—"Have to run, got work to do. I'll call you later!"

Only once safely in the car, Loki and Astrid moved to the back seat, did Leni heave a breath she must have been holding the entire time.

"Thank you," she said, her ice-cold hand pressing Aurelia's wrist for a second as they sped along the tree-lined road. "I don't know what I would have done if it weren't for you."

"Want me to turn around and set the dogs on his sorry tail?" Aurelia began to turn the wheel.

"No, no!" Leni cried, terrified at the prospect. "Just go, please."

Aurelia shrugged—*as you wish*—and pressed the gas pedal harder. "Who's the *Arschloch*?"

Leni was silent a beat, as if considering if she should reveal the name or not. "Goebbels," she said at last.

Aurelia turned to glance at her. Leni kept staring forward with glassy eyes, her teeth biting her lip relentlessly. Her shoulder-length chestnut hair was whipping wildly in the wind, but she didn't seem to notice it.

"As in, Propaganda Minister Goebbels?"

"The very same."

"What the hell did he want with you?"

"Exactly what you have assumed."

Holding the wheel with one hand, Aurelia dug in the pocket of her door and pulled out a silk scarf for Leni to cover her hair. Moving like an automaton, Leni did.

"How do you even know him?"

"His wife invited me over once Hitler delegated me the Horst Wessel documentary," Leni said, tucking her strands under the scarf.

Aurelia's hand tensed upon the wheel. "Are you aware that the said hero, Wessel, whom the Nazis are going to glorify by means of your documentary, didn't die a poetic death for the country? He was a drunkard and a pimp who was notorious for getting into brawls with the Reds but finally got into the wrong Red's face? That's all there is to it."

Leni shifted in her seat. "I'm just a hired hand, no different than you on Laub's set," she said, somewhat defensively.

"Max doesn't make me film propaganda."

"Every film is propaganda, when you think about it. Your *Caesar* is a liberal one; Horst Wessel is a nationalistic one. But propaganda all the same."

Aurelia shrugged. She had more important things on her mind than getting into dialectics with Riefenstahl. "So what's with Goebbels? He wasn't here to discuss Horst Wessel, I take it?"

Leni released an exasperated grunt to emphasize the point. "I wish he was. During our very first meeting, he took me aside and confessed that back when I was an actress, he was waiting outside a film theater at one of my films' premieres to catch a glimpse of me. His wife was sitting at the other end of the room as he said it, for Christ's sake!"

She stopped abruptly to take a cigarette, also fished out by Aurelia from the same pocket. After lighting one up, Leni proceeded, "I haven't the faintest idea how he got my address, but he just appeared with his driver—he left him by my house—

and told me that he needed to talk to me about something urgent, but privately. I thought there was some trouble with Horst Wessel..." She tossed her head, still struggling to get her nerves under control. "At any rate, I'm still building my house, as you know, and there are workers there, so he took me for a ride, began telling me how he and the *Führer* were just revisiting my mountain films and how I can have the brightest future and then he stopped the car and tried to jump on me. I got out as quickly as I could, but I couldn't just make a scene. He's the Minister, for God's sake! All of us artists work for him now. So I was in the middle of trying to talk some sense into him, remind him of his wife and his duty to the country that must always come first, and thankfully you pulled up and got me out of the situation."

Leni passed the back of her hand over her forehead. The slight shake of it didn't escape Aurelia's attention.

"You think he'll bother you again?"

"I sincerely hope he'll get the idea and switch his attentions to someone else."

"What if he doesn't?"

Leni made no reply.

They were driving through the city proper now. All around them, the leaves rustled gently in the warm breeze, yet the air was thick with an unspoken tension. Aurelia pursed her lips in distaste each time she noticed yet another colorful advertisement replaced by the new regime's propaganda posters. In place of fashionably dressed women, German mothers, attired in traditional dirndls, lifted blond babies in the air. In place of a cabaret advert, travel courses for aspiring pilots to, oddly, USSR. "Work and bread" everywhere she looked. Shovels, hammers, babies, and Jewish storefronts defaced with red paint.

"Mind the dogs, will you?" Aurelia tapped Leni's shoulder to get her attention. "I'll be back in a minute."

She stopped by the Romanisches—Berlin's bohemians'

favorite haunt, which also happened to serve Max's favorite Viennese pastries and whose waiters didn't mind filling Aurelia's thermos with their fresh-brewed coffee.

Initially, it was Art who had brought her here. She had just run away from home, not even a suitcase to her name, and Art was the first thing she'd noticed after emerging from the bustling train station. Mounted next to the statue of the Kaiser which was pelted with clumps of mud and missing the head, the young soldier in a tattered uniform devoid of any identification marks was calling in his clear, passionate voice to the revolt, but not the one the Bolshevists suggested.

"Down with the rotten Prussian militarism! Down with the wars and uniforms and leaders and organized religion and its servants—all they do is pit us against each other. All we need is air to breathe, sun to kiss our bare skin, water to wash down the thirst. We are all brothers and sisters, all the peoples under the sky. Down with the institutions of marriage—let us love who we want to love at this given moment and leave when we feel the need to move forward. Instead of weapons, we ought to create art. Instead of blood, let us spill paint onto canvas. Instead of orders, let us write love letters. Let us love instead of hate—whoever we wish, men, women—it's all the same as long as we love instead of running bayonets through each other's guts! Enough of this inequality, infighting, hate! Love one another, people."

The crowd had dispersed, but Aurelia still stood, mesmerized, her eyes riveted to this revolutionary who preached against everything her father and her name embodied. He had descended from his makeshift podium, finished shaking hands with the small group of likeminded folks, and noticed this young girl, unmistakably an aristocrat, in her white lace dress and pearl earrings.

"You lost?" he had teased.

"No. I think I have just been found."

The Romanisches was where he had brought her, the only girl among all former army men. In between the coffee, he had asked her what was with the dress. She had told him that it was her unfinished wedding gown and that her fiancé was sixty-one but very rich and Father needed money, and she was a girl and that was all she was good for in Father's eyes.

"I was watching the seamstress pinning my hem in front of the mirror and just couldn't take it any longer. Grabbed whatever little pocket change I was afforded, ran to the stables, seized the first horse I saw, rode it to the train station, bought the ticket to Berlin, and... now I'm homeless, I suppose." Aurelia had finished with a brave smile despite the fright in her eyes.

"I'm homeless myself at the moment, but if you don't mind bunking with us at a studio we're renting, you're free to come. Fair warning, we all sleep on the floor. There's only enough money for canvases and paint, not for mattresses. Best I can do is spare my overcoat."

An old army overcoat that had been through four years of the trenches and was probably still teeming with lice was a much better choice in Aurelia's eyes than any feather mattress her sixty-one-year-old future husband could offer.

"And here's where we work..." Art's comrade had gestured around himself. Certainly, almost every table was occupied with someone writing, typing, sketching or putting together a newspaper from a wild assembly of leaflets.

This was where she worked too soon after meeting Art, clearing the tables for spare change and witnessing the birth of Dadaism, Expressionism, Cubism, and modern theater. In one corner, the Reds could be conspiring to bring about world revolution; in the next, Bertolt Brecht was mounting the table to recite the punchline from his new play and, damn, did his words go straight for the jugular!

By the time Father had found her, she was already married to Art—not out of convention but out of necessity, so that Otto von Brandenburg couldn't claim her any longer. She wore her hair shorter than her husband wore his and a skirt just below the knees. With an army of artists behind her, Aurelia Nacht-nebel had told Otto von Brandenburg and the two uniformed goons he'd brought with him to go hang themselves and released a victorious cry into the smoke-stained ceiling when the door had closed after him, once and for all.

Now, as she crossed the familiar vast room to pick up Max's lunch, Aurelia couldn't help but notice how snatches of conversations her ear caught seemed to falter at the mention of politics. Friends who had once animatedly discussed the latest films or art exhibitions now exchanged cautious glances, their laughter tinged with uncertainty. People unfamiliar with her personally clammed up entirely as she passed by their tables. The vibrant chatter of Berlin's intellectual circles was slowly giving way to a heavy silence, as if the very essence of the city was holding its breath.

"Our best to Herr Laub," Ricci, the waiter who'd been a staple of the place since the mid-twenties, looked oddly pale without his usual, signature rouge. His hair was still pomaded but no longer waved.

Aurelia nodded her thanks as she collected the cardboard box tied with a colorful string. "Has Art been around?" She directed the question to Ricci's back while he was filling her thermos with coffee.

He shook his head without interrupting his work. "Saw him last time 'round May. Said, Romanisches is not the same anymore."

"He used to say the same about the Westens."

"He isn't wrong."

Aurelia sniffled quietly, directed her gaze at the ceiling, and just then realized that she was still wearing her sunglasses. Pushing them atop her headscarf, she studied the ceiling with disbelief.

"Have you scrubbed it?" she asked.

Ricci had to put the thermos into her outstretched hand, for Aurelia's eyes were still drawn upward. It had been a dark-gray color for as long as she could remember. So were the columns supporting it, bearing layers and layers of tobacco smoke like badges of honor. Was it Nomberg, who had said in jest that the air here was so thick and smoky, viruses were dying off?

"Some fancy peacock from the Health Ministry came over, showed me some new order on public health or some such," Ricci said and waved his hand. "Smoking is very much discouraged now. Apparently, it's a 'bohemian vice.'"

They exchanged knowing glances without saying another word and Aurelia headed for the exit. Art was right, Romanisches wasn't the same any longer.

The streets were no better. The uniforms of the SA and SS men stood out starkly against the everyday attire of passersby, their presence a constant reminder of the regime's tightening grip. Aurelia's grasp on the thermos grew stronger with a hateful feeling once she noticed how people instinctively altered their paths to avoid confrontation, suddenly very interested in the ground under their feet. The very atmosphere had shifted; what had once been a city of freedom and expression was beginning to feel like a place of surveillance and intimidation.

FOURTEEN

Having dropped off Leni, Aurelia went straight to the editing room, her wolf dogs left fastened securely outside. She pushed the door open, humming a tune under her breath, but ceased abruptly at the sight of the bare walls and table, stripped of everything except a pair of small scissors Max was presently twirling around his finger as he stared blankly into space.

"Max?" Aurelia called to him, her throat growing dry with suspicion. "Where is the film?"

Her husband slowly lifted his bloodshot eyes and stared at her for a very long time as though struggling to place her.

"Max?" Aurelia repeated, fear creeping into her voice. "*Caesar*. Where is it?"

"Gone," he uttered with eerie calmness.

"What do you mean, gone? Grown legs and left? Or have you had a Gogol moment and burned it?"

"Gone to wherever everything goes now," Max answered with the same indifference in his voice. "Two SA fellows turned up and said they had an order to requisition it. I told them that no one in Germany can requisition a Max Laub film, but if they wanted, they could try."

He gestured to the empty room, putting the rest of the story into that single, final wave.

In Aurelia's chest, her very heart sat heavy as stone. She made a move toward the screen, still lit up but robbed of ribbons of film that contained the Roman Empire's long-dead heroes in each frame, paused, turned to Max once again, her mouth opening but refusing to form any words. Had it really come down to this? It had only been months since Hitler had taken office and the old way of life had already been smashed with batons, pulverized to dust; it was slipping through her fingers like sand. With each new day, another right, another freedom they had taken for granted—dismantled.

Suddenly robbed of all force, Aurelia dropped into a chair next to her husband.

"You were raising the alarm an entire year ago and I didn't listen," Max said, moving the scissors back and forth apathetically. "You said it would eventually come to this, but I naively believed that a simple movie would sway the masses, the brainless, pompous raven that I am. And now there is no movie and there's no one to fight for us ordinary folk anymore. The only organized and armed group—the Reds—Hitler's SA were taken care of first. Now, all of their leaders are either dead or imprisoned and the rest are keeping to themselves—there will be no revolts from them anytime soon. The free press is all but gone as well: no more dissenting, leftist newspapers for sale at the newsstands, and even the centrist ones are disappearing when refusing to stick to the new regime's ideas."

Suddenly furious, Aurelia began tearing the paper in which Laub's lunch had been wrapped. "Not that it bothers Hitler's supporters in the slightest: look at them, thankful for free, brand new radios the Propaganda Ministry gives out to each household and they don't even care that out of the shiny new box poison pours straight into their ears. They no longer realize that they have been made into the Party's pet parrots, repeating its dogmas which have replaced their own opinions and any free thought."

A studio hand poked his head through the door but retreated at once after Aurelia threw a murderous look his way.

"The Party tells them that the Jews are vermin poisoning the country's blood," she continued, setting the food in front of her husband, who looked like he had lost all will to live, "and they nod compliantly, without realizing that their family doctor whom they love so much is Jewish and so is their tailor and so is half of the orchestra they gush over on opera nights. The Party tells them women don't belong in workplaces but at home and they nod again; only the women, who suddenly find themselves out of work, stare at the door closing after their husband each morning as he leaves for his job in stunned stupefaction. They prided themselves on being nothing like those feminist types; they voted for their *Führer*," she mocked them, her voice dripping with righteous venom. "Why were they pushed out, replaced by a man, when they did everything right? It should have never affected them... But the lunch won't prepare itself and the husband's clothes need washing, starching, and ironing and the floors also won't wax themselves. No, the irony is not lost on me that I have just brought you your lunch, so eat it, damn it! And so they work, for which they shall receive no pay and soon grow much too exhausted to wonder why it has all turned out this way and glare at women who still manage to keep their positions with unconcealed hostility and badmouth them to their just-as-unemployed, house-bound neighbors, and turn even more radical in their views and ask their husbands to push for more aggressive policy changes to put more women back where they belong—at home, in the kitchen—so that they don't have to agonize watching them march confidently to work from behind the immaculately clean kitchen window."

Aurelia finally breathed out, feeling oddly empty but lighter somehow after her impassioned speech.

"The Party tells them that the Party knows best and they agree without thinking, for thinking is out the window at this point. Besides, they did get their free radio, didn't they?" She finished in a much softer voice. "Life is fine and dandy. Democracy? An old Bohemian vice. No one misses it here."

Except for the very few, and for them, each new violation was like a hot needle under the nail.

"*Caesar* was supposed to pay for so many families' new homes in New York."

Max's words, full of unspeakable torment, called Aurelia back to the present. With a heavy hand, she once again pulled the second chair up and folded her hands atop the table. Now that the initial shock had passed, she was finding herself being able to think again.

"Maybe it will yet. Let me talk to my—"

"No," Max cut her off categorically. "It won't be of any use. Minister Goebbels' people confiscated it, not your brother's, and from what I hear, there's no love lost between the two. Even if your brother interferes, which I doubt, Goebbels will keep it just out of spite."

Aurelia thought of the scene in Grünewald that very morning but took a deep breath and put on her most confident smile. "So, I'll go talk to Goebbels then."

Only, she didn't get a chance to even schedule an appointment with the Ministry: when the couple arrived home, an official invitation from Herr Minister himself was awaiting Herr Laub on his golden mail tray.

FIFTEEN

The following morning, Max, dressed in his Sunday best suit of dark-gray wool with a matching silk tie, ascended the stairs of the Propaganda Ministry building. As he presented his identification and the official invitation to the sentry on duty, he couldn't help but feel like a character in one of the espionage films recently so *en vogue*. Only, there was no script to follow and no ending to know and, therefore, no fear, nor a director to guide him to safety.

"Up the stairs and to your left."

There was no visible recognition from the male secretary at the reception or the deference he'd grown so used to, either.

Surrounded by crimson banners streaming from the top floor to the bottom in an overpowering display of power and opulence, Max followed the directions, suddenly aware of the echo of his own steps.

Another sentry; another labyrinth of rooms, cold, despite the sunny day outside, with the oppressive chill of the ideologies permeating the air. At last, they admitted him. The reception area was elegantly furnished but dimly lit, as if following Max's own notes on set decoration. That's precisely how he would have staged it for his unsuspecting hero: a gilded trap full of shadows and the hushed whispers of clerks and aides, their eyes darting nervously as they moved about fulfilling their tasks. That's precisely how he would have presented the power dynamics at play to his audience.

The appointment time on his invitation said ten thirty, but he already knew that Goebbels would make him wait. Sit here and marinate until he was good and ready.

The scent of polished wood and stale cigarette smoke hung in the air, blending with the faint aroma of Max's French cologne and, underneath the collar, just a hint of sweat. In spite of his resolve to keep his nerves steady, Max felt his heart racing, a mix of fear and determination coursing through him. He was not in immediate danger, not quite yet. If they wanted to arrest him—for *Caesar*, or heavens know what else—they would have done it already. Goebbels must want something from him; else, he wouldn't bother with the niceties. But what could he, Laub, a simple director (all right, a well-known director, but still...) of mixed racial origin offer him, the man in charge of what the German public was thinking nowadays?

Lost in his thoughts, Max didn't initially hear a secretary calling his name to admit him to Herr Minister's office. When he did, he gulped, almost choked, but managed to pass the threshold and complete the seemingly interminable walk along the red runner leading toward the imposing desk and two visitors' armchairs.

"Please, be seated. Herr Minister will be with you shortly."

Shortly, his foot. Another thirty minutes passed. The faint ticking of Max's wristwatch resonated in his ears, each second amplifying the anxiety that swelled within him. With each passing minute, he grappled with the duality of his identity; he was a talented creator, yet he carried the burden of his heritage like a heavy cloak. Why, oh why, did he go and tell every publication that asked about his Jewish ancestry? His mother had converted; it could have been swept under the rug so easily!

Because only six months ago it had been perfectly fine to be Jewish. Who could have known that time, and public opinion with it, could shift so seismically fast?

"Herr Laub!"

Caught unawares, Max jumped in his chair, swinging toward a door he hadn't the faintest idea had existed before that very moment. Cleverly blended in with the pattern of the wallpaper, it was one of the inventions French kings had been so proud of, moving undetected inside the walls of their own castle. Only, the kings had ordered those secret passages made to visit their mistresses clandestinely. It was Max's profound suspicion, Minister Goebbels had much more nefarious plans in mind.

There he was himself, the Propaganda chief, walking toward Max with a noticeable limp and his hands outstretched, as if to greet a dear childhood friend he hadn't seen in years. A good head and a half shorter than Max, displaying his nicotine-stained teeth in a wide grin, Goebbels shook the director's hand with his two. Unlike Max's, his hands were dry and warm.

"Sit, sit, don't stand there; I can't bear when people stand in front of me."

Max sat, all well-bred compliance.

"Some coffee, perhaps?" Goebbels offered.

"Only if you have it with me."

Goebbels only had to smile and someone was already scuttling behind the doors, scrambling for coffee and cream. In no time, it was all arranged for them: the coffee, the cream, the sugar, and even the pastries. With a dash of a chill through his heart, Max recognized the exact kind he favored at the counter of the Romanisches.

Goebbels continued to play the good host. He talked obligatory weather, world politics, Laub's films.

"Did you know that your *Vikings* is one of our *Führer*'s favorite pictures?" Goebbels tilted his head to one side, his black eyes impish.

"I... was not aware of it, no." Max plastered on a smile as well. "It's a great honor."

"A perfect example of what a true Aryan film ought to be."

Max continued to smile despite the growing ache in his jaw, feverishly wondering where Goebbels was going with this. Taunting him and his Jewish mother? Or implying that everything about Nordic people was Aryan and therefore acceptable? Was this about *Caesar*?

"Such an important message, so cleverly hidden behind all that magnificent imagery," Goebbels continued. "And without any dialogue! In a silent film—genius! You, my friend, are indeed a genius."

What message? Sweat broke out on Max's forehead. There was no message besides the fact that he'd been infatuated with everything Norse during that time and had a producer who thought it would sell well. *Everyone's sick of the war, hunger, realism, and depression. Anything that will take them out of this bleak reality will sell like hot pies*—those were the producer's exact words.

"Thank you, Herr Minister. But, really, you are too generous with your praise," Max responded cautiously and tried to hide from Goebbels' piercing gaze behind a delicate coffee cup.

"Nonsense!" Goebbels suddenly cried, startling Max anew. "The new Reich have no use for false modesties. Our great German Empire is to be built from the ground up and is to last for a thousand years—wasn't it Caesar's intention for the Roman Empire as well?—we'll get back to Caesar. His time has passed."

He was suddenly on his feet, hands in pockets, strolling along the window, behind which Max could see the tall ornate clock belonging to a bank. Both hands were aligned on twelve.

"We are the generation that shall lay the foundation for this new Empire that shall eventually eclipse everything history has ever known. And it's our duty, as the founding generation, to give our all to our Fatherland. And for that, we need the best people in leadership positions." Goebbels' eyes caught Max's once again, holding him in their spell. "Out of the entire fleet of German directors, you are the person, Herr Laub. I want you to lead the German cinema office."

This was the last thing Max had expected. What a precarious situation to find himself in, caught between his artistic aspirations and the ideology that threatened his very existence. A joke? No, not a joke. Surely, Goebbels didn't know of his tainted racial origins—

—But he knows exactly what Viennese pastries I always buy?

In the silence that fell, Max was acutely aware that every word he spoke from that moment on could tip the balance between acceptance and annihilation. With rivulets of sweat running down his back under the tailored jacket, he decided to speak.

"Herr Minister, I fear no words shall be enough to express the extent of my gratitude, but I'm afraid some of your colleagues might look at such a choice as myself quite unfavorably."

For the first time, Goebbels' dark brows knitted together. In his tightly pressed lips, Max saw the portrait of a man who didn't like having his authority challenged.

"Why would they do such a thing?" he asked nevertheless, separating each word as if to underline the absurdity of such a suggestion.

Max wetted his lips and put the fine china cup down, not quite trusting his hands at the moment. "You see, Herr Minister, I'm afraid I can't boast as impeccable Aryan origins as they do. My mother was born to Jewish parents. She converted to Catholicism," he rushed to add, disgusted with himself for sounding apologetic, "long before she got married to my father, and I was born and raised in the Catholic faith, but when it comes to actual genealogy—"

"Herr Laub," Goebbels cut him off with a benevolent smile, "we decide who's Jewish here and who's not. Surely, you weren't thinking that I was unaware?" He regarded Max as one would an adorable yet infinitely silly child.

"No, Herr Minister."

"Good. The matter's resolved. Anything else you'd like to bring to my attention? Before you waste your time with them, you will be reporting directly to me and no one else. You, and only you, will be solely in charge of anything related to production of any film on the territory of Germany. Every script, every idea shall go through you first. All actors, directors, writers, studio chiefs shall be under your immediate command. Fire whoever you like. Hire whoever you like. I'll give you vague guidelines of what I'm looking for, but for the most part, you shall have free rein. You can also have your *Caesar* back, if you like. I went through it—it's perfectly salvageable. Just... tinker with the entire tyrannical dictator image a bit. I blame it on your wife's influence. She's a notorious leftist, and whether we like it or not, our better halves' influence seeps into our work." He accompanied these words with a smile even kinder than the previous one.

The dim lighting cast long shadows, creating an ambiance of foreboding that mirrored Max's internal struggle. He felt the weight of history pressing down on him, a reminder of the countless artists who had been silenced or persecuted under similar regimes. He had finally got the answer to his question: would he be embraced for his talent, or would his lineage overshadow his accomplishments?

Fate itself had granted him the position of power that came

to a few fortunate ones only once in a lifetime. No longer would he respond to anyone besides Goebbels himself. The entire German cinema would be under his sole discretion. Old Laub, the one from six months ago, would salivate at the prospect. This new one felt the dichotomy of hope and despair enveloping him. This moment could be a pivotal juncture in his career, a chance to wield his craft as a tool for influence, or it could spell disaster, casting him into the shadows from which he might never emerge.

He had expected anything that morning as he was fixing his silver cufflinks to his cuffs; anything but suddenly finding himself in Faust's shoes. And the devil, in such an innocent disguise, was already arching his brow at him, waiting for the answer.

All the power you want. Just pledge your soul to me, mortal.

"Thank you, Herr Minister, for your trust in my abilities," Max spoke at length. "I hope I shall make my country proud."

SIXTEEN

Aurelia was taking the sun in a chaise outside, with Astrid and Loki sprawled on the grass next to her, when they suddenly leaped to their feet and trotted into the house, all excitement. Grabbing her silk kimono to cover herself against the chill of the house—she always sunbathed in the nude—Aurelia followed them inside, calling Max's name. It was convenient having wolf dogs when it came to an early alert system: with their unsurpassed sense of smell, they could tell who was approaching their territory long before Aurelia could see the person for herself. She and Max once joked that they could sleep with the gates and the front door open—woe betide the unfortunate idiot who tried to venture inside.

"I take it, they haven't arrested you?" she said teasingly by way of greeting, but then she saw her husband's face, pale as a ghost, and felt her smile drop. "What happened?"

Max let go of Loki's ear he was rubbing, went to her, and grasped her with strength. It left her fresh-from-the-sun skin smarting. He'd shed his jacket at the door and as she closed her arms around him, Aurelia discovered that his entire body was wet with sweat.

"Max, what happened?" she repeated, feeling Astrid nosing between them with soft, plaintive whines.

Still holding onto Aurelia with one arm, Max reached down to caress the thick fur atop Astrid's head. Something caught in his throat. Had Aurelia not known him better, she would have sworn it was a sob.

"We have to leave, Ari. Now."

"Now?" Aurelia pulled back. "Now, meaning—"

"Now meaning *now*, Aurelia! Right this very second." He kissed her on her lips—hard—and charged toward the stairs. "Don't just stand there!" Max called to her as he took the stairs two at a time. "Pack the valuables, the necessities, and let's go!"

Aurelia ran after him, folds of her kimono flying after her like wings. In the bedroom, as he was hurling the contents of his wardrobe into his usual travel suitcase, he told her everything: Goebbels' offer, his response, and what it would mean for them both if he didn't report to the Ministry tomorrow morning.

"Max, stop!" Aurelia's sobering command halted him in his tracks, arms full of underwear. "You aren't thinking clearly."

"Oh, no?" He arched a mocking brow.

"No. You're panicking is what you're doing. Put the things down and let's talk."

"Talk?" He stared at her as if she'd just announced that she had descended from Jupiter. "There is no time to talk, Ari! We have to get to the train station and buy tickets before it closes—"

"Tickets where?" Aurelia asked in a perfectly collected voice, her arms crossed over her chest.

"To... London. Or Paris—I don't know!" Max moaned, throwing the stack of underwear into the suitcase.

"And then what?"

"Then?" He looked at her, seemingly at a loss. He clearly hadn't thought this through that far.

"Yes. Say, we're in London. Or Paris. We have just arrived in the city. Now what?"

"Now we go to the hotel."

"All right. And after? I'm talking a few months after. What do we do? Where do we work? Where do we live? How do we make money? I assume we won't be stopping at the bank on the way to the Bahnhof."

"No. It'll alert them right that instant."

Aurelia nodded. "I have about five thousand in cash here, at home."

"I have about the same."

"Taking into the account my jewelry, let's say another five. That gives us fifteen altogether."

"Enough to last us a few months, either in Paris or London."

"And after we run out of money?"

Max removed his glasses and ran his hands down his face. "Aurelia, we'll think of it once we're there. We'll figure something out. Someone will hire us—"

"With the current outpouring of German émigrés?" she looked skeptical.

"I am still Max Laub," he said, growing annoyed. Yet, there was visible hesitance in his eyes, peering into hers as though desperate for support.

"Yes. Here, in Germany. But they have their own Max Laubs in Paris and London, and I'm not even going to suggest Hollywood." Aurelia softened the blow with a kind smile. "Then there is the question of your films. Your intellectual property. The ones that we produced independently, with the UFA acting only as a distributor. They are all stored at the UFA. How do we get them out?"

"We don't." Max looked like he'd given it plenty of thought already.

"Just leave them all here?" Aurelia's voice caught. Their films were their children—they had poured all of their love into each one, nurturing them to perfection. Though they were most proud of *Caesar*, their unmatched creation so far. "To these jackals?"

Max shrugged. His expression remained impassive; only in his eyes did the unspeakable pain of an animal gnawing off its own leg to get out of a trap flash momentarily. "We'll make new pictures, Ari."

He tried to smile at her and press her hand, but his fingers felt like ice. Aware of it, he regarded his hand atop his wife's.

"I went through the war and I was never afraid, Ari. But I am, now."

"In the war, the fight was equal. Both sides had weapons."

"What do I do, if not leave? Stay here and create propaganda for the Nazis?"

"Of course not."

"Then what do you want me to do?"

His distressed shout tore at her heart. Yet, she remained calm and collected—because someone had to. "Leave."

"But—" He blinked a few times, dumbfounded. "That's what I just—"

"Alone. Without me."

Silence fell upon the room, louder than an exploding grenade.

Breathing hard, Max stared at his wife, as if suddenly unsure if she were a friend or an enemy.

"What are you saying?" he finally asked, deceivingly softly.

"Max..." Unable to withstand that agonized look in his eyes, Aurelia went to him, took his face in her hands, and began covering it with kisses. "You are absolutely right. You need to leave right now. You are the one in danger, I am not. I have Wilhelm, they won't touch me. You go and I'll stay. I'll see that Bibi and his family are taken care of, along with the rest of our employees; I'll work with Art to help them; I'll find a way to get our films out—including *Caesar*—and then I'll follow you. How does that sound?"

Pacified with her words of assurance and the warmth of her lips on his skin, Max calmed himself considerably.

"Yes," he managed with a nod of resignation. "I suppose it all makes perfect sense. Good thinking."

"I'm glad you agree."

"I hate to leave you here all alone though."

"I'm not alone." Aurelia smiled, jerking her chin toward the wolf dogs. "I have Astrid and Loki. They'll see to it that I'm safe and sound."

"I still hate it."

"I know. So do I."

Under the cover of twilight, Aurelia saw Max off at the Lehrter Bahnhof, still teeming with people despite the late hour. The train station was a cacophony of voices and the whistles of the conductors and the hissing of the departing trains, but all she could hear was the sound of her own thoughts, spiraling into despair.

Next to his sleeper heading to Paris, Max stood before her, his tall frame silhouetted against the pale light of dusk. He adjusted his favorite work jacket, the fabric worn yet familiar, and she could see the way his hands trembled slightly, betraying the calm he tried to project.

"We haven't said goodbye yet and I'm already missing you something frightful," he said, his voice low, as if afraid of disturbing the fragile moment they shared. The words hung in the air between them, heavy with the weight of reality.

Aurelia nodded, the lump in her throat making it difficult to speak. "I know, my love. Me, too," she managed, her voice barely above a whisper. The truth was an unbearable burden; while he was fleeing the clutches of a regime that would have undoubtedly destroyed him, had he dared to go against it, she remained tethered to the very heart of it through her brother's influence, if they both wanted to survive.

Max reached out, brushing a strand of hair behind her ear, his fingers lingering against her skin. She closed her eyes for a fleeting moment, savoring the warmth of his touch, wishing she could freeze this moment in time. They had shared countless sunsets and whispered dreams, but now it felt as though the sun was setting on their very existence.

"I'll call you as soon as I arrive in Paris," he promised for the hundredth time. They'd discussed it all on their way here, but he still felt the need to reassure her.

Aurelia's hand rested against his chest, feeling his heart beating wildly behind the hidden stack of cash. It was illegal to bring more than a thousand Reichsmark across the German border; Max carried ten thousand on his person—all they had left after pouring everything else into *Caesar*.

"Don't forget," Aurelia whispered meaningfully, "as soon as you board—"

"Go to the restaurant car, find the opportune moment when no one is looking, and hide it in the box where they keep the book with suggestions and complaints. And don't forget: nothing foolish from now on. Don't bait the SA, don't make enemies out of your brother's friends."

"I'll be good," Aurelia replied, her eyes on his, filled with a mixture of love and fear. "I promise." But the truth was, the walls around her were closing in, and every decision felt like a gamble with their future.

They stood in silence, the world rushing by around them, oblivious to the quiet tragedy unfolding. Each tick of the station clock felt like a countdown, a reminder that time was slipping away. She wanted to scream, to rail against the injustice of it all, but instead, she simply clutched his hand, feeling the warmth of his skin against her own, a fragile connection that seemed to defy the chaos surrounding them.

As the whistle of the train pierced the air, Aurelia's heart sank, heavy as a stone. It was time. The moment they had both dreaded had arrived. Max stepped back, the distance between them suddenly palpable, like a chasm formed by the very circumstances that tore them apart. He turned slightly, as if to glance back one last time, but she couldn't bear to see the resolve on his face, the pain etched in his features.

"Promise me," he said urgently, his voice cracking, "you will stay safe. Don't let them—"

"I promise," she interrupted, her voice steady despite the storm raging within her. "I love you. Till death and beyond."

"Till death and beyond," Max repeated and kissed her one last time, with all the love he carried in his heart that beat for her and for her only.

With one final, lingering look, Max was swallowed by the train's metal belly, and Aurelia was left standing alone on the platform, the rush of the world around her in stark contrast to the stillness in her heart. Tears brimmed in her eyes as she watched the carriages disappear into the distance, taking with them a piece of her soul.

In that moment, she felt the weight of everything—the love they had built, the dreams they had nurtured, now scattered like leaves in the wind. She was still a part of his story, but the ending was unwritten, and for the first time, the uncertainty of the future felt more daunting than the past they had shared. Alone at the station, Aurelia steeled herself for the fight ahead, but deep down, she knew that nothing would ever be the same again.

SEVENTEEN

It didn't take long for Goebbels to react. Not even a week had passed after Max's successful escape—he'd been calling her from Paris every night—before Aurelia received summons from the Propaganda Ministry. She'd considered ignoring it, but in the end decided against it, even if out of morbid curiosity.

To her surprise, on the appointed morning, she discovered Leni Riefenstahl already waiting in Goebbels' office in one of the visitors' armchairs.

"Am I interrupting anything?" Aurelia asked, hands in the pockets of her slacks, taking in the coffee tray, the cup in Leni's gloved hands, and Herr Minister himself leaning against the desk very close to Leni.

Goebbels smiled at Aurelia as if he'd just tasted something sour. "Aren't you always?"

Aurelia inclined her head with a smile of her own at the hint to the Grünewald scene and gestured toward the door the secretary was holding open for her. "I can always see myself out—"

"No, thank you. One of you Laubs already did." With a

dash of annoyance, Goebbels indicated the second chair for her. "Sit, please."

Aurelia obliged.

"Coffee?"

"Thank you, Herr Minister, but I would hate to waste your time. I'd rather get my dressing-down and be on my way."

Goebbels chuckled, studying her with his expressive black eyes as one would an extremely curious, although poisonous, specimen.

Unlike Leni, wearing a stylish floral dress with high-heeled sandals to match, Aurelia hadn't bothered to dress nicely for the appointment. She wore pale-green linen slacks and a simple white shirt, forgoing a bra as was her habit. No fancy updo either; just her hair, faded by the sun to platinum, pulled into a bun at the nape of her neck in wonderful contrast with her bronze skin with not an ounce of makeup on it.

"You know, Frau Laub, I remember back in the day your brother saying what a marvelous model you could be for the German women, had you not been brainwashed by that leftist ideology and turned by Nachtnebel against your own race, and I could never understand him. But now, I do."

It was under that probing gaze of his that Aurelia realized her mistake. Going for the casual look to show her indifference to Goebbels' office and influence, she had accidentally presented herself as the female Aryan ideal the Nazis were spouting forth about on every corner. She suddenly wished she'd worn her brightest red lipstick instead.

"And despite hearing so much about you, I just now realize that we have never been introduced properly." He put away his cup and, circling the chairs, stopped on Aurelia's side this time, offering her his hand. "Joseph Goebbels."

Instead of remaining seated and having to look up at him, Aurelia straightened to her full height to shake it. Now he had to look up at her. It was her turn to grin like a cat. "Aurelia Laub. My pleasure."

She did have to sit back down, but the balance of power was reset once again. Aurelia crossed her legs and leaned back in her chair, relaxed and at ease.

"Let's get to brass tacks then," Goebbels said, clapping his hands. "Seeing that Herr Laub decided to seek employment elsewhere, it leaves me with no choice but to appoint the next best thing to the position that would have been his. And seeing that you are the one who studied under him"—the double entendre and the smile with which he accompanied his words didn't escape Aurelia—"that makes you the next best thing, cinematographically. However, given your political inclinations, it goes without saying that the *Führer* was none too happy when I suggested appointing you to the position, despite your brother's insistence that you have been coming round in recent months and finally seeing clearly the error of your former ways."

Aurelia couldn't help but arch her brow. *Coming round?* This was certainly news to her. She wondered just what precisely Wilhelm had been feeding Hitler concerning her so-called compliance as there was nothing whatsoever to substantiate his claims. True, she hadn't attacked him in the press lately, but there was no more independent press for her to contact.

Goebbels, however, was too busy gazing at the portrait of Hitler dominating the entire wall of his office to notice her expression and the look she exchanged with Leni, who appeared to be just as stunned as her.

"So, we have arrived at a compromise of sorts," he continued, turning to face the women once again. "Fräulein Riefenstahl shall hold the official position and you, Frau Laub, shall be sharing responsibilities with her as the head of the German cinematography department. That is until you prove yourself to be politically reliable enough to appoint you both to the same position. Fräulein Riefenstahl has already proved herself to be a wonderful nationalist director who can produce just the films we want to see distributed to German public. I couldn't be more certain that you two shall make a splendid team."

Having lost all faculty of speech, Aurelia gaped at the smiling Propaganda Minister for an interminably long moment. She had expected to be told off and sent out; instead, she suddenly found herself facing the business end of a proverbial gun. Not even a semblance of the offer Goebbels had presented her husband with. What had just tumbled out of his mouth with such ease was a fait accompli; in his eyes, Aurelia and Leni were already a team, whether they liked it or not.

Still recovering from such insolence, Aurelia had finally opened her mouth to inquire just why he thought she would agree to such an appointment and where he could shove it as far as she was concerned, but then closed it just as abruptly. Goebbels was granting them the same powers, even if it would be Leni occupying the official position. As a leading cinematographer, Aurelia could get her hands on all of her and Max's films that UFA studios had in storage and no one would dare question her. She could travel to Paris with them in her suitcase and no one would dare search her. What had appeared at first glance to be a curse was in fact a blessing in disguise.

Before he could utter another word, Aurelia leaped to her feet and held her hand out to the Propaganda Minister, beaming with such joy, Goebbels eyed her with suspicion.

"Are you going to thank me for the offer, promise to do your best and run to the train station as soon as you're out the door?" he asked, holding her hand in his.

"Oh no, Herr Minister, I am very much staying," she assured him, all giddy and bright-eyed.

Goebbels continued to study her closely. It was obvious he had expected much more resistance on her part.

Leni, too, was shifting her eyes from the Minister to her colleague and back, just as confused as Goebbels.

"I am still working on my latest film—" Leni began in an apologetic tone, just to be waved off airily.

"Take all the time you need. I won't need you two until next fall."

Sensing something she wanted to be no part of, Aurelia forced her smile to stay in place as she asked, "What's happening next fall?"

"Why," Goebbels smiled like a snake, "the NSDAP annual Nuremberg Rally, of course."

EIGHTEEN

Fall—winter 1933–1934

With the first frosts arrived that inescapable grayness Aurelia dreaded and loathed in equal measure. It draped the city as if in a funereal shroud, suffocating and smelling faintly of rot. No wonder her mother had chosen this setting against which to set her dramatic exit from the world. Listening to the monotone pattering of the rain on the window as she tried to keep warm in that immense, deserted house of hers, Aurelia felt like kissing the barrel of a gun herself.

In September, it had been all right still, tolerable somewhat. She had Zara staying with her, even if her childhood friend had only arrived to close her German galleries—until further notice. Max had called every night too, talking to her until either of them fell asleep with the phone pressed against their cheek and shoulder, hugging the soulless metal instead of warm flesh.

His arrival in Paris had caused quite a stir, but the news of the newest German émigré celebrity soon grew old. He, too, had been alone and listless in his Ritz suite until an American producer approached him with an offer that was too good to pass.

"Two-year contract; they'll be paying me whether the work is done or not," Max had told Aurelia, speaking against the noise of the Ritz's bar. "Even if they don't give me a single project, I'll still be paid. Is it too good to be true?"

"Not at all," Zara had responded—a specialist in everything American. She had always listened in on their conversations, her welcome presence offering them a faint semblance of their former soirées. "It's Hollywood. They have more money than they know what to do with. Take it, don't be foolish."

Max had done so and now, in addition to the thousands of miles between them, there was the time difference to consider. His day was her night and when he called, exhausted from being driven around town with a real estate agent in search of a new home, Aurelia would still be sleeping, the shrill sound of the phone mixing with some disturbing nightmares tormenting her, and by the time she'd awaken and call him back, he would be fast asleep, having knocked himself out cold with the same sleeping pills Aurelia had been taking for years.

Unmoored and somewhat unemployed, she used her free time to probe and prod around the UFA archives for *Caesar*. The trouble was, all of the Laubs' loyal employees had been replaced with Nazi appointees.

"How does one to go about it?" Aurelia's hollow laughter echoed faintly around the Wolowskys' living room one evening. Lisl and Bibi were her only closest friends left in Berlin. She had tried Art's studio a few times, but he was nowhere to be found. Her only living relative, Herr Ministerpräsident of Prussia Wilhelm von Brandenburg, Aurelia wouldn't even consider visiting of her own free will. "I do have access to the UFA archives, but there is this obnoxious secretary minding it at all times, all helpfulness. *What precisely are you looking for,*

Frau Laub? You just kindly put the request into this form and I'll fetch it for you, Frau Laub."

Her mocking intonation and gaze, drawn to the ceiling in contempt, elicited amused snorts from both Berthold and his wife. Their newborn daughter in her arms, Lisl was positively glowing despite their family's precarious position. Just like her husband in Hollywood, Aurelia was getting paid for doing nothing—as long as she stayed put and within Goebbels' reach. If only Herr Minister knew that her very first Propaganda Ministry-issued salary had gone almost in its entirety to the Wolowskys, now especially in need of money with the new baby to care for. It had given Aurelia particular pleasure to part with that money, for that very purpose.

"I don't think they keep *Caesar* at the UFA," Berthold spoke, bouncing his eldest son on his knee. Unemployed as well, he had concentrated all of his attention on his little ones, much to their delight. "Back in the twenties, all confiscated material was stored at the censors' archives. And since the Nazi Party is the censor now, I would assume Goebbels' Ministry has them."

"What, inside the building itself?" Aurelia didn't fancy this new turn of events the teensiest bit.

"I would assume so."

She had had it planned out so nicely: stay a few weeks, sneak the film cans out, cross the border, and celebrate Christmas under the palm trees in Beverly Hills together with Max and the dogs while Max's new employer readied the film for release. Berthold's single remark slashed those plans, plunging a metaphorical knife into Aurelia's gut.

"Have you been inside?" she moaned in anguish, rubbing her face as if to wipe this never-ending nightmare from her eyes. "The building's security is tighter than a bank vault!"

"Yes, naturally, as a Jew, I have been inside," Berthold said deadpan. "Goebbels invited me personally and then we had coffee and cake and watched *Potemkin* together."

"Bibi, you would be of much more help to everyone if you applied your witticisms to filling out the essay section of your employment application for your visa," Aurelia grumbled with a dirty look in his direction.

Even with *Caesar* still out of reach, Aurelia could boast at least making Berthold see reason in the Universal Studios' offer. Together with Lisl, they'd been pressing him from both sides until he had issued a compromise: he would agree to it if his entire family could come with him. He wasn't leaving his wife and children here alone, not even for a short period of time. The trouble was, now he had to submit paperwork for an immigration visa instead of a simple work one and each time Aurelia visited, the requirements kept mounting.

"Speaking of which, I need another character reference from—" He checked the form, a stack of which was presently covering most of the dining table's surface, leaving only a small corner for the family to have coffee with their guest. "A neighbor or a community member of good moral and social standing. The lawyer said, the chances of approval are much higher if it's someone, and I quote, *with a recognizable name and preferably Aryan.*"

"Ours and the Whitbys' references are not enough?" Aurelia pulled back in surprise.

"They need five."

And who nowadays would vouch for a Jew, risking the wrath of the new regime? Aurelia heaved a sigh, raking her brain for options.

"I'll go and try Art again. He's more than popular in America now and I know for a fact he'll do it."

"As long as he doesn't get into trouble because of us," Lisl added, always worried about others first.

Already rising—why lose valuable time when friends were in need?—Aurelia quickly patted Lisl's shoulder with the baby muslin thrown over it. "It's a good kind of trouble—he's always lived for it."

Gray mist that had lingered over Berlin since the morning had turned into a nasty drizzle by the time Aurelia closed her umbrella at the entrance to the veterans' house where Art had lived and worked for the past decade. Taking two steps at a time, she hit the familiar old stairs until she reached the attic she used to call home. There, she came to an abrupt halt at the sight that presented itself to her stunned eyes: the door stood ajar, the wood around the lock splintered and gaping where a heavy boot must have kicked it in. Inside, an overturned bed with a mattress slashed to ribbons, the stuffing spilling out of it like gore from a bloated corpse.

Around the narrow room, broken bones of smashed easels lay, all fortunately empty after the Laubs had taken Art's works, including those in progress, for safekeeping. He hadn't bothered creating any more art ever since—why would he, if his name was officially banned and whatever he produced would only be seized by von Brandenburg (in the best-case scenario) or slashed and burned by Goebbels' people? Aurelia understood that silent protest of his all too well. Yet, with no works available to destroy, someone had still gone to great pains to snap each one of Art's brushes before smearing his paints all over the walls in a macabre display of hatred.

Death to race traitors!

Aurelia felt her stomach tie itself in a painful knot as she surveyed the graffiti.

Somewhere below, a door creaked opened. Seizing her chance, Aurelia ran outside and hung over the railing.

"Frau Holzer, is it you?" she called, hoping to see her and Art's old landlady who also managed the veterans' home's day-to-day upkeep. "It's Aurelia! What happened to Art?"

The door creaked further, instead of being slammed shut as Aurelia feared it would. Taking this as a good sign, she quickly ran down in time to see Frau Holzer beckoning her silently through the narrowly opened door.

"It was no SA," the old woman whispered, her eyes darting behind Aurelia's shoulder to ensure they were alone. "I remember those thugs from the civil unrest's days. These were all plain-clothed men. I called the police at once, but whatever identification they showed, the police saluted them and strongly advised me not to interfere if I knew what was good for me and to find a new tenant, as this one wouldn't be coming back," she added, her voice breaking.

Aurelia swallowed as she watched the kind old lady wipe her tears. Before Art had begun making money and sponsoring the upkeep of the entire building, Frau Holzer used to often feed them from her own table and didn't mind it when the rent was late. To express his gratitude and affection, Art once asked her to sit for him. That portrait was now on display in the Metropolitan Museum in New York, named aptly, *Mother*.

Forgoing an umbrella, Aurelia marched to her car and drove straight to her half-brother's office, where she demanded to be seen at once.

Soaked with rain and fuming, she stormed past some under-ling Wilhelm must have dismissed upon hearing his sister's name from his adjutant. At least in this sense he was still predictable, still very much a bored society prince, still loving a good scandal better than anything.

"The Cinematography Department Chief in the flesh! What an honor!" Wilhelm cried in mock delight, rising to greet her with open arms and a familiar air of smugness that made Aurelia's blood boil. "To what do I owe this unexpected visit?"

"Cut the pleasantries, Wilhelm," she snapped, her voice sharp. "Who's in charge of the SA or whichever plain-clothed thugs arrested Art?"

He dropped his arms, his eyes narrowing with amusement. "That would be me."

"Why am I not surprised?" Annoyed to the utmost, she dropped into a plush chair, unconcerned in the least with staining the expensive upholstery with rainwater. "Who are the new goons?"

"The goons would be the newly established Secret State Police. Or, for short, Gestapo." Wilhelm beamed at Aurelia, instantly transporting her back into the past. Only then he would boast of shooting a wolf—perfectly through the eye, so as not to ruin the coat he would spread in front of the fireplace—instead of snatching innocent people from their homes. "Efficient, aren't they?"

"They smashed the entire studio to pieces!"

"Precisely." Wilhelm's laughter echoed through the room, cold and devoid of empathy. "They are instructed and trained to operate in a manner that would deter any potential criminals from following suit."

That certainly explained the violence of the arrest and the door left purposely opened. Intimidation through the unrestrained display of power, with her brother's fingerprints all over it.

"Criminals?" Aurelia pulled forward, her nails digging into the armchair's velvet. "Just what crime did he commit, pray tell?"

An adjutant walked in, carrying a silver tray with a white towel neatly folded on it. "For your hair, Fräulein von Brandenburg."

Seeing that he wouldn't leave off, Aurelia snatched the towel from the tray and as soon as the adjutant snapped to attention and turned to leave, flung it across the desk, hitting her brother in his richly decorated chest. But he only laughed harder, positively delighted.

"You've got one husband, what do you need the old one for?"

"Your colleague Goebbels ran my husband off, in case you weren't aware," Aurelia responded poisonously.

"Ach, so you were feeling lonely and decided to visit good old Art?" Wilhelm raised his arms in theatrical apology. "Begging your forgiveness. Had I known, I would have waited with the orders."

"Shut your trap, Wilhelm! This is no joking matter."

Only it appeared his amusement grew in proportion with her fury. He had descended into a bout of belly-shaking laughter at Aurelia's last verbal assault.

"Was he really that good in the sack?" He heaved, wiping at the corners of his eyes. "All right, all right! Don't stare at me like you're trying to make my head explode. In my defense, Nachtnebel did it to himself." Having had his fun, Wilhelm straightened his uniform, assuming a more or less serious air. "He gave an interview to that American fellow, Shirer, one of their foreign correspondents here in Berlin, accusing the NSDAP of hypocrisy. Said the only reason we call ourselves a socialist party is to ingratiate us with the working class that would have overwhelmingly voted for the communists otherwise and not only here in Berlin, which has always been a Bolshevist hotbed. Said if we truly are working for the better of the German people, we should collectively donate our salaries to hospitals, schools, infrastructure and what have you, instead of throwing it at countless marches, expensive, tailored uniforms and the new Reichstag building he also said we burned."

Aurelia arched her brow.

"Which we did, you're right, but one can't just be spelling it out to the foreign press." Wilhelm didn't even deny it any longer. It was amazing what power did to people in only a few short months.

A cold shiver ran down Aurelia's spine at the thought of

where all this would go years into the NSDAP's regime with people like her brother at the helm.

"So, he spoke the truth," she summed it up for him. "To a news outlet. That's the reason for his arrest."

Wilhelm shrugged, unconcerned. "If he's foolish enough to challenge the regime, he deserves what he gets. This new world, it's not kind to those who defy authority."

Aurelia rose from her seat, her eyes shining wrathfully. "You'd better let him out, Wilhelm."

"Or what?" He grinned, pushing his swivel chair right-left, right-left with the heels of his tall boots.

Good question. It stung to know that he held all the cards. Still, Aurelia refused to back away, just like when they were children.

Not too long after her mother's death, Otto von Brandenburg had snatched Maria's cameo which Aurelia carried everywhere for comfort and threw it out the window. Aurelia had searched for it the entire day and had eventually found it. After her father's demands to hand it over so he could burn the damned thing once and for all, she had bolted out of the room and hid her little treasure so well, no servant could find it even after going through her room with a fine-toothed comb.

"You find out where she hides it," Otto had thrown over his shoulder to his son, his teeth set in helpless ire.

Wilhelm had pretended to drop the matter and Aurelia had begun to believe him until one day he had rowed their boat into the middle of the lake, dropped the oars by his sides and, with the kindest of smiles, told her that the boat wouldn't be going back until she told him about the cameo. Aurelia had shrugged and leaped into the water, dress, shoes, sunhat and all. Wilhelm's incensed curses had followed her all the way to the bank, where the governess was running around like a mother hen.

If she had such suicidal bravery then, surely Aurelia could conjure something up now?

With the same shrug, she smiled at her brother. "Or I'll go to this... what's his name? Shirer? I have a couple of things to say to him about you as well."

Wilhelm regarded her almost with respect, his opponent of old. For some time, his hands interlocked over his belly, he pondered his next move.

"I thought you wanted to leave Germany," he said at length. "Your friends certainly do. That family you're visiting so often. What are their names? Wolowsky?" he asked, mirroring her. "They happen to live in Prussia, of which, allow me to remind you, I am the President. My office is in charge of issuing exit visas. What good will an American office do, admitting them to their country, if they can't leave this one?"

Aurelia felt her chest tighten with rage and despair. "How do you sleep at night?"

"With the windows open," Wilhelm replied with a dismissive, self-satisfied grin. "Nachtnebel is toiling for the glory of new Germany in a new re-education camp called Dachau, still very much alive. If you want him to stay that way, I suggest you focus on your films and leave the politics to those who understand it."

Feeling a mix of defeat and fury, Aurelia turned on her heel, storming out of the office, out of the building—as far away from him as possible. Outside, she stood for a moment in the cool air, the weight of anguish settling heavily upon her.

Overnight, the city they called home had turned into a prison and she and Wilhelm into jailers and inmates, respectively. With rain streaking down her cheeks, Aurelia gazed into the gathering twilight, wondering on which side of the bars she belonged and seeing no answer.

Only darkness.

NINETEEN

Aurelia called every Jewish employee that had been dismissed from the UFA in the past few months and offered to sponsor the visas of those wishing to emigrate, but so far, aside from the Wolowsky family, there were no takers. It would all pass eventually, they thought. They were only fired temporarily, to appease Hitler's voters. They would hire them back soon; they were certain of it. Besides, immigration wasn't so easy when there was one's extended family to be considered. They couldn't just up and leave them, could they now?

In November, Aurelia tried testing the Propaganda Ministry archives but was met with silence and looks full of suspicion.

"Minister Goebbels assured me that I would have access to any facility and material in order to do my job," she declared to yet another Ministry employee, who—just her misfortune—turned out to be smarter than she hoped.

"That may be so, but the archives contain sensitive materials that can only be accessed with special authorization."

"Such as?"

"Herr Minister's."

Another dead end. But at least Leni agreed to write a reference for the Wolowskys—perhaps out of gratitude for saving Aurelia from Goebbels' advances—but, regardless, Bibi now had all five references. The lawyer had already informed him that the few visas allocated to German refugees in 1933 were no longer available, but if the Wolowskys moved fast enough, they could submit the documents just in time for the few available in 1934.

Just like Aurelia, they could do nothing but wait.

And now, with Christmas approaching and Zara gone, Aurelia felt so miserable and alone, she thought she could howl at the moon together with her wolf dogs.

"At least I still have you," she spoke to her loyal guardians, rolled in two tight circles on the bearskin rug in front of the fireplace. Pulling her socked foot from under the layers of covers, she stroked Loki's thick fur with her toes. On a small redwood table next to her stood a glass with brandy and yet another invitation from Wilhelm.

Of late, they came like clockwork, each one offering a semblance of connection amid the chaos. *"Come on over; you must be bored out of your mind and I know for a fact you aren't working on anything."* Zara's departure had left a gaping void and the laughter that once filled the air was now replaced by an oppressive silence; yet, the thought of stepping into his world—a world defined by the very regime she despised—was unbearable. Wilhelm had been nothing if not busy in the past year, turning his native Prussia into a police state. Between establishing the first few concentration camps, arresting and jailing the opposition, including Art—the very artist from whom he had profited so handsomely— and not even making a secret of rebuilding the army against the Treaty of Versailles, it was surprising he found time to call on his sister. Aurelia would have almost been flattered, had she not despised him so much.

She celebrated Christmas alone, with a phone as the only

lifeline to her friends and loved ones, drinking herself to sleep just to escape that everlasting chill invading her bones and the brittle silence that had descended upon her estate, turning it into a lifeless memory of itself.

On Christmas Day, instead of sending an invitation, Wilhelm called and refused to leave off, despite Aurelia telling him in no uncertain terms that she would rather eat nails than share a tea with his *Parteigenosse*.

"I'm at our family's estate, there's no one else here. Certainly, no Party members."

From her bed, Aurelia watched Astrid and Loki take up a position by the window, low growling emanating from their throats.

"I sent the driver for you."

"I know."

"He's already there?"

"No. He can't get in, the gates are locked. But I know he's by the gate. The dogs sense a stranger."

"Bring the dogs, too. Plenty of space for them to explore. Come on over, Hackelberg."

Like a sleeper agent spurred to action by a code word, Aurelia sat upright, covers sliding off her shoulders, suddenly awake. She hadn't heard the nickname for years; had all but forgotten Wilhelm had bestowed it upon her.

There was a legend of a man named Hackelberg who'd lived in bygone years on German land. Hackelberg had loved hunting so much that when the time came for him to ascend to heaven, he begged God to leave him on earth instead, so he could hunt for centuries to come. Not animals, mind you, but the wicked, whose souls he would collect for the lord of the Underworld. God granted his wish and, legend claimed, he still roamed the earth, and the more wickedness was in the world, the bigger the harvest he reaped.

"You always thought it was an insult," Aurelia said into the phone, "calling me that."

"Not an insult. Just a harmless tease. You've always been on a mission against authority, always looking to liberate the masses from their chains. How old were you when you let out all those pigs the peasants kept on your friend's estate?"

"Eight."

The year after her mother's death.

"Eight," Wilhelm repeated.

Aurelia pictured him nodding to himself.

"Father considered sending you away, you know."

She didn't.

"He was very concerned about your behavior," Wilhelm continued. "Thought you'd inherited your mother's madness and would embarrass the family name sooner or later. He even consulted that Austrian Freud fellow."

"Why didn't he?" Aurelia asked, shivering against the cold and memories of old. "Send me away?"

"Come on over," Wilhelm replied with sudden playfulness. "I'll tell you."

Aurelia cursed at the phone that had gone dead; cursed at Wilhelm and his games and then at herself—for climbing out of bed and yanking clothes out of the closet. A warm sweater and, after consideration, riding breeches and tall boots. She bet he still kept his horses.

On her request, Wilhelm's driver let Aurelia out at the edge of her family's sprawling estate, the grand manor looming like a specter against the gray sky. It had been over a decade since she last set foot on the grounds. She didn't want company as she navigated her way back into the past.

Loki and Astrid's chains around her wrist, she took a hesitant step forward, a wave of conflicting emotions washing over her. Gusts of icy wind over the expansive lands, faint smells of manure and horse sweat, the screams of ravens overhead—all her senses assaulted at once, nearly knocking her off balance. How hard she had tried to forget and how quickly she remembered it all—half of her life flashing before her eyes as if it had happened just yesterday.

Sensing small prey, the wolf dogs pulled hard on their chains and Aurelia let go, watching them charge toward the forest towering to her right. They were wild creatures, after all. It went against her very nature, trying to keep them confined when their very blood demanded freedom.

If only her father had released the chain that had held her mother fastened to his will.

"Lia!"

There he was, a sole horseman galloping toward her as if emerging from the days gone by as well. Wilhelm von Brandenburg, in all his glory.

"Hop on!"

She did and off they went, her arms around his chest, her face against his back—like the old days. He smelled different and yet familiar and Aurelia turned her head away. She didn't want this familiarity. She still couldn't explain what she was doing here, even to herself.

He hadn't tricked her into company. There was no one waiting at the manor's imposing facade besides a stable boy to take Wilhelm's stallion back to his stall. Not even a manservant to heat the living quarters. It was just as cold inside as it had always been, as if all the warmth had been sucked out of the air by the icy demeanor of her father, who used to rule their household with an iron fist.

His portrait greeted Aurelia: the last one of the many others watching over the vast marble hall with their long-dead eyes. One could trace the flow of centuries by their elaborate costumes and the attire of their war horses. Always war horses, the earliest one clad in iron from head to hoof next to its knight, the original von Brandenburg who had received the title from the Hohenzollern dynasty. Germany as a state hadn't even existed when he had charged the Pomeranian armies, his armor shining brighter than the sun.

"I'm a bit surprised Father didn't put up your portrait," Aurelia said, pulling her gloves off finger by finger. "You earned your place among the forefathers."

"I didn't."

Aurelia paused in her tracks to face him. She searched his face, but it told her nothing. "You fought your war."

"I *lost* my war," Wilhelm replied with a certain undertone, and all at once Aurelia was reminded what von Brandenburg House had always been about. Conquest and power, at any cost, all else be damned.

Emerge Victorious or Perish, her fingers traced the engraved motto on the miniature familial crest at the foot of the oldest von Brandenburg's portrait. "So, what now? You want a do-over? Under a different flag?"

A coy smile was the only reply she received.

He hadn't been around to tend to the estate of late. All furniture stood draped in white, its ghostly presence emphasized by the skeletal remains of old leaves, crushed underfoot and never swept. Aurelia's heart tightened as she recalled countless evenings spent in the ornate drawing rooms, where laughter should have flourished but was stifled by her father's cold, demanding presence.

They always bore a quality of performance, those nights when Otto chose to entertain. Long before guests would appear, he would enter his wife's rooms and select the gown she was to wear, pairing it with whatever jewels he considered appropriate. As little Aurelia had watched, he'd directed the maid on how to do Maria's hair. Aurelia was fortunate to escape such close attention to her wardrobe given her age and unimportance in her father's eyes, but she would still be summoned downstairs to sit on her father's lap for exactly five minutes as his guests cooed at her. As soon as the time was up, the governess would hustle her back upstairs, not to be heard nor seen for the rest of the night.

Unlike Wilhelm. Wilhelm had always been there, but even he, in the end, failed to earn Otto's approval.

"I remember when you returned from the war," Aurelia said, catching a faint whiff of roast meat and wondering if it was her imagination playing tricks on her. "I remember what Father said."

"He said, *Well. Here you are*," Wilhelm quoted Otto with an intonation to match and all the hatred Aurelia felt for this place surged within her, casting shadows over a childhood and youth marked by fear and resentment. "But then you threw yourself at me and I didn't feel so rotten for returning back alive instead of at least dying like a hero, which he would have much preferred."

"You stunk to high heaven." In spite of herself, Aurelia discovered that she was smiling. "It was raining and you were splattered with mud—"

"And you got it all over your white blouse," Wilhelm's own memories poured into the stream of hers; his hand found her palm and squeezed. He led her further inside.

With every step, Aurelia felt the weight of her dual identity pressing down on her—an aristocrat returning to a home that felt foreign yet familiar; a woman of a new social order who believed that all were created equal, grappling with the legacy of privilege that had been thrust upon her. The estate was a symbol of everything she had come to despise: the opulence, the entitlement, the blind adherence to tradition that had stifled her sense of self. Yet, it was also a place where her roots lay deep, tangled with the very essence of her being.

As they crossed the threshold into the dining room, Aurelia

was enveloped by the scent of burning wood, smoked meat, and freshly baked potatoes. By some invisible hands, the enormous dining table stretching from one end of the room to the other was set for two, the familiar silver confined to one corner of the heavy oak monstrosity. Red wine shone through carved crystal in two goblets, with a pitcher resting among the cuts of cheese and fresh bread.

"I do have your gin if you prefer it—" Wilhelm offered, but Aurelia stopped him with a toss of the head.

"The wine, it's ours? From the cellar?"

Wilhelm nodded, pulling the chair out for her. "I tasted it before serving. Don't fret, it hasn't turned to vinegar yet. Hungry?"

"Famished."

She dug into the food, unrestrained by the etiquette that used to dictate every moment of her life here. Holding the beef rib by the bone, she sank her teeth into the meat, hoping that her father's ghost was watching in helpless ire. She swallowed a mouthful and gulped down the wine, already sensing, suspecting why Wilhelm had lured her here.

"Father, he never changed the will, did he?" She stared around the room with a mixture of hatred and dread.

"No," Wilhelm answered. "He didn't."

So half of it was legally hers.

Aurelia put the goblet down with a dull thud. Her stomach turned. She had hoped she had thrown off the chains binding her to this land years ago and yet Otto managed to throw a collar around her neck once again, pulling her back into oppression. Sure, she could more than use the money—Aurelia was up to her eyes in debt after Max had mortgaged their house to produce *Caesar*, only for the film to be seized by the authorities. But the memory of her mother's suffering was much too strong within her. No money was worth tying herself to what she had fled with such abandon some thirteen years ago.

"Send your lawyer with the deed to me; I'll write my half off to you," she said before it could claim its power over her, this familial land her ancestors lived and died for.

"No."

Aurelia stared at him, just now realizing that his chair was positioned opposite hers, not at the head of the table.

"Why did you call me here then? What games are you playing now?" All at once, she felt small and defenseless, thrust back into the past, her half-brother the only buffer between her and her only surviving parent who had seen her as nothing but a well-bred mare to sell to the highest bidder. It was this place; it was reducing her to something she had sworn she would never again be—a woman at a powerful man's mercy.

Wilhelm considered the wine against the fire going in the hearth behind Aurelia's back. "No games," he spoke at length. "I want you to have it, I want you to stay *here*."

"Here, at the estate?"

"Here, in Germany." Wilhelm heaved a sigh and picked up a slice of a cheese but didn't bite into it. After a few moments of contemplation, he dropped it onto his plate and wiped his hand on an ornate, pristinely white napkin. "I know what you're planning, Lia. Poking and prodding the UFA stagehands for rumors as to where *Caesar* was taken, calling old employees, having tea with Lisl Wolowsky every Sabbath—"

"Spying on me then? With your Gestapo goons?" Aurelia hissed like a cat, all sentimentality for their shared childhood gone in a flash.

"Not spying, Lia—"

"It's Ari. Ari Laub to you."

"Aurelia, quit it with your revolutionary stance, for the love of—" Wilhelm caught himself raising his voice and ceased abruptly, wiping his hands down his face as though to wash off the annoyance. "This is how the new Reich works: people watch everything and, it just so happens, those reports end up on my desk. I haven't ordered anyone to do surveillance on you. And before you storm out of that door, listen to what I have to say to you. Can you please sit down and grant me five minutes of your time so I can continue to ensure that my desk is where those reports end up, instead of Himmler and his lovely underlings?"

"Who the hell is Himmler?" Aurelia muttered through gritted teeth, lowering back into her chair and staring at her brother askance.

"Tomorrow's Ernst Röhm."

Aurelia blinked, confused as to where Hitler's beloved leader of the SA was going, but Wilhelm only waved her off. *Don't concern yourself with it; it's none of your trouble.*

"Do you see Hitler as a leader of Germany?" he asked, beginning to separate delicate slices of meat from the bone, nonchalant as ever. "Some Austrian, not even a German?"

The sudden icy disdain in his voice threw Aurelia off track.

"Some uneducated lowlife," Wilhelm continued, his voice gradually rising, filling the room with barely contained anger, "who feigns contempt for anything intellectual simply because he doesn't understand it. Who feels the need to burn the books and paintings of those who made it into the galleries his unimaginative watercolors never did. Who strives for greatness but inspires nothing but scorn, with his idiotic mustache, his incomprehension of diplomacy, his anti-intellectualism. He parades around as if one of the people so that the ignorant herd can feel they finally have one of their own in the highest office."

Aurelia threw a glance at the servants' entrance leading from the dining room to the kitchen.

"They're all gone," Wilhelm answered her unspoken question. "My driver had orders to pick them up from the back entrance as soon as we stepped through the doors. It's just us here, Hackelberg."

"All right." Aurelia patted her lips clean and clasped her

hands atop the folded napkin. "I'll bite. What are you doing in his administration if you despise him so?"

"Simply acquiring enough resources and power until those who are ordained by divine right rule the German land again. If you remember your history, the House of Brandenburg emerged when one such ineffective ruler surrendered the crown."

"Hitler will never surrender the crown. Not willingly."

"Oh no, we don't count on that," Wilhelm smiled, a charming officer once again. "There will be war and it will not go as planned—they never do, those wars, something always happens—and here's where we step in. To replace an incapable leader."

"*We?*"

"The aristocracy." Wilhelm made a bridge with his inter-laced fingers and rested his chin on it. In the light of the fire-place, his eyes shone with lively mirth. "As the gods intended, from the dawn of ages."

Aurelia rubbed her forehead, chuckling. "Wilhelm, you do not really believe that, do you?"

"No, of course I don't, but the lower classes do. Not even two decades had passed since the Kaiser's abdication. What had been ingrained in them for centuries is simply dormant; it shall never be forgotten so easily. And your new chief Goebbels, he's a talented fellow, I'll concede that much. But I have already seen his methods. I know just how to take over when the time comes to steer that tremendous propaganda machine into some-thing old and familiar, like a pair of one's favorite slippers. And here's where you come in."

His smile still in place, he stretched his hand out, offering it palm up to Aurelia.

"That's why I need you to stay here in Germany, little sister. That's why I need you to continue working for the Ministry, so that you learn it inside out. So that when the time comes, we can rule it together. You'll bring your husband back, give him land, money, the entire Babelsberg, the UFA—whatever you want, I'll sign on it. He'll forgive you a few years of separation, trust me. Zara will open her galleries once again; hell, I'll gift her the spaces in gratitude for your services to the country. I'll even throw in Nachtnebel for you, slightly worse for wear but still with all of his limbs about him. He may well have to leave the country though; something tells me even Dachau won't re-educate him. So, what do you say?"

"I'm not interested in money or power, Wilhelm."

"I know that. That was the bare minimum I'm offering you. Just so you wouldn't storm out on me. Five minutes has long passed, after all."

Aurelia pressed her lips together in annoyance. Indeed, they had passed and yet, here she was, still sitting. Listening.

"Go on," Wilhelm prodded her gently. "Bargain away. Ask and you shall receive."

He was offering what he didn't have, and out of morbid curiosity, Aurelia played along just to hear what he would say.

"I want a complete reversal of Hitler's racist policies. I want you to reinstate all of those Jewish workers who lost their jobs and make it illegal to discriminate against them in any sphere of life."

"Consider it done. Personally, I have nothing against them as long as they don't mind paying taxes to the crown on time and neither does the aristocracy as a class. It was the king who granted them equal rights in the first place some centuries ago, if you remember."

"Good. Next, I want equal rights for women. And not the social democrat concessions that we used to have. I want German women to be equal to German men. In everything. Pay, hiring practices, higher education accessibility, land and property ownership—everything."

Wilhelm pondered with his index finger at his chin. "More

workers, more taxes, more money in the government coffers—
sounds fine by me."

"I want freedom of speech and assembly."

"Lia, I'm offering you a finger and you're trying to take off
my entire arm!" Yet, he was laughing, clapping his hands in
apparent delight. "Besides, freedom of speech shall concern
your department."

"Good. And I don't want it to be the Propaganda Department, I want it to be the Everyone Has a Voice Department."
Aurelia slammed the carafe down after refilling her glass. "Why
are we even discussing this though? It shall never happen."

"It shall never happen," Wilhelm repeated, savoring each
word. "Famous last words. Was it your party, the social democrats, who said as much during last fall's elections concerning
Hitler winning the vote?"

Aurelia made no response, eyeing her brother sullenly over
the rim of her wine glass.

"And who made that happen?" He arched his brow meaningfully.

Aurelia remained silent, acknowledging a certain logic to
his statement in spite of herself. Inside of her, an internal battle
raged on. To stay and fight for her country or leave and make a
home elsewhere? She had fled her ancestral land once. She had
made a home elsewhere—in progressive Berlin, with like-
minded people. But authoritarianism had followed her to that
new home, spreading like a cancer over the places and people
she loved, poisoning everything in its path. Who could guarantee that it wouldn't eventually creep over the ocean and put
roots in the Land of the Free?

"At any rate, I won't keep you here against your will,"
Wilhelm said, as if reading her thoughts. "You want to leave the
country, I'm only one call away. You still have European visas in
your passport—you can follow Laub's route. I'll make sure they
let you through on the border." He paused, pondering some-

thing. "I was hoping you'd be up for a challenge, Hackelberg. We share the same blood. You're a warrior just as much as I am. I thought instead of running, you'd want to stay and fight for your people, but it's up to you. Go to Los Angeles if you like, make your films. Maybe you'll be happy there."

He was a damned good orator, that half-brother of hers. Knew just how to stir the emotions Aurelia tried to smother inside. Sure, she could leave, go to a country that had already fought for its freedom and won. But who would stand up to the fascism raging through Europe like wildfire if all of them, the dissidents, left? Who would stop its spread all over the world if everyone decided to keep their heads in the sand and, as Wilhelm put it, go about their business and pretend that it didn't concern them?

Freedom was never easily surrendered by those in power. It could only be torn out of their hands by those who weren't afraid to lay down their lives for it. And retreat only worked as a temporary measure: sooner or later, one would have to face the enemy. She was an army child, she knew that much.

"You never told me why Father changed his mind about sending me away." Aurelia's eyes met Wilhelm's across the table.

In the silence that followed, both felt the weight of their shared history—a history now shadowed by the choices that had driven them apart.

He smiled faintly. "I asked him not to."

"Why?"

He gestured around with a mirthless chuckle. "Would you want to be alone in this prison?"

TWENTY

Los Angeles. Summer 1934

Max Laub found himself adrift in the sprawling landscapes of Los Angeles, a city that pulsed with energy yet felt achingly foreign. With the weight of his recent emigration, he navigated this new world with a heavy heart, feeling the absence of his beloved wife, Aurelia, who remained in Germany, caught in the shadows of an uncertain future. Each day, the sun rose over the palm trees, casting a golden hue on his small rented house in Beverly Hills, but the warmth did little to dispel the chill of loneliness that enveloped him.

His daily routine began whenever he felt like rising; no one to see, nowhere to rush to. Breakfast was a solitary affair, with Max often opting simply for toast with marmalade and coffee— no Frau Abel, the Laubs' loyal housekeeper, here to cook for him and Aurelia. After breakfast, he would don his tailored suit —a remnant of his past life—and make the journey to the studio. He didn't have to. No one monitored his comings and goings, just like they didn't worry about the schedules of the two other émigrés sharing an office with Max. Frank Harding, the MGM producer who had signed him up back in Paris, kept his word: Max indeed collected his paychecks at the end of each month without so much as lifting a finger for them. However, it was that very idleness that hung over him like a dark cloud—the only real presence against the backdrop of the artificial brightness of his sun-colored days. He had begged Harding for work throughout winter and mid-spring, only to be met with, "Give me a script I can sell to the studio."

June was nearing an end when it appeared that he finally did, even if he didn't plan on it.

His head on a swivel, Max sat at the MGM executives' desk, caught in the crossfire of the producer, the publicity liaison agent, and the studio boss. In the few months he had spent in Hollywood, his English had improved, but he still found himself lost when the trio fired away at each other in rapid succession, arguing over his script.

The publicity liaison agent was categorical. The Germans would never acquire it, and not only that, they would likely show their dissatisfaction by boycotting MGM films altogether.

Frank Harding waved the argument off with his fat cigar, sending the ashes flying over the script. The American public would lap it up instead. It was domestic sales they should worry about, not international ones. What Laub had here would sell like hotcakes. An insider's view of the family, two members of which now occupied positions of power. They would have to change names, of course, but the public would recognize the von Brandenburg siblings, all right. Wilhelm, the Minister-President of Prussia and one of Hitler's closest advisors, and Aurelia.

It took Max all his effort not to cringe whenever Harding pronounced her name. Not just pronounced, but let it roll off his tongue, tasting each letter with his eyes half-closed. After rejecting all of Max's scripts, he'd pounced on the idea of this one with an almost unhealthy interest. Max had never thought of submitting it. All he'd done was type out a few sketches of Aurelia's childhood on a particularly dismal day when he was missing her sorely and left them lying about carelessly in the office. By the time he'd returned from his lunch break, Harding was in his chair, devouring the scenes and demanding more.

"The idea is brilliant, but you shouldn't be so restrained. Turn all the dirty laundry inside out. And Wilhelm, he's a solved case. He was raised a martinet. No; tell me what happened to the little girl that made her first run from it all, spend years as a freedom-loving little anarchist who created films to match, only to do a one-eighty."

Max had tried to argue that Harding misunderstood it all; that Aurelia didn't do any such thing; that she had her reasons for staying. But Harding had looked upon him with such pity, the words had died on his lips.

"She left you, Laub. I know it's a bitch to admit, but she did. Don't try to justify it. The least you can do now is make money from it."

Max was mortified. He would never stoop so low. Only, it wasn't up to him any longer. Harding had reminded him of a clause in his contract which stated that anything Laub produced in the MGM facility was automatically considered MGM's intellectual property. Once green-lighted, the film would be made in any case. It was Max's choice if his name appeared only as a scriptwriter or as a director.

In desperation, Laub had called Aurelia that very night— her morning—and asked for her advice. Her voice, reaching through half of the world, had appeared distant and hollow, echoing Harding's advice.

"Make the film, Max. Make money."

"I didn't even mean for Harding to see the script. All I did was write down the things that you told me about your mother that day, at the cemetery, remember? I never meant for it to—"

"You don't have to explain yourself," she had interrupted

him mid-word. "I'm sorry, Max, I can't really talk right now. I'm running late for the department meeting."

He didn't understand. He had tried calling back for the next few days until Frau Abel answered the phone and, after inquiring after Herr Laub's well-being and health, explained that Frau Laub had left for Nuremberg to see how the rally preparation was progressing. She would be directing the rally in a few months. Would Herr Laub like to leave a message?

"Ari is set to direct the Nuremberg Rally?" Max's blood had run cold from the announcement. This couldn't be right. She had only stayed to save their *Caesar* and aid their former employees' immigration efforts; certainly not film any Nazi propaganda. And the Nuremberg Rally wasn't just any propaganda—it was the culmination of nationalistic ideas, a parade of goose-stepping soldiers to demonstrate to the entire world new Germany's growing power. The affair would last several days, during which the country's ardent Nazi population would be getting drunk on Hitler's and his underlings' nationalistic hatred as it poured forth from the rostrum. And Aurelia would be documenting it all—the torch-bearing SS, the mesmerized Hitler Youth, the standards and fireworks that made one dizzy— an orgy of fascism.

"I beg your pardon, not direct," Frau Abel's voice had torn him out of his frightful musings. "That other girl—Leni something—she will be directing it. Frau Laub will be filming it, if you know what I mean. Forgive the old crow, I'm not good with all that motion picture terminology."

"You aren't old, Frau Abel; you are fresh as a lily," Max had chided her kindly, his chest full of aching for their back and forth, the playful dynamic he so sorely missed.

"Not according to my back, I'm not."

"Tell Aurelia not to work you too much."

"As if! I'm bored stiff here without you to look after, Herr Laub. That child, she's running around all the time, not even eating at home most days. That new boss of hers works her to the bone, the poor girl."

It appeared he did, that scheming little minister who could sell cattle tickets to the slaughterhouse. Had he sold this new vision of Germany to Aurelia though?

No. Max had rejected the idea with a violent toss of his head. Not his Ari. There was a perfectly reasonable explanation for the ruse which she couldn't spell out on the phone. With the way things were progressing, with Wilhelm von Brandenburg's Gestapo sniffing around like hounds, no wonder one had to think twice before discussing any sensitive information.

He knew his wife. He trusted her.

"If you let us make it, we'll release it simultaneously with that Nuremberg film I hear Riefenstahl and von Brandenburg are working on." Harding's voice pulled Max back to the MGM office, full of cigar smoke and infinite loneliness. "Von Brandenburg's glorification of German nationalism against the insider family story told by none other than her Jewish husband, Max Laub, a persecuted minority himself," he spelled out, holding his hands up in the air to form a frame. "I see headlines from here."

The executive must have seen them too, plus the revenue such a picture would bring. The very next day, Laub and Harding were going over the budget.

TWENTY-ONE

The work Max had pleaded with Harding for was finally his, only the excitement of the project was dulled by the stark realization that everything he had known in Germany was now replaced by an alien landscape of Hollywood glamour and bravado. Upon arriving at the studio on his very first day as an MGM director, the yawning expanse of sound stages loomed before him, a labyrinth of creativity that felt more like a maze of confusion. Within the first couple of hours, Max realized that the language barrier had become a palpable obstacle; though he spoke English, the nuances of American slang often slipped through his fingers like grains of sand.

Technical terms were also out of his grasp, leaving him to snap his fingers and explain what he meant to a sound director, who stared at him with barely hidden contempt. The set was only being prepared for the rehearsal and Max could already hear the laughter of stagehands and the occasional snickers when they thought he was out of earshot. Their mocking imitations of his thick German accent stung deeper than any verbal jab, and it was a reminder of how isolated he truly felt in this land of opportunity.

As the work began in earnest, the chaos of actors and crew bustling about was a far cry from the disciplined environment he was accustomed to in Germany. The actors, stars in their own right, didn't follow his directions with the reverence he had hoped for; instead, they seemed to interpret his vision through a lens of indifference. Each miscommunication became a struggle, an uphill battle against the tide of frustration that threatened to drown his artistic spirit. He watched as scenes unraveled, his heart sinking with every take that fell short of his expectations.

"Cut!" he called from his chair, only to catch an annoyed *what-is-it-now?* look from his leading actress. "Miss Ashwood," he began, as politely as possible. "Maria—I mean Alexandra"— the name under which Aurelia's mother would be known to the audience; Max kept misspeaking and using her real one— "wasn't a hysterical woman. On the contrary, she was always perfectly collected. She doesn't say a word when her husband hurls the book she purchased into the fireplace. She doesn't say a word when he cuts off her allowance altogether. She keeps her composure when he shoots her favorite horse in front of her, blaming the innocent beast for Alexandra's early miscarriages. That's what makes the outburst all the more powerful later on, when it's not just her who's suffering, but her little girl. That's what—"

"Lunch!" The stagehands' leader called into a megaphone, cutting Max off mid-word, and before he knew it, everyone began to disperse in front of his eyes, open wide in astonishment.

Anger surged in him, propelling him to his feet. "Who said you could be dismissed?" he bellowed at them, the dam breaking under the pressure of their mocking indifference. "I'm your director! I'm in charge of the schedule on set."

"Not in America you're not," one of the stagehands called over his shoulder, pulling a cigarette from behind his ear and sticking it in his mouth. "We're in the Union. Union rules say lunch at twelve. It's twelve. So, lunchtime."

There was nothing else for it but to sit and chain-smoke for the next hour, wondering what the hell he was doing here in the first place. They made it clear: they didn't want him here. He had imposed on them, a foreigner who thought he was something else. As far as they were concerned, he could go back to where he came from and take his orders with him.

Max rubbed his injured eye behind the lens, swallowing in rapid succession. Aurelia would have made friends with them. Aurelia would have made them respect her without throwing her directorial authority around. Aurelia would make a joke on the fly, something along the lines of "Well, Aurelia rules say your fat tail stays where it is until I'm finished talking if you don't want to be socked in the mug. I'm still talking. So, your fat tail stays put and listens."

Aurelia... He felt like howling with despair.

Another day, another battle with the crew. Exasperated, Max leafed through the script, foreign words stringing together and melting before his eyes. Harding had stopped by earlier that morning to check on progress; saw the previous day's rushes and sucked his teeth. Max hadn't tried to defend the material. He couldn't bear watching it without cringing either. Schedules in Hollywood were much tougher than in Germany: five weeks to shoot the entire picture. Max had four left.

On set, Jean Ashwood was pulling hairpins out of her hair, holding a hand mirror in her other hand. The "frizzy atrocity" of the Edwardian era wasn't doing her any favors. It didn't go with her features. Now, if she would just let her hair fall onto one side just so...

The assistant director was mediating between Clark Armstrong, the male lead, and the costume designer. The uniform Armstrong had to wear was making him look too round around the midsection.

"Not the uniform's fault. Though I can always suggest a girdle," the designer muttered under his breath with a viciously sweet smile and Max's assistant had to physically restrain the male lead to prevent a fistfight.

"I demand that pansy fired!" Armstrong shouted in Max's general direction, his eyes still on the costume designer. "Either he comes to work tomorrow, or I do. But not both of us. Is that clear?"

He was in the middle of his dramatic exit from the set when Max suddenly leaped to his feet and planted himself in front of the actor. In his eyes behind the horn-rimmed spectacles was sheer murder. Old memories surged in him, placing him back in the mud-filled trenches of the Eastern Front. The new recruits he'd been given to replace those presently stuck on the barbed wire in no man's land had also tried to challenge his, officer's, authority. They had climbed out of the trench after Max and his white flag, seen the fat ravens circling above the carpet of corpses, in such numbers the entire sky turned black, and refused to take another step forward to collect the dead. Max had grasped the nearest greenhorn by the scruff of his neck and dragged him to the first line of the fallen, sticking the makeshift flag into the wet earth.

"We bury our dead. This is what sets us apart from animals." His voice had travelled far across the land, drowning out even the ravens. The first dead soldier lay prostrate with his eyes wide open, as if pleading for an answer from these two. *Why did I have to die? Why so young?* Max closed them gently before collecting his tag. "Grab the feet, I'll hold the shoulders."

They had worked their way further into no man's land bit by bit. On the opposite side, inspired by Max's example, the Romanians had climbed out as well to collect their fallen. Soon, more men had joined Max and his aide until the entire battalion was there. When the signal for an attack had sounded at dawn the following day, they had followed him into the battle without a word of protest.

Armstrong must have seen a shadow of those battles in Max's dark eyes. Confronted with the director, he suddenly hesitated.

"Get back on the set," Max said quietly but with such power in his voice, Armstrong made an uncertain step back. "You!"

Startled, Miss Ashwood dropped her hand mirror at Max's wrathful shout.

"Touch another strand of hair, I dare you."

His chest heaving, he stalked onto the set, his furious gaze taking in each member of the crew. One by one, they averted their eyes. For the first time in the entire week, dead silence descended upon the pavilion.

"Vain, pathetic little creatures, the lot of you! Do you even comprehend, with your tiny little minds, what we are doing here? Do you see any further than beyond the end of your own conceited nose to realize what's going on in the world?"

Still as scolded children, they listened.

"What do you think this is? A cute little historic picture, with costumes and hairstyles and horses and some German flair?" Max paused, his jowls clenching. "It's a warning tale to all of us, pointing precisely at the mindset of nationalistic militarism spreading all over Europe right now. You're damned right, Otto von Brandenburg was fat! His kind never descends into the trenches—we, ordinary people do. We are sent there as cannon fodder, to die in the name of their ideas! I should know, I was one of such trench rats for four damned years! See this?" He pointed at the scar above his eye. "Romanian shrapnel, an Eastern Front souvenir. I can barely see out of this eye. So, in the future, if you decide to mock me, by all means—this is the side from which you can do it safely."

None of the stagehands made a sound of protest. Neither did their regular scornful smirks follow Max's remarks.

"I have already fought one war for my country. Another one is coming, take it from me. I lived there; I recognize the early signs. Now, you can continue concentrating on your waistlines or flattering camera angles or lunch or you can put your talents to actual use and show the audience the good, the bad, and the ugly of what Germany is like. Otto von Brandenburg is Hitler. His orders are never to be doubted, his authority never challenged. Maria von Brandenburg is the German people, threatened into submission, with death as the only escape route."

"And little Aurelia?"

Max turned back to Jean Ashwood. Her entire countenance seemed to have changed in response to his speech. Her features softened, shoulders slumped a bit. Around her mouth, two sharp creases were showing as she eyed the crib in the corner of her set bedroom with pensive, extinguished eyes.

"Aurelia is the voice of dissent," Max said, hugging himself with both hands.

His assistant arched his brow skeptically. "She stayed, Max. You left. Isn't it you who's the voice of dissent?"

Max smiled at him with bitter melancholy. "I ran. She stayed. So, no, I'm just a director."

TWENTY-TWO

The dynamics may have changed, but all the same, this was no way to work. Aurelia had been right on that very last day they saw each other. This was no Germany. Here, Max Laub was a nobody and he should act accordingly.

The following morning, Max swallowed what was left of his pride and addressed the crew, his tone no longer that of a self-important German celebrity.

"I, uh... I would like to begin by apologizing to you for my outburst yesterday. I assure you, it was a one-time affair that will never repeat itself." He raised his head and gazed around, eyes full of newfound humility. "I want you to know that I deeply appreciate the fact that you welcomed me into your country and allowed me to work alongside you. I'm saying *alongside* because this is what any good film is—a collective effort. Back in Berlin, it was almost a family effort," he continued with a smile, his memory resurrecting fleetingly the shadows of the joyous past. "Most of my film crew had been with me for over a decade there..."

Lost in thought, he didn't notice the film crew members' eyes softening. The air of hostility was lifting like a curtain, giving way to sympathy instead. They regarded him differently now, well aware of how tough some Germans had it under a new regime. Foreign correspondents living in Berlin told enough stories of the countless professionals losing their livelihoods due to the new discriminatory laws, the so-called crackdown on crime which was mostly used to silence the opposition and give the Gestapo a reason to jail a few more dissidents who just couldn't seem to get it into their heads that the days of democracy were effectively over. And now Laub's own wife was photographed in Goebbels' and von Brandenburg's entourage more and more often... They felt for the poor bastard. And he was right, too: they hadn't cared all that much before, not until he had called them out on it. But this film *was* important. It would do the whole of humanity good if they really put their hearts into it.

"I don't have anyone here," hand on his heart, Max spoke endearingly earnestly, his eyes full of mist. "But I hope to get to know you all and make you my new family, if you will allow me. I'm not familiar with Hollywood labor laws, but I'm striving to learn. Your equipment is also different from ours, so forgive me in advance for my ignorance if I give directions that make little sense. Correct me, whenever possible, please, and I'll do my best to grasp it the best I can. Goes for my English, too," he ended with a chuckle, which, to his surprise, echoed amiably around the set.

"All you really need to know is how to use the most important word in America," the same stagehand who had always been the first to tell Max to piss off offered with a good-natured grin.

"What word?" Max inquired despite the crew already exchanging knowing looks.

"*Fuck*—what else?" The stagehand shrugged his massive shoulders, eliciting laughter from actors and fellow stagehands alike. "*Fuck you, fuck off and fuck this*—three magic combinations that will get you anywhere. Here, let me show you. Imagine I'm Harding, harassing you about the dailies. What do you say to me? Don't hesitate, say it with a full chest!"

"Fuck off," Max complied to the crew's utter delight.

"Good, Prussian, you're getting it!" The stagehand clapped his great paws, all enthusiasm.

"Fuck you, I'm Austrian!"

The entire set hollered. Laughing together with them, their hands clapping him amiably on his shoulders and back, Max felt that he finally belonged for the very first time in this strange, endless land.

They finished the picture just in time for the deadline. A couple of weeks later, the editing was done. The MGM executives, invited by Harding to the first private screening, sat in mortal silence for a few minutes after the final scenes before rising one by one and breaking into a thunderous applause.

No longer burdened with a tight schedule, Max returned home to his lonely house, the familiar silence greeting him like an old friend. On the set, among people, it had been all right, but now the feeling of being all alone in the world had redoubled.

He should get a dog. At least someone to greet him.

After discarding his clothes, Max turned the radio all the way up just to drown out the unbearable silence. Dinner was another solitary affair; used to cooking for himself by now, he sifted through the cabinets for ingredients, a cookbook with a smiling woman in a pink apron on its cover, splaying its pages open in front of him. He should hire a maid, too. He could afford a cheap one, who would only come to make his meals and clean up once a week. He kept promising himself that next week he certainly would: would go find some mongrel in the city streets and call one of the adverts in the local paper to arrange help. But come the new week, Max knew he would put it off for another week.

Because he already had two dogs back home and it was Aurelia who always hired help. And she would come. Soon, she would come. Then they would hire a maid together.

As he sat at the small dining table, alien, American music pouring out of the radio's speakers, Max desperately tried to fill the void Aurelia left behind. The chair across from him felt heavy with her absence and every bite tasted bittersweet, seasoned with nostalgia. He missed her contagious laughter, her recounting of the day's events on set, and the way she would have turned mundane evenings into cherished memories. The Hollywood lights outside his window shone like stars, yet they felt cold and distant, in stark contrast to the warmth of their shared life in Germany.

In the heart of bustling Los Angeles, lost among the glamour and chaos, Max Laub felt the weight of isolation pressing down upon him. His life had become a series of lonely routines, each day marked by the absence of the one person who made it all worthwhile. As he drifted off to sleep that night, the silence of his small house echoed with the memories of a love that transcended the distance, leaving him yearning for the day he could be reunited with Aurelia once more.

TWENTY-THREE

Nuremberg, Germany. Fall 1934

In early September 1934, the air in Nuremberg was thick with anticipation and the musky scent of sweat and dust. The city hummed with the fervor of the Nazi Party rally, an event that would be immortalized by the lens of a camera. *Their* camera.

Aurelia exchanged glances with Leni. Leni smiled. Aurelia didn't.

"We were given complete freedom and all the money we want," Leni said through that wide, false smile, barely moving her lips so that only Aurelia would hear. Her sharp elbow pronged Aurelia's side. "Don't ruin it with your sourpuss."

Their small film crew was an island among the throngs of eager party members and soldiers pitching their tents right in the open. Two teams of Hitler Youth boys played tug-of-war with a thick rope, shirtless and bronze-skinned. Even in her linen shirt and slacks, Aurelia felt herself sweating.

"Too much testosterone floating around," she muttered by way of explanation, though her facial expression didn't twitch.

"Precisely," Leni retorted through gritted teeth. "After all the women were chased back into the kitchen, we should be doubly grateful we're here, doing our work."

"I may just break into a celebratory dance right here and now."

"What's gotten into you? You did want to do this."

No. She didn't want to do this. Aurelia wanted access to the UFA labs and storages to rescue *Caesar* and be gone with it. Her brother's insane ideas about reconstructing German monarchy? Aurelia had seen it for the pipe dream it was as soon as she was out of the door of their estate, released from the spell of its influence. So, she had made a pact with herself: just a few more months and she'd be out of Germany at the first chance. Aurelia even knew the first thing she'd do once she was out of this rat trap: denounce her nationality and burn her German passport in front of the international press. Next, she would find her husband and make love to him until they both couldn't move. On lonely nights, his absence was a phantom limb: her entire body ached without him.

The sooner they wrapped it up here, the better.

"Let's do it then, Riefenstahl." Aurelia's fake smile was so bright and feral, Leni pulled slightly back, unsettled.

Each day began with the sun's rays breaking through the fog of early morning, casting a golden light over the massive parade grounds. Soldiers marched in perfect formation, their boots thundering like a heartbeat in the chest of the nation. Albert Speer, that young architect with wide black eyebrows and eyes drooping with sadness, like those of a bloodhound, really put his vision to work: grandiose designs, picture-perfect formations, endless crimson banners streaming into the cloudless skies—it was a cinematographer's gift tied up with a bow. Which gave Aurelia even more pause each time she adjusted her lens on Leni's orders: if even she, who loathed the regime with every fiber of her being, felt chills at this awesome display of national-istic pride, just how easy it would be for the common person to fall under its hypnotic sway? They would see these young, blond men, handsome as gods, with bodies as though chiseled from the hardest rock, and admire them in their idol-like glory. The fact that these same handsome men defaced Jewish busi-nesses, broke windows at synagogues and called for the deporta-tion of the entire Jewish race would remain undisclosed, and it was she, Aurelia, who was helping to make it happen.

Leni orchestrated the scene with an almost feverish enthusi-asm. With her striking presence and sharp, artistic gaze, she floated from one location to another, almost drunk on the sweeping grandeur of the rally.

"Film those athletes rising. I want it slow, in close-up. First, athletes, then the SS men climbing the stairs, and then we'll splice it with the ascension of the *Führer* himself as the culmi-nation." Her laughter rang out, a stark contrast to the grim atmosphere that surrounded them. "The entire nation, rising as one—I can already see it on the screen! Look at my arms, Lia." Leni's fingers grazed the chills of excitement on her bare skin.

Aurelia's stomach twisted.

It was good.

Much too good.

On the morning of the third day of the rally, Heinrich Himmler was set to speak. Aurelia was in a foul mood. The night before, she had drunk a bit too much with the crew and was nursing a headache. She had little patience for the fervent crowds today and their early-morning animation.

"Oh, give it a rest," she muttered at the sight of their faces alight with zeal, their fanatic chanting pulsing in her skull like a demented drum.

Willy, her assistant cameraman, who also looked worse for

wear after throwing back schnapps shots with Aurelia, snorted with sympathetic laughter.

As she set the camera to focus on the grand stage, the leader of the SS stepped onto it. After hearing of his prospects of replacing the SA leader Ernst Röhm from her brother, her impression of Heinrich Himmler was underwhelming. If he were among the crowd, she'd never film him voluntarily. He was neither tall nor handsome, nearsighted judging by the looks of it, with a nonexistent chin held by a helmet strap.

"Let's get the light just right for the *Reichsführer*," Leni instructed, her eyes sparkling with ambition.

Aurelia threw her a glance from behind the camera. The light was Albert Speer's domain. Leni and Aurelia controlled nothing.

"You know what I mean," Leni huffed. "Make sure to get his good side."

"He doesn't have one," Aurelia grumbled, earning a playful shoulder shove from Willy. He was staring through his lens, too; he knew precisely what she was talking about.

Aurelia hadn't known him prior to this trip, but his résumé intrigued her. Wilhelm Sonnenberg, still not a member of the Party, used to shoot documentaries for a French director interested in French Polynesia and, after that, for some scientific society digging out Pompei. He was scheduled to do a stint in Australia, filming aboriginal tribes for *National Geographic*, but had returned to Germany instead and joined the UFA as a regular staff member. Soon, he was shooting short propaganda films shown before each picture presentation at every German film theater, the ones about people with mental disabilities. They were disturbingly convincing: crisply dressed personnel trying to tend to empty-eyed, unkempt unfortunates with shaved heads, wandering around enclosures, not unlike those Aurelia saw at Berlin Zoo, with subtitles sharing just how much each of these "parasites" cost the German economy a year without contributing anything to it. They always ended abruptly, those films, without any call to action as they ordinarily did. Only an unsettling feeling remained.

When Aurelia had interviewed Willy the first time and asked about his sudden career change, he had mumbled something learned about duty and fatherland.

When they had a heart-to-heart last night, in Aurelia's hotel room, he had changed his story. He had a sister in Germany and she wasn't all there, if Aurelia knew what he meant. He wanted to be close in case of some new policy change or the other.

Unexpectedly, Aurelia had a new comrade.

At the podium, Himmler was going on about each German man's duty to procreate, and each German woman's duty to bring forth as many children as possible. The *Führer* was returning German women to the pedestal where they belonged. Down with hostile foreign influences trying to lure noble German women into a trap of so-called liberation.

"It's not liberation, it's exploitation is what it is," Himmler droned on, his voice as bland as his unimpressive appearance. Still, the message was met with roars of approval from the regime's supporters. Aurelia set her teeth. "Capitalists wish to chain a woman to a workplace. They promote the fashionable notion of a career just to pump more money into their dying economies. National socialism returns woman to her rightful place: at home, caring for her children. Unlike the insatiable international Jewry, we take the burden of worrying about anything but home from the shoulders of our German sisters. It is our—men's—duty to provide. Worry not, German woman. Delight at the child suckling at your breast—he's the biggest gift you may possibly bring to the Fatherland. The rest, leave to us."

"The filmmaking too?" Aurelia mumbled under her breath, unable to contain herself any longer. "Come on down and take my place then, if you're so good at it." She adjusted the camera's settings, forcing herself to concentrate on the technical aspects of the scene, but her heart raged against the very subject she was documenting.

Leni lingered nearby like a specter, her mind consumed by the aesthetics of the moment. "Do you see how the flags catch the light? It's breathtaking! This is art, Aurelia!" she exclaimed, her eyes gleaming with the thrill of creation. "We must capture the fervor, the energy of the people!"

But all Aurelia felt was nausea from the mixture of yesterday's gin and the weight of hypocrisy. To her, this entire spectacle was not art, it was a manipulation of reality, a facade that masked the oppressive regime. She recalled the faces of women she had known who had been silenced, their dreams buried beneath enforced domesticity. The fortunate ones simply left, Zara included.

"It's not just art, Leni. It's a weapon," she whispered, almost to herself, as she focused on a young mother cradling her infant amid the fervent crowd, her eyes blank. As she adjusted the camera for a close-up, her suspicions were confirmed: it wasn't a shadow under her left eye, it was a carefully concealed bruise.

"Deputy Führer's Chief of Staff Martin Bormann's wife," Willy commented as he saw the woman through Aurelia's lens.

"What happened to her eye?"

"Failed to fit into the dress Bormann wanted her to wear to the rally, from what I hear. This child is their fourth, by the way. She had her in late July."

"How old is she?" Aurelia asked, disgusted.

"Twenty-four, I think. He married her when she was nineteen," Willy responded and turned the camera away.

Inside Aurelia's veins, her very blood was boiling. Is this what Himmler meant when he spoke so highly of returning women to their rightful place at home? Something told her Frau Bormann wouldn't be walking around with a black eye because she had failed to shed baby weight in time for her husband's rally had she not been burdened by said husband in the first place. All of twenty-four years young and already the same dead look in her eyes that Aurelia had seen so many times in her mother's.

A glorious new regime, indeed.

Leaving the camera to Willy, Aurelia walked away for a smoke. The sun was at its zenith, but all she could see was shadows all around, slithering on the ground like serpents.

Spotting her from his place near the rostrum, Aurelia's brother winked at her, resplendent in his uniform and aware of it. In that fleeting exchange between brother and sister, she saw all of his plans laid out before her. This was what he wanted— power, awesome and unrestrained. Anyone who went against it would be swept aside.

Herself, included.

Eventually, the rally culminated in a breathtaking display of power, with thousands of hands raised in salute, a sea of zeal that both frightened and fascinated. As Aurelia captured the final frames under Leni's direction, she felt both accomplished and disemboweled somehow. The film would be an artistic masterpiece, two women's collaborative triumph. She wondered how quickly the Propaganda Ministry would wipe her name from the credits as soon as Aurelia held a match to her passport in the port of New York.

As the sun dipped below the horizon, casting a warm glow over the empty grounds, Aurelia stepped back from the camera and allowed herself a moment of reflection. In the midst of chaos, amid artistic ambition and ideological conflict, she still forged a path of her own, one that would resonate long after the final frame of their film had been cut. *The Triumph of the Will* would be remembered, but so too would the quiet rebellion of a woman who refused to be defined by the very ideals the film sought to glorify.

TWENTY-FOUR

The air in the film theater was thick with the chill of winter, a biting cold that seeped through the cracks in the old stone walls. Dim lights illuminated the lobby, casting ghostly shadows on the patrons who shuffled in, their breath visible in the frigid air. The theater, nestled in the heart of Vienna, was a relic of a bygone era, with its velvet drapes and gilded moldings whispering tales of grandeur from a time when films were more than just flickers on a screen, they were a cultural lifeblood.

As Aurelia slipped into the dimly lit auditorium, her heart raced with a mingling of dread and anticipation. It was risky, sneaking in here incognito, her face veiled with her hat's layers of netting. If anyone from the Propaganda Ministry discovered that their celebrated cinematographer had been to see Max Laub's *Father's Land* just before attending the premiere of *Triumph of the Will* hand in hand with Leni, they would certainly flip their lid.

Minister Goebbels' nearly hour-long rant on account of Laub's first American creation was still fresh in her mind. How dare he, the dirty Jew, attack the name of one of Germany's most noble families? It was libel, pure and simple; the subversive invention of Laub's scheming mind from start to finish. A revenge ploy to exact on his wife for leaving him. A smear campaign orchestrated by the Hollywood Jewry. Not only would the film be immediately banned in Germany, but anyone caught watching it abroad or even bringing it up in conversation would pay a fine and have a long talk with the Gestapo.

"I can't express the extent of my sympathies, Fräulein von Brandenburg." Goebbels had held her hand in between his, his head tilted to one side, eyes full of tragedy. "Neither you, nor your brother, and especially your late parents, deserved to be treated in such a bastardly manner. I would understand completely if you decided to divorce him right here and now."

Aurelia had managed to wiggle her way out of the suggestion—"I appreciate it, Herr Minister, truly, but I wouldn't want anything to distract the public from the *Triumph*'s tour"—but the cold intent in Goebbels' eyes still lingered.

Hence the veil and the fact that she had snuck in here after everyone had already been seated. Gestapo or not, it was Max's film—about her. She wouldn't miss it for the world.

The scent of cigarette smoke hung heavily in the air, mingling with the musty aroma of aged wood and faded upholstery. The soft hum of whispered conversations faded away as she settled into her seat at the very back, the plush velvet cushioning embracing her like a long-lost friend. The screen flickered to life, casting a glow that danced across Aurelia's intent face, illuminating her eyes full of hope, nostalgia, and sorrow.

Aurelia's breath caught in her throat as the film began to unfold. The familiar strains of music enveloped her like a warm embrace.

Here's her mother, just a fifteen-year-old girl—before Aurelia, before Otto even—competing in dressage in England and beating her much more experienced opponent. Her smile is radiant as she poses for photos, her hand on the neck of her mare —a new sensation from the continent, such a future ahead of her!

Next scene, fast-forward five years and here she stands at the corpse of the same horse, her new husband's hand holding a shotgun just visible in the frame. That was the last time the damned beast had taken his unborn son. As though cut down by a scythe, her mother drops to her knees and weeps as she hugs the horse's lifeless form.

"I wish you mourned my children with the same passion!" Otto's voice boomed through the speakers and Aurelia's heart broke into a thousand pieces in her chest—for her mother, for herself, for Gerda Bormann and countless women all over the world tied by the same invisible chains of suffering.

Each frame felt like an echo from her past, memories of childhood intertwined with the painful reality of her family's history. Who knew that Max had listened so closely to Aurelia's memories of the past? She'd kept them mostly to herself; only a few painful snippets had slipped from her tongue in the rare moments she'd allowed him a glimpse into the world that had borne her, most of them at her mother's grave. But not only had he listened, he must have felt her pain as his own; else, he would never have been able to put it in such vivid frames onto the silver screen.

Enter newborn Aurelia, the apple of her mother's eye—a disappointment in the eyes of Otto. A fine trick she had played on him: finally giving birth, just for it to be a girl. No, he didn't wish to see it, let alone hold it. With a mere sliver of her former fierce spirit, Maria followed her husband's exit from her bedroom; rose on her elbow against the doctor's protests, rummaged through her night table's contents to produce a diamond brooch. Precious stones shone in the close-up of her hand slipping it into the doctor's.

"*Make it so I don't bring any more children for that monster*

to torment." And, as he hesitated, her small hand closing on one
of his obstetrician's instruments. "*Or I shall do it myself.*"

Tears streamed down Aurelia's cheeks, warm against the coldness surrounding her. They were tears of grief, of longing, and of
fierce pride. As Maria finally stood up to Otto, her defiance
igniting a spark of rebellion that resonated deeply within Aurelia,
a wave of emotion washed over her. The parallels between the
film's narrative and the current political turmoil in Germany were
stark and haunting. The oppressive atmosphere of fear and
control that had driven Max from their homeland loomed over
her, a specter that cast a shadow on the lives of countless families.

*Little Aurelia, pleading with her mother for a pony for her
fifth birthday. The breakfast table set on the terrace, all bright
and airy in the shimmering August sun. Otto von Brandenburg
barely looking up from his newspaper to categorically forbid it.
The only thing the girl is good for is marriage and he will not be
embarrassed when she fails to produce an heir for her husband.
Much like Maria did. A pointed look at mother and child, the
camera lingering for the effect.*

"Good on her, paying that doctor for permanent steriliza-
tion," some girl commented from a few rows down.

"Yes, screw that pompous ass and his opinion," another one
added to approving murmurs. "Whatever is he good for?"

"Jawing about politics and smoking cigars," some fellow
opined.

Aurelia grinned, swiping at her face under the netting in
silent triumph. Her choice of a theater favored by the working
class was a good one. Even if the bourgeois class approved, they
wouldn't be so open about sharing their opinion and Aurelia
was hungry for it; she devoured it like a person starved. No
wonder Goebbels had it banned. Max had produced something
truly powerful.

One could just look at the audience: they were transfixed,

absorbed in the story that seemed to transcend the screen, weaving its way into their hearts and minds. Aurelia felt a connection to each viewer, a shared understanding of the pain and resilience depicted on screen.

Maria's very first outburst came when Otto decided to discuss six-year-old Aurelia's future engagement with a son of the Austrian-Hungarian ambassador. The boy was nine; left alone with Aurelia's playroom, he instantly smashed the head of her favorite porcelain doll and laughed at the little girl's tears. Over Maria's dead body would that lout ever come near her daughter again. When Otto tried to tell her to mind her tone, Maria hurled his brandy decanter at his father's portrait and a six-candle, silver candelabra as a follow-up. House servants and stable workers managed to put out the flames before they could spread from Otto's study to the rest of the house, but Maria's point was made. His authority challenged, Otto made it a point of honor to restore it and he proceeded to do it by taking it out on little Aurelia—Maria's weak spot.

Aurelia sobbed silently as she watched her mother lash out like a wounded, cornered animal with her last reserve of strength to protect her little girl from Otto's coldhearted abuse and renewed scheming. This time, he had a bigger fish than an ambassador's son interested in the girl he couldn't wait to get rid of. Feldmarschall von Brauch, recently widowed, expressed great interest in the "little angel." He longed to see the young woman she'd grow into in just a few years.

"Forefathers married them off as young as twelve," Otto remarked to Maria, lips around his pipe.

"Foremothers spiced those forefathers' wine with belladonna," Maria responded, baring her teeth. "Try to let von Brauch near her again, see what happens."

"You're mad!" Otto cried from the screen. "I would have long locked you up if it wasn't for the family's reputation. Who will take your spawn off my hands then, if her mother is in the sanitarium?"

The film was reaching its tragic climax. Aurelia knew what came next and yet seeing it all unraveling on the screen—her mother's fierceness, her bravery, her selfless love—contradicted the real story. This silver screen Maria would die for her daughter but not abandon her. Did Max take too much of creative license with the portrayal? No; so far, everything he had shown his audience was perfectly accurate—Aurelia's life story, told to him in her own words.

For the first time in her entire life, a shade of doubt crept into the back of Aurelia's mind. On screen, Otto was cleaning his shotgun; really polishing it with an odd look about him.

Aurelia's breath caught. She pulled forward in her seat, eyes riveted to the screen as Otto called her mother's name. The entire theater was holding its breath.

No. It couldn't be. Her mother was alone in the study when Aurelia discovered her body.

Maria enters, wearing the dress little Aurelia loved on her the most.

Aurelia always wondered why her mother had chosen to end her life in it. And by a shotgun, no less. Her father always claimed it was due to her psychosis and flair for the dramatic. But today, as a grown woman herself, Aurelia suddenly remembered that her mother hated guns. She wouldn't go near them, not after Otto had shot her beloved mare. Now that she thought of it, Aurelia was certain that Maria didn't know how to shoot.

"It appears we have arrived at an impasse," Otto says, locking the door and slipping the key into his pocket. "I can't institutionalize you. I can't have you threatening my life either, each time I decide on how best to run this household. And the more you act out, the more she emulates you, the little she-devil. I want her to practice piano and dancing, she runs out on her tutors to play Valkyries with that other girl, whatever her name

is. You're raising her into some feral thing who already defies her father. That just won't do."

Aurelia's fingers dug so deeply into the upholstery, the cloth was beginning to tear. She was on the verge of a revelation much to terrible to even comprehend.

Maria realizes it too, but much too late. She takes a step back, holding a hand in front of herself in a futile gesture. "Otto, please —" Her lips form and, instantly, the frame switches to Otto, gun raised to his shoulder in a practiced gesture.

The collective yelp of terror echoed around the theater after the deafening gunshot. In her seat, Aurelia's hand stifled her own wild cry ready to tear from her lips.

Young Wilhelm bangs on the door of the study. Perfectly composed, Otto unlocks it.

"Is the girl still at her drawing lessons by the lake?" Otto asks.

Wilhelm's hands shake. He notices his father staring at them and clasps them behind his back. "Jawohl." He swallows once, twice as he stares at his dead stepmother, but regains control of himself. "Would you like me to fetch her?"

"No need." Otto positions the gun in Maria's lifeless hand, lays the barrel across her bloodstained chest. "Let her discover for herself what her mad mother has gone and done."

The final credits rolled, and the audience remained silent, much too stunned by the film's profound message. From several different rows, sobs broke out. Someone rose to his feet unsteadily and began clapping.

Several more people joined in, rising from their seats, weeping and applauding and looking around as though to ask how such cruelty was possible in the civilized world. These people, the von Brandenburgs, they weren't just characters: this entire story was their reality.

Her back against the wall, Aurelia, too, clapped so hard, the skin on her palms was ringing. She could barely catch her breath through the sobs, choking her. Her husband's name swam before her eyes in all its true glory.

He had listened. And he had put together what her own mind refused to acknowledge.

The entire theater was awash with wild applause. It was both a celebration of her mother's bravery and a lament for the lives crushed beneath the weight of tyranny. Max had captured the von Brandenburgs' tumultuous history with such raw honesty, the film would resonate powerfully beyond the walls of the theater. Aurelia wished desperately to tell him how much his work meant to her. Though they were separated by thousands of miles, she held onto the belief that soon she'd have him in her arms—to tell him how proud she was, how his art had transcended their struggles, and how she would live to make her late mother proud.

As she left the theater, the chill of the winter night wrapped around her and together with it, the image of the last scene from *Father's Land*. Wilhelm had known all along. He'd known and said nothing. The betrayal stung like a red-hot poker against her very heart. From beyond the grave, her mother's spirit was calling for vengeance.

Aurelia could always burn her passport, safe on foreign shores. But first, she had scores to settle.

TWENTY-FIVE

United States. February 1935

An excerpt from *The New York Times*:

"Last night, the Hotel Astor exuded an air of grandiosity. Gathered for the unveiling of Leni Riefenstahl's latest work, the provocative *Triumph of the Will*, press found themselves waiting in the famous 9th-floor Large Ballroom purposely redecorated for the hosting of the event. Hung with crimson banners and stills from the documentary, the ornate architecture cast a spell that was both captivating and foreboding. The space buzzed with an electric tension as the journalists prepared their notepads and cameras, eager to interview the film crew that had just finished their European tour and finally made it to the New World.

"As Miss Riefenstahl took her place at the podium, her presence transformed the room. With a determined gleam in her eye, she radiated enthusiasm, her voice clear and passionate as she spoke of her artistic vision. Each word dripped with conviction, her excitement infectious as she painted vivid images of her film. She gestured animatedly, her movements a dance of zeal that captivated the audience, drawing them into her narrative. Yet, amid the fervor, there was a stark contrast—Miss von Brandenburg, her cinematographer, sat slightly apart, her demeanor cool and composed.

"At times, one could almost sense slight resentment from Miss Riefenstahl whenever the press directed their questions at the cinematographer instead of the director. It came as no surprise, given the number of journalists openly admitting that they had obtained the press pass for the event precisely because of Miss von Brandenburg.

"An enigma bigger than Miss Riefenstahl herself, Aurelia von Brandenburg used to be one of the faces of the revolutionary German Dadaist movement and a vocal defender of democratic institutions and civil rights before making a sharp turn right.

"True to her newfound nationalist ideology, Miss von Brandenburg appeared in a subdued black ensemble and wore no jewelry except, notably, for the wedding band on the ring finger of her right hand. She answered the questions related solely to the film production and refused to elaborate on her political stance or her private life. To my own question, whether she had seen her estranged husband Max Laub's film, she responded with her usual, 'No comment.'

"A UFA representative, Fritz Heine, expanded on Miss von Brandenburg's statement, saying, 'German people don't watch that sort of propaganda. Frankly, Herr Laub ought to consider himself fortunate that Wilhelm and Aurelia von Brandenburg are too noble to consider the libel suit the UFA suggested they bring up against Laub personally and anyone affiliated with the film.'"

"So?" Aurelia sighed into the receiver, rubbing the grit out of her eyes.

Still out of sorts after her transatlantic journey and the frantic US tour schedule, she had no patience for lectures. Unfortunately, hanging up on Minister Goebbels himself was not an option, no matter how attractive.

"So?" he drawled mockingly before issuing an oath away from the phone. "Stark contrast to Riefenstahl's fervor? Cool and composed? A wedding band?!" His voice rose an octave, turning into outright screaming: "The only thing missing is an SS man holding a gun to your head, according to that article!"

Aurelia snorted softly. *Great imagery—no argument here.*

"Do you find this amusing?"

"No, Herr Minister."

"Then why do you act this way?"

Aurelia drew her eyes to the clock on the wall of her luxurious hotel suite. Only an hour left till the Los Angeles press conference. She wouldn't have to endure this for too much longer. Downing what was left of her martini, she gripped the phone even harder, picturing Goebbels' neck in its place.

"I'm afraid I don't understand what you mean, Herr Minister. If I didn't display enough enthusiasm, it's solely because I would never dream of stealing the spotlight she so rightfully deserves from Leni. You have just read the article to me; you saw what they were saying, those journalists. They were openly admitting that they were much more interested in my personal life and the scandal with that film than in *Triumph of the Will*. I simply didn't want the conference to turn into a circus."

Goebbels was silent for a few moments, mulling it over. "Fine," he finally grumbled his verdict. "But do me, and yourself, a big favor. Take that damned ring off."

.   .   .

At the Biltmore Hotel, which was about to host its 7th Academy Awards in just a few days, the scent of polished wood mingled with the faint aroma of expensive perfume, creating an ambiance that felt both luxurious and heavy. Even more press here; more cameras aimed at her—the woman who never smiled for them, unlike Leni. She was in her element today, drinking in the attention with an insatiable thirst. In her sequined gown, with her hair done by a Hollywood stylist, Leni sold white supremacy to the masses with a bright smile on her beautiful face.

As the questions flew, Aurelia leaned back in her chair, her eyes scanning the crowd. She felt like a ghost in the midst of a celebration, her heart heavy with unspoken disdain for the ideology that fueled their work. She had expected much more resistance from the freedom-loving Americans. Instead, their small German delegation was greeted by members of the budding American Nazi Party in New York and even bigger enthusiasm in Los Angeles.

"Miss Riefenstahl, how did you find the courage to put into vivid imagery such a powerful message?"

"What message is that?" Leni asked the reporter with playful innocence.

"The purity of the people that benefits the entire nation in the end. There were no actors in your film, ordinary people only. And, frankly, neither me nor my wife could tear our gazes off the screen for one sole reason: are you truly a nation of superhumans? I mean, how is everyone so perfect?"

The press corps chuckled in agreement. It took a lot of effort for Aurelia not to roll her eyes.

"I'm not a politician," Leni was chirping with false modesty, "I'm only a director. I film what I see. And I do agree that the message of purity is an important one. But I'm not the one to take credit for it. Our *Führer*, Adolf Hitler, is. As for purity benefiting society, it is true. The *Führer* has been in office for only two years and we have already seen a great improvement in our quality of life. People are healthier, happier. We promote physical activity, healthy eating, the great outdoors—in short, the closer to nature one is, the more beneficial it is for that person in particular and society in general. Healthy people produce more healthy people. It's simple eugenics."

A reporter raised his pen. "Ben Cohen, *Illustrated Daily News*. To expand on the previous question: how does the German minority population fit into this picture? I'm talking about those of Jewish and Negro race, for instance. From what we hear, ever since Hitler took office, German Jews have been fired en masse and marriages and even non-marital relations between Aryans and non-Aryans have become almost criminal."

"Again, I'm not a politician and therefore not the right person to answer this," Leni responded with the same sweet innocence in her dark eyes.

"The German government is not in favor of mixing of the races, that is correct," Fritz Heine, the UFA publicist, answered coolly, pushing his glasses back onto his nose. He paused for effect before adding, "Just like the American government."

Cohen wouldn't have it. "We don't shave the heads of our girls for kissing a Black boy, nor do we tar them and parade them round with placards around their necks, calling them traitors of the race."

"No," Heine said, examining his nails. "You don't. You lynch the Negro boy instead."

In the grave silence that followed, the reporter's penetrating gaze shifted to Aurelia. "And how do you feel about all this, Mrs. Laub? It's still your name, isn't it? Where are all the Jewish and African movie crew members you and your husband used to employ, or did you drop them just as you did the inconvenient last name?"

The Wolowsky family were waiting for the exit visa from

Germany, German bureaucrats purposely dragging their feet despite Bibi and Lisl sitting quite literally on their suitcases for the second year in a row, American entrance visas stamped in their passports. Some in Austria or Czechoslovakia, where film studios gladly offered them employment. The rest, back in Germany, were making do with the money Aurelia supplied them with monthly, waiting it out, just like she was. Hoping for Germany to regain its sanity. Only, she couldn't say any of that.

"I'm pleading the Fifth."

"Your English may be excellent, Mrs. Laub," Cohen said with a smirk, "but that is something someone would plead in order not to self-incriminate."

A criminal, the reporter's eyes implied what he omitted.

"I know." Aurelia nodded and noticed a slight pause of hesitation in the journalist before he retook his seat.

Someone else was asking a question, but Cohen was still staring. Like a mathematician trying to solve a formula and getting contradictory results.

"Don't listen to that Jew!" someone from the throng of spectators crowding at the back of the hall called. "We love you, Aurelia! You're a Norse goddess!"

Three things happened simultaneously: Leni's stare hit her sideways like shrapnel, a soda bottle sailed past Cohen, hitting the chair of the journalist in front of him and staining Cohen's light-beige jacket with brown—

—And Aurelia's gaze, seeking Cohen's assailant from the crowd, landed on someone she hadn't expected to see—certainly not here, definitely not now.

Max Laub, her estranged husband.

Time seemed to suspend as their eyes locked, a jolt of electricity coursing through the air. In that fleeting moment, the noise of the press conference faded into oblivion, replaced by the silent symphony of emotions swirling between them. Max's expression was a mix of longing and vulnerability, his eyes reflecting the depth of feelings that had been buried under years of separation. Aurelia felt her throat tighten, an overwhelming rush of memories crashing over her with seismic force. Her hand reaching for the tightly buttoned collar of her blouse of its own volition, Aurelia noticed her own frantic pulse on the side of her neck. She held onto her emotions with a vise grip in order not to betray herself. Not to jump from her seat and run to him and throw herself into his arms, weeping with relief and love that knew no time nor borders.

Recognizing the reflection of the same passion that shone in his own eyes, Max smiled at her from under the rim of his hat, pulled low onto his face. Tears threatened to brim in Aurelia's eyes, but she blinked them away, resolute in her composure. Surrounded by Goebbels' spies, hustled from one conference to another, always under a watchful eye, she'd had no chance to make a phone call, let alone arrange a meeting.

Wilhelm must have seen a glimpse of such an idea in his half-sister's eyes for his parting words, whispered in her ear at the *Triumph*'s Berlin premiere, were, "When you go on your international tour, keep one thing in mind, little sister: SD, the security service, listen to all phone calls any German official makes. Don't say anything stupid."

She'd been so good up until now...

As the press conference continued, the atmosphere shifted. Leni, unaware of the emotional whirlwind brewing between Aurelia and Max, remained engrossed in her narrative, rallying the crowd with her fervent declarations. But Aurelia was suddenly back in Berlin in the mid-twenties, when it was only just starting between them; when they would stand on the opposite side of the pavilion and he'd look at her with those dark, hungry eyes and heat would instantly break all over her skin. They barely touched each other back then, but each inci-dental brush of the fingers was a slow, sweet torture, building to something so explosive, they instinctively knew that neither of their lives would be the same again.

She'd grown addicted to him worse than opium and he'd drowned himself in her like a drunk; it was mad and dangerous and impossible to bear at times, but, as she found herself losing herself in Max's eyes once again, Aurelia knew that a life without him was simply not worth living.

She was just about to call his name, but suddenly, he wasn't there any longer. Aurelia just caught Max as he shifted his eyes toward someone to her left, pulled the hat even further down and disappeared into the crowd. One of the plain-clothed SS goons keeping order was staring ahead with rapt attention like a hound who'd just caught a scent. Frantic with fear at being whisked away before she could at least talk to her husband, Aurelia sought Cohen in the crowd and stared at him with such intent, he must have sensed it. With immense relief at having his attention, Aurelia nodded at him almost imperceptibly and motioned her head toward the exit before drawing her eyes to the ceiling. Twice she tapped her index finger atop her other hand, then pressed three fingers to her mouth as if deep in thought. To his credit, Cohen didn't betray himself with a single muscle movement on his face.

Aurelia didn't have the time to change before she heard an urgent knocking—on the window of her room.

"Damn, lady!" Cohen breathed out as she helped him inside, his legs shaking visibly. "Eleventh floor, with my love of heights! I'll have some strong words with the administration for not designing adjoining balconies in their suites."

"I'm so terribly sorry!" Aurelia's own hands were shaking as she dusted off his slacks, just then realizing that there were no balconies whatsoever in the hotel, adjoining or not. "How did you even get here?"

"From the windows of suite 1102, after bribing the maid for the key; how else?" He looked at her, sarcasm masking the fright he must have gone through. "One can't just go and knock on your door with your Teutonic knights hanging about the floor." He rolled his eyes. "I assume we also have to whisper?"

"Again, I am so sorry. And yes, it would be best to keep our voices down."

"Keep the window open then."

He sat, cross-legged, right under the sill. Having an escape route this close must have given him comfort. Aurelia followed suit.

"I assume I'm not here for an official interview," he said, studying her closely with eyes that were more amused than hostile. "What is it that you want?"

"My husband."

Cohen's dark brows flew up.

"He was just here, in the conference hall. He must be some-where around still. If he isn't, could you call him, please? I'll give you his number and address."

The smile that had slowly been growing on the journalist's face during her impassioned speech turned into a veritable Cheshire Cat's grin.

"You're still Mrs. Laub then?"

"Of course I am. What idiot would leave that angel of a man?"

Cohen rubbed his forehead, his shoulders shaking slightly with chuckles. "Can't you just come out of the door? It's Amer-ica, you know. Even your thugs in ill-fitting suits posted outside won't shoot you in the open. Bad for publicity, you know, and all that rot."

"I know, yes." Impatiently, Aurelia grabbed his brown-stained sleeve. "But there are people in Germany... They depend on me. If I just up and leave—"

"Didn't drop them after all?" He didn't make a move to free

himself. In his eyes, warm mirth danced. "Your husband, is he afraid of heights?"

"No. He's Austrian. He climbs mountains for fun."

Aurelia was right about Max: he hadn't gone far. Not even fifteen minutes passed when the curtains to her bedroom parted and her husband climbed in, holding onto his hat and laughing.

"You're turning me into the lead from one of my—"

She didn't let him finish, just pulled him to herself, her hands clutching the back of his neck. Their lips met in a fierce collision, a desperate mingling of breath and longing that spoke of all the nights spent apart, filled with dreams of each other.

Max's hands found her waist, drawing her against him as if he could meld their bodies into one. She felt the heat radiating from him, the urgency in his touch igniting a fire deep within her. The world outside—Germany gone mad, the chaos, the lies —faded into insignificance. He tasted of salt and sorrow and home—an intoxicating concoction going straight to her head like no alcohol could. His fingers were digging into her flesh even through the layers of clothing.

Stumbling backward to the edge of the bed, Aurelia let herself fall and laughed like a midnight witch when he climbed atop her. It was like their very first time, back in Babelsberg, in some storage room, atop the rolls of carpeting: she'd been making eyes at him the entire day and he had followed her into the room to which he himself had sent her and locked the door behind him as if sealing the deal. With the same animalistic hunger, she welcomed him now like she'd welcomed him back then—her legs wrapped around his waist, his teeth against the wildly pulsing vein in her neck.

. . .

The moon hung low in the sky, casting silver beams through the thin curtains of the Biltmore Hotel's suite. The air was thick with tension and unspoken words, a tangible reminder of the distance that had stretched between Max and Aurelia for far too long. When he had climbed through her window, the world outside had faded, leaving just the two of them in this flickering sanctuary of shadows and whispers. Now, as Aurelia lay across her husband's chest with her leg draped around his legs, it was slowly coming back into focus.

"I missed you so much, I could die," she said, drawing slow circles on her husband's skin. He'd grown more tanned under the Los Angeles sun. Leaner. But stronger somehow, like Loki upon his return from his yearly disappearances into the forest for mating season. He'd leave, domesticated, well-fed, and lazy, and return all muscle and slender sides, still bearing scars of his enemies' teeth.

"I missed you so much, I felt like I did," Max whispered into her hair, in which his hand rested, tangled. "It's all one big hell, the world without you."

"It is."

Time slipped away, minutes stretching into eternity as they clung to each other. Earlier that evening, Heine's messenger had knocked on the door, reminding Aurelia about the dinner reception. She'd sent him away without opening it, claiming a migraine. Leni had knocked hours later, hoping for a nightcap. Aurelia had sent her away as well, this time through the slit in the door.

"You look terrible," Leni had commented, taking in Aurelia's hair all in disarray and the slight rash marring her otherwise perfect skin. No matter how closely he shaved, her husband always ended up with a five o'clock shadow precisely by that time.

Aurelia had pulled the ends of her robe closer around her neck. Things were much worse there, just like across her chest, her stomach, and her thighs. "I must be coming down with something."

She'd pulled the phone cord out after sending Leni on her way and dropped the robe back to the floor to climb back into bed, into her husband's waiting arms.

"What do we do now?" he had asked her then.

Hours passed and she still had no answer for him. All Aurelia knew was that in that sacred space, no matter the world outside, they were home. The future could wait.

TWENTY-SIX

"Is this what I think it is?" Max's hand betrayed his excitement with a slight shake as he caressed the film cans neatly stacked in Aurelia's suitcase.

"Yes. Our *Caesar*, as promised."

With *Triumph* successfully in the works, Goebbels had relaxed his control on Aurelia's access to the Ministry departments significantly. A visit to the archives?

"If possible." Aurelia had smiled, all compliance. "I'd love to go through all the Party archival footage to get a better sense of the mood you're striving to deliver."

Without a second thought, the Propaganda Minister had stamped her pass and slashed it with his signature. No one had questioned her entering the archives or taking a few film cans every now and then to watch at home in her projection room. No one had checked what she'd brought back the next day, as long as the number of cans returned coincided with those taken out. And after the film's release, no one had even thought of checking her luggage at the German border. She had produced a marvelous piece of propaganda. As far as Goebbels was concerned, she had proven her loyalty. All doors were open to her now.

Aurelia was more concerned as to how her husband would get the film out of the hotel.

"I suppose I'll just have to shack up here with you until it's time for you to leave," he said, assembling the cans on the floor.

"Don't you have plans for this weekend?"

"Ach." Max playfully tapped his forehead. "The Oscars. Completely escaped my mind. I don't really have to go."

"Max, you're nominated as a best director and scriptwriter."

Max waved it off, as if such an accomplishment was of no consequence. "They won't give it to some German émigré for the very first film he made on American soil."

"What happened to 'I'm still Max Laub' and all that?" Aurelia teased, reaching toward the breakfast tray for a fresh bun. Thank God for room service: she didn't have to drink her coffee in the presence of Heine and his goons.

"Hollywood knocks the attitude out of you pretty quick."

"You like it there though?"

"It's better than where you are."

The words hit her right in the gut.

Max saw her wince as if after a slap and rushed to gather her hands in his to cover them in kisses. He didn't mean it; it came out the wrong way, but Aurelia only shook her head and kissed the top of his. No, he was right—she no longer recognized the country she used to love so fiercely either.

Kneeling in front of her, Max lowered his head to her knees, wrapping his arms around her folded legs, holding onto her like a savage onto his idol. Only, she was no idol. Just a relic of bygone times.

"I spoke to my brother." The words turned, heavy as stones, on her tongue.

"Before or after you saw the film?" His words were muffled by the folds of her robe.

"Before."

A pause.

As they remained locked in their embrace, Aurelia told Max all about Wilhelm's grandiose plans—of the war, of doing away with Hitler, of restoring monarchy and declaring himself a new Kaiser.

Her husband listened without interrupting and without releasing her either. All he asked in the end was, "Do you believe him?"

From Aurelia a soft snort. After Wilhelm had helped her father cover up her mother's murder? She didn't believe a word coming out of his mouth. He had made Aurelia think her mother had abandoned her. That she'd been mad and weak when she'd been neither. He was complicit in her mother's murder; he knew and he said nothing.

"I can walk out of this door, claim asylum, stay here with you, make movies, and cross Germany out of my memory entirely. Cross my mother's murder out. Our dogs they will shoot and print the photos on the front page of every government-controlled edition just to spite me. Cross Art and Bibi's entire family out of existence. Later, when I'm old—because I will have the privilege to grow old in this wonderful land of abundance—I will claim that I had done all I could but the fate wasn't so kind to them as it was to me and there was nothing doing. I had to look after myself. And you."

With his head in her lap, he was looking at her from the side of his eye, already knowing what she was about to ask.

"My question is, will you be able to live with me? With this version of me, for the rest of your life?"

Slowly, Max straightened and fixed his glasses, regarding her wistfully. Atop his eye, his wartime scar stood out like a pale lightning bolt in contrast to his sun-kissed skin.

"I didn't want to fall in love with you, Ari. I didn't even want to hire you because I knew how it would all end. Astrid and Loki took you for their mother because you're just like them. One could never domesticate you, you're much too wild. I was afraid to love you because I knew you would eventually leave. And it hurts like hell when you do, I won't lie, but damn it, it would have hurt a million times worse never to know you at all. To answer your question, I would love you no matter what. Just like you still love me after I ran away with my tail between my legs."

Aurelia smiled through the tears.

"The real question is, will you be able to live trying to pass for a husky when it's wolf's blood that runs in your veins?"

TWENTY-SEVEN

Germany. Spring 1935

As the train rolled into Berlin's bustling Hauptbahnhof, the air was thick with the scents of diesel and fresh rain—a stark contrast to the sun-drenched landscapes Aurelia had traversed in South America and Mexico. Instead of the excitement of returning home, an unsettling weight pressed on her chest as soon as she stepped onto the platform. German press were here to welcome the film crew and yet, amid the camera flashes, Aurelia felt like a convict hustled back into prison after an unsuccessful escape attempt.

Leaving Leni to sign autographs, Aurelia clutched her handbag tightly as she made her way through the crowd. The porters knew where to deliver the rest of her suitcases. She didn't have anything valuable in them anymore: *Caesar* was safe and sound, with Max.

An official UFA studios car awaited outside, but Aurelia dove into a taxicab instead. Let Leni have the car all to herself. After months of promotional madness, all she wanted was some peace and quiet.

The flickering neon lights of the city flashed outside the window, lulling her to sleep. Aurelia was jolted awake by a sharp honk of the horn. Confused and still warm with sleep, she rubbed her eyes to see that they were already in Grünewald, outside the gates of her house. On the grounds, snow still lay. The leafless carcasses of the trees reached into the dark sky, light from the two first-story windows throwing long shadows of their twisted forms.

Heinz, their groundskeeper, was already trotting along the driveway, immaculately cleared as always.

Smiling, Aurelia pushed the door open and handed the driver the fare. He didn't need to wait for her to be let in, she was home.

The heavy gate creaked open after Heinz's ministrations and slammed back into place after admitting the mistress of the estate inside. Dressed in a sheepskin hastily thrown upon an old sweater, Heinz began apologizing at once. He'd been oiling the lock and the hinges regularly, but now with this dampness—

Aurelia refused to listen, scooping the old man into a hug instead. Barely reaching her shoulder, he patted her on her back awkwardly and extracted himself from the embrace. He was an old Prussian, their good Heinz. Not used to such displays of affection. He expressed his love for the Laubs differently: by keeping the kindling for the hearth stocked, by watching their hounds when they were gone, by minding the deliveries and running the water at scheduled times to ensure the pipes didn't freeze.

After letting Aurelia inside the house, Heinz stood with her handbag while she had her back against the wall, Astrid's great paws on her shoulders, the wolf dog's rough tongue all over her face.

"Loki gone looking for a girlfriend?" Aurelia asked Heinz, barely catching her breath in between the licks Astrid kept showering her with.

Heinz nodded in reply. "You really ought to fix him, Frau Aurelia, like you did with Astrid. I don't like him running into the forest by himself one bit. Lots of hunters outside nowadays and they don't know him to be yours."

"I wanted to, but Max was against it." Just uttering her husband's name brought a rush of nostalgia.

Heinz averted his eyes, muttering something along the lines that it didn't matter anymore what Herr Laub thought now, did it?

Wrenching herself from Astrid's grip, Aurelia took a step forward. "What's that supposed to mean?"

Heinz made no reply, only glanced at the stack of newspapers on the mail table and looked away once again.

Suspicion turning her stomach, Aurelia grabbed the fresh *Beobachter* from the top. The bold headline screamed at her like a siren in the night: "Aurelia von Brandenburg Divorces Jewish Husband!"

Her breath caught in her throat, she felt the ground shift beneath her feet. Aurelia's fingers trembled as she read the article, her vision clouded by a mixture of rage and betrayal. The gleeful article detailed her divorce from Max on racial grounds, painting her as a patriotic figure and a role model for Aryan women, who were also urged to sever ties with their Jewish spouses.

The words twisted like a dagger in her heart. The very thought of being used as a symbol of Nazi propaganda left her stunned, her mind racing with disbelief and anger.

"A divorce? I've never even considered a divorce, let alone agreed to one!" she cried, wounded and furious, hurling the paper onto the floor.

Heinz's expression changed from subdued and wounded to confused. "You didn't?" he uttered at last, shifting from one foot to another.

Aurelia shot him a glare of reproach before yanking the phone from its cradle.

"Aurelia von Brandenburg. Propaganda Ministry, please," she barked at the operator, feeling her entire body beginning to tremble with righteous anger.

"Do you have an extension?"

"Give me Minister Goebbels!"

"Just a moment."

Aurelia waited, foot tapping.

"I'm afraid he's already—"

"I know he's there!" Aurelia screamed into the phone, properly furious now. "The *Führer* doesn't go to sleep until three in the morning and neither does Herr Minister." She spit out the title with more venom than she perhaps should have, but at this point, Aurelia didn't give two damns about anything. "Put him on the phone or I'll go there in person and make such a scene, his head will spin—"

Heinz yanked the phone out of her hand and dropped it back onto the cradle. His lips didn't move, his eyes said everything instead.

"Don't be so upset," Wilhelm said with a dismissive gesture toward the paper Aurelia had dropped onto his breakfast tray the very next morning. "You two aren't *really* divorced." He was more concerned with his cake being ruined than Aurelia's marriage. "It's just good publicity. The Propaganda Ministry had to do something. The Amis not only produced his little picture but gave him a damned award for it. Your old friend Goebbels had to knock Laub down a peg or two."

Sitting opposite her half-brother in his gilded Minister's office, Aurelia was turning a marble paperweight in the shape of an eagle in her hands, considering quite literal murder. He took no notice, busy removing the part of the cake the newspaper touched to resume his attack on the rest of it. He'd gained even more weight in the past two years, Aurelia noted. Odd, considering how obsessed the Nazis were with their perfect physical specimen ideas.

Once again, she pictured the sweet sound the paperweight would make connecting with Wilhelm's skull, but then she remembered that *Caesar* was now in her husband's hands, likely getting ready to be released, and set the eagle down, biting back a smile.

"Besides," he continued in a conspiratorial whisper, pulling close and still chewing, "didn't I promise to reinstate your better half as soon as I'm in power? How about we make him a new Minister of Enlightenment?" His pale eyes gleamed as Wilhelm got a hold of Aurelia's hand. "That will really get Goebbels' goat before his date with the hangman! What do you say to that, little sister?"

Now that he was so close, Aurelia nearly jumped with an epiphany. How had she not noticed it before? All the signs had been there all along. But it was the eyes that finally betrayed him, after she'd missed all the rest, pupils unnaturally constricted against the pale-blue of his irises—the telltale sign of a morphine addict. The paperweight appeared a crude device compared to the fresh idea flashing through Aurelia's mind. She still remembered how many veterans had died back in the twenties after overdosing on the drug. Why not Wilhelm? Even if with just a bit of her help...

"I say," Aurelia responded, feeling like a gambler whose luck had just turned, "you, Wilhelm, now have my full attention."

TWENTY-EIGHT

"My brother wants to kill you."

Minister Goebbels choked on the coffee he was sipping out of a delicate cup and slammed it down with such force, the china cracked.

"I beg your pardon?" he responded, drying his lips with a napkin.

In perfect possession of herself, Aurelia crossed her legs and opened her clutch bag, looking for a cigarette.

Unlike the meeting with her brother, she had come prepared for this one. She had even requested that they meet "in private," if possible. Less bureaucracy to deal with at his private house. Besides, it was unlikely the Propaganda Minister's living quarters were tapped.

As Aurelia had entered, she at once noticed the juxtaposition of beauty and menace that pervaded the space. Goebbels, with his piercing gaze and charismatic demeanor, had welcomed her with a smile that seemed rehearsed yet genuine. He had gestured for her to take a seat at the polished mahogany coffee table that had already been set, his movements fluid and deliberate.

Now, though, all of his self-possession was gone.

"You heard me." Aurelia held the flame to her cigarette and inhaled deeply, narrowing her eyes, lined with black, at the Minister.

It was just past noon. The heavy, draped curtains framed the tall windows, filtering the sunlight into a muted glow that cast shadows across the room. The air was thick with the scent of expensive cigars and polished wood, a reminder of the high stakes that played out within these walls.

"And you have this information from..." He shifted in his chair, making every effort to recover himself. "Where exactly?"

Aurelia shrugged as if it was obvious. "The man himself, of course."

"He..." Goebbels licked his lips, apparently still reeling from such a brazen admission. "He told you that?"

"And more."

It was almost pleasant, watching him squirm in discomfort. Aurelia had never had any illusions concerning the inner workings of the highest echelons of the Party. Like every political organization, it was a vipers' nest, pure and simple. Everyone schemed and plotted against each other; everyone vied for Hitler's attention; everyone was ready to step on the corpse of yesterday's comrade to prop himself up to a higher position—one didn't have to look far for an example. The Night of the Long Knives, with its purge of the SA to consolidate power in Hitler's hands without having to share it with the SA leader Ernst Röhm, was still fresh in everyone's memory.

And there was certainly no love lost between her brother and Goebbels. The Propaganda Minister was secretly envious of the Minister-President of Prussia's background and the fact that von Brandenburg enjoyed Hitler's full attention concerning all things military. Wilhelm, on the other hand, couldn't stand "the big-mouthed clubfoot" and his influence on the information spoon-fed to the German people. If Aurelia wanted the downfall of one, all she had to do was to secure the alliance of the other.

She had heard tales of Goebbels' ruthless ambition and manipulative genius, yet here he was, suddenly silent and on the defensive.

"Let's say I believe you," he began cautiously, "why are you telling me this?"

"I want something, of course."

"I already gave you everything I could that was within the Propaganda Ministry's sphere of influence." He appeared genuinely confused. "Unlimited budgets, access to any location, your own salary—"

"Herr Minister..." Aurelia tilted her head, in a fashionable hat, to one side. The light in her eyes was positively impish. "Surely you don't think I'm after money or power?"

"What are you after then?"

The living room, with its opulence, felt a stage set for Aurelia's own warfare. And by now she had directed enough films to know just how the plot would unravel.

"Have you seen my husband's latest film?" She could almost see herself through the lens, playing a femme fatale who would definitely get a couple of murders to her name in the second act. "Oh, drop the act, Herr Minister, really. I know you did. And I can bet you secretly loved it. To see how depraved the von Brandenburg clan actually is. And the finale?" She arched a lively brow at the color touching Goebbels' sharp cheeks. "You know you watched it several times in your personal theater, right here, under this very roof, while your wife and children slept peacefully."

Goebbels moved his mouth as if to show distaste, but Aurelia couldn't help but offer him a knowing grin in response. Publicly denouncing the picture didn't mean he couldn't savor it privately—they both knew it all too well.

"He helped cover up my mother's murder," Aurelia said

after a pause. Her eyes turned to hard steel. "I want him gone. Seeing that he wants you dead, I assume you want to see him gone as well. I'll take care of that if you agree to take care of a few things for me."

"Name them."

"I want you to get my former husband out of jail." She slid Art Nachtnebel's information across the table along with his photograph. "I want safe passage for him out of Germany, together with the Wolowsky family. Berthold Wolowsky is our former employee, a brilliant man, who my husband and I are very fond of. They already have US visas, it's the German side that keeps stalling them despite the fact that their taxes are paid and they agreed to relinquish all of their property to the state."

Goebbels was already shaking his head. "Impossible. I can try to get your Jews out, but Nachtnebel—no. Too big a name just to slip through the net unnoticed. Besides, he's in Dachau from what I hear. Concentration camps are under your brother's jurisdiction."

"Don't think of them this way, think of them as just six people in exchange for one very influential minister who wants you dead. *And can have you dead.* Only I will know when and how since I'm the only person he trusts with this information. And only I can bring about his downfall."

This moment was more than just a meeting, it was a fork in the road from which history itself could go either way. Goebbels must have sensed it too. His mind at work, he tapped his long finger on his wristwatch as if measuring time itself. Impossible? There was nothing impossible for this man. If Aurelia could craft dreams, he could twist them into a tool for control.

"To move out such a big group of people without raising suspicion will require special circumstances. Exit visas are not in my jurisdiction, they are in Himmler and Heydrich's and they—" He flicked his wrist in annoyance, his mouth twisting in unconcealed disgust. "Let's just say, if you don't want anyone asking any questions, you will have to wait till the laws are temporarily relaxed." He finally regained his charming exterior. His voice flowed smooth as silk.

"And just when that will happen?" Aurelia wanted out of this rat trap of a country sooner rather than later. Waiting for some special occasion that may or may not occur anytime soon was not in her plans.

Goebbels smiled and Aurelia couldn't help but feel the pervasive influence of his, which sought to shape not just the art of cinema, but the very fabric of society itself. He was a master in weaving webs of deceit. She sure had come to the right person; only, who could guarantee she wouldn't be the one caught in them in the end?

"Why, Fräulein von Brandenburg, during the Olympics, of course," he replied, his merriment knowing no bounds any longer. "Which you will be filming for Fräulein Riefenstahl."

"Do I have to?" Aurelia muttered, barely restraining herself from rolling her eyes.

The Propaganda Minister's smile remained in place, only his eyes fixed Aurelia with chilling attention.

"For us to keep our communication this intimate, without arousing anyone's suspicions, you have to be either working for me or sleeping with me. So, I suggest, you start scouting your location."

TWENTY-NINE

Berlin. Summer 1936

The sun hung low over the Olympiastadion in Berlin, casting long shadows across the vibrant green field where history was about to be made. Leni Riefenstahl stood poised and resolute, her dark eyes scanning the throng of athletes. Aurelia snapped a few photos of her and the crew, capturing the emotion on the director's face. Leni's heart must have been racing with the excitement of creation despite being out of her depth.

"A sports film?" Leni had initially outright rejected the idea of having anything to do with the Berlin Olympics whatsoever. "I haven't the faintest clue of how to even go about making one!"

"What do you mean?" Aurelia, with her own interest at stake, had invited Leni for a weekend at a ski resort in Austria she and Max used to frequent—"a girls' mountain trip to celebrate the Yuletide," Aurelia had claimed. In reality, she had wanted to ensure that Leni wouldn't have a chance to make a quick escape. "You directed *Triumph of the Will* just fine—look at all the critical acclaim that got you."

"*Triumph of the Will* was not a sports film!" Leni, her short, wavy hair wet with sweat and snow after their descent from the mountain, had taken a long pull on her spiked cider. They were enjoying a break at the concessions stand manned by a sweet Austrian couple in traditional costume. "It was a rally. Sports films are a different beast altogether." She had suddenly narrowed her eyes at Aurelia. "Was that *Herr Minister*, by any chance, who suggested it? I don't imagine the response is at the bottom of your mug, Laub."

It was strangely refreshing, the fact that Leni hadn't dropped Aurelia's surname from her vocabulary, unlike the rest of Germany with Aurelia's brother at its helm. Neither had she ever said a bad word about Max. Not even when *Caesar* had been released in the late summer of 1935, after which Max was officially declared persona non grata.

"I'll tell you precisely why he suggested it," Leni had continued in the meantime, her sculpted cheekbones flushed with brandy and the blood still pumping wildly in her veins. "Ever since I told him in no uncertain terms that his advances will lead nowhere, he's had it in for me. I'm lucky the *Führer* took my side and told him to leave off—I'm telling you this in confidence, so don't go repeating it."

Aurelia could never understand the fierce admiration Leni had for Hitler or her near-fanatical protectiveness of him. He embodied everything Leni, personally, rejected. He professed that women belonged at home, with children, and a childless, unmarried Leni—the country's leading director—filmed him and applauded. He declared the supremacy of the Aryan race and Leni diligently filmed his "Aryan supermen," shrugging off his blatant racism as a mere difference of opinions. When Aurelia tried gently prodding her for logic—*it's not like he likes white wine and I like red and we just agree to disagree, we're talking human beings here*—Leni would just clam up and refuse to see reason. Hitler could do no wrong in her eyes. Aurelia, who had more than her share of battles to pick, left that one well alone.

"So yes," Leni had continued, "the only reason Goebbels wants me to direct the Olympics is for me to fail and for him to gloat over it. No, thank you. Much obliged. I'm not doing him any favors."

Aurelia saw her point and yet she needed Leni. Because *Herr Minister* didn't lie: Germany was indeed changing before her very eyes in preparation for the Winter Olympics set to take place in a little over a month. The international athletes hadn't even arrived yet and the government had already temporarily relaxed the oppressive laws that had marginalized Jews and other minorities, creating an atmosphere of tolerance for the nation to get used to. In summer, with the international press here, the Wolowskys would have no trouble getting their exit visas. Goebbels had guaranteed it himself. As for Art, the Propaganda Minister had promised to see what he could do. Perhaps he could persuade the *Führer* that a pardon of the anarchist Nachtnebel would create a marvelous piece of propaganda just in time for the world to lap it up.

She'd felt rotten to the core in pushing Leni to create yet another propaganda film, but this was indeed a sports film. True excellence wins—they would just be there to film it. After her last sip, Aurelia had gone in for the kill.

"It wasn't Goebbels' idea, it was actually the *Führer*. He asked for you."

Now, as Aurelia adjusted the focus on her camera, she caught Leni gazing at her beloved *Führer* again.

"Riefenstahl." She nudged the director with her elbow. "We're waiting."

"Right you are." Leni laughed, embarrassed, and got to work.

Aurelia had to give it to her, the filmmaker's passion was palpable, contagious even. Her voice cut through the cacophony of cheers and chants that celebrated the best athletic feats each country could offer. One could breathe freely here, in this little oasis of international comradery and friendly competition. And, propelled to action by those last few words Aurelia had uttered at the Austrian resort, Leni tackled the challenge head-on, set on making her idol proud. Camera rails were laid out in front of the track to follow the athletes' process in real time; all sorts of contraptions awaited Aurelia's camera to soar into the air to catch the flight of the disk.

"Looking good there, Laub!" Leni called to Aurelia, barely balancing herself and the camera atop the narrowest plank set up in front of the gymnasts' bars. "The French team say they wish you were wearing a skirt!" she added, cupping her hands around her mouth.

Sweating with effort, Aurelia flipped her the bird—the gesture both women had picked up during their US tour—and chuckled good-naturedly despite nearly losing her footing. "Tell the French team to mind their own business."

Things were looking up. Bibi's family had finally left Germany a day ago after a tearful goodbye, thanking Aurelia profusely for not abandoning them to their fate. On the other side of the pond, Max was already waiting to welcome them with open arms, his home—their home for the time being. On the German newsstands, the international press reappeared. Coca-Cola billboards framed Unter den Linden. In cafés and parks, from the entrances to which "For Aryans Only" signs had been removed, songs in French, English, Spanish, and Portuguese poured out of speakers. Berlin was Berlin once again, the one Aurelia used to love and remember, and she couldn't get enough of it.

Everyone in their crew felt it too: work was, once again, a pleasure. Without a Nazi Party watchful eye scrutinizing their every move, they came alive. They teased one another and laughed and almost believed that the worst for their country was over.

Only the news of Art's fate had arrived like a shockwave, shattering Aurelia's illusions and slamming her square in the chest.

"Dead?" she had whispered, hand against her heart, as if the wind was truly knocked out of her. "But just days ago he was perfectly fine; you said that much yourself!"

Goebbels had merely regarded her gloomily. "He was. But as soon as I gave an order for his release, signed by the *Führer*, as promised, he suddenly suffered a heart attack—according to the camp commandant, who reports to your brother."

Her eyes swimming with the memories of the sweet, innocent past, of Art's studio that had become her first true home, of the woman she had become thanks to his ideas, Aurelia had asked if she could at least give her ex-husband a proper burial. To have a grave to visit, next to her mother's—also murdered by a member of the same cursed clan.

"They cremate them there, I'm afraid." After clearing his throat, Goebbels had moved a small cardboard box across the desk to her. "You can take it if you wish. I wouldn't count on this being his ashes, though; from what I hear, they cremate them there en masse. This could be anyone. Or a hundred different people, depending on how you look at it. No personal belongings, either. They are all distributed among the German families in need." Encasing his handkerchief into her hand, Goebbels had added, "No one comes out of those camps."

Aurelia had cried herself to sleep that night, but the next day awoke with a redoubled determination to stick to her end of the bargain and leave Germany once and for all. The country which kidnapped its own citizens from their homes, which threw them into concentration camps from where there was no escape, and murdered them without any repercussions was beyond any help. At this point, staying around to see if it mirac-

ulously recovered its senses amounted to suicide. She'd film the
Olympics with as little Nazi propaganda involved as she could
and leave with the last international ship.

The trouble with this plan was that Hitler still saw the
Olympics as a tool to prove his theory of Aryan racial superior-
ity. Goebbels hinted that the lens should mostly be aimed at the
German athletes, but the stadium was their little world, even if
for only a few idyllic days. They would film what they wanted.
As if to test the crew's resolve, fate offered them just the
opportunity.

As the events of that day unfolded, Leni directed her crew
to the track. Jesse Owens, the African-American athlete, radiated confidence as he lined up for the 100-meter dash. From
their booths, the SS elite with Heinrich Himmler and Wilhelm
von Brandenburg at the head stared down at the athlete with
visible distaste. Aurelia had seen Owens train—he was fast as
lightning! She felt her pulse quicken; she had to capture this
moment.

The gun fired, and the athletes surged forward, their bodies
a blur of motion. Aurelia's fingers danced over her camera
controls, her heart pounding as she focused on Owens. With
every stride, he became a beacon of triumph against the backdrop of a regime that sought to diminish him. As he crossed the
finish line, arms outstretched in victory, the stadium erupted
into applause, a sound that drowned out the festering hatred
that had permeated the air.

Aurelia, caught in the moment, could not help but shout,
"Yes! Yes! Go, Jesse!" Her voice, a defiant ripple among the
waves of nationalistic fervor, surprised even herself.

Annoyed with the Black American's triumph, Hitler turned
his back on the stadium and stormed off, his immediate
entourage following suit.

Good riddance to bad rubbish, Aurelia thought to herself.
No one will miss you here.

She continued to film, capturing the raw joy on Owens' face as he celebrated, and the genuine smile of his German competitor, who approached him, extending a hand in camaraderie—a silent rebellion against the ideals that threatened to envelop them all.

"Look at that!" Aurelia called to Leni and the rest of the crew, her voice a mixture of awe and triumph. "This is what the Olympics should celebrate! This is what the whole world should aspire to be."

In Willy's eyes, tears shone. He, too, was clapping loudly from behind his camera, cheering the friendly exchange. At that moment, humanity itself shone brightly amid the darkness of the regime.

As the competition wound down, Aurelia captured another touching moment between Owens and his competitor. Climbing down from their stand, gold and silver medals shining on their chests, they embraced one another warmly and exchanged a few words Aurelia would have loved to hear. The camera whirred softly and Aurelia felt a swell of pride—this was the truth she sought to portray, a fleeting glimpse of unity in a country engulfed in hatred. Hitler's followers could stare and grunt their disapproval all they liked. History would obliterate them like the inconsequential, hateful maggots they were. It was moments like this that would live on for centuries to come, inspiring new generations to live up to their forefathers' loving nature. How honored she felt witnessing something of this sort. How honored she was to capture it on her film.

The competition came to a close until the next day. The sun dipped below the horizon, painting the sky in hues of orange and purple.

"What a great day," Willy said, passing his forearm over his forehead, tired as a dog and looking it, yet smiling all the same.

The spectators and the athletes were long gone, only the film crew remained to dismantle their intricate devices. In everyone's mind, the events of the day undoubtedly flashed. They had risked everything for a moment that might not be welcomed by those in power, yet unanimously, they understood the importance of its role. In a time when their country was spiraling into darkness, capturing glimmers of light, no matter the cost, was a small act of resistance still available to them.

With the last rays of sunlight shimmering across the stadium, Aurelia whispered softly, "Let this be remembered."

The rest of the crew toasted their beer bottles to hers.

On the way to their temporary home—they shared a hotel by the stadium—Leni suddenly cleared her throat.

"I'm not making any more films for the Party."

The announcement took Aurelia's attention from the road long enough for her to notice the telegraph pole just in time to avoid the collision.

"Way to go, Laub! I'm trying to turn my life around and you're trying to kill me?" Flung against Aurelia, Leni laughed and stayed where she was, her head in Aurelia's lap.

Aurelia didn't mind her colleague using her as a makeshift pillow—Leni must have been exhausted more than she was. "What did they put in your beer?" Aurelia asked instead. "The spirit of American democracy?"

"Americans are no better than us," Leni countered, playing with her bracelet. "We segregate our Jewish population, they segregate their Black one. The very idea of eugenics we took from them—just ask Willy, he'll tell you all about it. They hate communism even more than we do and, frankly, prefer fascism because our uniforms are smarter." She shrugged. "I know they imagine themselves the torchbearers of democracy, but they aren't immune to what's going on here."

"I thought you liked what's going on here," Aurelia said with a quick glance at Leni. In the shadows thrown off by the lampposts, she appeared to be the same young girl Aurelia had met in Babelsberg many years ago. Before Hitler, before the Party. Before all this... *rot*.

"I'm still convinced that our *Führer*'s heart is in the right place," Leni said at length. "All he wanted was for Germany to rise from her feet and be a great, respected country once again. It's all those other people around him—Himmler, Goebbels, Hess... don't take offense, but your brother, too."

"Oh, don't you worry, none taken. He's a piece of work, all right." Aurelia chuckled but felt her smile slip at the look on Leni's face—disappointed and wistful and slightly lost.

"Still, he shouldn't have walked out today. I somehow always thought he was a bigger man," the filmmaker whispered so softly, Aurelia could barely hear her. "At any rate, I'm done with the Party requests. Let them find themselves someone else."

"Yes," Aurelia echoed, passing her hand over Leni's dark curls. "Let them."

THIRTY

Goebbels took the news of both women's "resignations" surprisingly in his stride. When Aurelia and Leni met in the editing room, hung with stills from *Olympia*, they immediately began comparing notes.

"I was ready for him to have an apoplectic fit and instead he gave me seven million Reichsmark for the next film of my choosing," Leni said, arming herself with a magnifying glass and a pencil.

"Same with me," Aurelia said, leaning over the editing table with her portion of film. "Shook my hand, thanked me warmly for my cooperation, and wished me all the best in my future endeavors."

Aurelia omitted the part of the conversation that included the terms of such an amiable parting. After the Olympic rings had come down and the international press had returned to their countries of origin, the oppressive atmosphere of an authoritarian state had settled over the country once more, palpable tenfold. Eager to leave, Aurelia had gone to her immediate boss with her passport at the ready.

"I want to leave. Keep the house and everything in it, but let me go, together with my dogs and my groundskeeper. I want a clean exit visa, no catches."

Goebbels had considered, his head slightly cocked. "That can be arranged. After you finish your job on *Olympia*. I liked your idea of making albums with stills for sale—cards, books, merchandise in general. Your Jewish husband's business savviness must have rubbed off on you."

Max was the least money-savvy person Aurelia had known, but she wisely held her tongue. No need to alienate him now.

"Leni can finish it herself—"

"No," he had cut her off categorically. "The deal was, you give me *Olympia*, I give you your Jews. I held up my end of the bargain. How can I trust you with this next one if you're already going back on your word?"

"Fine," Aurelia had grumbled, acknowledging superior force. "You'll have your *Olympia*. *Then* I go. Right after it's released."

"By all means." He had spread his arms, all smiles and goodwill. "I'll even give you something extra, to see you through the next couple of years. How does a budget of seven million Reichsmark sound?"

"Too good to be true," Aurelia had muttered, rather to Goebbels' delight.

"My, you are far too suspicious, Fräulein von Brandenburg! I'm giving the same amount to Riefenstahl—my way of thanking you both for your efforts. Take it and spend it how you see fit."

"I can just take it and go?" Aurelia had eyed him with mistrust.

"Yes."

"To any country of my choosing?"

"That's correct."

"And I can film whatever I like?"

"You may film the Bolshevist revolution for all I care." Goebbels had laughed, positively amused. "If you can find a market for that sort of thing, outside of the Soviets."

Aurelia had requested the money transfer to the Swiss bank. To her great surprise, a telegram with a confirmation had reached her promptly—the money was in her account, ready to be withdrawn at her request.

Thinking back to it, Aurelia still believed it was some sort of extremely elaborate trap on Goebbels' part, but for the life of her, she couldn't figure it out.

"So, I am thinking of making *The Lowlands*," Leni began, marking her portion of the film for cutting. "Remember that opera that played just about everywhere, back in the twenties? I want to make it into a movie."

"If you mean the early twenties, I was mixing with a different crowd." Aurelia grinned, splicing the frames with the roaring crowd and a springboard diving athlete. "We went to see Brecht."

"I entirely forgot you were a little anarchist back then!"

"What can I say? Escaping the sort of household I was born into does that to a person."

Leni was silent a beat. Then, "I saw your husband's film." Very quietly.

"Who didn't?" Aurelia glanced up from her work with the tug of a grin at her mouth.

Leni returned it. "I cried," she admitted. "I mean it. I bawled. Hysterically."

"I know. Me too."

"Is it true then?"

"About my mother? I mean, I will never know, unless my brother dearest admits it to me—fat chance of that happening—but I assume so. Funny that it took my husband's writing skills to open my eyes to it and yet the German public thinks it's all Jewish slander and lies."

"The German public doesn't think, that's the entire trouble."

"Why should they? They have the Propaganda Ministry telling them what to be outraged about. And so instead of being outraged about our loss of free speech, civil freedom, bodily autonomy, the right to an education and work, they are outraged about Jews 'stealing' their jobs and the 'perverts' walking around with powder on their faces and leading the pure, German youth astray."

Aurelia thought back to the conversation she had just had with the Romanisches barkeep, Ricci. The SS had raided the last Berlin club he and his friend frequented, setting fire to the place after they had chased the patrons outside with wooden batons and vicious kicks of their steel-lined boots. Ricci had touched a yellow bruise, nearly invisible under the masterfully applied layers of makeup, with his fingertips and admitted that he was considering marriage. The neighbors kept throwing him and his "roommate" more and more looks. Ricci and his "roommate" thought that if they each married these gals who used to frequent the same club and also "roomed" together, they could possibly just keep out of the slammer, the four of them. *Anyway, enough of his troubles; how was Herr Laub doing in Hollywood?* Old, faithful friend... he hadn't once thought they were divorced, Aurelia and Max, and no amount of *Beobachter* headlines would persuade him otherwise.

"I regret making the *Triumph*," Aurelia said, cutting the film with the chilling finality of her own complicity.

Leni shifted her pose, growing uncomfortable. "I wasn't keen on making it in the first place but it did come out good—visually, that is—didn't it?"

"It did. That's the trouble. We made the regime look good, glorious even."

"But it's just one silly film." Leni tried to smile, almost apologetic. "It's not doing anyone any harm."

"The destruction of an empire never starts with an explosion, it starts with a whisper." Aurelia nodded a few times at those heavy, burdensome thoughts of hers. "And we turned that whisper into a war cry."

THIRTY-ONE

Vienna, Austria. Fall 1937

Aurelia stood in the lavish suite of the Hotel Sacher—a gem nestled in the heart of Vienna. The golden fall sun cast a warm glow through the large, ornate windows. The room was a tapestry of elegance, adorned with rich burgundy drapes that framed the view of the bustling streets below. The plush carpet muffled her footsteps as she paced restlessly, the soft sounds of classical music wafting from a gramophone.

As she held the receiver to her ear, her fingers traced the delicate edges of the polished mahogany desk, which was scattered with freshly picked flowers in a crystal vase, their perfume mingling with the scent of the fine tobacco from the cigar her husband often smoked. The phone call felt like a lifeline, a connection to the man who was her whole world, even if for the past few years that world had felt distant and unreachable.

"So, it's all set then?" Max's voice echoed through the line, tinged with excitement. His words wrapped around her like a familiar embrace, yet the distance between them felt palpable, stretching across the miles like the fog that settled over the city.

"Well, we already had the script," Aurelia replied, the cord coiling around her finger. "We just never had the budget for the damned thing."

"I still can't believe he just forked it out."

"Neither can I, and yet I've just filed for the permits to film and paid for them in full. When is your train leaving?"

"Tonight. I'm staying at this quaint little hotel right by the station. Came with rats and fleas in the blanket."

"Quit boasting! Mine didn't come with any wildlife."

They both shared a laugh, still unable to fully grasp the fact that they were finally on the same continent—she in Austria and Max in Italy—to be reunited in mere hours.

"How is Vienna?" he asked, his voice taking on a nostalgic tone.

Aurelia gazed out the open window. The skyline was dotted with spires and domes, a timeless portrait of the city's grandeur. The air was crisp, filled with the faint aroma of roasted chestnuts from a vendor below. The laughter of students returning from their lectures reached her ears, an echo of simpler times. Yet, as she pondered her response, Aurelia felt the weight of uncertainty pressing against her heart, a reminder that the world outside was changing in ways they could scarcely imagine.

"Beautiful, as always," she replied, her voice steady despite the turmoil inside. The gilded details of the room—the chandeliers sparkling like stars overhead, the sumptuous silk bedspread —felt almost surreal in contrast to the anxiety that gnawed at her. "Just a bit too close for comfort."

"A bit too close to Germany?"

"You sure we don't want to film in Hollywood? MGM are distributing the entire affair after all. And I've just shipped Loki and Astrid to Los Angeles. I'm not so sure Bibi will be thrilled looking after them."

"You said it yourself, they'd grown used to Bibi and Lisl over the years and the children adore them. As for the location, we talked about it," Max reminded her of the countless conversations they had shared over the summer. "It'll cost an arm and a leg to pay for the costumes as it is; recreating the entire set, building the whole city from scratch will drive the budget no end. It's much easier to film on location. The set is there, all we have to do is put actors in front of the camera. And don't forget, we also have Hungary to consider—that's another whole new set to build."

"Yes, I know."

"It's just not worth it."

"I know, I know." Aurelia pinched the bridge of her nose. They'd been over it for weeks now and still, she questioned the decision.

"You're not in Germany anymore. Austria is an autonomous country, I still hold its citizenship. It's fine," Max reassured her.

"Yes. All right."

Still, Aurelia found herself torn between the luxurious cocoon of her surroundings and the emerging shadows that loomed over Europe. The rich history of Vienna, a city that had seen both brilliance and despair, echoed in her thoughts. She longed for the days when she and her husband would stroll through the gardens of Schönbrunn, hand in hand, without a care in the world. He'd point out haunts he'd frequented as a student, the coffee houses that served the best stuff around, the small theater in which he had first discovered his love for the burgeoning cinematic art.

"We'll be fine, I promise," Max soothed her, his voice imbued with resolve.

Aurelia smiled gently, knowing that promise was as fragile as the leaves fluttering past her window. He hadn't just escaped Germany's clutches, he'd been living in his *freedom-land* for far too long to remember what it was like here, in Europe, under the spreading shadow of fascism. Yet, in that moment, surrounded by the opulence of the Hotel Sacher, she let him talk her into it.

"I'll be there first thing tomorrow," Laub assured her once again. "Wait for me in the dining room, don't you dare meet me at the station. Leave the key for me at the reception. I'll come up, shower, shave, shake all the fleas out of the seams—in short, make myself presentable—and then I'll join you just in time for your poached eggs to be served. What do you say to that?"

"I say, I don't mind one bit joining you and your fleas in the shower."

He laughed. "See you tomorrow. I love you."

"I love you more."

As she hung up the phone, Aurelia turned her gaze back to the window, the golden light of the setting sun casting a magical glow over the city. She took a deep breath, allowing herself to savor the beauty of the moment, even as the world outside began to shift beneath their feet.

Let him be right. Please, let him be right about everything.

The golden beams of the rising sun filtered through the ornate windows of the Sacher's dining room, casting a warm glow over the elegantly set tables adorned with crisp white linens and delicate crystal glassware. The soft murmur of conversation and the clinking of cutlery created a harmonious backdrop that felt both enchanting and surreal. In the corner, a pianist played a gentle waltz, his notes floating through the air like whispers of nostalgia. It was in this intimate atmosphere that Max Laub stepped through the threshold and, just like in one of his films, made his lead heroine gasp with profound emotion.

It had been years since Aurelia last laid eyes on him, her beloved husband, whose absence had left a gaping void in her life. He stood there in his crumpled suit, a trench coat hanging on the crook of his elbow, fedora at his heart, and Aurelia couldn't remember a moment when he had looked more hand-some. Instantly on her feet, she rushed to him across the room, her breath catching in her throat. The years apart melted away as she approached him, her heart pounding like a drum.

"Max," she breathed, her voice full of tears and joy.

"I had every intention of showering and shaving," he said, smiling, "but then I saw you sitting there and..."

They stood there for a moment that felt suspended in time, the air thick with unspoken words and emotions.

Max reached out, his fingers trembling as they brushed against her cheek. "I thought I'd never see you again," he confessed, his voice cracking under the weight of his feelings, and, dropping both his coat and hat to the floor, scooped her into his arms and kissed her hard enough to make her head swim.

Too absorbed in each other, they didn't notice the first claps and teasing cheers. Only after their tide swelled to the crescendo of an applause one could no longer ignore did Max lower his wife back down and mock-bowed to their audience. Her cheeks ablaze—from the kiss, not embarrassment—Aurelia was gazing at him with adoring eyes, her lip between her teeth.

"Allow me to take this, Herr Laub." The maître d' was already snapping his fingers at the bellboy after collecting the director's things off the immaculate floor. "We'll have it cleaned and pressed for you. And welcome back to Sacher."

"Home away from home," Max responded to the warm greeting, taking the maître d's hand in his.

"Will you be staying in Frau Laub's suite?"

Aurelia and Max exchanged glances. No Fräulein von Brandenburg nonsense here. No matter what Germany claimed, in the eyes of the rest of the world they remained very much married—to the delight of the local public at least.

"Yes, tell them to get a room already," one of the guests quipped, only to be slapped on the arm by his own spouse. She might have acted scandalized, but Aurelia saw that the woman was smiling all the same. Max Laub was their national treasure. Austrians had a special love for their celebrated compatriot.

"Yes, if you could take my suitcase up there, please," Max replied, slipping a generous tip in the maître d's gloved hand.

"Hungry?" Aurelia asked, steering her husband toward her table.

"Starving," he whispered in her ear and bit it lightly, turning Aurelia's very blood to molten lava.

As they shared their breakfast— the first of many, Aurelia was certain of it—she forced herself to believe that the worst was behind them; that this was a promise of a new chapter waiting to unfold. In Max's presence, she felt alive again, two souls entwined once more.

THIRTY-TWO

Vienna, Austria. March 1938

In the sun-drenched streets of Vienna, Aurelia stood at the edge of a bustling film set, her heart racing with trepidation. The air was thick with the smell of horse sweat and the distant echoes of laughter from the crew, but all she could focus on was the official figure weaving his way through the multiple cables lining the street like the roots of a great tree. Busy with filming, neither she nor Max had paid much attention to the news until the referendum booths sprang out all over the city, which were impossible to ignore. And now this uniform clicked his heels in front of the couple, handing them an official notice prohibiting work the following day.

Max regarded the paper, dark brows drawn together. "But we have a permit from the city valid until the end of the month. Weekends and national holidays included. We paid extra for it, specifically."

"This order supersedes it," the official retorted, examining the meticulously crafted costumes and the grandiose sets that echoed the opulence of the Austro-Hungarian Empire. The crew that was bustling around them moments ago, preparing for the next scene in which Empress Sisi would ride through the streets to the cheers of welcoming crowds, came to a standstill. "Tomorrow is the national referendum. All of these people need to go and vote either to join Germany or not. They can't do it if they're occupied on your set. Speaking of, you need to go vote too."

"I'm only visiting," Max responded, crossing his arms over his chest. "I'm going back to the States as soon as we're done."

"Do you hold dual citizenship?"

"Yes, but what does it—"

"If you're still an Austrian national, you must go and vote."

With that, he clicked his heels again and set off, leaving Aurelia and Max staring at each other in charged silence.

"*Herr Direktor?*" Willy, whom Aurelia had brought over from Germany to work on their *Sisi* as a cinematographer, cleared his throat. This was his first historical film in a long line of documentaries, but even out of his element, he was showing up to work with a big smile and his sleeves rolled up, feeling liberated and free to create what his heart desired without the oppressive presence of the Propaganda Ministry. "We can start from midday tomorrow, so we don't lose it entirely. You, Austrians, go vote; I can always shoot scenery in the meantime under Aurelia's direction. She's also German; she doesn't need to show up for that circus."

"That's not what's—" Aurelia stopped abruptly and rubbed her eyes. To hell with the lost day, she didn't relish one bit this referendum idea that had sprung into some Hitler-likeminded head. She turned to her husband: "Shall we go to the Embassy?"

"The American one?"

"No, the German. Yes, Max, the American! Let's go ask them what we should do."

"Right now?"

"Yes, now!"

He motioned his head toward the carriage, the horses, the guard, and the crowd, all dressed in the costumes created from scratch specifically for *Sisi*. "We're in the middle of the scene."

"To the devil with the scene!" Aurelia hissed at him, grasping him by the elbow. She'd almost forgotten how obsessive he was with his filming: always the first on set, always the last one to leave. She had cursed that self-imposed work ethic of his throughout the first weeks of assisting him, back in Babelsberg. The crew would have been long gone and he would still crawl on his hands and knees, marking the grid according to which the rails for the camera would be laid out the following morning. And once the scene was all laid out? He was like a dog with a bone. He wouldn't leave it for anything. "Do you understand that tomorrow this country will be voting on becoming a part of the blasted Reich?"

Max exhaled audibly. "It's just one idiotic vote. Even if— and I doubt that it shall be so—the majority votes on joining Germany, nothing will happen outright. Remember 1933, when Hitler's party was just elected? Even then it took them a few months to implement their policies and by that time we'll have wrapped it all up here and be gone."

They would have continued to bicker if it wasn't for the actress playing Sisi.

"Are we filming anytime soon?" she called through the opened door of her carriage. "I don't know what the handlers have been feeding this horse, but we're all suffocating here!"

The girls playing her ladies-in-waiting giggled in confirmation, holding their delicate handkerchiefs to their noses.

His hair tousled in the wind, Max winked at Aurelia and pinched her cheek. "Let's get back to it before they start dry-heaving—that will really ruin the shot."

Despite all of her senses screaming alarm, Aurelia picked up her horn and called for silence on the set. *Sisi* the film was their labor of love; the empress herself—their patron saint, as they jokingly claimed. With the force of her love—not war—she had united Austria and Hungary into a grand, thriving empire, which, in turn, had made it possible for Max's parents to meet and get married. Had it not been for Sisi, the man Aurelia loved so fiercely wouldn't exist. Max would never abandon her story; certainly not now when they were so close to its completion. How could Aurelia possibly live with herself if she tore that dream out of his hands?

As the first scene unfolded, the camera rolled, capturing not only the grandeur of the story they were telling but the infinite love that intertwined their fates. In that moment, with the world fading away and dreams becoming reality, she knew that no matter the challenges ahead, they would face them together.

"Till death—" eyes on the set, Aurelia whispered barely audibly, grasping his hand in hers.

Without tearing his own gaze from the rolling camera, Max brought her fingers to his lips and kissed them with ardent emotion. "—And beyond."

Max protested that it was unnecessary and foolish, but Aurelia refused to listen to any reason: she was going to the polling station with him whether he liked it or not. They left their hotel early—the sooner they were done with this moronic affair, the better. In the streets an almost palpable sense of unease hung in the air like the heavy fog that often enveloped the city. The sun struggled to break through the overcast skies, casting a dull light that mirrored the somber mood of the day. Lines snaked outside the polling station, filled with men and women clutching their identification papers, their faces etched with a mix of apprehension and resignation.

"At least we aren't wasting daylight," Aurelia muttered, pressing closer to her husband. "The weather is dreadful. If it doesn't clear up, we'll have to film interior scenes only today."

He grunted in agreement and wrapped his arm around his wife. "Cold?"

"Mmm," Aurelia lied.

She wasn't cold, she was overcome with a suffocating sense of déjà vu. This was how it had all started for Germany—with elections and polling stations and nationalistic young men shouting their propaganda from every corner. With promises to clean up the mess after the social democrats, to bring Germany back from her knees, to put her interests first. The rest of Europe could stick their judgment where the sun didn't shine: Hitler told his followers that they didn't need anybody. To hell with tolerance, empathy, and women's liberation. They burned books and jailed their authors. They fired Jews and, right after them, everyone else who refused to toe the line. As for the elections, they were no more in Germany. And now Austria was heading down the same slippery slope.

Near the station itself, Aurelia was loath to discover members of the Austrian SS standing sentinel, their uniforms sharp against the drab walls of the hall. They loomed over the line of voters, their expressions fierce and unyielding. At times, they cast threatening glances at those who simply looked like they could vote against the proposition.

"Hey, pansy, don't forget: you're Aryan first," one of the thugs addressed an extremely handsome young man with a silk knot of a tie tucked under his leather jacket. "Don't you go voting against your nation's interests." With his great paw, the SS man pointed the young man in the direction of a voting booth, which wasn't even curtained. "We'll be watching."

It was clear they were there not just to maintain order, but to enforce a compliance that felt increasingly like coercion. The air crackled with the tension of a society on the brink. Each vote cast felt like a step deeper into an abyss, a surrender to a regime that made it abundantly clear that dissent would not be tolerated.

His sense of justice outraged, Max stepped out of the line and positioned himself square in front of the SS men. "Gentlemen, I must protest! This is entirely against all regulation. Voting has always been anonymous in Austria and voter interference and suppression is simply unconstitutional."

"Who says we're interfering?" The same SS man grinned, displaying a revolting view of nicotine-stained teeth. "We're maintaining order is all."

"Yes, so that the anarchists don't interfere," his comrade supplied, cackling like a hyena.

The vein rose in Max's forehead. "The anarchists haven't been around for over twenty years," he hissed.

"Get back in line, Father," the SS man advised.

"If you know what's good for you," his hyena friend quipped.

Aurelia was about to make a move to insert herself between the two parties but forgot that Max had faced things far worse than some uniformed youngsters. He drew himself to an impressive height, shoulders squaring. Behind his glasses, his gaze narrowed, sharpened, like an unsheathed bayonet. It took all but two seconds to transform a director from Beverly Hills back into the Great War soldier who still remembered the trenches.

"You insolent dung beetle!" he bellowed in a voice that rolled over the station like thunder. "Opening your beer trap at a superior officer? Stand to attention when a *Hauptmann* addresses you, numbskull!"

To Aurelia's amazement, the SS men pulled their arms along the seams.

"Whose brilliant idea was it, putting circus clowns into uniforms?" Max continued, his assault inches away from the SS men's faces. "You're protecting the polling station?" His finger pushed in the tall SS fellow's gut, which he tried to suck in, but failed miserably. "You're about as useful here as a screen door on a submarine! As for you, mentioning anarchists"—Max turned his attention to the formerly cackling hyena, now quiet as a mouse—"you're another shining example of what happens when evolution takes a day off. If brains were dynamite, you wouldn't have enough to blow your nose! I suggest you start using what little you have before it completely evaporates. There's a library around the corner: do yourself a favor, pick up a recent history book. In fact, pick up *any* book. Because if you get any denser, you'll turn into a black hole. Judging by the dumb look on your face, the joke is lost on you, so pick up a textbook on physics as well. Dismissed!"

Stunned and yet visibly impressed, the duo made an about-face only to catch more flak from Max.

"Trot faster, you lazy scum! You're so slow, I could put a rock in front of you and it would finish a marathon before you do!"

With the SS men's departure, the crowd cheered up considerably. Poll workers also appeared to heave a sigh of relief. Someone offered to hang his own coat as a poll curtain. A woman volunteered her scarf to partition the other booth. With an ache in her chest, Aurelia watched Max's compatriots shuffle toward the ballot boxes to cast their honest votes. Here and now, a few dozen could mark the box "no" without facing consequences. She wasn't convinced that the rest of the country could boast the same.

THIRTY-THREE

The following day, the air was thick with the scent of freshly painted backdrops and the excited chatter of crew members bustling about. With the skies finally clear, Max hoped to get as many of the exterior scenes shot as he could before dismissing the crew for their day off. Her back already wet with sweat, Aurelia ran about the set, adjusting the lighting and delegating the director's commands to the crew.

But as the camera began to roll, the sound of a distant rumble made them turn their heads in a westward direction, one by one. Aurelia felt Willy pull her sleeve.

"Call *cut*," he whispered barely audibly in her ear. "The mic is picking up whatever it is. The scene is ruined."

"Cut!" Aurelia called to the actors.

Willy had long stopped the camera, his eyes on the horizon.

"What in the hell?" Max muttered, rising from his director's chair. Shielding himself from the sun with the script, he peered at the streets radiating beyond the set's enclosed rectangle. One by one, windows were flying open. From the open cafés, patrons were spilling onto the streets. It was not the clamor of thunder threatening to ruin another day of filming but the heavy boots of soldiers marching. From the platform on which the camera stood, Aurelia could just make out the first few rows of them—and then an entire sea of field gray.

In the distance, a public announcement speaker coughed to life.

"The glorious day we've all been praying for is here! The results of the referendum were overwhelming in their support of this long-awaited union. Welcomed by their southern brothers, German troops have crossed the border. The Anschluss is upon us. Austria is now officially part of the Third Reich."

Aurelia's heart sank like stone as the weight of this announcement settled over her like a suffocating blanket. "No," she whispered, her voice a mixture of disbelief and dread. "How did they—" Her hand flew to her mouth, her blue eyes wide with terror. "So soon!"

"I suppose we may as well pack up for the day," Max spoke to the crew, dazed but still in control.

"Everyone, pack up. Actors, change and go home. Stagehands, take all the equipment back inside until—" The truth was, Aurelia hadn't the faintest idea until what. "Until further notice, I guess."

Left alone amid the crew dismantling the set, the couple exchanged a frantic glance, the reality of their situation crashing down like a tidal wave.

Looking like a scolded dog, Max tried to soften Aurelia's severe expression with a timid smile. "Would you look at it? You were right, as always."

"Oh, shut your mouth, Max!" Gathering their things, Aurelia shoved her husband's valise into his hands, together with the script, now absolutely useless. "Where do you think you're going?" She yanked his sleeve after he made a step in the wrong direction.

"To the hotel." He blinked at her, sheepish.

"We're going straight to the train station," Aurelia stated in a no-nonsense tone, pulling Max after herself as she set off.

"But our passports—"

"I've been carrying them around this entire time," she called, picking up the pace. "Because what do you know? I always happen to be right and you never happen to listen."

Max caught up with her, the remnants of their film world fading behind them like a distant dream.

As they made their way through the cobblestone streets, the atmosphere thickened with chaos. From the windows, crimson banners began to stream, following the Laubs' escape like an avalanche sweeping the capital. People were pouring out of buildings, their faces etched with excitement. Many donned traditional dress. Small swastika flags clutched in their pudgy hands, children rushed toward the action, attracted by the military music and the cheers of the crowd.

Those sharing the couple's fear and uncertainty were a rare sight. Heading in the opposite direction of the swelling crowds, Aurelia sometimes caught snippets of conversations, the frantic whispers of neighbors and friends, all sharing the same dark realization.

"Chaim, ask the Rabbi what will happen to us," a woman, dressed modestly all in black cried, clutching her child close to her chest. "Are we still citizens of Austria or Germany now?"

"You aren't citizens of anything, you ugly sow!" one of the flag-waving children called. He couldn't have been older than twelve, but he spat in the woman's direction with the confidence of a seasoned SS thug. "Get out of our country, Austria is for Austrians!"

"Ugly sow!" one of his friends repeated with wicked delight as he picked up a stone and hurled it at the woman's small boy with his long blond sidelocks. She turned her back to shield her son and didn't cry out when the stone hit her in the shoulder blade. Her husband rushed her back inside and locked the door after himself.

At long last, after the mad sprint, the train station loomed ahead of Aurelia and Max, a monument of hurried desperation. Upon arrival, they were met with a scene that felt like a nightmare. The station was a sea of humanity, bodies jostling and pushing against one another, all vying for a chance to escape. The air was thick with the scent of sweat and anxiety, punctuated by the distant wail of a whistle signaling an approaching train.

"Look at this madness," Max breathed, his eyes scanning the crowd. "We'll never make it through."

Aurelia's grip tightened on his arm. "Yes, we will. Follow me."

Tension crackled in the air as they pushed their way through the throng, the cries of families and the shouts of porters blending into a cacophony of desperation.

Aurelia's heart sank as she caught sight of the departure board, the words written in chalk blending into a death sentence. Most trains were delayed or canceled altogether, and the few that remained looked as though they were filled to capacity. The ticket booths were under veritable assault, impossible to get to. Not that it would do them any good: it was obvious that no one was having any success purchasing anything from the tellers.

"Ari! Over there!" Max shouted, pointing to a train that was just starting to board. They dashed toward it, weaving through the crowd, adrenaline fueling their every step.

Just as they reached the platform, a conductor shouted, "Last call! This train is leaving in minutes!"

Fighting his way through the crowd, Max positioned himself in front of the conductor, slipping a fat wad of dollars into his pocket as their eyes locked. "There's a thousand dollars there. I don't care if we sleep on the floor by the privy. Get. Us. In."

It took the conductor a second to assess the situation. "Welcome aboard," he announced, producing two tickets from his breast pocket. "Sleeper. Twelve. Good luck."

With no time to spare, they clambered aboard, their breaths ragged as they squeezed into the tight space.

As the train lurched forward, leaving the station behind, Aurelia caught Max glancing out the window at the city he had loved, now overshadowed by an impending darkness. The faces of those who remained blurred into the distance. A wave of sorrow washed over her.

"Do we even know where it's heading?" Max barked a nervous laugh, wiping the sheen of sweat from his forehead with the back of his hand.

"Budapest," supplied one of the fortunate ones sharing the last train out of Vienna with them. "Thank God."

"Thank God is right," Aurelia chuckled as well, her voice strung with nerves. "Come, Max, let's find that sleeper."

As they made their way to their car, their new status of fugitives evident in their disheveled appearance and meager possessions, Aurelia prodded her husband in the small of his back. "Where'd you get the money from?"

With a coy look over his shoulder, he grinned. "Given multiple precedents of you being right before, I decided to take certain measures. You were carrying our passports around, I was carrying my American cash."

But even as they laughed about getting out by the skin of their teeth, the reality of their situation loomed like a specter. The startled look on the faces of the two other couples sharing their compartment—the conductor must have turned quite a profit on selling a single sleeper to six people instead of just two —was another unrelenting reminder that the world they once knew was slipping away, replaced by an uncertain future filled with shadows and fear.

In that moment, amid the chaos of the train, Aurelia took a deep breath, steeling herself for the challenges ahead. They were no longer just a couple creating art, they were now absconders, fighting for survival in a world that had turned against them. The journey was only beginning, but they were ready to face whatever lay ahead together.

THIRTY-FOUR

The train rattled through the twilight, the rhythmic clattering of wheels against tracks underscoring the tension that hung heavy in the air. Aurelia sat beside her husband, Max, their hands intertwined, a fragile lifeline in a world that felt increasingly precarious. The two other couples that shared the compartment with them held onto each other with the same mute desperation —Austrian citizens just hours ago; now, refugees without any rights, hoping to outrun the Nazis that had poured over their country's border earlier that day. The landscape outside the window blurred into a series of indistinct shapes, a haunting reflection of their own lives—once vibrant, now marred by fear and uncertainty.

Finally, the last stop before the Austrian-Hungarian border. Suddenly lightheaded with nerves, Aurelia looked around. The air itself seemed to vibrate with anticipation. Her foot tapping in time with her wildly racing heart, she sensed the same unease radiating from the other passengers. Whispers floated through the compartment, a blend of hope and anxiety. Aurelia felt her heart pound against her ribs like a caged bird desperate for freedom.

"Do you think we'll make it?" she asked, glancing at Max, whose face was etched with concern.

He squeezed her hand, his eyes steady. "Our papers are in order. We should, just stay calm."

But as they pulled into the station, Aurelia's heart sank at the familiar sight of plain-clothed men standing on the platform. The Gestapo. She'd seen enough of them in Berlin in the past few years to instantly identify them even without their uniforms. It was the manner in which they carried themselves, assured of their unchecked power, and also the eyes. It was the eyes that always betrayed them: cold, searching, utterly devoid of all emotion—those were the vultures' eyes, just waiting to pounce on their prey. Through the window of their car, Aurelia watched as they moved with purpose, their faces impassive, eyes scanning the train with predatory intent.

"The Germans only crossed into Austria this morning," Max murmured, his grip tightening around her hand. "How in the hell are they already here?"

Aurelia tossed her head, her throat dry with mounting fear. Because the elections before the Anschluss had only been for show. They'd known the outcome for months now. They'd been preparing, implanting their agents everywhere. And as for the Austrian SS? They were just as old as the German ones. Frankly, she would have been surprised if they weren't here. And in her own twisted way, she, Aurelia, had helped make it all happen.

As the train came to a halt, the doors slid open. The Gestapo officers boarded, their heels thudding against the metal floor—each step a nail in their communal coffin. Naturally, they began with the private compartments: people who could afford them had the most to hide and the most to lose.

"Papers!"

Aurelia jumped as she heard one of them bark in the next compartment. The atmosphere shifted, a palpable tension filling the air. Their fellow passengers scrambled to comply, fumbling with documents, their expressions a mixture of fear and resignation as they waited for their turn. Aurelia's blood drained from her face as she listened to the steps move down the aisle, nearing their compartment's door.

"Max," she whispered, "what if they—"

"Shh," he whispered back, his expression a mask of calm. "Don't forget who you are. We'll be fine."

As if she could ever forget. It was that cursed name of hers that had got them into this mess. How desperately she'd tried to shed it, but it kept coming back, like a snake's skin, enveloping her anew and strangling her all the same.

"I'm Aurelia Laub—" Aurelia tried to speak, but the door slid aside, cutting her off.

The officer in charge—a tall man with a sharply defined jaw and ice-cold blue eyes—fixed Max and Aurelia with his piercing gaze. He recognized them; Aurelia could see it at once.

"Papers," he inquired, politeness personified.

Still, his voice sliced through Aurelia's hopes like a knife.

She reached into her bag, retrieving their passports, together with Max's American certificate of naturalization. Should she have just produced the certificate alone? But he didn't have a visa to travel to Hungary as an American citizen; as an Austrian, he didn't need one. No, she did everything right.

Meanwhile, the officer scrutinized the papers, his eyes narrowing as he flicked through the pages. "Herr Laub," he said, looking up at Max. "Would you kindly step off the train, please?"

Aurelia's heart sank. "What? No! His papers are in perfect order!" Panic surged through her as she stood, gripping Max's arm tightly. "He's done nothing wrong! Why are you taking him off the train?"

The officer remained unfazed, gesturing for Max to follow him. "I'm merely following orders, Fräulein von Brandenburg," he said with the same mock-apologetic smile. "They give me a list with names, I check papers against the list. Apparently, Herr Laub is needed by one agency or the other for further questioning."

"Further questioning?" Aurelia echoed, her voice rising. "You can't just detain people without good reason! Besides, he's an American citizen."

"He's also an Austrian one," the Gestapo man pointed out, smiling wider. "So, Austrian law holds." He quickly caught himself, chuckling. "I beg your pardon, *German* law. Austria is a part of the German Reich as of today but I'm sure you've already heard that much."

He motioned for two other officers to approach. They moved with a practiced efficiency, gently but firmly guiding Max away from her. Aurelia felt her entire world tilt on its axis, her heart racing as she struggled to keep a grip on reality.

"You have no right!" she cried, trying to prize their hands from her husband's shoulders in the narrow passageway. "What are you charging him with? He's done nothing wrong! Just let us leave; you'll never see us again anywhere near Europe, I swear! We just want to leave, that's all!"

Half-turning to her, the Gestapo leader beamed at her as his underlings led Max through the car door. "Oh, you are welcome to proceed with your travels, Fräulein von Brandenburg. You aren't on the list."

In a last surge of desperation, Aurelia lunged at the Gestapo agents, set on prizing her husband away or dying in the attempt. Momentarily surprised, they subdued her, though, with the utmost care not to inflict any injuries, for which there would be hell to pay. She screamed at Max to use his chance and run— she'd just keep fighting them if needed—but he only stood there, the believer in human rights, the damned idealist she loved more than life.

"Ari, quit it, please," Max urged, smiling at the agents

almost with embarrassment. Despite the angst in his eyes, his voice remained steady. "You'll only make it worse. Go to Hungary like we planned. I'm sure it's a simple misunderstanding. As soon as they let me go, I'll find you."

But as the leader escorted him to the unmarked car, the memory of Art's fate settled heavily upon Aurelia. Wilhelm had already killed her first husband. Over her dead body would he be getting her second.

The officers repeated their mantra, "You're free to go, Fräulein von Brandenburg," as if their words could erase the horror unfolding before her.

Aurelia's resolve hardened, fueled by a fierce determination. "Like hell I will!" she declared, her voice unwavering. "Wherever you take him, I'm coming with you."

The lead officer raised an eyebrow, clearly taken aback by her defiance. "That's not how this works. You can leave now or—"

"Or what?" Aurelia interrupted, her voice rising. "You'll arrest me too? I don't care! You think I'll abandon my husband to whatever fate you have in store for him? Take me with him!"

The officers exchanged glances, momentarily unsure of how to proceed. But Aurelia stood her ground, the fire in her eyes burning through the veil of fear. She couldn't lose him—not now, not when they were so close to freedom.

With a resigned sigh, the Gestapo leader put his mask of a smile back on. "As you wish, Fräulein von Brandenburg. As you wish..."

THIRTY-FIVE

The air in Vienna was thick with a tension that seemed to grip the city tighter with each passing day. March 1938 had marked not just the Anschluss but also a palpable shift in the atmosphere—a prelude to something far more sinister. Aurelia stood in a dimly lit office, commandeered, no doubt, from one Austrian official or the other, the smell of stale tobacco and polished oak filling her senses, and yet it was the weight of fear that pressed down on her chest. Across from her, Joseph Goebbels sat behind a grand desk, his eyes glinting with a mixture of ambition and malice.

Only a day had passed since that fateful stop at the Hungarian border.

Only a day since uniformed men had pulled her away from her husband and forced them into separate cars.

Only a day that felt like an eternity of nightmares.

"Fräulein von Brandenburg," the Propaganda Minister began, his voice smooth, almost honeyed, yet laced with an unmistakable edge, "such a pleasure to see you again."

"I wish I could say the same," Aurelia growled, her eyes glowing like those of a wild cat ready to pounce. "I thought we had an agreement, *Herr Minister*. Why in the devil did your agents stop me and my husband at the border? And where did you take him?"

Goebbels pressed his hand to his chest, all innocence. "My agents? No, no, dearest Fräulein von Brandenburg. You are quite mistaken. That would be your brother's doing. I'm in charge of radio, film, and press—I have no police under my control."

"Where is my husband?" Aurelia repeated, in no mood for his games. The moment of their detention kept replaying in her mind like a demented record. The thought of Max in the Nazis' claws gnawed at her insides, replacing all instincts of self-preservation with an urgent need to protect him at all costs.

Goebbels shrugged. "I can't say for a fact—again, kidnappings are not quite my sphere of operations—but I can vouch for his safety, if that's any consolation."

"And how would you know he is safe?"

"It would be utterly foolish of your brother to kill him, now that he can use him as a bargaining chip instead."

The lightness with which he uttered those words and the actual message behind them turned Aurelia's legs to jelly. Feeling as though the ground was going from under her feet, she sank heavily into the visitor's chair, her fingers clawing at the upholstery.

"Oh no, there's no need to be so distraught," Goebbels continued, circling the desk. "He wants you for whatever reason," he said, placing his hands on Aurelia's shoulders. "We had quite a fight over my letting you go, your brother and I. He called me an idiot. You don't believe me? I wrote it all in my diary—I'll be more than happy to show you—"

"I don't care what rows you have among yourselves," Aurelia groaned, burying her face in her hands. "We had a deal, you and I!"

"Did I break it?"

"No, but—" She swallowed the lump in her throat, the full realization of her helplessness dawning on her, pressing her down, together with those reptilic hands. "It was all a trap. One elaborate trap, from the very beginning. You knew German troops were going into Austria and yet you said nothing."

Goebbels paused a while, his thumb brushing the exposed skin on her neck. "What can I say in my defense? I'm only a man—a man in desperate need of individuals with extraordinary talents, and you, my dear, are one of the finest in your field." Shifting his pose once again, he bore his gaze into her, searching for a flicker of hope or despair that might betray her thoughts. "I didn't orchestrate the entire thing, I merely took advantage of the situation."

"And you expect I'll continue working for you." Aurelia stared at him, her voice steady despite the tremor in her hands.

Returning to his chair, Goebbels leaned back in it, his fingers steepled together thoughtfully. "I have only respect and fondness for you, Fräulein von Brandenburg, but in times such as these, the needs of the state transcend my own personal feelings. Austria was only the beginning. The new German nation needs room to expand and thrive. And now that we have our eyes set on the rest of Europe, we need someone to turn our vision into a powerful tool. Art is a weapon, my dear. It shapes minds, influences the masses. And in this new order we are building, we need artists who can wield that power for the Reich." He paused, allowing the weight of his words to settle between them. "I can assure you that your husband's safety is contingent upon your cooperation."

The coldness of this statement sent a chill through her spine. "You can't be serious," she stammered, her breath catching in her throat. "You're holding a virtual gun to my head to make films promoting the war you're about to unleash on an innocent population?"

"A gun to *your* head?" Goebbels echoed, feigning surprise.

"My, Fräulein von Brandenburg, your head is far too precious! It's more of a metaphorical gun to your *husband's* head." His gaze turned steely, a predator sizing up his prey. "You have a choice to make. The regime values talent, and we could create something extraordinary together—a series of films that will galvanize the people, rouse their spirits, and solidify our power."

Aurelia felt the walls of the room close in around her. The flickering candlelight cast shadows that danced ominously, mirroring the turmoil within her. Her mind raced with images of Max, his arms around her, his laughter, his creativity, the way he would move masses of viewers with his passion for story-telling. She felt the weight of desperation creeping in. The thought of losing him, of his spirit being crushed in the clutches of a regime, gnawed at her.

"And if I refuse?" she asked, though she already knew the answer.

Goebbels leaned forward, his expression darkening. "Take it up with your brother, Fräulein von Brandenburg. He's the one who ordered your detention, not me. You may refuse to work for the Ministry, but think of it this way: I'm the only man who has the *Führer*'s ear when it comes to protecting people I like. It pays to be my friend."

In that moment, Aurelia realized the terrible truth: she was caught in a web spun by two men whose thirst for power over-shadowed any semblance of humanity. The room felt smaller as she grappled with the gravity of her situation, torn between her love for Max and the dark path laid before her.

"I need time to think," she finally replied, her voice barely above a whisper.

Goebbels smiled, but it was a smile that did not reach his eyes. "Take all the time you need, my dear. But remember, time is a luxury you may not have. Consider your options carefully."

As he dismissed her, Aurelia stepped out of the office and into the corridor, her heart a tumultuous storm of fear, anger, and resolve. She had entered a world of shadows and now she had to navigate the darkness—not just for herself, but for Max, whose fate was intricately tied to her choices. The weight of her decision loomed over her like a spectral presence, and as she walked away, she knew that the battle for her soul had only just begun.

THIRTY-SIX

Berlin

Max stepped off the transport vehicle with a jolt, the cold Berlin air biting through the thin fabric of his clothing. The chaos of his arrest at the Austrian-Hungarian border felt like a distant nightmare, yet the stark reality of his surroundings quickly grounded him in a new, horrifying truth. Tegel prison loomed ahead, its imposing structure casting long shadows under the gray sky. So, back to the capital then—at least they didn't shoot him someplace in the woods on the way here.

With two guards close on his heels, Max crossed the threshold into the prison yard, his stomach tensing with each step. The place was a fortress, encased in high red walls that seemed to absorb the very light of day. The sound of heavy iron gates clanging shut echoed ominously, a finality that sent a shiver down his spine. It was then that he caught sight of the sentries patrolling the roof—stern-faced men clad in dark uniforms, their expressions unreadable, hardened by the brutality of their duties. They moved like wolves, their guns at the ready.

In the moments that followed, Max felt a whirlwind of emotions crash over him. Fear was the most prominent, followed closely by a fierce anger directed toward the circumstances that had led him here. He had only been trying to leave Austria with Aurelia, to escape the tightening noose of the regime, yet here he was, ensnared in its clutches. The thought of her, waiting in uncertainty, gnawed at him. He should have listened to her when she first sounded the alarm, but he was too pigheaded, too self-assured, too wrapped up in the illusion of his invincibility granted by the dual citizenship. Now he was lost in a place where hope seemed to flicker like a dying candle.

The guards lined him up with the others who had been recently detained, their faces a tapestry of despair, confusion, and resignation. Max stood silently among them, taking in their haggard appearances and the pallor of their skin—a collective suffering that spoke of nights spent in fear and days filled with uncertainty. He instinctively straightened his posture, a remnant of his pride as an artist, even in the face of such dehumanization.

A guard barked orders and they were herded into the building like cattle. The scent of damp concrete mingled with something metallic, a smell that hinted at violence and despair. The fluorescent lights flickered overhead, casting an unflattering glare that illuminated the faces of the men around him; some were older, their faces lined with worry, while others were younger, eyes wide with disbelief. Max felt a surge of empathy for them all, a shared understanding of their precarious fates.

As he entered the cell block, the heavy metal doors creaked open, revealing a long corridor lined with cells. The sound of iron bars clanging shut echoed menacingly, a reminder that freedom was now a distant memory. He was led to a small cell, barely large enough to accommodate a narrow bed and a toilet. The walls were cold and unyielding, adorned only with peeling paint that seemed to flake off like the hopes of those who had been confined within.

He stepped inside, the door slamming shut behind him with a finality that resonated in his bones. The echo of the lock turning was like a death knell, sealing him in a world of darkness and uncertainty.

Max pressed his back against the wall, feeling the chill seep into his bones. He inhaled sharply, the air thick with the scent of despair, and closed his eyes.

"Good day, neighbor."

A pleasant, polite voice, though muffled by the wall separating them, pulled him out of his unhappy musings.

Quickly scanning the cell for its origin, Max discovered the hole formed in the chipped cement surrounding the ancient, rusted radiator.

"Good day," he called into it.

"Are you a political prisoner as well?" his invisible interlocutor inquired. He was a German, but not a Berliner. A Bavarian likely, if Max ventured to guess the accent.

"I haven't been charged with anything," he confessed, patting himself for cigarettes and remembering that they'd been confiscated, together with everything else the border guards had discovered in his pockets. The valise was a lost cause entirely.

"Not a single one of us was," the man chuckled humorlessly. "Not in this wing, at any rate. What crime did you commit against the state?"

"I haven't committed anything!" Max protested.

"I'd say save it for the prosecutor, but the joke would be on me: without charges, there is no court of law—whatever court of law remained in this country. Allow me to rephrase it: on which circumstances were you detained?"

Max puffed out his cheeks. "My wife and I, we were trying to cross into Hungary."

"Only, it isn't Austria any longer but Ostmark." The faceless inmate appeared to be well informed on the current state of affairs. "A German province with no autonomous power. Why were you running?"

Max considered his response for a moment. "I'm Max Laub," he said at length.

"*Ach*," his interlocutor said with a mirthless chuckle. "You're not a prisoner then, you're a hostage."

A moment passed, during which Max was taking in the man's verdict. "A hostage," he repeated, opening his eyes to the stark reality of his surroundings: the dimly lit cell, a small window barred with iron preventing any semblance of freedom. Outside, he could hear the distant sounds of the city—life continuing, unaware of, or perhaps unconcerned by the turmoil behind the prison walls. He sank down onto the hard bed, his mind racing. "What was your crime against the state?" he asked his invisible neighbor.

"I quoted directly from the Bible."

"Is that a crime now too?" Max suddenly felt very tired, his head a dead weight in his hands.

"Not if one cherry-picks what the regime likes to hear." The same soft chuckle, oddly comforting in this drab, cold place. "Let me clarify: on the first day when Hitler was installed as Chancellor, I delivered a radio address to the German public. You're a Catholic, if I remember correctly?"

"I am, yes."

"So, you know your Bible. Can you tell me who God warned against worshipping?"

"False idols, for the devil is behind them."

"And what's the word for a false idol?"

"*Verführer*." Max discovered that he was grinning. "*Führer*, the leader. *Verführer*, the seducer. The devil." Chuckling, he shook his head at the brilliance of it. At the simple logic of it. "No wonder they arrested you. How long have you been here, Father?"

"About five years now," the man responded.

Blood draining from his face, Max stared at the hole in the wall. *Five years.* He had built an entire new life in America in those five years. Five years might as well have been an eternity. Would he ever see Aurelia again? Would he ever come out of here?

"Don't despair, Herr Laub." His prison block neighbor must have sensed his anguish. "Not all is yet lost."

"How can you say that?" Max's hollow, bitter laugh echoed around the small rectangle he would call his home for the next few years—or decades. "We're stuck here like rats in a trap."

"That's one way to see the situation. One can always curl up and die. But one can also live and resist the evil by sharing his light with those who need it most."

"Easy for you to say," Max grumbled. "You're a priest."

"A minister," the man corrected him seemingly without taking offense. "But it's of no matter. You can be an atheist for all I care, so long as you keep being purposely, defiantly *good*."

"Good?" Max repeated.

"In the times of darkness enveloping the world, the smallest spark of empathy, love, friendship, sacrifice or kindness is considered resistance. We aren't powerless, Herr Laub. Even here, we can make a difference."

Max felt surprisingly uplifted on hearing the minister's words. He would not let the regime break him, he would find a way to outlast the darkness that threatened to consume him.

As he sat in the cold silence of his cell, a fiery resolve began to kindle in his chest. He would survive this, not just for himself, but for Aurelia, and for the art that still burned within him.

THIRTY-SEVEN

Paris, France

The streets of Paris, once a symphony of life and art, now felt like a haunting melody played in a minor key. Aurelia moved through the city with a heavy heart, her spirit weighed down by the oppressive atmosphere that had descended upon the French capital. It was June 1940, and the echoes of the recent capitulation still reverberated through the cobblestone streets, mingling with the whispers of despair and defeat that lingered in the air.

As she walked, the remnants of Parisian elegance clashed grotesquely with the harsh reality of occupation. Boulevards once vibrant with laughter and the clinking of wine glasses were now lined with German soldiers, their sharp uniforms in stark contrast to the delicate architecture of the city. Aurelia's heart twisted at the sight, each soldier a painful reminder of her forced complicity in a regime that threatened to suffocate all that she held dear.

Officially, she had been summoned to Paris by the Propaganda Ministry, tasked with creating films that would glorify the Nazi regime and its conquest of France. Unofficially, her presence here was her half-brother's doing. Each frame she captured felt like a dagger driven into her conscience, a betrayal of her art and everything she had ever believed in. But as long as Max remained a hostage in Tegel prison, she had no choice but to comply. The thought of her husband languishing behind bars haunted her every waking moment.

"Cheer up, little sister," Wilhelm had told her on the train trip here, as he was busy pouring champagne into their respective glasses. "You'll be filming history itself. Who else can brag of such a thing?"

"Where's my letter?" she had demanded instead, her eyes sheer murder.

In the privacy of the luxurious compartment they shared, Wilhelm had pulled out an envelope from the inner pocket of his uniform. Recognizing her husband's handwriting, she had reached across the folding table between them, only for him to snatch it just out of her reach. He kept teasing her with it several times until she slammed her palms into the table, sending one of the glasses tumbling to the floor.

"Give it to me!"

He had surrendered at last with drunken laughter—*fine, have it, don't get yourself all worked up*—before reminding her to be on her best behavior while in Paris. Her husband's well-being depended on it.

"As if I could forget."

"This is not some *Wehrmacht* recruitment ad you've been filming for Goebbels for the past couple of years." Wilhelm's voice had been low and cold, just like his grip on her wrist. "I've arranged for you to follow Hitler and his entourage around with your camera. After Paris fell within weeks thanks to the army I have built, he loves me like a fucking son and I won't have you spoiling it with your loose tongue and the dirty glances you like to throw. After I'm the *Führer*, after you get your Laub back, do it all you like. But not now, not when so much is at stake. Understood?"

Understood? Wilhelm's eyes seemed to warn her once again as she fell into step with her half-brother and a small entourage following Adolf Hitler on his tour of the city. The *Führer*, flanked by his inner circle, seemed to revel in the spectacle of his victory, a puppet master delighting in the destruction of a great city. Aurelia raised her camera, her stomach churning as he strode through the famous Arc de Triomphe, his presence a spit in the face of the proud nation. She felt nauseous, her skin prickling with a mixture of anger and revulsion. She had grown used to watching the dictator over the past few years, though never quite so close, always with a camera lens separating them, sanitizing the relationship to that of an impartial photographer and an object to capture. But now, forced into Hitler's immediate orbit, Aurelia couldn't help but stare at him with a naked eye and wonder how a human being could be born to be so vile, so full of poison. Earlier that day, just before the French surrender was signed in the same train car as the 1918 Armistice, at the same Compiègne Forest, she'd watched him clamber atop the black granite slab commemorating the Allied victory and read its inscription with eyes full of pure hatred and disgust. He had no respect for his valiant adversaries or memorial commemorating their sacrifices. He had ordered to drape the Alsace-Lorraine memorial, with its defeated German eagle pierced by the Allied sword, in swastika flags so as not to offend his delicate senses and later to dynamite it along with all other war memorials. The man was not only a sore loser, but a sore winner no matter how ridiculous it seemed. Even with France at his feet he could feel no joy in "restoring Germany to its former greatness." It was Aurelia's profound conviction that he simply wasn't capable of joy—or empathy or gratitude or generosity for that matter. Of anything making a human, human.

And now the grandeur of Paris—its historic monuments, its art, its very soul—was eclipsed by the dark shadow of tyranny created in his image. As they passed the Champs-Élysées, Aurelia caught a glimpse of the once-bustling cafés, now eerily silent, their patrons replaced by the stoic faces of German officers.

With each click of her camera, she felt like a traitor to her own people, a betrayer of the very art that had defined her existence. Each photograph she took was a moment captured, but it was a moment that now belonged to the oppressor, a fragment of beauty twisted into a tool of manipulation. She longed to destroy the images she had taken, to unearth the truth buried beneath the propaganda, but the reality was that she was trapped, her artistry commandeered by a regime that demanded compliance.

As the tour continued, Aurelia's thoughts drifted to Max, locked away and helpless. She imagined him standing in their old bedroom in Grünewald, the walls adorned with their shared dreams and the remnants of their life together. She could almost hear his voice, the way he spoke of stories yet to be told, of films yet to be made. In her mind's eye, she saw him smile, a glimmer of hope that felt impossibly far away.

What she wouldn't give to be by his side—in jail, anywhere, as long as they were together. Instead, each click of the camera felt like a betrayal, and with every shutter release, she felt a piece of herself wither away.

Wilhelm, the self-appointed art connoisseur, wouldn't have been Wilhelm if he hadn't suggested an art museum to be included in the tour.

"I fear the Louvre is a bit of a mess at the moment," he explained to Hitler, whose small eyes glimmered from under the visor of his military cap. Even victorious, in Paris, he still managed to appear sour and discontent. Aurelia snapped his picture. Let future generations see what a lack of a soul does to a person's face. "The French whisked half of it away, but this gallery—"

"I have no use for galleries," Hitler said loftily. "And particularly French ones. All they harbor is the sort of degenerate art we've thankfully purged from Germany. I suggest you do the same here," he added, gesturing with his gloved hand in Wilhelm's general direction. "Go through it and see if there's anything useful there. If there is, bring it to Berlin. Speer has plans to build a grand museum to exhibit all great Aryan art, from all over Europe."

"And the rest?" Wilhelm asked.

"Burn it."

With that, the tour concluded—for Hitler, at least. Apparently, he'd seen all he wanted to see. Looking just as annoyed, he climbed into his car and drove off with his personal guard, leaving the rest of his entourage to their devices.

"Well, I'm still going in for a quick inspection." Wilhelm cleared his throat, recovering himself. It couldn't have been easy for him, hiding his emotion at such an offhand dismissal by some former lowly corporal he detested, but this was what he had signed up for, Aurelia thought to herself. "Anyone up for a tour before we head to The Ritz?"

It was either the promise of champagne or the idea that it was best to be on Minister von Brandenburg's good side after his victorious conquer of the capital, but no one peeled away from the group.

THIRTY-EIGHT

The air in the museum was cool and still, the hushed reverence of the space amplifying the weight of history that surrounded Aurelia. Following Wilhelm, she wandered through the grand halls, her senses dulled by the oppressive atmosphere that had settled over Paris. Before her camera, traces of the chaotic evacuation revealed themselves: some exhibits had been taken down but remained standing by the walls, still in their frames, open crates stacked nearby. Those that hadn't been touched hung like silent witnesses to the turmoil of the present, their colors vibrant against the dark tapestry of occupation. Aurelia's heart ached as she passed the masterpieces, recognizing the famous names and unmistakable brushstrokes.

Burn it, the hideous, blasé verdict singed like a brand in the back of her mind. The failed, talentless artist, condemning century-defining pieces to a pyre out of sheer envy and spite.

"Matisse." Reichsführer Himmler squinted through his thick lenses at the name of the artist.

Aurelia caught Wilhelm's expressive glance—*can you believe that idiot had to read the plaque to deduce who painted the* Joy of Life? Even Goebbels drew his eyes skywards.

"A three-year-old could have painted better. The French must indeed drink too much if this is the so-called art they decide to display in their galleries. Take it off the wall right now," Himmler ordered in disgust, motioning to two SS men of his personal security detail as he groped for his ceremonial dagger. "It'll be my pleasure to make the first slash before sending it to the pyre outside, where it belongs."

"*Reichsführer...*" Wilhelm physically positioned himself in front of the much-too-eager SS guards. "With all due respect, there is a process to follow. My agency, together with the Propaganda Ministry, will need to properly catalog the entire contents before sorting them. And condemned pieces ought always to be photographed—for the history books so that our youth can better appreciate our efforts in purging the world of such filth."

With a shrug, Himmler surrendered—to Aurelia's great relief. She couldn't stand the sight of her half-brother, but at that moment, she was grateful for his self-serving interest in art. Certainly, he would never burn the work but hoard it until it was safe to sell it, but at least the irreplaceable piece would survive. She could live with that much.

"Herr Minister, if I may."

Swinging round to the sound of the melodic voice, Aurelia stood stock-still at the sight of a familiar face—Zara, her childhood friend, standing just a few feet away, her hands deftly adjusting the lighting.

"If it's not too forward, I would suggest to go a step further." Zara shifted her frank, alert gaze from Wilhelm to Goebbels and back, a sure smile on her face. "You could organize an entire exhibit out of this degenerate art. A traveling exhibit, so not only the students but all the people of Germany could see it for themselves."

"Displaying this filth?" Himmler regarded the gallerist as if she had just said something entirely moronic. "Instead of burning it? And... who are you, at any rate? You aren't French."

"I'm Zara Whitby. I used to own galleries in Germany but was forced to close them due to my husband's insistence. He all but held me hostage in the United States, but as soon as our brave troops crossed the French border, I knew I just couldn't sit idly when my country needed me. I left everything I owned in New York and came here with only the clothes on my back and my old German passport—if Germany will still have me, of course."

Aurelia's breath caught in her throat, disbelief washing over her. *Zara? Here? In the heart of the occupation? Spouting this nonsense?*

Yet, here she stood, her childhood friend, all dignified humility, hands folded modestly as she awaited their verdict.

Wilhelm, his brain likely already calculating just how much money he could make out of such a connection, was the first to take a step forward and gather Zara's hands in his. "Frau Whitby, Germany always welcomes its children—and particularly such outstanding ones. Gentlemen," he said, addressing the rest of the group, "for those of you unfamiliar with Frau Whitby, she's a well-known expert in modern art and will certainly make a wonderful addition to our department of visual arts. I can recommend her services personally as I have known her family for quite a number of years. The von Neumann family—which is Frau Whitby's maiden name—are still our neighbors." The group's guarded expressions turned to smiles at such a glowing recommendation and the fact that the elegant brunette with an English name turned out to be one of their own—and one with pedigree at that. "My sister and Frau Whitby grew up together and I truly couldn't have imagined a happier reunion here, in Paris of all places. Welcome home, dearest Zara!"

Aurelia quickly masked her astonishment, adopting a nonchalant demeanor as she approached. "Zara," she said, feigning ignorance, "what a surprise to see you here! I didn't expect to find you in Paris."

Zara's expression, as she took Aurelia's hand in hers, remained unreadable. "Aurelia, it's been a long time."

"Yes, it has," Aurelia replied, searching her old friend's face. The moment felt surreal, a collision of past and present that she was unprepared for. Zara's presence was a reminder of a time when life had been filled with possibility, untainted by the shadows of war. When it was four of them instead of just two. When she and Zara laughed hysterically as Max and James tried to drunk-teach each other English and German. When Zara wore her hair in a short straight pageboy cut instead of styling it in soft, feminine locks. When they got into mischief together, cackling as they took obscene photos in front of the SA propaganda truck and running along the streets they still called their own instead of being reduced to hunted shadows of their past selves.

They exchanged pleasantries, but Aurelia could sense the weight behind Zara's smile. The sparkle in her friend's eyes was dimmed, replaced by a steely determination that spoke volumes about the choices she had made. They parted ways and Aurelia followed the group out, feeling more confused than ever.

Later that evening, unable to shake off the encounter, Aurelia returned to the museum. The dim lights cast long shadows across the marble floors. The air felt charged, as if the very walls were holding their breath. Whatever motives Zara had for coming here, she needed to know. She hadn't seen her friend for years, true, and people did change, but Zara would never leave James. Yet, here she was.

Here she was...

Zara appeared from behind a large canvas, her expression shifting from surprise to guarded acceptance as she recognized Aurelia. "You came back," she said, her voice low, reverberating in the quiet space.

"I had to see you," Aurelia replied, her heart pounding. "Can we talk?"

Zara measured her coolly with her dark eyes. "I suppose." She motioned for Aurelia to follow her outside. In the small courtyard, away from any metaphorical ears in the walls, Zara produced a pack of local French cigarettes and offered Aurelia one.

"What are you doing here, really?" Aurelia asked once they lit up.

"Same as you." Zara shrugged. "Doing my patriotic duty."

Her poker face, which Aurelia had always found unmatched, was beginning to grate on her nerves.

"I'm not here because of some idiotic patriotic—" With an annoyed huff, Aurelia exhaled away from Zara's face and poured the truth out to her, beginning with the Anschluss and the arrest at the border. "My *Arschloch* of a brother is holding Max hostage in jail. You can imagine what will happen if I don't cooperate. Now, why are you here? Last time I checked, James was safe and sound, across the ocean."

Zara's gaze softened despite her dark brow knitting in concern. "I didn't know about Max. Your press reported that you both returned to Germany of your own volition. Max had to retire to some resort due to his health issues, where you visit him regularly, and as soon as he's well enough, you'll be working together again for the prosperity of the Reich."

"What?!" Aurelia found herself at a loss for words. All she could do was stand and blink at her old friend, pale as ash, the cigarette trembling lightly in her hand.

"Where are they holding him?" Zara asked softly.

"Tegel."

Zara blew the smoke out of her nostrils as she uttered a curse under her breath. "Some resort. I'm sorry."

"Thank you."

With a sigh, Zara glanced around, ensuring they were still alone. "I couldn't sit idly in New York while everything was falling apart here. When the rumors of war began to swirl, I felt compelled to act." Her words were steady, but the underlying pain was palpable. "When I arrived in Paris, I offered the French to evacuate their most valuable pieces to the south of the country. We believed we had enough time to get them aboard a ship sailing from Marseilles. The plan was to get them away from the Nazis and store them in my galleries in America until it was safe to bring them back, but..." She gestured around, indicating the occupying forces that had swept through the country faster than anyone could have predicted and all the art which was still, tellingly, here.

Aurelia breathed a sigh of relief and caught Zara's hand in hers, chiding herself for allowing even a shadow of doubt on her best friend's account. "And now? You're stuck?" she whispered, stroking the back of Zara's hand with her thumb sympathetically. How well she understood her predicament. "What's the plan?"

Zara's jaw tightened, determination etched into her features. "There is no plan. I'll have to play it by ear from now on. Today was the test. Your brother seems to be on board."

"Sure he is," Aurelia hissed. "He remembers how much money you made him for saving Art's paintings. He doesn't care why you're here, all he sees is dollar signs."

"Fine by me. People without principles are much easier to deal with. If he continues to cooperate, I'll remain here in Paris as a guardian, cataloging and tracing everything that Germany will most definitely confiscate. It's not much, but it's something."

The weight of these words bore down on Aurelia. "You're sure you don't want to leave? You still can."

"I know," Zara replied, her voice steady but tinged with vulnerability. "But you've seen what can happen if one high-ranking *Arschloch* is too pyre-happy. If I have Wilhelm's and your boss Goebbels' ear, together we can just keep these treasures safe. I'll go into the pyre myself before I let them burn Matisse. So, no. To answer your question, I just can't leave."

Aurelia felt a swell of emotion at her fierce resolve. "I missed you so much, Zar-zar."

The childhood nickname brought the warmest of smiles to Zara's face. She pulled Aurelia toward herself and buried her nose in the folds of her trench coat. "I missed you too, Li-li. Though I'm still mad you traded me for that other brunette—whatever her name was."

Her hands around her best friend, who was more blood than her own brother, Aurelia chuckled softly, inhaling full lungs of Zara's perfume. "Don't be. Leni meant nothing to me, I've always loved you the best."

Wiping her face with the back of her hand, Zara pushed her away with a playful swat. "Quit your clowning about before someone arrests us for 'unnatural' relations."

"They only arrest men for that."

"Why not women?"

"They need women out in the open to breed, lesbians or not. The Nazis don't need a woman's consent to impregnate her for the glory of the Reich." Disgusted, Aurelia spat on the ground.

As did Zara. "Back to the barricades then, old comrade?" she asked, outstretching her hand—just like Aurelia had done decades ago before they had set off on the quest to liberate the von Neumann farmers' piglets.

Aurelia shook it with great emotion. "To the barricades."

In that moment, she rediscovered the threads of her past entwined with the present. Evil persisted but so too would they —until victory or death, whichever came first.

"*Vive la résistance.*"

THIRTY-NINE

Theresienstadt, German-occupied Czechoslovakia.
Summer 1942

The sun beat down mercilessly as Max stepped off the transport train. After spending several years behind the fortress-like walls of Tegel prison, the sense of sudden freedom—even if such freedom meant climbing aboard a train going devil knew where —had gone straight to his head. He still swayed on his feet slightly, taking in his surroundings. Not a prison, but a small town opened up in front of him, oddly quaint, despite the presence of barbed wire around the perimeter and the omnipresent eyes of the guards. As more and more people poured out of the transport, the air grew thick with the scent of despair, mingling with the dusty remnants of a life once lived in freedom.

"This is it, ladies and gentlemen," one of their SS guards announced with the slap of a riding crop against the palm of his hand. "Theresienstadt ghetto. Last stop. Make yourselves at home."

His underlings guffawed as if they were in on the jest. Soon,

Max would see for himself the reason for such mirth on the part of the SS.

As they lined up for processing at the gates of the ghetto, Max felt a familiar presence beside him. It was Friedrich Wenz, the Lutheran minister he had befriended during their time in Tegel prison, but whom Max had only seen for the first time two days ago when the guards urged them out of the cells and into the trains. It was Wenz, with his gentle demeanor and unwavering faith, who had made Tegel tolerable. He, and Aurelia's parcels—with food, clothing, cigarettes, and books—kept Max from losing his mind and fashioning a noose out of a towel. Throughout the four years of his incarceration, she'd only been allowed to visit him twice—under a guard's supervision, for an hour, on opposite sides of a table screwed to the concrete floor. Max had refused to wash his hands for days afterwards in order to keep the faintest traces of her perfume on his skin.

"Hmm," Wenz cleared his throat, pushing his glasses back onto the bridge of his nose. "What do you think, old fellow, have they transported us here by mistake?"

"What do you mean?" Max asked, shifting a pillowcase serving as a suitcase from one hand to another.

"Look at our fellow travelers' attire," Wenz motioned his head toward the family, all bearing the same mark with a yellow star on their chest. "From what I heard, Theresienstadt is a Jewish ghetto."

"I'm half-Jewish." Max shrugged.

"I'm not. And they didn't put a star on you, so to them, you're not either." Wenz chuckled as the line moved closer toward local officials of sorts. Seated on folding chairs at small tables, they were busy taking down the new arrivals' information before directing them someplace else. "I've been telling you that for years, but you still won't get it into your head: you're here not because of your poor mother. You're here because you're a political hostage and as long as it pays to keep you alive, you shall be alive."

Indeed, the SS appeared mighty confused when Max's and Wenz's turn came to produce the temporary traveling papers issued at Tegel. For some time, they quarreled among themselves about putting gentiles together with Jews, then motioned for Max and Wenz to step aside while they sorted the mistake out. Someone went to call someone else, only to return with yet another paper.

"No mistake has been made," the SS man announced. "You, Jew-copper," he called to one of the civilian ghetto officials with an armband bearing a blue star on his bicep. Max bristled at the speed with which the man scrambled to his feet with a servile expression on his face. "Take a few of your people and clean out this barracks here," he barked, shoving the paper into the ghetto official's shaking hands. "These two are the first ones. There will be more of them arriving and they must have their own quarters so as not to mix with you, Jew scum."

Max, having never been witness to such blatant disrespect—the official, with his wise eyes of an intellectual, was old enough to be the SS pup's father—was just about to open his mouth and protest. However, Wenz's hand clasped around his wrist like a vise, saving him from a beating he had no idea he was close to.

"Apologies for our ignorance, gentlemen," Wenz's melodic voice, designed for the pulpit, drowned out whatever Max was about to say. "But could you perhaps explain to us just where exactly we are and what is expected of us? I am well aware that each place of confinement has its own set of rules and I would hate to even consider breaking any of them by mistake."

"No need to apologize, Father," the SS man's attitude, so vicious just moments ago, changed as though by magic at the sight of Wenz's ministerial white collar. "This here is the Theresienstadt ghetto. Lots of Jews, the good kind," he added, wrinkling his nose, unhappy with the term but unable to come up with anything better, "our own, German ones, they have Iron Crosses from the Great War and all that. Army veterans, you understand?"

Wenz nodded.

"Well, the higher-ups thought it unseemly putting them together with those Eastern Jews in those other ghettos. And now that we have transports from Holland and France—those Jews are not like Soviet ones, surely, you agree—at any rate, a place for them was needed. And also for those prominent ones as well, the artists and musicians and writers and such-like. I'm not quite sure why you're here, the clergy—"

"I quoted the Bible on the radio," Wenz supplied with a disarming smile.

The SS man, who must have been religious, to his own chagrin cleared his throat and averted his eyes. "Yes, well... I don't decide these things, but it's a good barracks they're cleaning out for you. And the ghetto itself, it's quite all right, too. We have a library, a concert hall, a playground for the children. A school, a hospital, some shops even. It's better than in other places; trust me, I've been. I know."

He was smiling his stupid smile as he praised the ghetto into which the government he served was presently herding war heroes and it took Max all of his self-control not to slap it off his stupid, stupid face.

In the days that followed the grim reality of their circumstances settled over Max like a shroud, suffocating and inescapable. He spotted familiar figures, artists, and intellectuals, their spirits dulled but not entirely extinguished; made friends with deportees from all over Europe. All of them had known the vibrancy of life outside these walls and now they were trapped in a grotesque parody of existence. But about one thing the SS guard was right: the ghetto was indeed not so bad. Max rediscovered comradeship here; he drank the pitiful reminder of a civil life thriving against all odds in this truly strange place like the rarest of wines. In the midst of the bleakness, slowly he began to carve out a semblance of purpose.

In the evenings, he and Wenz gathered with small groups of fellow prisoners in hidden corners of the ghetto, sharing stories, laughter, and the remnants of their fading hopes. They formed a makeshift community, a refuge within the confines of their bleak new abode. Max, with his passion for storytelling, often led these gatherings, weaving tales that transported them to a world beyond the barbed wire.

One evening, as the sun dipped below the horizon, casting long shadows across the ghetto, Max sat before a group of children, their young faces weary, their eyes reflecting a mixture of longing and despair. Their beloved teacher had just passed away from a fever and the Jewish council couldn't find a substitute in time. Max hadn't the faintest idea of what to do with children—he had never had his own and neither did he have to work with them on his sets—but when one of the council members pleaded with him, he just couldn't say no.

He was writing down numbers on the wall serving the makeshift class as a blackboard and wondering what good math would do these tiny mites—Count all the bread they weren't getting? Or the centimeters they were lacking according to the old growth charts in the parody of a hospital where people went to die instead of getting better?—when from behind his back a teeny voice called out, breaking through the heaviness of the air: "Tell us a story, Herr Laub."

Max half-turned, unsure, but smiled at the ocean of the saddest eyes ever produced by the world, which tore at his very heart. "A story?"

"Yes," a little girl, her dark hair in neat braids, said from behind the table she shared with another. "*Vati* always talks about your stories when he comes back home to the barrack."

"My stories?" Max repeated, at a loss.

"Yes. About the city of angels where the sun always shines and where palms grow taller than the tallest building in Berlin. And about the desert with the pink sand and Indians who dance in front of the fire at night and cowboys who jump off their horse and right on top of the train..."

Her voice trailed off, but Max's smile only grew, the warmth of connection swelling within him. Those weren't stories, they were descriptions of different sets he had visited in that old life of his which had long since ceased feeling like his own. Who would have thought that sharing them with the local folk at their little gatherings was making this little girl get through her dismal, hopeless days?

"A story then? Very well," he said, putting the chalk away. "Once upon a time, but not that long ago, in a land far, far away, there lived a brave Navajo chief whose name was Running Horse. The land on which he lived was all thriving green pastures to the east for the Navajo horses and sheep to graze and the tallest mountains to the north that only the Navajo could navigate. To the west, the endless ocean rolled over the white-sand beaches under the sun that shone bright and warm every single day. Running Horse's people tended their sheep and crops, but they took particular pride in the peach orchards they had cultivated for years, which yielded the softest, most delicious fruits that were like a feather to touch, yet melted on one's tongue like sun-infused sugar."

Max swallowed, losing himself momentarily in his reminiscing of the days when he could stop at a fruit stand on his way home from work and buy one of those peaches and bite into its supple flesh as he watched the sun dipping into the Pacific Ocean from the porch of his house on Beverly Hills. Was it ever real or just a fever dream, and was this his reality? This nightmarish existence, from one gaol to another until he wasn't needed anymore...

With the sheer power of his will, he tossed his head, grounding himself in the moment. It had just now occurred to him how much the room had transformed in the eyes of the children fixated on him, the walls of the ghetto fading away, replaced by the vibrant landscapes of his imagination.

"But then one day, a commander came from the east with his army and saw the beautiful land on which the Navajo lived. He wanted it for himself and for his people and so he gave Running Horse a choice: to abandon the land and leave with his people or to be killed by a superior force. Running Horse held council with his people for all decisions were made by the entire tribe, not just the chief himself. Should they pick up and leave or stay and fight?"

"Stay and fight!" one of the children called and was instantly supported by his classmates' cheers.

Trying to hide a smile and failing miserably, Max continued, "They decided to stay and fight." More cheers; more smiles than he'd ever seen on those little ones' faces. "Now, the army commander, whose name was—"

"Hitler!" the girl who had asked for the story suggested.

Max shrugged after a moment's consideration. Why not Hitler? It was befitting enough. "As soon as the war was declared, Hitler ordered his men to slaughter the Navajo's sheep and horses and burn all of their crops so that they would starve to death and freeze without the wool their sheep always supplied."

"Like us," another young boy mumbled quietly, poking his entire fist through a hole in his woolen vest, which was all but coming apart.

"Yes," Max acknowledged with a sigh. Perhaps, he should have told a fairy tale instead, not an actual history he had heard firsthand from those very Navajo now working as stuntmen on Hollywood sets—if they were fortunate enough to secure such a position. Most had to make do as stagehands and only if a producer didn't mind them being there. "But even then, Running Horse refused to surrender. After taking the women and children to the mountains, he and his men began to plan how to fight back and defeat Hitler and his soldiers. The trouble was, they weren't warring people. All they had for weapons were bows and arrows, with which they hunted small prey, whereas Hitler and his men had guns and bullets. But Running Horse had a plan..."

Just then, the mothers came to fetch their children: after a long laborious day, they could finally have their first real meal, no matter how laughable the rations.

"Off you run." Max shooed his new students with a warm smile despite their protests. "Running Horse is going nowhere, we'll finish the story tomorrow."

Only after the room had emptied out and Max was about to head out himself did a shadow peel off the doorframe. It was Wenz.

"You, my friend, have a most marvelous gift," he said quietly, clapping Max on his back. "All that those children have seen their entire lives is sorrow, hunger, and persecution. And you remind them that hope lives in the stories we tell. This is what I meant when we spoke on that very first day of your arrival in Tegel. Keep spreading light even in the darkest of times. Don't you ever stop doing that."

FORTY

Ukraine, USSR. Summer 1942

The sun hung high in the sky over the Eastern Front, casting a harsh light on the devastation that stretched as far as the eye could see. Aurelia stood at the edge of the war-torn village in her *Propagandakompanie* uniform, her heart pounding in her chest as she adjusted the strap of her camera. The air was thick with the acrid smell of smoke, mingled with the distant echoes of gunfire and the cries of the wounded. When she had volunteered as a war correspondent for Germany, during the *Führer's* birthday celebration she'd been forced to attend, Wilhelm had outright rejected the idea. He had plans for his "little sister" for after the war and the risk of her being killed by a stray bullet would ruin them. However, Hitler and Goebbels had both displayed quite an enthusiasm for their best cinematographer to travel to the front: it would boost the troops' morale and the pictures and films she'd produce glorifying the victorious German forces would inspire people on the home front.

"She's a woman." Wilhelm had desperately grasped for straws against the superior force. "The German army isn't equipped to accommodate a woman within its ranks, not even the Propaganda Company, which is essentially still Wehrmacht, only with cameras and notebooks in addition to guns. Where would she sleep? Where would she shower? In their barracks?"

Reichsführer Himmler had waved his concerns off as the SS waiter in his white tailcoat refilled his champagne glass. "The SS will be more than happy to accommodate Fräulein von Brandenburg. She can travel with one of our *Einsatzgruppen*, behind the actual frontline; I assure you, she'll be more than safe there. My men will see to it. As for the living quarters, *Einsatzgruppen* are ordinarily stationed in towns or villages, but at any rate, Fräulein von Brandenburg will have plenty of room of her own, in the most suitable quarters for a woman of her status."

"Thank you, *Reichsführer*." Aurelia had produced a smile worthy of the Oscar her husband once held in his hands. "I promise to do anything within my power to make my country proud."

"I wish my *Feldmarschalls* could boast the same attitude instead of '*warring on two fronts is disadvantageous, we ought to subdue the English first, Napoleon's example showed us why one shouldn't wage war with Russia*,'" Hitler had jested, instantly triggering a round of servile chuckles around the table.

Aurelia had laughed too, almost genuinely when she saw her brother gritting his teeth on the opposite side of the table.

"I don't know what new scheme you've got into your head now," he told her on catching her alone after dinner, "just like your little friend in Paris, but I'm watching you both very closely. Don't forget where I have your husband."

"Come, Wilhelm," Aurelia had countered, smiling at him sweetly. "Just what could I possibly do at the front except take my photos? Run off to join the partisans? I'm too old and lazy for that. I couldn't live in a forest. I like my late mornings and breakfast in bed; you know that much—you're like that yourself."

She hadn't lied when she claimed the plan only to take photos—that's precisely what she was doing. Except Aurelia had omitted the fact that she was keeping copies of certain photos for herself. While sending photos of victorious German troops to Goebbels and more nefarious pictures of the SS death squads executing innocent civilians en masse to Himmler, she was slowly gathering evidence of all the crimes she witnessed. So far, Germany had been winning on all fronts. Europe was one mass grave, brutalized and laid to waste. But such evil couldn't possibly sustain itself. Soon, justice would prevail and when that day came, she would be ready.

All Jews and anyone holding a position in the Communist Party are ordered to present themselves with their paperwork at the Kommandantur *at 1200 sharp.* A sign in both German and Russian came into focus in the frame of Aurelia's Leica.

All around, buildings lay in ruins, their charred remains standing as hollow sentinels to the lives that had once filled them. The ground was littered with debris—broken furniture, shattered glass, and the remnants of lives abruptly interrupted. Aurelia felt her very heart ache at the sight, but she steeled herself, knowing she had to capture the truth that lay beneath the surface.

She moved cautiously through the wreckage, her camera poised and ready. With each click of the shutter, she documented the devastation, the faces of the local civilian population lining up in front of the lone surviving building with the swastika flag mounted on its roof. They were frightened of the Germans but even more terrified of what the Germans would do if they defied them. The men were mostly silent, detached from reality in their helplessness. Children huddled together, their eyes wide and frightened, while mothers clutched their little ones, tears streaming down their cheeks. A few called to

Aurelia in a language that wasn't quite German but very similar —"Please, *gnädige Frau*, you must be a mother yourself..."—only to receive a backhanded slap from one of the SS men maintaining order.

"Quit your swine language, you Jew sow! How dare you address an Aryan woman without being spoken to! Insolent Jew-bitch! I'll show you how to mind your manners!"

Aurelia walked away hastily, self-loathing rising together with blood in her burning cheeks. It was because of her that a woman was being beaten and she couldn't do a damned thing to help her without revealing herself. Best to stay away from people altogether then. Best to cut her hair and hide her face behind the uniform cap's visor so that they didn't recognize her as a woman any longer.

An SS barber stared at her in mute horror, his scissors frozen in the air as she let her long, golden tresses down, but there was nothing doing. He obliged her that very day, so that the next morning she could set off after the column of Jewish women—out of the village and into the open field. Before too long, a great, deep trench appeared like a gash in the fertile soil: the Jewish men had been digging all night. As Aurelia stepped closer, she saw their bodies filling the mass grave they'd been forced to dig for themselves. At least they didn't have to see their families die.

But the women saw them, and their anguish rose in a communal wail aimed at the mockingly blue sky and the indifferent god in it. Aurelia's breath hitched in her throat, a knot forming in her stomach. She could feel the darkness of the SS death squad's actions creeping into her own soul, threatening to suffocate her. But if there was nothing she could do to save these people, she could at least document it all—to keep their memories alive, to make their murderers pay for their crimes... to warn future generations of the horrors that follow a murderer's ascent to power.

The death of thousands around her didn't begin with the death squads.

It began with a far-right newspaper calling all Jews filthy rats.

It began with regular Germans hearing SA men sing songs about Jewish blood running off their bayonets and saying nothing in order to keep the peace.

It began with police dismissing a free press editor's complaint against the SA thugs that ransacked his office and beat him up and the judge refusing to side with the newspaper because he wished to keep his job.

It began with the dismissal of the officials who criticized the government and the public that shrugged it off.

It began with Hitler and his followers calling Jews criminals and rapists and agitating for their deportation.

It proceeded with racial laws forbidding an "Aryan" man to marry his Jewish fiancée.

It proceeded with the arrests and imprisonment of the men whose crime was loving each other.

It proceeded with the SS removing Jewish citizens from their homes as their neighbors watched indifferently or cheered.

It proceeded with the clergy filling prison cells because they dared to preach Jesus's love and forgiveness when it was Hitler who was the only god Germans needed.

It proceeded with the euthanasia program to rid society of its disabled population that didn't contribute anything and therefore didn't deserve to live.

It proceeded with concentration camps, torture, and war.

It began with a whisper and ended with a gunshot—into a defenseless mother's back who, even in her last moments, was still trying to shield her child from imminent death.

Tears blurring her vision, Aurelia photographed it all. She forced herself to remain composed, to maintain her facade as a loyal correspondent, while inside, her heart burned with rage.

"Congratulations," one SS soldier jeered, gesturing a boy of barely twelve toward the mass grave into which his mother and baby sister had just tumbled. "You're officially the last Jew of Zarechye. This is quite an occasion, which calls for commemoration!" He pulled a bottle from his comrade's hands—they always drank, the death squads, crates of alcohol following them whenever they went on Reichsführer Himmler's orders—and shoved it into the boy's hands. "Come on! *Prost!* Drink to the victory of the Reich and smile into the camera."

With trembling hands, Aurelia aimed the camera at the child at the same time the SS man raised his rifle to his shoulder.

A snap. A gunshot—and there was no more Jews left in Zarechye.

As night fell, Aurelia lay in her cot, her heart longing for Max as it always did at this hour of silence. She wondered how he was faring in Theresienstadt, whether he was safe, whether he had to face his own share of terrors he would never recover from. The darkness of the night seemed to echo the uncertainty of their lives, a reminder that the world they had known was slipping further away with each passing day.

But even in that darkness, Aurelia felt her blood burn with purpose. She would document the truth, no matter the cost. She would ensure that the stories of those suffering would not be forgotten, that they would one day rise from the ashes of this nightmare.

In the days that followed, Aurelia immersed herself in her work, capturing the grim realities of the war. With each photograph, she felt the weight of her mission grow heavier, yet she pressed on, determined to expose the truth.

She was not just a witness, she was a voice for those who couldn't speak.

FORTY-ONE

Theresienstadt ghetto, German-occupied Czechoslovakia.
Fall 1943

Max stood in the center of the dimly lit room that had been hastily converted into a makeshift studio. The oppressive walls of Theresienstadt loomed around him, reminding of the horrors that surrounded him. He could feel the weight of despair pressing down on him, the specter of suffering hanging in the air like a thick fog.

"Well? What do you say to that?" The ghetto *Kommandant*, Obersturmführer Burger, asked Max, slapping the professional film camera as if it were the flank of a running horse. "Neat, eh?"

Max had heard that Burger loved his drink, but surely he couldn't have been inebriated to the point of constructing a film set in the middle of a ghetto as a joke?

"It's... nice," Max ventured cautiously.

"Just nice?" Burger raised his brow, hitching the belt with his service pistol on it. "I thought you'd pounce on the idea of getting back to it."

"To... what precisely, *Herr Kommandant*?" Max prodded politely, still confused to the utmost.

"Making films, what else?" Burger regarded him like an idiot. "You're a director, aren't you?"

"I was, yes, *Herr Kommandant*."

"You must miss it."

Max looked at the man in the uniform. Was this some daft attempt at a joke? Ever since things had not quite gone according to plan on either front and the population of the ghetto had swelled with the new influx of Dutch and French Jews, starvation and disease had run rampant among the ghetto. Hospitals were overcrowded; the elderly died right where they sat—by the walls of their respective tenements, surrounded by fat black flies. The summer of 1943 had been particularly brutal; the only salvation from the heat was outside, in the scant shade. The water had always been contaminated and caused dysentery more often than not. By the time the corpse carrier detail would arrive after a shift on their SS-managed work detail, rats would have already gnawed on the corpses' exposed extremities and, often, their faces as well. Just what did Burger think Max would film here?

"Those pesky people from the International Red Cross voiced their *concerns*"—Burger drawled mockingly—"after certain rumors surfaced about the horrendous conditions in the ghetto. Apparently, a few of those sneaky Jew-rats smuggled some accounts from the inside to the—" He stopped abruptly, waving it off. "No matter. All you have to worry about is making a nice film about the wonderful life the German and European Jews live in the idyllic town of Theresienstadt. Get some war veterans, make them put on their Iron Crosses and whatever decorations they have. Tell mothers to put their brats in their finest—you get the drill. We'll deliver books for the library, sets and costumes for the theater, food for the canteen, equipment for the playgrounds and gymnastic halls; you don't need to worry about any of that. All you have to do is make them act as they should, both for the film and for the Red Cross people's visit as well. Explain to them, together with your pastor friend, how it's in their interest to be on their best behavior. Remind them that the train is already waiting to take them further east if they decide to forget it."

At first, Max rejected the idea outright. How could he lend his artistry to such a grotesque facade? The very thought of creating a film that would mask the truth, that would manipulate the reality of the suffering inmates for the sake of the regime, was nauseating. He had imagined the faces of those around him—the artists, the dreamers, the survivors—whose lives were being stripped away piece by piece. How could he face them after betraying them in such a dastardly manner? But as the days passed, the oppressive silence of the ghetto grew louder, and the whispers of rumors began to swirl around him.

Then, one afternoon, the air in the ghetto shifted dramatically. Burger's people came for Max once again to escort him back to the studio he'd been avoiding like the plague. As they stood to attention on both sides of him, the heavy clang of metal echoed through the courtyard. An armored vehicle pulled up, and Max felt himself swallow hard as he recognized the figure stepping out: Wilhelm von Brandenburg, his brother-in-law. The man who had thrown him in here.

With his head held high despite his racing pulse, Max watched Wilhelm approach, flanked by a cadre of guards. The sight of him stirred a cauldron of emotions within him—fear, anger, and a heavy sense of betrayal. It was a meeting he had dreaded, knowing that the man before him was not just a figure of authority but someone more than capable of murder—if not with his own hands, then by issuing orders, that was for certain. The late Art Nachtnebel testified to that.

"Laub, you old fox!" Wilhelm greeted him with a cold smile, his voice dripping with condescension. "Still alive and kicking?"

"Apologies, Herr Minister." Max bowed in mock regret to hide the defiance burning bright in his eyes. How his fist ached for the bastard's jaw! It would almost be worth getting shot for. If only it was just him, Laub, to be considered. But what would happen to all the inmates witnessing such open revolt? Von Brandenburg would order their execution there and then, just so they wouldn't get any ideas. Max continued to look down.

"Still have the fighting spirit in you! I can respect that." Von Brandenburg slapped him on the shoulder and turned him forcefully around to lead the director inside. "I hear you've become quite a thorn in Burger's side. He has finally appealed to me directly, asking for my intervention, given that you just won't see reason. I almost gave him permission to persuade you like the SS usually persuade people who just won't listen, but oftentimes things get out of hand in the heat of the moment. Someone loses his teeth or an eye or drops dead altogether of a weak heart and then what I would say to the Red Cross Commission?"

Max clenched his jaw, struggling to maintain his composure. "Do what you please to me. I won't do it," he replied, his voice steady despite the storm raging inside.

Wilhelm's smile faded, replaced by a chilling seriousness. "However did you and Aurelia get married in the first place, two pigheaded donkeys that you are? Or, shall I rephrase it, how did you two not murder each other given that neither of you budges an inch once you get something into your thick skulls?"

"I learned early on to move more than an inch as far as Ari is concerned." Max took pleasure in the distaste that crossed von Brandenburg's face at the nickname. "Life gets abundantly easier for husbands as soon as they realize that their wife is always right."

Von Brandenburg measured him up and down. "You have my sympathies. What inferior thinking for a man!"

"Ari left you and all the riches and power you had to offer to be with me. Which one of us is really inferior?"

"You watch your fucking mouth, half-breed," von Brandenburg growled, his finger inches away from Max's face. "Nothing would give me greater pleasure than putting a bullet between your eyes."

Max smiled at him almost pityingly. "And then how are you planning to rein Ari in? The only reason she hasn't obliterated you yet is because of me. Go on then, kill me. See what happens next."

In the silence that fell, von Brandenburg stepped back to regroup. Behind his pale-blue eyes, Max could almost see the cogs turning.

"Two can play this game," he said at last with an alarming calm. "You made that film, *Father's Land*. You deduced quite correctly what happened to Maria von Brandenburg, Aurelia's mother, when she refused to submit to my father—he shot her. I have no qualms about doing the same to your wife if you don't cooperate."

The words hit Max like a physical blow, stunning him with their cold, methodical horror. Wilhelm von Brandenburg didn't bluff—Max saw that much in his indifferent, ruthless eyes. His father's blood ran in his veins. As a child, he had covered up a murder. As an adult, he wouldn't hesitate to pick up a weapon himself. All blood draining from his face, Max regarded the man in front of him for a long time.

"You're a monster," he said finally, the words escaping his lips in a shaky breath. The mention of Aurelia, the threat against her life, shattered his resolve.

"Not really." Von Brandenburg grinned, self-satisfied. "I'm just a man. A man the way a man ought to be. A man who isn't burdened by empathy for the weak. A man who puts the interests of his country above all. A man who can never be blackmailed into making a film to feed to those stupid Swedes from that stupid Red Cross because he has stupid feelings for his stupid wife. Who's inferior now, Laub?"

Von Brandenburg was expecting humiliation and shame but instead received a collected response from the man with nothing to be ashamed of.

"History will show, von Brandenburg. History will show."

After a moment's faltering, Wilhelm's smile returned, though devoid of warmth. "Whatever makes you sleep at night. You'll begin immediately. The Red Cross will be here soon and we need to present a facade of normalcy—see that we do."

As Max walked away, his heart felt heavy with despair. He had made a choice, one that gnawed at his conscience, even though he had done it to protect Aurelia. Trapped in a web of manipulation, he was forced to dance to the tune of a regime that was annihilating the very people among whom he lived. *Whatever makes you sleep at night*—what a fine joke. Nothing would make him sleep at night, not with this task at hand.

In the days that followed, Max threw himself into the project despite the weight of his decision suffocating him. He wrote the script, crafting lines that glorified the supposed benevolence of the Nazis, all the while feeling the bile rise in his throat. Each word felt like a betrayal, every scene a distortion of the truth. He directed with a heavy heart, forcing himself to smile as he instructed fellow inmates to act as if they were receiving aid, while all around them, reality painted a different picture altogether.

As the cameras rolled, he fought back tears, his heart breaking for the men, women, and children whose lives were being so callously manipulated. He watched as they feigned smiles, their eyes hollow with despair, and he felt their pain as an echo of his own. It was a grim theater, a tragic play staged for the benefit of those who had no understanding of the suffering that lay beneath the surface.

"Cut!" he shouted, finally allowing the tension to seep from his voice as the cameras halted. The inmates around him sagged with relief, but the heaviness of what they had just done lingered in the air like a fog.

The day of the inspection arrived. Max stood behind the camera, somber and guilty as the members of the Red Cross entered the ghetto. He watched as they surveyed the conditions, their expressions a mixture of concern and curiosity. Instructed by Wenz and frightened by the repercussions spelled out by the SS, the inmates knew to smile, to wave, to create an illusion of life thriving amid the despair.

As the Red Cross representatives moved closer, one of them brightened in recognition. He stood out among the commission, not just due to his tall stature but the manner in which he carried himself, reminding Max of the refined elegance of European aristocracy of prewar years.

"Herr Laub!" He seized Max's hand and shook it warmly. "What a fine surprise! Folke Bernadotte, Vice-President of the Swedish Red Cross. I'm here with the international inspection."

Under the watchful eyes of the SS, Max took the man in. Bernadotte's hair was light blond and neatly combed back, revealing the high forehead of an intellectual. He had a strong jawline and high cheekbones, which lent him an air of authority and sophistication. In the diplomat's intelligent blue eyes, a sense of calm determination though unlike his counterparts who were regarding the Nazi-imposed theatrics with appeased smiles, he appeared genuinely concerned with the ghetto's situation.

"Is everything all right here?" he inquired without releasing

Max's hand. "If there is anything you would like to say, now is the time to do it."

Max's breath caught in his throat. In a flash, his years of incarceration passed before his eyes. The Swede was holding his very fate in his hand. *Tell him everything, ask him to whisk you away from this hell—he'll do it too; too many international eyes on the Nazis. Too big a scandal to cover up, even for Goebbels' well-oiled propaganda machine. But what of all the others? With the best will in the world the Red Cross won't be able to secure an entire ghetto's release. SS reprisals shall come, swift and ruthless, while I'm still on the road under Bernadotte's protection. And the main question, what will happen to Ari?*

That, Max refused to even consider. He had to maintain the facade. "Oh yes," he replied, forcing a smile that felt like a mask. "As you can see, Herr Bernadotte, this isn't a prison or a concentration camp. We have an entire town generously given to us by the German government. We have many elderly here, quite a few of them war veterans and their families. They spend their retirement vising the theater, joining chess clubs or reading groups, or even playing sports if their health permits it. We have guests from Holland and France living with us, but from what I understand, it's for the duration of the war only. As soon as it's over, they will be returned to their native countries and assigned living spaces according to the Reich's plan for future development."

The diplomat scrutinized him for an interminably long moment. Max felt exposed, as if the Swede could see right through him with those piercing, honest eyes. For the first time, he wished the official in front of him didn't care for humanity with such obvious passion.

"Frankly, I was quite surprised to find your name among the list of Theresienstadt's inhabitants," Bernadotte spoke, studying the famous director's threadbare vest and frayed cuffs. "We all thought you were undergoing treatment in some spa town..."

"I was." The lie slipped easily off Max's tongue. All it took was imagining Aurelia staring down the same barrel her mother had stared down just before von Brandenburg took her life. "But it was growing a tad too dangerous there, with the Allied aerial raids." He forced a chuckle. "My brother-in-law, Minister von Brandenburg, generously offered to transport me here, knowing how much my safety means to my wife. Theresienstadt is a peaceful town; we haven't had a single raid here, so I couldn't be more grateful to the Minister."

"Perhaps no aerial raids, but we've heard troubling reports about conditions in the ghetto," Bernadotte pressed the issue. Obviously, he was much too well-versed in diplomacy to buy the Propaganda Ministry's lies uttered by one of the regime's hostages.

Max fought to keep his composure. "Conditions are not ideal, but your visit brings hope. We are working together to improve our situation," he lied, the words tasting bitter on his tongue.

"Herr Laub, I can offer you asylum in my native Sweden. I assure you, you will be perfectly safe in Stockholm. And whatever health issues you have"—the look he gave Laub's thin frame was more than telling—"we shall address them as well. All you have to do is say the word."

Max felt a wave of nausea wash over him. The tension in the air was palpable. He could sense both the scrutiny of the Red Cross members and, on the opposite side, the SS. If they saw through the illusion, if they uncovered the truth, it would spell disaster not only for him but for everyone in Theresienstadt.

Say the word.

One word, and you're free.

Seal the fate of your wife and your friends but walk out of these gates—if you can live with yourself after.

Max smiled gently at the Swede in front of him. One day, if

he was alive, he would tell him the whole story. But not this afternoon—this afternoon too much was at stake. "I truly appreciate your concerns, Herr Bernadotte, but I don't know what else to tell you. By wartime measures, we are more than well off. I'm sure Stockholm is a great refuge for those hoping to avoid aerial raids, but so too is Theresienstadt. And I have my new film studio here—I'm already planning a new project. Hopefully, I'll bring it to Sweden after the war, if you'll have me."

Even if Bernadotte intuitively sensed something was amiss, there was nothing outwardly warranting any further investigation. The children skipped the rope and played marbles under the peaceful sky. The library was well-stocked. The stores boasted a wider selection of goods than most German ones. Old war veterans were indeed alive and well, their medals and orders shining with pride in the September sun. And Max Laub was very much fine, contrary to the conspiracy theories some sources were beginning to spread.

Reluctantly, the Red Cross members departed.

As soon as the gates closed after their staff cars, Max slid down the wall to the ground with a crushing sense of guilt. He had played his part in a horrific charade, even if for the sake of his wife's survival. The realization gnawed at him, a relentless reminder of the cost of his decisions.

He covered his face with his hands, shielding it from the people whose eyes he couldn't meet. It felt as though the weight of the entire world was pressing down on him—a burden that could not be lifted. The shadows of Theresienstadt loomed larger than ever. In the silence that followed, he clung to the hope that he could still fight back against the tide, that he could one day make amends for the choices he had been forced to make. But for now, he was trapped in a world of lies and the path forward felt impossibly dark.

FORTY-TWO

Paris, France. May 1944

The clouds over Paris hung heavy and dark, pregnant with the storm ready to burst any moment. Breathing a sigh of relief at making it before the downpour, Aurelia pushed open the familiar heavy door to the museum curated by Zara Whitby—Wilhelm von Brandenburg's favorite person as of late. Having passed off the administration of the concentration camps to the RSHA—Reich Main Security Office—he had all but retired from the bothersome war, happy to watch Hitler's regime implode from the sidelines.

It was all going perfectly according to his original plan: after the disastrous Battle of Stalingrad, Germany's fortune on the frontline had turned. From the East, Soviets were pushing back, regaining lost territory with frightening speed. Africa was almost entirely under Allied control. Italy was still hanging on, but by a thread. Waiting for it all to go entirely belly up so that he could assume power, Wilhelm von Brandenburg busied himself by transferring priceless art pieces from the occupied territories to his familial estate. If at first Aurelia had been appalled at the sight of Zara personally checking the inventory loaded onto *Herr Ministerpräsident*'s train against her list, she soon saw reason in her friend's scheme.

"We're already getting the odd bomb dropping here and there in Paris," Zara had explained at their subdued Christmas celebration during a rare visit to Berlin. It was just the two of them at Aurelia's home. "From what I hear, the Allies are getting ready to open a second front soon. Once they do, the bombs shall rain on us full force. Seeing as your brother doesn't do much to stop that from happening, all of those artworks will be much safer in his estate. He's out in the country. Paris museums are... well, in Paris."

Only five months had passed since that conversation and numerous pieces had already found their way into Aurelia's cellar—for safekeeping. With the extent of his looting, Wilhelm had run out of space in the von Brandenburg familial estate.

At Zara's museum, the familiar scent of oil paint and varnish filled Aurelia's lungs. Near the entrance, sandbags were piled high, reducing a beautiful limestone building to a shadow of its former self under siege. The elegant gallery, once a sanctuary for artistic expression, now felt like a sanctuary of secrets, where whispers of resistance mingled with echoes of despair.

"Curator Whitby!" Aurelia called into the silent sanctuary, loud on purpose. On her person she carried enough compromising materials for her brother's own Gestapo to string her up nicely from the first lamppost they encountered. After witnessing their methods for years, she had learned by now that the more inconspicuous one tried to act, the more suspicion one would invite. It was the loud ones, the brazen ones who treated the world like their doormat that got a free pass. Her last name and Propaganda Ministry credentials certainly helped too: "Propaganda Ministry official von Brandenburg, with the inspection. Report to the front immediately or I'll have your hide."

Before too long, out of the depths of the museum, Zara ran to greet her, arms open wide. "You made it!" she cried, kissing her friend on both cheeks. "I was worried you'd be stuck on the border. The French blew up another set of train tracks," she added, annoyed, for the benefit of the invisible ears that might be listening—Aurelia had schooled her well on that matter too after witnessing firsthand how swiftly the Gestapo dealt with all the unfortunates reported by informants.

"Trains are for peasants," Aurelia said deadpan. "I have a personal plane."

"Must be nice, having the Airforce Marshall for a big brother," Zara responded in the same manner, guiding her back toward the entrance.

"I can't complain."

"Good. Since you're so rich, you're buying lunch."

"It's about to pour out there—" Aurelia began to protest but stopped at once at the pointed glance Zara threw over her shoulder.

"The place is just around the corner. We'll make it."

Once outside, muggy air standing still all around them, Zara pressed Aurelia's elbow meaningfully.

"Berlin sent some odd characters to help me out with the museum. Know anything about it?"

"They finally appointed someone new to Heydrich's old position," Aurelia replied in an undertone. "French Resistance was such a thorn in the Nazis' side, they wanted to transfer Heydrich here, to Paris, to deal with them, just days before his car got blown up by the Czechs last May."

"Heroes!"

"They are."

In the distance, the first crack of thunder. Both women simultaneously looked up and hastened their pace, Aurelia clutching her travel bag closer to her side. If only the weather would hold another few minutes. The negatives of the SS atroc-

ities captured on the Eastern Front would survive the rain, it
was the concentration camps' quarterly reports from her brother's desk Aurelia worried about. Unconcerned with the death
machine he had conceived and manufactured, Wilhelm
scarcely bothered skimming through the paperwork his subordi-
nates supplied him at his home office, leaving it for his adjutant
to file and organize later. For Aurelia, swiping a few such
reports off Wilhelm's desk was never a problem—the real
trouble would be for Zara to pass them to the Allies.

"So now, the Resistance hot potato landed in this new
appointee's hands," Aurelia explained, thinking of her own hot
potato she was about to hand over to her friend. "Smart of you,
suspecting those new helpers of yours. I bet they're from his
department."

"Anyone I know? The appointee, that is."

"Some Austrian, never heard of him before. Heydrich's staff
all hate him from what I hear." Another crack of thunder, closer
this time. "How far are we? I have papers on me and they absolutely must not get wet."

"You ever come to see me empty-handed?" Zara protested
in mock annoyance, but the mirth in her dark eyes betrayed her
excitement.

She basked in the role of conduit between an insider within
the highest echelons of Nazi power and the British intelligence.
Certainly, preserving art was nice, she had confessed to Aurelia
when the latter first voiced the idea of passing evidence of the
German war crimes to the Allies through Zara, but this—this
made her feel like she was actually doing something truly
useful.

At last, they dove into a bistro bearing the name Le Refuge.
At first glance, it appeared to be an overtly pro-German and
pro-Vichy establishment. Aurelia's brow arched at the sight of
its menus plastered with slogans that celebrated the new regime
and the walls adorned with flags and propaganda. From the

radio, German music blared, a barkeep singing along as he cleaned the glasses. He must have recognized Zara as he nodded to her with a wide grin and announced that her usual table was waiting.

"Well? What do you say?" Zara giggled, all mischievousness, as they were seated at the corner table under a stag's head mounted on the wall.

"I say, what under God's blue sky..." Aurelia couldn't even finish explaining the extent of her puzzlement at the setting.

"Not only do you hide in plain sight, it's the local brass's favorite watering hole, which is coincidentally operated by the French Resistance," Zara explained, speaking in Aurelia's ear against the loud music. "Genius, isn't it? The owner, he's the one who's been helping me pass your information along to the British. He should have been an actor, I tell you. A veritable master of deception, with a charming smile that could easily disarm the most vigilant occupier. If you saw him drinking champagne with the Germans and praising Vichy, you would never know he's the one who created a safe haven for the resistance fighters. They use the menu to communicate—a sprig of parsley tucked beneath a plate or a subtle change in the daily special signal an urgent meeting or a new supply of contraband. It's really amazing if you think of it! And with this Bavarian noise blaring, you don't have to worry about any listening devices or informants."

"That's for sure—I can barely hear myself think!" Aurelia laughed in response, gazing about the place with newfound appreciation. How perfect for them to eat here as well, two German women working diligently for the regime! Suddenly, she felt the sense of camaraderie permeating the air, a thread of resilience woven through the laughter and conversation. In this hidden corner of Paris, they found solace from the chaos outside, a brief respite where they could eat and talk freely under the watchful gaze of the Resistance.

"This is Étienne, the owner," Zara effortlessly switched to French as soon as the same barkeep, who turned out to be the proprietor, approached their table with an aperitif. "Étienne, this is Aurelia, my friend from Berlin."

"Oh, I know who she is." He winked at Aurelia as he placed the drinks in front of the women.

"Aurelia has something for you."

"Come to the kitchen," Étienne said, gesturing for Aurelia to follow. "I'll show you around."

As soon as they stepped through the doors, he held out his big palm to Aurelia. "Anything urgent?"

"No," she explained, producing a small envelope. "It's mostly evidence. You know... For later."

The Frenchman nodded, the envelope disappearing into the pocket of his apron. "I'll keep it stashed until one of ours heads across the Channel. Anything useful you have to tell me?"

Aurelia considered. "I just told Zara, they appointed someone to Heydrich's position. Watch your back. He'll likely be sending new agents to infiltrate cells and what have you."

"What about Allied landings? Where are the Krauts expecting them? No offense."

"None taken. As of now, the High Command are betting on either Normandy or Pas de Calais."

Étienne stepped a bit closer, suddenly looming over Aurelia like one of those thunderous clouds outside. "Be a lamb," he said quietly, peering directly into her eyes. "Try to persuade them it will be Pas de Calais."

Her heart in her throat from the mixture of anxiety and exhilaration, Aurelia nodded her understanding.

On stiff legs, she returned back to her table, leaving the resistance leader inside to hide her precious intelligence some-where it would safely wait for its hour.

"It's happening then," she said, downing her drink in one go. "The landings. The second front. It's truly happening."

Zara threw back her drink as well. "Better yet—though I don't know how much of it is true—I hear there's growing dissent within the army ranks. Not just regular soldiers, but high military brass. Have you heard anything your end?"

"The military wouldn't talk to me," Aurelia confessed. "Neither would they approach me, if anything was really going on. I'm too much of a turncoat in the general public's eyes," she added with a melancholy smile. "An aristocrat turned socialist turned full-blooded Nazi... no one in their right mind would trust me."

"They're men though. Men still like you very much."

Aurelia arched her brow. "After I got my first husband killed and the second arrested and thrown into a ghetto?"

Zara reached across the table and caught her hand. "How *is* Max?"

Aurelia sighed, rubbing her eyes with her free hand. "Max directed a fine piece of propaganda about Theresienstadt after Wilhelm threatened him with putting me against the wall if he refused. Big Brother conveyed their conversation to me in gleeful detail. Goebbels had me watch the film together with him in his projection room. Lamented such a great talent going to waste in the Jewish ghetto instead of working for him as he should have. God, how I hate them all!" She finished with an anguished moan, dropping her head on her folded arms. "How does the earth carry such scum? How are they not stricken with God's wrath?"

As though on cue, a bolt of lightning pierced the sky outside, hot-white and multipronged in the open windows, followed by a thunderous explosion. In an instant, the clouds burst open, spilling torrents of cool rain onto the suffocating streets.

Watching waiters scramble to close the windows against the

powerful onslaught, Aurelia felt a flicker of hope ignite in her for the first time in years. "Do you think they'll pull it off? The Allies?" She stared at Zara, almost pleading.

Zara dipped her bread in olive oil—restaurants catering to Germans could still boast their choice of foodstuffs—and munched on it pensively. "I think they will, but we must also do our part to aid them in any way we can."

Pas de Calais, Étienne's words reverberated through Aurelia's mind. Newfound focus in her eyes, she grinned at Zara. "Mind if I use your husband as my source as to where the Allied landings will likely commence?"

The same fire reflected, bright and quick, in her friend's eyes. "Be my guest. Lay it on thick, too: tell them he's with the Office of Strategic Services now."

"Oh, you know I will. Goebbels' *Lies Department* taught me well."

As they huddled over the dishes placed before them, outside the twilight began to disperse. Ever so slightly, just enough to remind them that the sun still existed, but persistently, purging the streets of Paris of oppressive heat.

Soon, victorious troops would follow, purging them of a different kind of oppression. The toughest of battles still loomed ahead, but Aurelia was ready to fight them—for Max, for the memory of the perished, for a world finally free of Hitler's bloody yoke.

FORTY-THREE

Theresienstadt. Summer 1944

The sun beat down mercilessly on the Theresienstadt ghetto, casting stark shadows across the cobblestone pathways that wound through the makeshift community. In the oppressive heat, the air hung thick with tension and a sense of dread as the inmates scurried about, trying to maintain a semblance of normalcy amid the grim realities of their existence.

Max stood beside the new Kommandant Rahm and his entourage as they surveyed a small group of fellow prisoners working diligently on the ghetto's "beautification." The SS men's faces were so gloomy, one would think they were the ones incarcerated here instead of the Jews, who were presently sweating and hammering away with feverish abandon. First, the news of the Allied landings in Normandy; then, an order from Berlin authorizing the second Red Cross inspection.

Kommandant Rahm flicked his cigarette to the ground and extinguished the butt with his heel. "Well?" He turned to Max, who, in spite of himself, pulled himself up to attention. "You're the big Hollywood hotshot director. We're installing several shops and cafés. Tell me what else needs to be done to pass this rat hole for a European spa town?"

Max was about to remind the new commander that this would be a set designer's job, but Rahm didn't seem to be in the mood for arguments. Unlike the former Kommandant Burger, he cared little for technicalities and operated with brutal efficiency: *Children from the new transport refuse to go through the delousing process, thinking that the showers are concealed gas chambers? Back onto the transport with them and ship them all east. Let them find out where the gas chambers are real, in Rahm's Theresienstadt or in Auschwitz.*

The children's cries as their transport pulled out of the ghetto still echoed in Max's ears.

He cleared his throat. "I would suggest playgrounds for children. At least a couple of different ones, fully equipped."

Next to Rahm, his adjutant began scribbling eagerly. "Yes, children—that's good, that's always a fine idea."

"What else?" Rahm barked, his horsewhip twitching against his tall boot impatiently.

Next to the SS, who was clearly in such a foul mood, the Jewish painting brigade redoubled their efforts in coating a newly erected fence with bright blue.

Within Max, a deep sense of resentment boiled. Once again, he'd been dragged into the rotten business of concealing the horrors that lay beneath the ghetto's surface. But this time he was given a phone call as an incentive and a promise of a visit afterwards—if he behaved, that was.

Just that morning, Aurelia's voice had reached him through the thick black cord in the *Kommandant's* office, so achingly familiar and yet so very distant.

"Max, love, how are you there?"

"I'm all right, everything's all right." His eyes welling up despite his best intentions to keep his composure, Max had clutched at the phone in a desperate attempt to reach for the woman his heart beat for. "I'm with Pastor Wenz here, our accommodations are very good and we're treated just fine—"

"Max, you can speak freely with me. It's Wilhelm's personal, secured line. No one is listening in. Wilhelm is here with me. He'll talk to your *Kommandant* right after, tell him to treat you like gold if he knows what's good for him." The words had rushed out of her in an urgent stream. "You'll probably hate me for this, but I made a deal on your behalf. On the ghetto's behalf. Now that the Allies have opened the second front, the question for Germany is no longer *if* it will lose the war, but *when*. Now, Theresienstadt is not just any ghetto, but the ghetto in which Europe's artistic and intellectual elite is gathered and the world is doing anything possible—and impossible—to keep you alive and safe. Granted, Wilhelm sees you as more of a bargaining chip for the future—" Max could vividly picture the dirty look Aurelia must have thrown her high-ranking sibling—"but the point stands: he knows he needs you all alive. *I* need you alive. And I swear to you, I'm doing everything in my power to keep you safe, no matter the cost."

Max had kept nodding, swallowing hot, salty tears, knowing that she couldn't see him and yet nodding all the same—relieved to hear her voice once again, relieved to know she still loved him just as much. "Where are you, Ari?" he'd managed, doing his utmost to keep his voice steady. "Are you in Berlin? How is the situation there? We hear they bomb you there sometimes?"

"Don't you worry about me, I'm fine."

But Max couldn't be persuaded. "Are you still with the Propaganda Ministry?" he'd pressed. He hadn't heard her name in a while, hadn't heard Riefenstahl's name either. Knowing Goebbels, he could have just gone and said something to Hitler and what if both women were in one of von Brandenburg's prison systems—

"Yes, but I work as a war correspondent now." Aurelia's

response had interrupted the frantic spinning of his thoughts. "I travel all the time, so the bombs have yet to catch up with me."

He'd heard her chuckle on the other end and felt his heart spasm with such a rush of love for her, he thought he would fall over where he stood.

"Bibi Wolowsky made his first film."

"What?" It had taken Max a while to resurrect the familiar name from the good old days' memories' grave. "Our Bibi?"

"Our Bibi, all grown up," Aurelia had confirmed, her voice full of fondness. "I saw it the other day with Goebbels."

"What is it about?"

"An antifascist picture, about Heydrich's assassination in Prague."

"Was it good?"

"More than. Goebbels was so annoyed with how good it was, he kept slapping his armrest: *do you see how well they make their propaganda? Everything is so subtle, so poignant, so wonderfully veiled.*" Aurelia had mimicked the Minister's voice with remarkable precision. Max felt his lips stretching into a grin. "*And look at what the UFA is turning out—nauseating! After you and Riefenstahl left, there are no more decent directors left.* I reminded him that Berthold Wolowsky would have been a German director, had the Nazis not run him off his native land. Just like his teacher, a certain Max Laub."

Max had gone silent, his good eye glazing over with the memories of old. In the periphery of the bad one, Kommandant's Rahm's uniform was a gray, shapeless blotch.

"I wish I could tell him how proud I am," he'd said.

"You will," Aurelia had replied and repeated it again as Max tried to interject something. "You will. But for now, do what they tell you—"

"That's right," Wilhelm von Brandenburg's voice had cut into the conversation, laced with arrogance and disdain. "Do what they tell you and if the Red Cross leaves the ghetto happy, you'll all stay alive for a while longer. I think it's in everyone's interest. Now give me Rahm—I have orders to give him."

"Tell Ari I love her, please."

"You can tell her yourself, after the inspection," von Brandenburg had replied, suddenly all benevolence. "I'll bring her to Prague, you know, for a visit if all goes well. Or for the nearest transport east; Auschwitz is close by as well."

Hours had passed and von Brandenburg's words still hung over Max like a blade. Wiping sweat from his brow, he collected himself, focused on the task at hand.

"Vegetable gardens would look good. Also, a cinema or a theater—maybe even two, combined. A barber shop for men and a hair salon for women. Granted, you'll need to stock the shelves at the stores—"

"Germans are on a strict ration system," Rahm spoke through gritted teeth, "and you want me to stock shelves for those Jewish rats? Besides, with what?"

"Von Brandenburg authorized all expenses," Max countered, his jaw clenching as well. The war that had brought all this scarcity and near starvation to the German population was their own doing. And if the SS, under von Brandenburg's charge, wished to use the ghetto population as hostages, he would be damned if he didn't squeeze them for all he could. "I imagine he'll supply you with everything you ask."

Later that day, as Max peeled a single potato for a soup that would sustain him and Pastor Wenz for the next few days, he outlined his plan to the minister.

"I'll ask Bernadotte to take you with him. You're a gentile, there's no use for your services here. You were never charged with any crime. The SS will have no choice but to let you go. Gesture of goodwill and all that rot."

Wenz tried to protest, but Max silenced him with a look full of urgency.

"I know you're noble and good and want to share the plight and all that, but Fritz! They have to be made aware of the situation. And the only way they will be made aware is through you. Don't shake your head at me and suggest passing them a note or some such nonsense: the blood by the wall is still fresh where those Czech gendarmes got shot for the several measly letters they tried to smuggle out of here. And don't suggest I go either. He'll kill my wife; out of sheer spite, he will. You go and you tell them the truth, so they can bargain with their eyes open, knowing precisely what's at stake."

They shook hands as the sun dipped lower in the sky, casting long shadows over the ghetto. The facade of Theresienstadt may have been carefully constructed, but they would not allow it to stand unchallenged. They would fight for the truth, for the lives that hung in the balance—to expose the horrors that lay hidden beneath the surface and, eventually—hopefully—to break free from the chains that bound them.

FORTY-FOUR

Theresienstadt. July 1944

No matter the SS's mercantile plans for the ghetto inhabitants, for the first time in years, the inmates breathed somewhat free. Upon Max's insistence—"no inspection shall believe your ruse if you present them with walking skeletons"—half-starved people began to receive slightly better portions of food, including bread, potatoes, and occasionally vegetables. Prominent figures within the Jewish community, including artists, musicians, and intellectuals, were allotted better living quarters to showcase the SS's supposed benevolence.

In a further effort to create the illusion of normalcy, playgrounds were constructed, complete with swings and slides, adding a veneer of innocence to the grueling life in the ghetto. Only, frightened of the SS that had herded them there, the children stood like petrified lambs for slaughter, much like their counterparts who had refused to go into the showers, suspecting the worst from the uniformed men with eyes cold and hard.

"Go play, damn it!" Kommandant Rahm shouted, a vein rising in his forehead. "Have you not seen a swing? Toss that ball! Act normal, blasted rats, or I'll have you all shipped east with the next transport!"

Seeing that the inspection was scheduled to arrive in three days, Max knew Rahm would rather go through with his threat rather than risk poor performance.

"Children, come round!" Max rushed to intervene. Gathering the small, frightened flock around him, he spoke with them in the same voice he told them his stories. "We'll be rehearsing a scene for a film today; what say you? I'll tell each one of you what to do and you'll follow my directions, just like you did when we were preparing for the play *Münchausen*. Don't forget to act as natural as you can, don't oversell it, all right? Because—and I'm letting you in on a secret—the important people who are coming, they are from Hollywood. They'll be filming and taking photos of you and later decide who to invite to America. You want to go to America, don't you?"

"To the palm trees and peaches?" Estee, the little mouse who had first prompted Max to tell her class a story, looked up at the director with such frank, trusting eyes, he felt rotten to the core for lying to these little innocents in such a manner.

But what else was there for it? Rahm had made his intentions more than clear. And if the Red Cross departed satisfied, von Brandenburg could keep his word and keep them all alive, as hostages, but alive nonetheless. Max would take this deal any time of the day—the alternative was much too frightful to consider. And so he shoved the pangs of his conscience into the furthest corner of his mind and nodded. "Yes. To the palm trees and peaches."

As the International Red Cross delegates arrived, the Theresienstadt that greeted them was something out of a fairy tale. While bombs rained over Europe, the sky over the old fortress town remained perfectly azure and at peace. Flower beds bloomed, fat bumblebees and butterflies had their choice of flower pots in the tenements' open windows. In vegetable gardens, tomatoes were gaining color under the generous sun. In the central square, a fine orchestra played as a few couples danced, smiles plastered to their faces under the SS's hawkish eyes.

"Here's a bakery and here's a pharmacy, much better stocked than any Prague one." Kommandant Rahm proceeded with the staged tour, showcasing the improvements made to the ghetto and highlighting the cultural activities flourishing within. The carefully orchestrated facade was designed to convince the world that the inmates were being treated humanely, that they were living productive lives under the watchful but benevolent eye of the German authorities. "As you can see, the Dutch-Jewish population are our guests, not prisoners," he said as he led the commission through the Dutch Jews' barracks that had been scrubbed, painted, and decorated for the occasion. "As soon as the war is over, they will be resettled to the Palestine, according to their wishes."

"They all wish to go to Palestine?" Count Bernadotte—Max had only been made aware of the Swede's aristocratic title before the inspection—once again at the head of the inspection, narrowed his eyes at the SS *Kommandant*.

Rahm only smiled and gestured the Swede toward the Dutch Jews, also scrubbed and attired for the occasion. "Ask them."

Schooled for days under the muzzle of Rahm's gun, they began to nod vigorously. Yes, Palestine was their historic home-land, they all wished to resettle there. No, they didn't want to return to Holland, they wanted to start new lives on their sacred land, in Jerusalem.

Bernadotte looked around, searching his fellow commission-ers' faces for doubt, but met only smiles, mirroring those of the "benevolent" SS. Apparently, the reports of Jewish extermination turned out to be false, after all, they spoke among themselves. Look at these people—they are all well taken care of. And Theresienstadt is certainly no prison, just a town like many others. Even better in some respects...

Rahm was already gesturing toward the limousine waiting outside to continue on with the tour before anyone could notice the cracks in the carefully presented facade. "Gentlemen, if you please, our local theater troupe prepared a performance for you. And after, a lunch at our most popular café, Europa. I hear the chef is making something exquisite for our dear guests."

"I hear it's the pheasant," his adjutant promptly supplied.

It was pheasant—Max had seen the birds being unloaded from the same transport that had brought crates with *Top Secret: RSHA Archives* on them. An entire barrack had been cleared out to make space for them. From the window of his and Wenz's dwelling, Max had watched the barrack's inhabitants shoved onto the same transport with SS batons. With the chalk, an SS man had marked its new destination: KZ Auschwitz.

Just before the inspectors departed, Bernadotte once again insisted on speaking with Max. He must have sensed that the improvements were a temporary illusion, a desperate attempt to mask the ongoing atrocities and the deep-seated fear that permeated every aspect of life in Theresienstadt. He wanted to give Laub one last chance to escape.

"Today I'm acting on behalf of the United States government as well," the Swede spoke in a grave voice. "They asked me to facilitate your return to your new homeland, of which you are a rightful citizen. Since you have been charged with no crime and reside as a guest here, I understand that you are free to go at any time." This was directed at Rahm. The SS *Kommandant* nodded with the sincerest of smiles, a uniformed jailer parading as a tour guide. "Herr Laub, would you like to leave with us today? You may either stay in Sweden or return to the United States, of which I shall be happy to assist."

Max thought of his home in Beverly Hills—a mere sweet dream that had faded after years of his new ugly prison life—of sunny beaches and fruit stands with those damned peaches a cent apiece. He thought of freedom, freedom to get in his car and drive as far as Mexico or Utah and stare at the sunset from the pink expanse of the mountains. He thought of trains to New York and Broadway shows, and James' and Zara's home at Long Island and the sailboat they could take out on a gorgeous day like this... He thought of it all and then of his wife here in Prague. The decision came plain as day.

"Thank you kindly, Herr Bernadotte, but until the war is over, I would rather stay here and make myself useful to the community. After they leave, I will leave as well. However, if you have a free seat in your car, take Pastor Wenz with you." Before Rahm could intervene, Max pulled the minister out of the crowd and almost physically handed him over to the Swede. "He was also transferred here to avoid the bombs, but I fear, as a Protestant, he's bored stiff here. You'll do everyone a favor if you take him off our hands." With a good-natured chuckle, he grasped first Wenz's hand and then Bernadotte's. "Find my wife and speak to her," he whispered in the diplomat's ear before releasing his hand.

Bernadotte nodded and climbed into the limousine, Wenz following him with one last look over his shoulder and a sign of the cross for all of those remaining. Shadowed by the looming specter of death and despair, Max stayed.

FORTY-FIVE

Berlin, Germany. January 1945

The winter of 1945 clung to Berlin like a shroud, the air bitingly cold and filled with an unsettling silence. The war had come to Berliners' doorsteps at long last. The once-bustling capital was now a city on the brink of collapse, the echoes of battle reverberating through its crumbling streets. As the Allies advanced from both fronts, squeezing Germany from west and east, the atmosphere in the capital was thick with desperation and fear, particularly after the world's reaction to the Soviet troops' liberation of Auschwitz. With each liberated town in the east, more and more horrors perpetrated by the Nazis revealed themselves to the appalled humanity. However, even confronted with photos depicting mounds of emaciated corpses, Goebbels dug in his heels and decried the enemy propaganda despite knowing for a fact that the photos were as authentic as they got. Instead, he sent Aurelia to the east to document reports of widespread rape "those Soviet Asiatic hordes are inflicting on defenseless German women."

"Liberators!" he spat out, crushing a report in his fist. "They liberate lots of things from what I hear, starting with silverware and ending with women's silk underwear."

Aurelia thought of all the silverware and women's silk underwear the SS had "liberated" over the years from the Jews both here and in the occupied territories but said nothing. Why waste energy on empty discussions now? God willing, it would all be over soon, one way or another.

"Shall I set off immediately?" she asked against the air-raid siren whirring to life. They were growing bolder, the enemy fliers: only three in the afternoon, not quite twilight yet, and here they were, probing the capital's air defenses.

One of the Propaganda Minister's aides burst inside, ready to whisk Goebbels into the underground shelter.

"You may as well," Goebbels threw, annoyed, as he gathered the rest of his correspondence and deposited it into the valise the aid was holding out for him. "The Soviets are only seventy kilometers from here, you'll be back before dinner."

Aurelia followed the two men and the rest of the Ministry's employees to the first floor but instead of descending further into the air-raid shelter, strode outside and scrunched up her face at the sky. Pale arches of anti-aircraft fire traced an enemy bomber somewhere on the outskirts. More would come, but from the north-west by the looks of it.

After assessing the situation, Aurelia climbed into the staff car issued by the War Ministry after her personal one had been seized for precious metal and set off east.

The Soviets indeed stood just across the river—even with the rapidly falling darkness, Aurelia spotted their positions through the field binoculars gallantly offered by the local *Wehrmacht Hauptmann* holding the front. She didn't ask him how it was looking for them, the Germans: the sheer size of the enemy forces amassing on the opposite bank against the pitiful leftovers of the eastern front divisions painted the picture clear enough.

"Big mistake, that entire Ardennes offensive was," the major spoke to her unprompted. Under the upturned collar of his overcoat, the beginnings of a beard. Three of his fingers poked through the holes in the gloves when he took the field glasses back from Aurelia. *"We shall turn our fortune around; the German people deserve a Christmas miracle and I shall deliver it. First, we'll deal a fatal blow to the western powers and after that—"* He proceeded in a mocking tone aimed at their "glorious leader"—an unfathomable expression of defiance that would have gotten him shot mere months ago. Not anymore. Things had changed after the July plot, no matter how much Hitler and Goebbels tried to deny the fact. The high-ranking officers' attempt to remove the dictator from power by assassinating him could have failed, but no number of SS men dispatched to deal with the rebels could silence the sentiment behind it. It was easy to shoot people, not ideas. And ideas, once taking root, grew, trickled down through the ranks until they reached regular soldiers. "He should never have taken a single man out of the eastern front army group. Now how are we supposed to contain that tide?" A spasmatic jerk of the chin at the Soviets, just a frozen river separating them from the open road to Berlin. "More and more of them pull up every day. And all we have is a few Howitzers and fifteen-year-old boys manning them!"

Aurelia nodded, shivering against the gusts of Arctic wind whipping along the bank. "How do I get to the other side?"

The *Hauptmann* regarded her as if she had grown a second head.

"Propaganda Ministry assignment," Aurelia explained, feeling her lips crack as she stretched them into the semblance of a smile.

"I'd ignore it if I were you." After digging in his pockets, he produced a stack of leaflets. "Enemy propaganda. We use it for latrines, but... here," he said, handing Aurelia a list of some sort. It didn't take her long to make out her own name right under her brother's, along with her immediate boss Goebbels and his aides, Himmler and his Gestapo goons, and just about half of the Nazi top tier. "Heads they'd like to collect, preferably before the western Allies pipe in with some sort of humanitarian sh—" He caught himself just in time, mustering a meek smile at Aurelia. *Begging your forgiveness; too many years commanding soldiers with the only language that gets them moving,* his embarrassed expression seemed to read. "And you're a lady, on top of things. They won't just shoot you, they will..." He waved the repulsive idea off. "Go back to Berlin, Fräulein von Brandenburg. Or, better yet, go west. Surrender to the British or Americans. They'll treat you fairly."

If it were just herself to be considered, Aurelia would have done exactly that. But there was a certain Max Laub, without whom this whole damned life wouldn't be worth living, and so she returned to Berlin—back to buildings scarred by bombs and to its inhabitants, weary and hollow-eyed, moving like ghosts through the remnants of their lives.

Aurelia had returned home under the cover of night, still processing the beginning of Germany's imminent collapse which she had witnessed. The air-raid siren hadn't appeared to shut up in her absence, but instead of going down to her home's cellar, Aurelia remained seated in her car, wasting precious gas on heating her frozen hands and brooding—brooding among the echo of distant explosions...

The news of her own name being on the same list as the criminals she would give her right hand to watch being shot didn't upset her as much as she would have expected. True, over the past few years her work as a war correspondent had morphed into something far more dangerous; she had become a conduit for truth, supplying the Allies with evidence of Germany's war crimes. Up until a few months ago, before the victorious Allied had troops rolled through the streets of Paris, she'd been smuggling rolls of film into Zara's museum, under the guise of visiting an old friend. Little did the German command know, Zara Whitby, their esteemed art expert who supplied not one high-ranking Nazi's home with invaluable paintings, supplied the French Resistance with Aurelia's films in her spare time. Also true, outwardly, Aurelia von Brandenburg remained the face of the Nazi Propaganda, almost just as recognizable as its Minister Goebbels. And if the Soviets got to her before the western Allies...

A gentle knock on her window startled her, pulling Aurelia out of her musings. Only now, in the silver light of the moon, did she notice the vague outline of a vehicle parked directly behind her. How did she not hear it pull up? *Ach*, yes. The bombs and that damned siren wailing.

The stranger's face in her driver's window was also a mere shadow. Too exhausted from the drive to give a damn, Aurelia merely jerked her head toward the passenger side. After circling the hood of the car, the stranger got in, bringing with him the faint scent of an expensive aftershave and warm cashmere.

Not a Berliner then; not even a German, Aurelia concluded in an instant. Germans were issued a single piece of shaving soap for each quarter and it reeked of lye and fat. Certainly no one from the eastern parts either.

"I hope you'll forgive me the intrusion, Frau Laub," the man began in very good German.

Aurelia's half-closed eyelids snapped wide open at the name no one had used in years.

"My name is Folke Bernadotte. I'm the vice-president of the Swedish Red Cross. I met your husband in Theresienstadt, when I visited there with the inspection," he said with his soft, whispering accent. "He told me Minister von Brandenburg had offered to transfer him there, away from the air raids."

"Air raids, my foot," Aurelia snorted softly, shaking her head.

"That was my feeling as well." Bernadotte sighed, shifting in his seat. "I didn't think he could speak freely, but what I can't conceive is the reason why he refused to leave under my protection. I did offer him a chance—"

"I'm sure you did, Herr Bernadotte. And you were right: Max couldn't speak freely, but not out of fear of reprisals for himself. It's all because of me. My brother did transfer him to Theresienstadt, but not out of the goodness of his heart. My brother needs him alive to make me do his bidding. I'm a flight risk, you see: first, I left my familial home, then—Germany altogether. Couldn't make it out of Austria in time. He got us both there." She lowered her eyes, her finger tapping against the wheel. "See my brother's dilemma? I don't tend to stick around without a proper incentive."

"And the other people there?"

"Hostages as well." Aurelia sighed and rubbed her eyes, tired of explaining the things that should be obvious. "Theresienstadt is a model ghetto—or camp—whatever you wish to call it. Exceptional for propaganda purposes. Fooled you, didn't it?" She nodded when Bernadotte hung his head in shame. "Frightening thing, propaganda is. With enough time, you can persuade people that black is white and top is bottom and the SS are fine, upstanding fellows and Jews and gays and intellectuals and whoever else they've put in their camps or slaughtered by now are what's wrong with the world. Trust me, I've been working for the Ministry for as long as it's been established."

Bernadotte considered it for quite some time. "All right. So they are hostages, but hostages are kept with a purpose. I'm guessing the purpose is to exchange them for someone."

"Exchange? No, not really," Aurelia replied. "Unless you

count favorable surrender conditions for a certain person as an exchange." She regarded the Swede pointedly, meaning her brother, of course.

But that was enough hope for Bernadotte to latch on to. "So you think it would be possible to secure their release eventually? As gesture of goodwill?" he asked.

"Not as long as Himmler is in charge of the SS. After the July plot, Hitler has grown mistrustful of everyone except for Himmler's SS. Himmler wouldn't do anything to jeopardize it and he knows that Hitler will lose it if he even hears of any concessions to the Allies. Hitler is waging a total war now. It's all or nothing for him. So, to answer your question, they would rather kill all of those people than make any deals with the west. They'll go down with the ship and everyone they've locked on the lower deck."

"What about you?" Bernadotte asked her.

Aurelia shrugged, indifferent to her own fate for quite some time now. "I'm not leaving without my husband. As long as he's alive, I'm staying here."

"It's very likely you'll both die."

"Very likely, yes. But while I'm alive and while you're visiting our forsaken corners, allow me to give you something valuable. For *after the war*, you understand?" After finally shutting off the engine, Aurelia climbed out and motioned the Swede after herself.

Inside the house, it was colder than in an ice box and just as dark. Navigating her way by memory, Aurelia entered her husband's former office, perfectly preserved as on the day he had left it, and unlocked the bottom draw of his desk. Not the best hiding place, to be sure, but it wasn't as if someone would be searching her home—not without her brother's direct authorization.

"Here." Pulling a thick folder out of the drawer, Aurelia handed it to the Swede. "It's all developed films documenting crimes committed by the SS detachments as they were pulling out of France, plus whatever documents I swiped from my brother's desk."

She smiled, but her smile came out pained and washed out, like a watercolor left in the sun for too long. Bernadotte briefly caught her hand over the invaluable evidence.

FORTY-SIX

Berlin, Germany. March 1945

The Reich capital will be defended to the last man and to the last bullet—the new directive from the Propaganda Ministry declared to the besieged population of Berlin. Much like Aurelia, most of them groaned at yet another call to arms against the formidable enemy armed to its teeth.

As the Soviet Army approached the city from the east and the Allied armies from the west, a palpable sense of dread and resignation enveloped the city. Distant sounds of artillery echoed through the night, reminding Berliners of the chaos closing in around them. But the last of the rabid Nazis, hardened by fear and propaganda, got swept up in the fervor of Goebbels' call. They wrapped *Volkssturm* armbands around their biceps and armed themselves with whatever they could find—rusty rifles, old pistols, and even kitchen knives—ready to fight against an enemy that was standing at the gates of their city.

Dispatched by Goebbels, Aurelia filmed German women hoisting antitank grenade launchers onto their shoulders and

Hitler Youth children drowning in adult uniforms as they lined up for a troop inspection. After reviewing the footage, Goebbels rejected most of it: the faces of Berliners, once filled with pride and hope, now wore expressions of resignation and despair, which they didn't bother to conceal from the camera. They were fighting not just against an invading army, but against the very regime that had led them to this precipice of ruin. Only the regime's blindest followers made it into the final cut.

"It's difficult to describe, frankly speaking," Aurelia said to Folke Bernadotte during yet another one of his visits. With the Western Allies on German soil, it didn't take Bernadotte long to travel to Berlin. His visits were still incognito and mostly to Aurelia's home under the cover of the night, where he exchanged US Army SPAM (specially processed American meat) for the precious information and the evidence for the international court already collecting material for their future cases. Tonight, Aurelia gave him an assortment of what she'd been fortunate to pick up after an air raid on the Reich Main Security office. With one of the wings obliterated, papers had been flying everywhere. It was only prudent of her to collect them as she emerged from the shelter in the Propaganda Ministry's department facing the damaged building. "They've one foot in their grave with Hitler and Goebbels is shoveling dirt onto them with these 'Berlin defense' directives, but instead of realizing that this is very much their end, they're still parroting the Propaganda Ministry's latest spiels assuring them that their *Führer* is the greatest chess player and that this was their strategy all along, and that now that he has his enemies so close by, he'll annihilate them all with his miracle weapons."

"But there are no 'miracle' weapons, correct?"

Aurelia only rolled her eyes, not even dignifying the question with a response.

"And what of Hitler himself? How's his mood these days? Still not considering the possibility of peace?"

"Hitler's in his bunker under the Reich Chancellery. Since he moved there after evacuating from his East Prussian head-quarters, I haven't heard of him coming out even for a breath of fresh air. And it stinks in that bunker," Aurelia groaned, scrunching up her face into a grimace of distaste. "Imagine stale air, body odor, cigarette smoke, and food being cooked, all contained in concrete quarters!"

Bernadotte's upper lip twitched in empathetic disgust. "And Himmler? Still loyal to Hitler to a fault?"

The question the Swede really wanted to ask was, can I make an offer for the release of Theresienstadt's hostages?

How Aurelia wished she could say yes—to that unspoken question. Instead, she nodded to the one he had actually voiced. "He is, I'm afraid."

Each time they parted on this pessimistic note, and each time, a tiny part of her died. With the SS evacuating the remaining concentration camps as the Allies closed in from both fronts, Max's chances of survival were shrinking. Because there was no evacuation, only corpses along the forced march's roads which no one cared to even conceal anymore.

Another day; more graffiti declaring Berlin's new "never surrender" motto; more corpses swinging from the electric poles, hanged for defeatism or refusal to pick up arms—uniformed and civilian alike. Just this very morning in his office, Goebbels swore to personally drag out and execute any Berliner hanging a white sheet off their window.

After leaving the Ministry, Aurelia wandered about the city that used to be so vibrant, so deliciously free, making short videos and snapshots of street barricades and lines of fresh corpses dug from under yet another entirely obliterated street. Berlin was singing its swan song. Aurelia made sure future generations would hear it—to learn the bitter lessons from the past.

Later, in the dim twilight of her home—the days had grown longer, but this particular one had dawned cold and misty—she unraveled the scarf from her neck, feeling the weight of the world pressing down on her. The air was tense, still ringing with the howls of distant air-raid sirens. The Allied fliers came during the day too. There were simply not enough anti-aircraft defense positions around Berlin to stop them.

Aurelia made her way into the kitchen, her stomach grumbling at the thought of the last SPAM can left from Bernadotte's previous visit. Dry leaves crunched underfoot inside the vast hallway. Without Heinz, long gone to tend to the fields on the Reich War Ministry's orders, there was no one here to rake them. Last fall, she had still swept whatever the November winds would push inside, but this time she simply couldn't find the will to care. After months of neglect, with Aurelia often away on her correspondent's excursions, the house was slowly falling into disrepair. With Frau Abel conscripted a year ago to some munition factory like the rest of the domestic laborers, dust accumulated everywhere, dulling each surface to gunmetal. Plaster peeled off the ceiling and hung in coils overhead. The walls shed their patterned wallpaper in clumps; on the top floor, the roof was leaking, turning the wooden floor into a puddle of black rot. Aurelia rarely ventured there these days. Like most of the Berliners chased underground by the Allied bombers, she slept in the cellar.

"Aurelia." A voice called out of the shadows, low and grave.

Startled, Aurelia whipped around with her gun drawn, nearly dropping the precious American chow.

"Damn it, Wilhelm." She shoved the gun back in its holster, facing her brother. He sat perched on the countertop like an ancient gargoyle with his gun in his hands. "I could have shot you." To be fair, shooting him had been the first idea that crossed her mind as soon as she was issued the weapon. International war correspondents didn't carry any, but it had been obvious for quite some time that what applied to the rest of the world, didn't apply to Nazi Germany. They armed whoever was ready to do their bidding, no questions asked, and they trained their war correspondents to take part in action, if such was their desire. Naturally, Aurelia had no inclination to partake in any such thing.

"Would have given you pleasure, wouldn't it?"

She met his gaze with a mixture of wariness and defiance. "What do you want? I'm tired and want to sleep."

"I would imagine, keeping dates with the Swedish," he scoffed, pocketing his gun. "Not even an effort to look surprised or insulted? Little sister, I'm beginning to fear you're growing a pair bigger than mine."

Pulling the dagger from its case—another present from the Wehrmacht along with a correspondent's uniform of the *Propagandakompanie*—Aurelia stabbed the top of the can and began prying it open. Whatever Wilhelm had to say could wait as far as she was concerned. She was starving.

"Why would I deny anything?" she mumbled, the first heavenly smear of pinkish meat paste exploding with sweetness in her mouth. "You were the one who initially approved Bernadotte's request for the Red Cross inspection. He has never made a secret out of his desire to secure a hostage deal. I'm sure I'm just one of the few people he's been visiting."

"Yes, only that's not all he's been coming for."

Picking up another cut of SPAM with her dagger, Aurelia paused just long enough to feign mock insult. "Are you insinuating I'm cheating on my poor husband, dear brother? Truly, I'm scandalized. I assure you, our relationship is purely platonic."

"Cut the nonsense, Aurelia," Wilhelm snapped, his eyes narrowing. "I know what you're doing, all I want is a way in."

The dagger with another slice froze inches from Aurelia's mouth. "Pardon me?"

Jumping off the counter, Wilhelm landed heavily on his feet and began to pace. "We talked about it, a very long time ago. In case you've forgotten, it's been my plan all along: to replace that impotent corporal who has lost the last of his marbles after his own Wehrmacht tried to blow him up. And to make sure the Allies install me as Germany's new ruler, I need to get into their good graces. Which you've been doing all along without bothering to inform me."

Bored once again, Aurelia returned to her improvised dinner. "Tough nuts, brother. You're a wanted war criminal and you shall die like one."

He was suddenly upon her, his gun once again in her head, pointing at her jaw. "Oh no, I don't think so. You're forgetting one little thing." The barrel of his gun tapped the metal of the wedding band on her ring finger. "Before I die, I'll make sure Laub is quartered, you hear me? I'll personally ask the ghetto *Kommandant* to torture him for days before he finally offs his sorry behind. And I'll bring you there so you can witness it. I've already sent one of your husbands to the great beyond. It'll be my utmost pleasure to extend the same courtesy to the other."

The vivid picture he painted chilled her very blood, even if outwardly Aurelia remained perfectly composed. "How do I even know he's still alive? I haven't received anything from him in the past two months."

"The postal service is collapsing, you daft bat! Come to my office tomorrow, I'll schedule you a phone call."

Her spirits momentarily soaring at the prospect of hearing Max's voice, Aurelia nodded, licking her lips. "What do you want then? A meeting?"

"To the devil with your meetings, I'm not getting shot by Hitler's goons for treason!" Wilhelm stood opposite her, a sinister grin spreading across his face. "No, I'll supply you with documents from Hitler's and Himmler's own desks—no one can get close to those, you must admit. And you shall take them to your Swede, telling him exactly where they came from, so when all this is over he knows who's been helping him win this war and liberating his damned Jews."

Aurelia considered her brother's ultimatum. Did it really matter now, Wilhelm's eleventh-hour move? He could deliver stacks of valuable documents to the Allies through her; still they would never believe he was doing it out of the goodness of his heart. And if that simple assurance secured Max's life? Fine by her.

"I suppose I don't have a choice." Aurelia shrugged, looking annoyed just enough for it to be believable. "Keep my husband safe and you have yourself a deal."

Wilhelm stood, smiling triumphantly, his figure looming over her like a dark cloud. "See, little sister? We make a good team, you and I. Wait till you see what I make out of this country!"

As he left her house, Aurelia exhaled audibly, working the feeling back into her shoulders that had been locked with tension. He had already done everything he could to this country. The Allies would be mad to install the man behind the creation of concentration camps as Germany's provisional leader. Just like Wilhelm was keeping her alive for as long as she was useful to him, so too would she. As soon as Max was out of his reach, Aurelia would give her brother to the Allies personally, whichever side got to them first.

FORTY-SEVEN

Berlin, Germany. April 1945

As the last days of the war drew to a close, the Russians and western allies tightened their grip around Berlin like a vise, leaving only a narrow pathway to the south—a last, desperate escape route. With the showers of late April came the thunder of artillery and the echo of collapsing buildings—the final act of a truly Wagnerian symphony underscoring the fall of a regime that had once brought the world to its knees. Berlin lay largely in ruins, a once-proud capital now reduced to a haunting picture of utter annihilation.

If Art was still alive, what a timeless masterpiece he would have made out of this, Aurelia contemplated as she witnessed the dying agony of the city she used to call home. Every corner of Berlin bore witness to the horrors inflicted by the war. Bodies lay strewn in the rubble, some covered with makeshift cloths, others left exposed to the elements, their vacant eyes staring blankly into the gray, indifferent sky. The once-illustrious boulevards, where Berliners had strolled with hope and ambition, now resembled a graveyard, with debris, twisted metal, and street barricades all around. In the air, the acrid scent of smoke mingled with the metallic tang of blood and the sweet smell of horses rotting in the spring sun. The very spirit of Berlin appeared to be crushed under the weight of its own history.

Inside Hitler's bunker, the atmosphere was just as grim. The dimly lit hallways echoed with the frantic footsteps of high-ranking officials, their faces pale and drawn, eyes wide with fear. As Aurelia and Wilhelm descended inside, the walls around them seemed to close in like a tomb, encasing the last remnants of a regime crumbling into dust. The air was stale, infused with the stench of sweat and alcohol—a revolting concoction making Aurelia's stomach turn.

Summoned by the *Führer* for his final orders, Wilhelm von Brandenburg paused in front of a group of his fellow high-ranking Nazis, his expression a mixture of contempt and resignation.

"Brave Teutonic knights," he muttered, glancing around at the scattered groups of officers, their uniforms in disarray, eyes bloodshot, singing popular songs from the twenties as they drank themselves into oblivion. "Annihilating brandy instead of the enemy."

From inside Hitler's war room, shrill curses. One of the revelers paused, made a move to rise, only to slump back in his chair. With a wave of resignation, he fished another bottle from the crate and threw his head back, gulping down as much as he could.

An artillery shell exploded overhead, sending tremors through the concrete walls. Aurelia welcomed each one with suicidal joy and reckless abandon. Let them pound it all to smithereens. The nation that allowed the atrocities she'd witnessed to be committed deserved to be obliterated. There were no innocents left here. They had either left early on or perished while resisting. Only the perpetrators remained and

those who stood by and did nothing. And the latter deserved
their punishment just as much as the former.

She had no illusions on her own account either. She wasn't
any better, using her talents to boost the image of sheer evil.
She, too, deserved to die along with the old regime—but not
before she saw to it that justice was served.

Crimson-faced instead of his ever-present air of calm
detachment, Reichsführer Himmler shot out of the war room,
forgetting to close the door after him. It must have been him
who had just received the magisterial dressing-down for
collapsing the last front on which Hitler had been pinning all
his hopes.

"Where are you off to?" Wilhelm called to him as Himmler
rushed past him, adjusting the cap back on his head.

"Back to the front, where else?"

"What front?" Wilhelm laughed, and the nearest group of
drunkards laughed along with him.

One of them continued longer than the others, but then
suddenly began to weep, wiping his face with the back of his
hand with his service weapon in it. "This is the end," he sobbed,
his shoulders slumping with each shuddering exhale. "We're all
dead and buried. Dead and buried, I tell you..."

Moved by morbid curiosity—the war correspondent in her
hadn't died yet—Aurelia peered into Hitler's last command
room. Once a proud dictator with most of Europe under his
rule, he stood hunched over a massive table strewn with war
maps, fingers trembling as he traced imaginary lines of attack
across territories long lost. Under the unforgiving fluorescent
light, his pallid skin glistened with sweat and his eyes, once so
hypnotic with power and ambition, now reflected a haunted
abyss, filled with paranoia and disbelief.

"Send an immediate telegram to General Wenk demanding
to counterattack the Russians here," he muttered, pushing
meaningless figures around the map of Berlin. "They over-

stretched their front when they rushed on Berlin, now they will have to pay the price."

Behind his back, his generals exchanged frightened glances. *Who's going to tell him?* Keitel's expression read just before Jodl and Krebs quickly averted their eyes. *Certainly not me.*

"Yes, Wenk with his Twelfth Army attacking from the west and Steiner from the east will cut off the Russian supply lines and have them right where we want them." Hitler continued his deluded mumbling, nodding with satisfaction at his plan. "Once we have them encircled, we'll deal with them swiftly and without remorse. Has Wenk reported his movements yet?" Once again, his eyes fixed on the radio operator, who was sweating so profusely, Aurelia nearly sensed his physical discomfort.

"My *Führer*." Wilhelm cleared his throat as he stopped opposite Hitler and his entourage, saving the radio man the explanation. "Wenk's army has been all but destroyed on the Elbe. He's likely unable to report the army's movements because there is no army anymore. Steiner also hasn't had the strength to counterattack. He's in full retreat, leaving no front in his wake in the west. Zossen is taken." Unceremoniously, Wilhelm moved the pins on the maps no one except for Hitler had ever dared to touch. "Stahnsdorf is also about to fall. In the east, the Soviets already reached Mahlsdorf, Karlshorst, and Lichtenberg. On the north, the enemy is currently between Frohnau and Pankow. There is still a small corridor on the south, but it's only a matter of days before Berlin is completely encircled."

For a spell, there was nothing but dead silence in the room. Aurelia couldn't as much as hear a single person breathing. All blood draining from his face, Hitler stared at von Brandenburg across the desk for an interminably long moment. Aurelia couldn't quite tell what he was hoping: for one of his oldest comrades to break into laughter and announce it to be a joke?

Or for one of his generals to correct the minister of Prussia, for certainly this had to be a mistake. Only, no one said a word to the contrary. Neither did von Brandenburg crack a smile.

At last, Hitler's face contorted in murderous rage as he slammed his fists down on the table, sending maps and nonexistent army groups flying across the floor.

"This is treason!" he bellowed, his voice ringing off the cold, concrete walls. All of the military commanders pulled their heads into their shoulders, wincing visibly at the shrill screams and abuse that poured on them. "Why is von Brandenburg more informed than *Reich Führer*?! You've been lying to me. Traitors, every single one of you! Incompetent cowards. Not a drop of honor between the lot of you! I should have had all high-ranking officers executed like Stalin did in '37! Treason is all I've ever seen from you! The July plot and now this! Ignoring my direct orders! You are the reason we are losing the war! You are the ones who doomed the German people to annihilation!"

The generals around him listened with a mixture of fear and resignation.

"Treasonous cowards!" Hitler's saliva sprayed as he continued to rage, shaking his fists in the air in impotent fury, glaring about him with a manic gleam in his eyes. "If you had any conscience, you would have put a bullet through your head instead of planning your escape like frightened rats! I explicitly ordered you to fight to the last man! This was a direct order and you ignored it! Ignored it and lied to me about ignoring it, leaving me in the dark! It's a conspiracy, the worst one yet!"

As the tension reached boiling point, Aurelia felt her own stomach tighten into knots. At first, she'd taken a certain pleasure in watching the dictator and his entire regime crumble to pieces in front of her eyes, but the weight of the harrowing reality was finally dawning on her. This was the end. This was truly, irreversibly, the end.

As if on cue, Hitler lowered slowly into his chair, moving

his greasy lank hair out of his eyes with a hand that shook something frightful. In the space of a single minute, he seemed to age twenty years. With the gleam gone out of his eyes and his cheeks suddenly hollow, his face was a death mask—a plaster cast of someone no longer living.

"It's all over," he muttered, his voice just as dead. "The war is lost."

Despite being aware of the fact more than anyone, the generals started at the admission, desperately searching one another's face for clues. In the corner, Krebs was patting his forehead with a handkerchief.

"Do what you want," Hitler said, addressing no one in particular, his eyes riveted to the bare concrete floor. "Run. Save your skins. Just don't insult me any longer with the suggestions of my evacuation. I'm staying here, in Berlin. If you have no honor among you, I still do. When the time comes, I'll die along with Germany. Now, go. Leave. All of you."

Wilhelm was the first one to go, without bothering to salute. If anything, he seemed relieved and almost giddy with anticipation of Hitler's Reich's finale when he motioned Aurelia to follow him back outside.

With a final glance at the broken man—not out of sympathy but to commit the historical moment to her memory—Aurelia turned and left the threshold of the suffocating chamber. Inside the corridor, the echoes of despair faded behind them, but the oppressive atmosphere of the bunker lingered like a ghost, desolate and all-consuming.

Suddenly, a commotion erupted at the staircase entrance and Goebbels descended from the upper level of the bunker, his face flushed with fervor. "Tell the *Führer* I'm here!" he ordered the adjutant minding the war room's entrance. "We all are."

To Aurelia's growing horror, Frau Goebbels strode it, dressed as if off to a fancy outing, and following her, all of the Goebbels' children, accompanied by their nanny.

Stepping in front of the woman, Aurelia blocked her path. "Are you completely out of your mind?" she hissed at Magda Goebbels by way of greeting. "This is no place for children!"

Frau Goebbels measured Aurelia coldly with her perfectly made-up eyes. "This is the only place for them: here, with their parents and their *Führer*."

She *was* mad. There was no other explanation in Aurelia's eyes. Who, in their right mind, would bring their little girls into a bunker that was the main target of the Allied forces?

Helga, the oldest of the brood, almost a teenager now, with her intelligent dark eyes and disproportionally long limbs, stared at Aurelia in mute horror, hearing her words and pleading with her eyes *to do something.*

"Wilhelm and I, we're leaving for our estate," Aurelia spoke again through her teeth. "We can still get to it in time. It's far from the frontline and has a huge cellar. Let us take the children —they will be safe, I promise."

Magda Goebbels regarded Aurelia with cold condescension, her eyes almost pitying. "*Safe?* Safe from what? The bombs? The Soviets? You don't seem to understand, Fräulein von Brandenburg: without the *Führer*, without National Social-ism, there is no future for them. So, as their mother, I'm doing what's best for them—to live out their final days together with the country they love and when the time comes, take their last breath along with it."

"I don't care what you've decided for yourself," Aurelia pressed on, "this is your life—do as you please. But don't drag them into the grave along with you. What kind of mother are you?"

Magda Goebbels drew herself up to her full height. "One who loves her children too much to make them suffer in Germany without their leader to protect them. I don't expect you'd understand—you've always been too selfish to have children for your country. Now, move. The *Führer* needs me and I'm not wasting any more time on empty talk with you."

With that, she shoved past Aurelia, her hand clasping Helga's like an iron cast.

"Wilhelm," Aurelia tried to appeal to her brother's reason, but he only shrugged with an indifference that turned her stomach.

"I think we've seen enough," he said instead and set off, taking two stairs at a time.

Seeing no other choice, Aurelia followed him and a small group of like-minded officers who were ready to abandon the sinking ship. Once on the upper level, they moved toward the exit, the weight of their choices heavy in the air, leaving Goebbels to rant in the bunker, his family trailing behind him like shadows.

Wilhelm's adjutant holding the door for her, Aurelia climbed into her half-brother's staff car, her half-brother following her with a sigh of relief.

"Finally!" He slapped the back of the driver's seat once the young man got inside. "Get us out of this rat trap and make it snappy."

Snappy wasn't on the cards in a city shrouded in a pall of despair. The streets were overrun with refugees from the west and east and regular Berliners who didn't fancy witnessing the joining of the Allied forces on the ruins of their homes. As they navigated through the throngs, Aurelia felt her heart ache for the suffering around her. Children clung to their mothers, tears streaking their dirt-stained faces, while men and women shuffled forward, their spirits crushed beneath the weight of war. The streets, once so full of life, now issued cries of sorrow and regret—a ghostly lullaby for the country that had forgotten how to dream.

"Wilhelm," Aurelia said, licking her lips as the car crept

forward. "It's almost over. He'll kill himself soon, leaving you as his successor, just as you planned—"

"Oh, I'm not waiting for him to put a bullet through his skull to take over," her stepbrother responded, full of morbid cheer, clashing so drastically with the oppressive atmosphere of the city under siege. "As soon as we get home, I'm telegraphing the bunker with the announcement that I'm in charge now. Then, as soon as we establish connection with the western Allies, I'll begin negotiating peace as Germany's new leader. Once they sign a ceasefire with us, you'll employ all your Propaganda Ministry experience to persuade them that it's in the West's best interest to unite with Germany against the Bolshevists. And once they turn on Stalin—"

"Wilhelm!" Aurelia cut off the stream of carefully assembled plans he had been nurturing for years, if not decades. "This was not the deal. I promised to tell the Allies through Bernadotte that you've been helping, in exchange for Max. I fulfilled my part of the obligation. It's your turn now. Make the call and have him released. Or let me go; I'll make my way there myself."

Wilhelm only groaned, rolling his eyes. "Lia, we are about to usher in a new dawn for our country and this is all you can think of? I'm offering you the world on a silver platter. Show some gratitude."

Her chest tightening up—she knew he couldn't be trusted, always had!—Aurelia, nevertheless, refused to surrender. "I never wanted your damned world," she said through gritted teeth. "All I wanted was my husband. Give him back."

"Are you really that daft? How am I to do that if I have no communication with half of Berlin?"

Lies, bold and inexcusable, right in her face. "Yes, you do," Aurelia growled. "Your communications post is better than the one at the bunker. That's how you received all those reports before Hitler did. Most of the lines going there are already cut.

Yours, on the other hand, are outside city limits, safe and sound."

"Aurelia, quit your droning. I have no time for this now."

"But—"

"One more peep out of you and I may just use one of those lines to make a call—to order them to shoot the bastard instead of letting him walk. Would you like that?"

There was nothing else for it but to bite her tongue—for now. It was all right. Even if he didn't keep his word, the Allies would still come to arrest him and once they did, she would jump on the first skinny mare she could find and ride to Theresienstadt without stopping. Just a few more days. She'd been waiting for years. Just a few more days wouldn't hurt...

Even with the windows rolled up, a cacophony of sounds filled the creeping vehicle. Families huddled together, clutching tattered belongings, their expressions a haunting reflection of despair and hopelessness. *Volkssturm* soldiers trudged beside them, their faces gaunt and hollow-eyed, their bodies burdened with the weight of their losses. Only small groups of *Hitlerjugend* boys with antitank rocket launchers on their shoulders marched in the opposite direction, singing patriotic songs in their still-unbroken voices.

"Step on it, will you?" Wilhelm urged the driver, his tone brisk. "We must reach the estate before they close off the roads entirely."

"There's too many of them, *Herr Reichsmarschall*," the driver tried to explain, laying on the horn. "They just won't move."

"Run over a couple," Wilhelm suggested without a trace of humor. "That'll make them jump out of your way quicker."

"Don't you dare do anything of the sort." Aurelia pulled forward, her hand grasping the driver's shoulder. "I'll personally bash your skull in if you hurt anyone."

"Don't listen to my sister. She's just mad I wouldn't let her see her husband before he kicked the bucket. In my defense, I knew she wouldn't stick around if I let him go." Wilhelm regarded Aurelia with mirth dancing in his eyes before uttering the words that would obliterate her entire world to dust. "So I ordered him to be shot a few days ago—you know, as an insurance policy to keep her around."

Red haze rising before her eyes, Aurelia threw herself at him, pummeling her half-brother with her fists and throwing kicks at his shins as much as the backseat allowed.

"Quit it, you banshee!" Wilhelm grunted, trying to wrestle her off. A few of her punches landed: blood was gushing out of Wilhelm's split lip and nose. "I ought to have shipped you east as well. If the SS didn't shoot you, the Ivans would pass you around for a couple of days before they did." He finally succeeded in pinning her down to the seat, holding her in place with the weight of his entire body. "You're on their *Wanted* list, in case you missed it. They didn't forget how you took pictures of their partisans hanging nicely for Goebbels' propaganda. Should I let you out? The Soviets will be here in no time. Want to wait for them together with this herd?"

Silent tears slipped down Aurelia's cheeks, staining the upholstery against which her face was pressed. In the past few weeks, she'd been demanding Wilhelm either let her travel east or bring her husband here, to Berlin. Too busy with his own affairs, Wilhelm had appointed one of his men to mind her at all times, so she wouldn't run. "He's fine," her half-brother had replied to each of Aurelia's inquests about Max. "Let him stay where he is, it's safer for him there. The Ivans shall liberate him soon enough."

And now this confession that had plunged into her very heart like a knife...

"Let me out then," she whispered through tears that stung like poison. "Let me out, shoot me on the side of the road for all I care. I have nothing left to live for."

"So fucking dramatic," Wilhelm huffed, annoyed, searching for something in his pocket. "Just like your mother. I wish I could do away with you, but I do need you to be by my side when the Allies come. Besides, I'll look like a hero, pulling you out of the burning city in your hour of need. Don't you agree?"

"Go hang yourself, Wilhelm."

"Let's spend the rest of the way in silence, shall we?" He shoved something bitter in her mouth and held a hand over her face until she swallowed. Within minutes, her limbs turned to cotton as her head began to swim.

Should have poisoned him with his morphine while I still had the chance—the last thought flashed through Aurelia's mind before everything faded to black.

When Aurelia came to, the familiar surroundings of her father's old study came into focus before her eyes. She lay on the settee under a bearskin throw. The adjutant must have covered her to shield her from cold, she guessed. Her brother had no care for such comforts. He had no care for human life either.

There he was, sipping cherry brandy at her father's old desk. He must have moved it back here from his office to avoid losing the heirloom to the bombs. On the corner, a portable telegraph machine stood, Wilhelm's adjutant working it without the convenience of a chair.

"...being the next in the line of power succession, it'll be my honor to see Germany through its last days and sign the conditions of surrender on your behalf." Wilhelm took another sip as he flipped the page of the message he must have prepared long before Hitler had even ascended to power.

"We only left the bunker a few hours ago and you're already stabbing the old man in the back?" Aurelia croaked, her voice hoarse from tears and the vile narcotic.

"Look who's up!" her brother replied, mock-toasting Aurelia

with his glass. "Why waste time? You heard him rant. The old corporal is cooked, time for the new command and leadership."

"He still has a few loyal men," Aurelia said, her voice flat. She didn't care what happened to him—to any of them—but wanted to argue solely to ruin the moment for Wilhelm. "Wait till he sends them here with machineguns."

"He'll send no one," Wilhelm scoffed, his arrogance palpable. "We barely made it through, the city is encircled."

As she watched her half-brother's delusions of grandeur unfold, Aurelia felt nothing but cold indifference. With the news of her husband's death, nothing mattered anymore. She almost wished she had remained in the bunker herself—to be buried alive under the rubble during the shelling. A much more merciful death than existing with this open wound of suffering in place of a heart which she felt had been ripped out of her aching chest.

FORTY-EIGHT

In the fading light of the late April of 1945, the von Brandenburg familial estate once again turned into a bastion of intrigue. While besieged Berliners had been chased into cellars by the constant artillery barrages, Wilhelm von Brandenburg rose at his leisure, rode one of the two remaining horses before a breakfast prepared by the cook he had managed to hide from the last Goebbels' conscription for the defense of Berlin, and sipped brandy as he dictated yet another telegram addressed to Count Folke Bernadotte.

"You're wasting your time," Aurelia claimed each time she happened to overhear her stepbrother trying out different versions of the text on his long-suffering adjutant. "You have no right to negotiate anything on Germany's behalf. Not after Hitler stripped you of your rank and ordered your execution. The Allies know you hold no power in this government."

"Foolishness," his voice scoffed from the depths of his "war room." "It's the old corporal who holds no power. It's been what, three days since he ordered my execution? I am yet to see a single SS man with a machinegun at my gates following up on his order."

Of course not. Berlin was completely encircled. No one was getting in or out—SS or not. Indifferent to everything and fully committed to the idea of ending it all once she saw Wilhelm getting what he deserved, Aurelia only shrugged and returned to the stables, where she tended to the horses, their gentle nuzzles the only comfort in the empty, broken husk of her life.

"Hungry, are you?" Aurelia murmured to the horses, her fingers brushing their manes as they devoured what little feed she could offer. "I'm sorry. Your owner had thought of stocking up on food and drink for himself but forgot all about you. But don't fret, you won't starve as long as I'm here. When we run out of oats, I'll steal bread and vegetables out of the kitchen for you. Stab the cook if he tries to stop me, but get you the food; hear me?"

Tears would always start to suffocate her after uttering those promises. It was guilt, pure and all-encompassing, strangling her anew the first moment she opened her eyes. It slithered like a snake, injecting fresh venom into the wounds that refused to close with each painful beat of her heart: she hadn't done enough, hadn't tried hard enough, hadn't sacrificed enough. She didn't deserve to live now that Max had died—because of her. And so, in the final days before the self-inflicted curtain dropped, Aurelia had thrown her all at the two helpless creatures. At least they would get through this war. At least they would survive the damned von Brandenburg clan.

But just as she was certain that Wilhelm's machinations would come to nothing, he burst into the stables, his face animated and rosy with glee.

"Take a guess who decided to be my new best friend, little sister!"

"The devil?" She barely bothered to entertain his charade.

Slightly annoyed, Wilhelm stalked over and virtually shoved a telegram under her nose. "Reichsführer Himmler," he announced victoriously.

Aurelia regarded him with mistrust. Ever since his appointment as the leader of Hitler's personal bodyguard—the black-clad SS—Himmler had been loyal to his master to a fault. True, he had left the bunker even before the von Brandenburg siblings did, but from what Aurelia remembered, he had been heading to the front, to command the remaining units of the Waffen-SS defending the capital.

Then again, that was three days ago.

"Come, ask me why," Wilhelm taunted, waving the paper in front of her eyes. "I know you're curious."

Aurelia sighed, dusting her hands off before folding them over her chest. "I suppose you won't leave off until you tell me."

He grinned, the scant light flickering across his face. "Himmler may be a Nazi, but he's not a stupid Nazi. He knows the war is lost. Hitler has admitted that much himself. Also, Hitler promised to put a bullet through his head before he would surrender, which leaves our beloved *Reichsführer* unemployed and rather defenseless. So, sensing the shifting tides, Himmler sought to align himself with me, hoping to leverage our combined influence to negotiate a favorable outcome. He also realizes that the Soviets will have our collective hides if we surrender to them. So, he wants to present a united front to... let's put it this way, salvage what remains of Germany."

"Salvage?" Aurelia echoed, a bitter laugh escaping her lips. "What remains is a shell of a nation bombed into oblivion and left without a semblance of order. Do you truly believe that you two can negotiate with the Allies while your hands are stained with blood?"

"Oh, we are already negotiating," Wilhelm said with confidence. "Bernadotte still wants to save his Danish Jews from Theresienstadt. Himmler and I are giving them to him as a gesture of goodwill—so that we can start discussing terms of peace in earnest. Their train is leaving as we speak. I'm sorry your husband won't be on it."

Aurelia didn't even bristle at the extremely low blow. She had long lost all capacity for feeling anything but resignation in the face of the approaching end.

"If you and Himmler believe the western Allies will negotiate separate peace with you against the Soviets, you are both just as delusional as Hitler. You'll end up like him, too. At least you will, Big Brother. The old gypsy said so."

Perhaps it was only a play of the shadows, but it looked as though Wilhelm's face paled a bit at the mention of the von Brandenburg curse.

"If the curse is true, it means you'll die too, little sister." He narrowed his eyes at her, hoping for a reaction.

Aurelia only smiled serenely in response. "I sure do hope so. The sooner, the better."

He backed away from her and stalked off, a mixture of annoyance and fear creasing his brow.

The next morning, as the "family" sat down to breakfast, the old radio crackled to life, Aurelia's former boss's voice filling the vast dining hall.

"Our beloved *Führer* Adolf Hitler has fallen," he announced, his voice steady and grave. "He died a hero's death, defending his capital from the enemy until his last breath."

With a cry of cheer, Wilhelm clapped his hands toward the cook waiting by the kitchen entrance. "About damned time! Well? What are you standing there for, like a Carmelite monk on leave? Bring the champagne! This calls for a toast!"

However, the cook didn't even have chance to fetch the champagne when the next announcement came, dampening Wilhelm von Brandenburg's spirits considerably.

"According to the *Führer*'s last will and testament, both Wilhelm von Brandenburg and Heinrich Himmler are expelled from the Party and their offices of state. Grand Admiral Karl

Dönitz is appointed Reich President and Supreme Commander of the Armed Forces. Joseph Goebbels is appointed Reich Chancellor and Martin Bormann Party Chancellor."

At the sight of her brother's darkening expression, Aurelia broke into scornful laugher. She kept laughing while Goebbels announced his own decision to rather die defending Berlin than run like other traitors had done; she still laughed when Wilhelm rose to his feet, overturning his chair and stormed off, muttering curses under his breath. She laughed until the laughter turned to tears and after the tears ran dry, she wiped her face and went to the window—to wait for the end.

The atmosphere in the estate shifted dramatically as the rumble of Allied vehicles echoed on the outskirts, the sound growing louder with each passing moment. Aurelia watched them come from behind the glass, ready for the resolution—whatever it may be. She'd been living in bondage of the regime for far too long. Her shoulders had grown numb from carrying the guilt of her complicity. Her heart beat for no one any longer, pumping useless blood into the shell of her body.

When the first Allied soldiers, military police in tow, spilled out of the army jeeps, it was Aurelia who opened the door for them. Strangely enough, there was press with them, already snapping photos of her talking to the officer in charge.

"Aurelia von Brandenburg?" He touched two fingers to the rim of his helmet. "First Lieutenant Moore, 36th division of the Seventh US Army. We have information that Wilhelm von Brandenburg is here."

"He is."

"Is he armed?"

"He carries his service gun, but he'll surrender it."

She escorted them into her father's old study, where Wilhelm sat at the desk in full regalia, his pose one of bored royalty. At the sight of the camera, his smug grin grew wider. He was basking in the attention, still naively believing that the military had arrived to negotiate the terms of the country that lay in ruins—owing in great part to him and his insatiable hunger for power. He had never cared for common people, like his ancestors had never cared for the soldiers under their charge. Everyone was dispensable; everything was a means to an end. Just like his forefathers had sucked the blood out of German peasants to feed their empire's ambitious war machine, he sucked the blood out of common folk to wage war and enrich himself. It was never about making Germany great, it was only about advancing himself. It was never about people, only about himself.

Aurelia watched him, and with him, her entire bloodline, face the culmination of their parasitic existence and felt her very soul rejoice when First Lieutenant Moore addressed her brother.

"Wilhelm von Brandenburg, you are under arrest for war crimes and crimes against humanity. You will surrender your weapon and come with us to face the International Military Tribunal."

Wilhelm's face went pale, disbelief flooding his features as he stammered, "You have no right to arrest me! I am the leader of the sovereign country—"

"Hitler is dead; the leader is Karl Dönitz," Moore cut him off, motioning for Wilhelm to rise. "Hitler ordered your arrest and execution for treason, by the way, before he appointed Dönitz as his successor. Surrender your service weapon."

As they disarmed Wilhelm and tore the epaulets from his shoulders, Aurelia felt a surge of immense relief. Her half-brother had left no heir to carry on their warmongering name. As for herself, she had long ago decided to bury the von Brandenburg bloodline with her.

As she followed the group out of the estate, she paused in front of the long line of her ancestors' portraits.

"You don't have to come with us," one of Moore's men advised. "You aren't under arrest. I imagine the Tribunal will summon you all the same for testimony, but you're not charged with anything."

Aurelia winced slightly. She didn't want to prolong her miserable existence, she had no business to be on this earth any longer. But, on the other hand, she did owe it to the perished and the survivors—to shed light on the regime she'd carefully documented as an insider, for this very purpose.

"The Soviets are looking for me," Aurelia said at last, arriving at a decision. They stood in the vast hall, contemplating the men of the von Brandenburg family scowling at her from above. "They don't know I've been helping."

"Ah." The soldier cleared his throat. "Then, I suppose, it's best if you come with us. Stay under the protection of the US until we clear the matter with our Soviet allies."

He was about to set off to join his corps outside, but Aurelia caught him by the sleeve. "Can I borrow a light?"

"Sure." He offered her his pack and the engraved silver lighter.

Aurelia took a cigarette out, lit it up, took a long pull, and before he could stop her, held the lighter to the bottom of the first canvas. Old oil went up in quick flames, soon spreading to the wooden paneling and igniting the rest of the portraits and with them—the entire estate.

"Just finishing my mother's job," she said with a smile as she passed ashen-faced Wilhelm and his escort staring at the fire devouring the old world.

As they drove through the outskirts of the city, the air felt different—charged with a sense of impending change. The sounds of gunfire and chaos had faded, replaced by the distant cheers of liberation. Soldiers moved through the streets, their faces a mix of weariness and triumph, yet Aurelia felt an ache deep within her. The Berlin she had known was in ruins, a landscape transformed by the horrors of war.

Waiting at one of the checkpoints, Aurelia took one last look at the devastated city she was leaving behind. The skyline, once proud and majestic, was now marred by the scars of war. Memories flooded her mind—her childhood, her dreams, and the love she had shared with Max. One particular recollection stood out among them all: her husband's fingers caressing her skin on the very first night they had spent together after reuniting in Austria.

"I was so afraid you'd see those newspapers and find yourself a new American wife," Aurelia had confessed, her lips against the stubble of his cheek.

"I knew you loved me," Max had said with an inexplicable confidence about him. "Not because I'm so great," he'd laughed between the kisses he was peppering her hair with, "but because I felt your love deep in my very marrow. If anything happened to you, I would know."

"I would, too," she had said then and meant it.

A flicker, a mere grain of doubt, made her turn and look back at the ruins of the country she was leaving behind. She hadn't felt anything before the hideous, mocking words Wilhelm had hurled in her face. She searched herself as closely as she could and, once again, felt absolutely nothing out of ordinary.

What if her brother had lied, like he had—through his teeth —for the entirety of his miserable life? What if Max was still alive, trying to make his way to her as she was driving away?

Aurelia closed her eyes, willing herself to remain strong. She had fought too hard to give up now. The Allies were finally here, and with their arrival came the promise of a new beginning, a chance to reclaim what had been lost.

"Excuse me." Aurelia touched her escort's wrist. "Do you have access to the Red Cross lists by any chance? The ones with the names of the people liberated from the camps?"

"Sure do." His eyes crinkled at the corners as he eyed her knowingly. "Looking for your husband?"

Aurelia nodded, her lip between her teeth—too afraid to believe and too afraid not to.

"If he's alive, we'll find him," he said, patting her hand, and resumed his whistling.

With a determined heart, Aurelia stared straight ahead, her eyes once more opened to the future. She would find Max; she would not rest until she had reclaimed her family from the ashes of despair. Her husband and her friends and the colleagues of old and the wolf dogs she'd saved and raised as her own—a real family, the ties of which ran thicker than blood. And once united, they would rebuild—the new world where everyone was welcome, where neighbor helped neighbor, where truth was universal, and love trumped hate.

The change wouldn't come fast and wouldn't come easy, but she was an old, experienced soldier. She was ready to fight.

FORTY-NINE

London. Summer 1945

The streets of London were a patchwork of resilience and scars, the shadows of war still visible in the rubble that lay strewn across the city. Aurelia Laub stood amid the debris, her hands covered in dust as she worked alongside other volunteers, clearing away the remnants of destruction. The air was filled with the sounds of shovels scraping against stone and the murmurs of determined voices, each person contributing to the rebuilding of a city that had faced its own trials. This wasn't something imposed on her—quite the contrary. With the highest-ranking Nazis locked in the Tower of London while the International Tribunal worked on gathering evidence, there was not much for Aurelia to do except wait. Wait for her turn to tell the world the story of a nation that had strived for greatness but ended with genocide and self-destruction instead. Wait to face her half-brother in court. Wait to discover the truth of the one question that stole her sleep, one angst-ridden night after another: was she still a wife or a widow?

That was the reason she worked so hard, tearing the skin on

her hands to blood—to silence that ache deep within her. Helping restore the city her brother's bombers had reduced to rubble offered temporary salvation from the relentless question that haunted her every waking moment: What had happened to Max? Each day, she begged for news, and each day she was met with the same reply: "We have heard nothing yet." The words felt like a heavy weight, a chain binding her to uncertainty and fear.

As she worked, she found solace in the shared effort of those around her. Londoners were resilient and their spirit inspired her to push through her own despair. She helped clear debris from homes, assisted in distributing supplies, and offered her strength to those who needed it most. Yet, the pain of her solitude redoubled each time she left the site for the day, the silence of her temporary quarters almost too much to bear.

Today was one of those days. With the sun setting behind the shattered form of the city's horizon, Aurelia untied the kerchief from her head and wiped the brick dust off her face and hands, waiting for the Londoners to wash up at the nearest water pump. She always held back, staying well away from them and pumping her own water out of shame for her own complicity in what she was presently trying to restore. No charges had been brought up against her, but without court proceedings, no one knew of her exact role in the regime or the resistance. To Londoners, she was Wilhelm von Brandenburg's sister and Goebbels' employee. If she was entirely frank, Aurelia was surprised the locals tolerated her presence in the first place.

"Hey, Kraut!"

Aurelia looked up, startled, and discovered the women from her clearing group gesturing her toward the water pump.

"Come here. Wash up."

"Don't fret, we won't waterboard you."

Like a nervous colt, she approached the group and,

painfully aware of everyone's eyes on her, held her hands under the water stream. Ice-cold water shocked her for a moment, stinging the sunburnt, peeling skin on her arms and neck.

"Here, let me help you." One of the women held Aurelia's hair so she could wash her face properly.

It was then that she broke down at last. First, her eyes began to fill; then, her throat was caught in a spasm that stole her breath at this unexpected kindness she knew she didn't deserve. Before she could get a hold of herself, Aurelia was on her hands and knees, weeping at the feet of these women who were so much better than her, than her entire people, offering a helping hand to the former enemy with graciousness of someone truly human.

A couple of weeks later, as the July humidity settled over the city, Aurelia was lost in thought, her hands moving mechanically as she cleared a section of rubble. There was talk of moving the defendants to Nuremberg, where the Tribunal proper would take place.

"Why go to all that trouble?" Jane, the same woman who had initially called Aurelia Kraut—still did, but good-naturedly now—and invited her to the water pump, blew an errant curly red hair away from her face. "Dust off the good ole ax from Henry VIII's days and chop their heads off right here! I'll provide the head basket."

"Or ask the French for the guillotine—I bet they still have a few squirreled away from the Revolution's days."

Each woman in the clearing line provided her own opinion until it was Aurelia's turn. Kate, a lucky wife whose husband had not only returned to her from the war but returned in one piece and with medals for bravery, ceased mid-word as she turned to pass the brick to Aurelia. With the interruption of their seamless work, the lively chatter died down, the women's eyes on the foreigner among them once again.

"If it were up to me, I'd do the same to them as they did to their victims in the camps," Aurelia said with an indifferent shrug, holding her hands out for the piece of rubble Kate was still clutching to her chest. "The ax and the guillotine are too easy. No, I'd lock them in the gas chamber, where they would watch each other claw at the walls for nearly half an hour as they suffocate slowly. Or make them dig a trench all night for their own families to tumble into as they wait their turn. Only then would they understand what they've done—" Her voice broke off mid-sentence, losing itself in righteous anger and the nightmarish memories she'd carry with her to the grave.

"Kraut for Prosecutor General," Jane observed, impressed.

A few women snorted with laughter, as did Aurelia, trying not to think that another reason behind her words was the image of her husband meeting the same fate as so many of the Nazis' victims.

With a shake of her head but also chuckling, Kate finally passed Aurelia the long-suffering brick. Offering merely a glance in the direction of the next person in line, Aurelia tossed the brick and turned back to Kate for another when it suddenly dawned on her that this wasn't the usual girl who occupied the spot beside her. Instantly frozen, she felt the next piece of broken plaster scrape her hands and miss them as it tumbled down.

As though in slow motion, Aurelia turned her head, the realization dawning like the first ray of sun breaking through a long and dark night.

"Max?" she breathed, disbelief and hope intertwining in her voice.

There he stood, alive and whole, the eyes behind the spectacles crinkling at the corners with mischief.

Overcome by a torrent of feelings, she threw herself at him, burying her face in the folds of his clothes, her tears flowing freely.

The world around them faded away as she held him close, feeling the steady rhythm of his heartbeat against her cheek. The chaos of the city, the rubble, the uncertainty—all fell silent in that moment. She was home again, wrapped in the embrace of the man she had fought so long to find.

"I once crossed the ocean and half the continent to get to you," he spoke into her hair, stroking it softly. "Did you seriously think that hiding across the Channel would stop me?"

EPILOGUE

Los Angeles. July 1950

On the silver screen, against the backdrop of bombed-out London, the actress playing Aurelia Laub slowly turns her head. Up close, her eyes widen; she pauses momentarily, barely daring to whisper her husband's name.

With the camera on the actor playing Max Laub, the audience gasps at the dramatic change in his appearance. The man who stands before them bears little resemblance to the director they last saw in Theresienstadt over a year ago. His frame is gaunt, almost skeletal, and the pallor of his skin betrays the toll of the months spent in the overcrowded confines of the camp. His hair, which must have been shorn a few months ago, is just beginning to grow out and nearly half of it is streaked with gray. Yet, amid this stark transformation, there is something unchanged— the piercing clarity of the eyes behind the glasses. They hold the same quiet strength and resilience that shone through even the darkest of days.

"I once crossed the ocean and half the continent to get to you," he speaks as the two lose each other in the tightest embrace.

"Did you seriously think that hiding across the Channel would stop me?"

The theater was silent for a few moments as the picture faded to black to the crescendo of the closing chords of the orchestra. Not a dry eye in the place, the audience froze as authentic photos along with captions began to appear on the screen.

"In the spring of 1945, Theresienstadt became one of the last German ghettos/camps to hold evacuees from other concentration and extermination camps. By May 1945, thousands were dying daily due to the severely overcrowded conditions, starvation, and disease. On Folke Bernadotte's special request, Max Laub's name was included by Himmler in the list of Dutch Jews released from Theresienstadt, against Wilhelm von Brandenburg's knowledge. However, Max Laub refused to leave the children under his care and remained in the camp until its liberation. On the day of liberation, he weighed only 45 kilograms—about 90 pounds. It took the International Red Cross over three months to nurse him and the other fortunate survivors back to life.

"Wilhelm von Brandenburg, the man responsible for the inception, implementation, and maintenance of the concentration camps on German and occupied territories, was sentenced by the International Military Tribunal to death for war crimes and crimes against humanity. One of the prosecution's chief witnesses was Aurelia Laub, who had been diligently gathering evidence of her half-brother's crimes over the years. Along with other criminals, he was hanged in Nuremberg in October 1946.

"Heinrich Himmler killed himself by swallowing a cyanide capsule as he was being apprehended by the Allied forces.

"Joseph Goebbels and his wife Magda remained in Hitler's bunker, along with their children. Magda Goebbels poisoned every single one of them before the couple committed suicide following Hitler's example.

"Leni Riefenstahl was declared a fellow traveler by the Denazification court but was acquitted of any other charges.

"Besides working with the French Resistance, Zara Whitby saved countless priceless European art pieces by 'gifting' them to Wilhelm von Brandenburg and later advising him to store them in the Austrian mines to avoid losing them to bombardment. Every single piece was recovered by the Allied group from the Monuments, Fine Arts, and Archives program and returned to the appropriate museums.

"Aurelia Laub made it possible for the director of this picture to emigrate to the United States in 1935 by trading her freedom for his.

"Max Laub opened his home to him and his family.

"This film is about them, for them, and for all of you.

"Berthold Wolowsky."

The applause that exploded around the couple in the front row thundered through the crowded theater. Embarrassed by all the attention, Aurelia and Max rose from their seats, tears glistening in their eyes as they waved at the audience. From the stage, Bibi —the director—applauded as well, elegant as ever in his coat-tails. It had been a long road, but they'd made it. Now, it was up to future generations to carry the torch.

A LETTER FROM ELLIE

Dear reader,

I want to say a huge thank you for choosing to read *To Save Her Husband*. If you did enjoy it, and want to keep up to date with all my latest releases, just sign up at the following link. Your email address will never be shared and you can unsubscribe at any time.

www.bookouture.com/ellie-midwood

I hope you loved *To Save Her Husband* and if you did, I would be very grateful if you could write a review. I'd love to hear what you think, and it makes such a difference helping new readers to discover one of my books for the first time.

I love hearing from my readers—you can get in touch through social media, or my website.

Thanks,

Ellie

www.elliemidwood.com

instagram.com/elliemidwood
facebook.com/EllieMidwood

ACKNOWLEDGMENTS

First and foremost, I want to thank my incredible editor, Lydia Vassar-Smith, for helping me bring Aurelia and Max's story to light. Out of a hot mess of a concept, she helped me turn it into a coherent story I'm not ashamed to put my name on. This was our first project together and after the very first round of edits I already knew I was in incredibly capable, wonderful hands! I truly couldn't be more grateful for her guidance, unwavering support, and encouragement.

To everyone in my lovely publishing family at Bookouture for working relentlessly to help my book babies reach the world. Imogen Allport, Mandy Kullar, Jade Craddock, Jane Donovan —thank you for shaping my ramblings into a coherent novel! Richard and Peta, you made it possible to have my babies translated into twenty(!) languages. I know I'm an author, but I honestly have no words to fully express my gratitude to you.

Huge thanks to Jess Readett and Sarah Hardy for organizing the best blog tours ever and securing the most interesting interviews for each new release. Even for an introvert like me, you make publicity a breeze. Working with you is a sheer delight!

Ronnie—thank you for all your support and for being the best husband ever! And for keeping all three dogs quiet when I work. I know it's not easy, given how crazy they are. I love being on this journey with you.

Vlada and Ana—my sisters from other misters—thank you for all the adventures and the best memories we've already created and keep creating. I don't know how I got so lucky to have you in my life.

Pupper, Joannie, and Camille—thank you for all the doggie kisses and for not spilling coffee on Mommy's laptop even during your countless zoomies. You'll always be my best four-legged muses.

And, of course, the hugest thanks, from the bottom of my heart, to all of you, my wonderful readers. I can never explain how much it means to me that not only have you taken time out of your busy schedules, but you chose one of my books to read out of millions of others. I write for you. Thank you so much for reading my stories. I love you all.

PUBLISHING TEAM

Turning a manuscript into a book requires the efforts of many people. The publishing team at Bookouture would like to acknowledge everyone who contributed to this publication.

Audio
Alba Proko
Sinead O'Connor
Melissa Tran

Commercial
Lauren Morrissette
Hannah Richmond
Imogen Allport

Cover design
Eileen Carey

Data and analysis
Mark Alder
Mohamed Bussuri

Editorial
Lydia Vassar-Smith
Imogen Allport

RAISING READERS
Books Build Bright Futures

Dear Reader,

We'd love your attention for one more page to tell you about the crisis in children's reading, and what we can all do.

Studies have shown that reading for fun is the **single biggest predictor of a child's future life chances** – more than family circumstance, parents' educational background or income. It improves academic results, mental health, wealth, communication skills, ambition and happiness.

The number of children reading for fun is in rapid decline. Young people have a lot of competition for their time, and a worryingly high number do not have a single book at home.

Hachette works extensively with schools, libraries and literacy charities, but here are some ways we can all raise more readers:

- Reading to children for just 10 minutes a day makes a difference
- Don't give up if children aren't regular readers – there will be books for them!

- Visit bookshops and libraries to get recommendations
- Encourage them to listen to audiobooks
- Support school libraries
- Give books as gifts

There's a lot more information about how to encourage children to read on our websites: **www.RaisingReaders.co.uk** and **www.JoinRaisingReaders.com**.

Thank you for reading.

hachette
UK

Printed in Dunstable, United Kingdom

66865854R00211